WILD CARD

ONE-EYED JACKS

The Wild Cards Universe

WILD CARDS VIII

♠ ◆

ONE-EYED JACKS

♥ ♣

**Edited by
George R. R. Martin
Assistant Editor
Melinda M. Snodgrass**

And written by

*Walton Simons
Chris Claremont
Kevin Andrew Murphy
Lewis Shiner
William F. Wu
Victor Milán
Carrie Vaughn
Stephen Leigh
Melinda M. Snodgrass
John Jos. Miller*

A TOM DOHERTY ASSOCIATES BOOK
New York

This is a work of fiction. All of the characters, organizations, and events portrayed in this novel are either products of the authors' imaginations or are used fictitiously.

WILD CARDS VIII: ONE-EYED JACKS

A Tor Book
Published by Tom Doherty Associates
175 Fifth Avenue
New York, NY 10010

www.tor-forge.com

Tor® is a registered trademark of Macmillan Publishing Group, LLC.

The Library of Congress Cataloging-in-Publication Data is available upon request.

ISBN 978-1-250-16809-2 (trade paperback)
ISBN 978-1-250-16808-5 (ebook)

Our books may be purchased in bulk for promotional, educational, or business use. Please contact your local bookseller or the Macmillan Corporate and Premium Sales Department at 1-800-221-7945, extension 5442, or by email at MacmillanSpecialMarkets@macmillan.com.

First Edition: August 2018

Printed in the United States of America

0 9 8 7 6 5 4 3 2 1

to Mike Cassutt

WILD CARDS VIII

ONE-EYED JACKS

Nobody's Girl

by Walton Simons

THE LATE-AFTERNOON SUNSHINE WARMED them. She lay naked on the bed, hands folded on her stomach, eyes closed. He looked down the outline of her body, trying to hold on to the ecstasy and contentment he'd felt with her only moments before. But it was already slipping away. Women kept it a bit longer. Afterglow. But they lost it, too.

"You could stay awhile," Jerry said. He tried to make the four words sound like it would be more fun than two people could stand. Not that they'd been pushing the limit in that area lately.

"Nope." Veronica opened her eyes and sat up, her long, sweat-soaked brown hair plastered to her face and neck. Jerry hoped it was his technique and not the August heat seeping in. She waited a few seconds, then stood and walked into the bathroom, closing the door after her. "Call me a cab."

"Okay, you're a cab." Jerry hadn't expected a laugh and wasn't disappointed. He heard her turn on the shower.

He pulled on his shorts and walked across the carpeted floor into the next room. A five-hundred-dollar bill was in the top drawer of the mahogany bedroom dresser. Along with a new pair of black silk panties and matching underwire bra with cutout front. It was their ritual. Maybe she'd wear the lingerie next time, maybe not.

He picked up the phone and paused for a second, stopping his finger from making a rotary motion. He hadn't adjusted to push buttons yet. Twenty-plus years as a giant ape could do that to you. A cold, sick feeling spread through him. Even Veronica couldn't help when it hit him. He tried hard to push the thoughts away, but that only made it worse when they finally broke through. The world had changed during those years, drastically and unalterably. His parents had moved to Pass Christian, Mississippi, and been killed in Hurricane Camille. Some idiot psychic had told them he'd been kidnapped and taken there. The bodies wound up in a tree three miles inland. All the time he was in Central Park Zoo, fifty feet tall and covered with hair. He bit his lip and punched in the numbers.

"Starline Cab," said a bored voice on the other end of the line.

"Thirteen East Seventy-seventh Street. A lady will be waiting."

A pause. "That's Thirteen East Seventy-seventh. Five minutes. Thank you." *Click.*

Jerry walked back into the bedroom and stretched out on the bed. The sunshine drove the cold from his skin, but not his insides.

Veronica stepped out of the bathroom. She picked up her clothes and pulled them on in a quick, awkward manner.

"It's not against the law for you to stay sometime," he said. "We could go out to dinner every now and then. Or a movie."

"If it's not illegal, I don't bother with it." She turned her back on him to button her blouse.

"Yeah." He rolled over on his stomach, not wanting her to see the pain on his face. She could be a real bitch at times. Most times, nowadays.

"Sorry." She ran a finger down his calf. "I'll see what I can work out, but no promises. I'm a busy girl."

The intercom buzzed.

Jerry sat up straight. Almost nobody ever visited him here, except Veronica. He ran across the apartment to the intercom and pushed the button. "Hello."

"Jerry, this is Beth. I'll bet you forgot about the fund-raiser tonight. You can't abandon me to all those lawyers and politicians."

"Oh, Jesus. I did forget. Hold on. I'll be right down." Jerry walked quickly over to the closet and snatched out a shirt and pants. "My sister-in-law. You should meet her. You'd like her."

"A lawyer's wife?" Veronica shook her head. "You must be kidding."

"You might be surprised. She's really terrific."

"I'm out of here," said Veronica, heading for the door.

Jerry struggled into his alligator shoes and hopped across the carpet after her. "Okay, I love you."

Veronica waved without turning around and closed the door behind her.

Jerry sighed and went into the bathroom. He combed his too-red hair and dabbed on a few drops of cologne. He heard the elevator stop. He waited a few seconds until it headed back down. It wouldn't do for Beth to see him with Veronica, who'd probably just say something snotty.

He checked to make sure he had his wallet and keys, then hustled out into the hall and punched the elevator button.

Beth was waiting for him downstairs. She was wearing a floral print shirt and light blue pants. Her blond hair hung just past her shoulders.

"Let's get moving, bro. I'm double-parked." She grabbed him by the elbow and guided him toward the door. "I just saw a cute little brunette number leave." She arched an eyebrow. "Anybody I should know?"

He did his best to look shocked. "Nope. Anybody I should know?"

Beth smiled. "You could do a lot worse. You probably have, too."

"A safe bet. Let's go and get this over with."

♣

The ballroom was filled with smoke and noisy, rich Democrats, most of them trying not to appear drunk. Yet. Koch and Jesse Jackson had appeared together earlier in the day to show Democratic solidarity, such as it was. There was a rumor that Jackson might show up to speak, but it wasn't in the itinerary. Jerry hated going anywhere he was required to wear a tux, but Beth had promised him three movie dates in return.

The three of them were the only ones at their table. Kenneth had his arm around Beth, whose shoulders were bare except for the thin straps of her blue silk dress. Jerry was jealous. He and Veronica were never to appear in public together. Veronica had made that much clear.

"I can't believe the party nominated Dukakis," Kenneth said. "Even Richard Nixon could beat him into the ground."

"Bad luck at the convention," Beth said. "Hartmann might have had a chance."

"Then again he might not. Public opinion on wild cards being what it is. That issue would probably have sunk him. You should be glad you're not a well-known ace." Kenneth stood. "There's a few people I need to talk to. Back in a minute." He kissed Beth on the forehead and made his way into the crowd.

"I'm not an ace at all, anymore." Jerry took a large swallow of wine. "Which is for the best, I guess."

"Hello, Mrs. Strauss." A young man stood behind Kenneth's empty chair. He was tall, blond, and could probably have passed for a Greek god even in good light. Jerry hated him instantly.

"David." Beth smiled and motioned to the chair. "I didn't know you were going to be here. How nice to see you. Do you know Kenneth's brother, Jerry?"

"No." David extended his hand.

"Jerry, this is David Butler. He's the intern working with Mr. Latham. Even St. John is impressed with him. Has David working all hours."

Jerry shook his hand. There was an almost palpable energy in David's touch. Jerry withdrew and managed a smile. "You do what, David?"

"Whatever Mr. Latham requires." David smiled at Beth. "You look lovely tonight. I can't imagine your husband being foolish enough to abandon you."

"Oh, I'm well taken care of, David." Beth put her hand on Jerry's sleeve.

David gave Jerry half a glance and drummed his fingers on the table. "I'd better be going. Mr. Latham expects me to mingle with the heavy hitters. Says it should be good for me." He got up, rolling his eyes. "Nice to see you, Mrs. Strauss." David left.

"He must be gay," Jerry said.

Beth chuckled. "I don't think so."

"Is he rich, then?"

"I'm afraid so."

"There is no God." Jerry emptied his wineglass and looked for a waiter.

"You don't need to be jealous, Jerry." Beth adjusted the straps on her gown. "Just because he's young, rich, and gorgeously handsome."

"I'm rich and young, sort of." Jerry hadn't aged physically in the twenty years he'd been an ape. Legally, though, he was in his forties.

"Feeling sorry for yourself again?" Kenneth said, reappearing and sitting back down.

"Constantly," Jerry said.

"Right. Did you ever contact any of those film people I mentioned your name to? You have talent. Beth and I are both impressed with your abilities."

"I'll get around to it. I have a lazy muse," Jerry said. "I know you went to a lot of trouble."

"Not as much trouble as proving that you weren't legally dead when you showed up last year." Kenneth smiled. "Nobody wanted to believe you'd been a giant ape for over a decade. Too many precedents."

Jerry sighed. "Sorry I was so much trouble."

"It's not that and you know it. When you're born into wealth like we were, there's a larger obligation to society that comes with it."

Jerry shrugged. "I like to think I'm keeping my bank from going under. It's the romantic in me."

Beth smiled, but Kenneth shook his head. "The romantic in you is going to get you into trouble someday. You can pay people to not call you Mr. Strauss, but you can't make them give a shit when it's crunch time. People don't love you for money, they love you in spite of it."

Jerry didn't need to hear this right now. He turned to Beth. "Why did you marry this guy?"

Beth smiled and held up her hands, palms about a foot apart.

"Nasty girl," Jerry said. "I guess it runs in the family."

Kenneth fingered a cuff link. "I don't want to be a pain, but you can count on me keeping after you about this. You need to find something to do with your life."

There was a burst of applause and people began standing. Jesse Jackson was making his way slowly from the back of the room, shaking hands as he went.

"I suppose we can expect a speech now," Jerry said, rubbing the back of his neck. "I'd rather be home watching a movie."

"Democracy is hell, bro," Beth said.

"I'll drink to that." Jerry snagged a waiter's arm and indicated he needed more wine. The only thing that numbed his butt quicker than politics was alcohol.

♠

After rubbing elbows with the rich and powerful, he felt like staying up late. Jerry split time between his apartment and his room at the family house on Staten Island where Kenneth and Beth lived. He'd had to overhaul the place when he got back. His sixteen-millimeter projectors were shot and the neglected cans of film had gotten brittle with age. He'd replaced them with a large-screen TV and videotape. Nobody collected actual films anymore. But there was no romance in video. It was cheap and easy. He was hardly in a position to be judgmental about people who went that way, though, considering his relationship with Veronica. Although she wasn't cheap and was getting less easy all the time.

He was watching *Klute.* It was a bad choice. At least Veronica didn't wear a watch while they did it. She probably never came either, though.

There was a soft knock at the door and Beth stuck her head in. Jerry paused the tape and motioned her in. "*Entrez.* I'm watching *Klute.* Ever seen it?"

"Twice, at least." She sat down on the sofa next to him. "I love the scene where she licks the spoon after eating the catfood." Beth licked her lips.

"You're sick."

"Afraid so." She picked up two other tapes off the table. "What have we got here? *Irma La Douce* and *McCabe and Mrs. Miller.*" She paused. He knew she expected him to say something.

"Yeah, well. I like to mix it up, you know. Murder mystery, period piece, comedy. I try to get a bit of everything." He shrugged. "I've got lots to catch up on."

She patted him on the shoulder. "You don't want to talk about it. I can tell. I always feel better when I talk about things. If I hadn't had some good friends and a decent analyst a few years back, Kenneth and I would have wound up divorced."

"I didn't know you two had any problems."

She laughed. "It's tough being married to a lawyer. You always have the feeling that anything you say can and will be used against you. And sometimes he did. I know he didn't mean to, or at least I hope that, but at the time it was hard to tell. You can't ever be another person and know how they really feel. That's kind of scary. But eventually you just decide to believe in them or not. I decided to believe in Kenneth and I'm not sorry."

"I'm glad." The words sounded flatter than he'd intended. "Really. You've been a big help to me. I know I'm not adjusting very well, but I will."

Beth kissed him on the cheek. "You can talk to me any time you feel like it." She pointed to the TV screen. "Want to know who the killer is?"

"No, thanks. I don't want to cheat myself out of guessing wrong and then feeling stupid."

"Good night." She closed the door.

Jerry shut off the TV and VCR. He didn't much like the way this one was headed, anyway. He crossed the floor to his dressing room. It hadn't changed much in thirty years. Back when he was the Projectionist, he'd practiced his Humphrey Bogart and Marlon Brando in front of the same mirror. Bogart died even before Jerry had drawn the wild card, and Brando was old and fat. He sat down, opened a drawer, and pulled out a picture of Veronica and a wig. The hair was as close a match as he could find for hers.

He stuck the picture in the corner of the mirror and looked at it for a second or two, then at his own reflection. His features began to change; his skin darkened. Hair was still a problem. He couldn't quite get it to do what he wanted yet. In the old days he could actually have turned into a woman, but that had always made him feel weird. He pulled on the wig and closed his eyes, waited a moment, then reopened them.

"I love you."

It was even less convincing than the few times Veronica had said it herself. He pulled off the wig and changed back. Beth was right, you couldn't know what another person was thinking or feeling. Couldn't ever actually be them. He tossed the wig and picture into the drawer and slammed it shut.

Who the hell would want to, anyway?

♠ ♥ ♦ ♣

Luck Be a Lady

by Chris Claremont

ONCE THEY HEARD WHERE she was going, nobody would take her. Some cabbies were apologetic, others curtly dismissive, a couple offered rude gestures and ruder words. If the plane had arrived on time, when the dispatchers were on duty, she might have fared better—but mechanical delays and rotten weather en route had delayed the flight so long it was well past midnight before she finally landed, and there was nobody official to turn to.

One asked point-blank why Cody was going there and, hoping it might persuade him to change his mind, she told him: "A job interview."

"Where fo'?" he asked. "Ain't nobody hirin' down there."

"The clinic," she said.

"Shit, missy, you got better places to go an' better things to do wit'chu life than waste it down 'at shithole, trust me."

"Absolutely," a friend chimed in, his accent so thick Cody barely understood the word.

"Decent lady got no bizness goin' there," the driver continued, hands weaving a fascinating pattern in the air before him as he spoke, took a sip of coffee, spoke, took a drag on a Marlboro, without ever missing a beat. "Shit, nobody human got any bizness there.

Unless . . ." Suspicion dawned and he looked narrowly toward her. "Maybe you're one of 'em."

The way he asked, far too deliberately casual, trying to mask the sudden burr of fear and hostility barely hidden underneath, caught Cody's attention and she tilted her head to give her one eye a better view of him.

"One of what?" she asked, genuinely confused.

"Them," as if that was the most obvious reference in the world. "Jokers, aces—whole fuckin' crowd."

"I'm a doctor."

"Cops got a name for their precinct down there, 'Fort Freak.' Fuckin' fits, y'know. Ain't there enough sick people needful amongst your own, why you gotta go take care o' them? Pardon me for sayin', lady, but you ain't got the look o' no Mutha Teresa, know what I mean?"

"Absolutely," his friend chimed in.

"Look . . ." She sighed, fatigue from her trip combining with apprehension to put steel in her voice, an edge that made the cabbie stiffen ever so slightly and take a reflexive half step backward. "All I'm looking for is a way into the city. If none of you will take me, can you at least point out some other way?"

"Sure," the other cabbie said, striking out with some humor of his own, "walk." Nobody laughed, and when Cody turned her eye on him, with a look she'd learned within forty-eight hours of landing in Vietnam and perfected over twenty years as a surgeon, he promptly wished he'd resisted the impulse.

"Hey, life's a bitch. Only other option is to take the Q33 transit bus over to Roosevelt Avenue/Jackson Heights, then catch the F, take you right into Jokertown."

"F what," she asked.

"F *you*," muttered the jokester, but she ignored him.

"Subway," said the first man. "Sixth Avenue line, that's what the letter stands for, take it downtown."

"Thank you," she told him, hefting shoulder bag and briefcase and following his pointed direction along the sidewalk to the bus stop.

"Better watch your step, Doc," he called after her, "they're animals down there, you got no idea." (And you do, she thought.) "They see a nice piece like you, sonsabitch freaks'll prob'ly eat 'chu!" And on cue, came his friend's stolid "Absolutely!"

Cody didn't argue. For all she knew he might be right.

At the station she scrambled into the next-to-the-last car, surprised to find it crowded. Where'd all these people come from? she wondered. The bus driver said this station's supposed to be one of the main ones on the line and there couldn't have been more than a half dozen of us waiting. She shrugged. Isn't my city, this could be the only train they run this time of night. The thing was, as it had rumbled past her into the station, the other cars hadn't registered as being so full.

It was standing room only—there was room to move, but not much else—the passengers about as wide and wild a mix as could be imagined, the night people of this city that loved boasting to the world that it never slept, everyone locked tight in their own miserable little private worlds, not caring a damn about what was outside and praying with all their hearts to be left alone. No one looked her way. No one knew she existed, or cared. Good. Right now, anonymity was a most valued friend.

She twisted a little sideways to get more comfortable and caught a glimpse of herself in the door glass, turned black by the dark tunnel roaring by outside. Tall, too tall for a woman, her height and the power of her rangy frame working against the clothes she was wearing, the only thing in her wardrobe that qualified as a power suit. First time she'd worn anything like it in years. Christ, she wondered, sifting back through the years, was it when Ben died, has it really been that long? In-country, she'd gotten into the habit of fatigues and T-shirts, of dressing for comfort rather than fashion—if for no other reason than what sweat didn't ruin, the blood surely would—and one of the things she'd loved about Wyoming was the casual nature of the people. They took her as she was—at least, she thought with sudden bitterness, when it came to how I looked. And here she stood, trading that in for a world where the package was at least as important as what was inside. Wha' fuck, she shrugged, a small smile twisting the corner of her mouth at how easily she adopted the cadence of the taxi driver, maybe the change'll do me good. Except, perhaps, for the effing heels. Too long in hiking boots and sneaks; dress shoes were going to take some getting used to. And she eased one foot free to rub-massage the arch on the opposite shin.

Automatically, she continued her inventory, hoping her brief visit to an airport washroom had repaired most of the damage done by the seemingly endless flight. The hair was black, except for a smattering of silver splashed above her right eye, unruly as ever despite her best efforts with hairspray and comb. The years had taken the harshest edge off her scars, but to Cody they still stood out in stark contrast to her tanned skin, one running across the crest of the right cheekbone and up beneath the patch, where it branched to three that continued up into her hairline. The round should have taken her head off—but she'd flinched a split second before it hit, without knowing why, the firefight had been total chaos, shells and shrapnel tearing the night to shreds, coming from every direction, things so crazy you didn't know where to duck. So instead of her life, she'd only lost the eye. Lucky, they'd told her in Da Nang—and later, in the big Pacific Hospital at Pearl—fantastically fucking lucky. She hadn't thought so then, she wasn't convinced now.

That side of her head throbbed like the devil—always happened when she was stressed, no matter that the cause was probably psychosomatic—rubbing it didn't help, but it was better than nothing. She curled her hand into a half fist and pressed the heel gently against patch and empty socket. She'd never been beautiful and the wound had made sure she'd never get the chance.

The brakes came on too hard at Queens Plaza—there was a cry of pain as someone's body wouldn't give, a curse as someone else got stepped on—she heard a smattering of apologies, saw a lot more rueful grimaces, this was no surprise to these people, the grief came with the ride. Then, the doors popped wide and Cody struggled out of the way, to let passengers pass.

Out of the corner of her eye, she noticed the people waiting by the last car suddenly rush toward the front of the train. A few who'd stepped inside quickly retreated, faces twisting in embarrassment and disgust. As the tide of passengers turned and those waiting on the platform bulled their way aboard, Cody twisted, snaked, finally shoved her way back to the rear connecting door. To her amazement, the car was empty—except for a gray, shapeless mass plopped on the bench seats, halfway along the right-hand side. At first, she thought it was a derelict.

As the train pulled out of the station, it bounced across some switches, sashay-swaying from side to side—and a tentacle dropped out from under the rags.

Without thinking, Cody yanked open her door and stepped across the tiny platform into the rear car. The smell was like a wall, blocking her way. She remembered Firebase Shiloh, that last morning, waiting for the dust-off choppers, the air filled with blood and rot, gasoline-soaked smoke and charred flesh. She'd taken a twelve-gauge and one of the walking wounded and searched the compound, making as sure as she could they wouldn't leave any breathers behind. She'd been fine until they reached divisional headquarters. She'd spent a month in a charnel house but it wasn't until she walked into the mess hall and smelled fresh food that it finally struck home how unutterably awful it had been. Two steps in the door, one decent breath, and she'd doubled over onto her knees, puking her guts bloody.

This was worse.

The joker made a gargly hiss with each breath, and when it rolled over in its sleep, she saw that it was naked and male. The legs were more like stumps, ending in viciously twisted scar tissue, and she realized that they were really flippers, worn down by years of trudging across concrete and asphalt. The skin was mottled gray and blue black, gleaming with oily secretions, with two sets of tentacles attached to the shoulders. The primary was thick as a human arm, but half again as long, broadening at the end into a flat pad whose inner surface was covered with cephalopod suckers. Nestled in each armpit was a secondary nest of limbs, a half dozen each side, shorter and much thinner than the main tentacle, constantly in motion, writhing among themselves, picking at whatever came in reach, almost as if they had minds of their own. Its head was little more than a bump growing out of the top of the torso, but the jagged teeth she saw when it snored convinced her this was as close as she wanted to get. The eyes were closed, and for that she was thankful. Maliciously, after twisting so much else, Tachyon's virus had spared the genitalia; the joker had a very human penis.

Without realizing it, Cody had slumped down on her heels, unconsciously making herself as small and inconsequential as possible, afraid without knowing why when her rational self told her that all she should be feeling for this poor creature was pity. Over the rumble of the train, she heard rude voices—passengers in the car ahead, looking through the window as she'd done, making fun, demanding action.

As the train trundled down into the tunnel beneath the East River, the joker stirred. Perhaps, Cody thought, he senses the presence of the water? What's he doing still on land, anyway—unless, my God, to give him a body designed for an aquatic environment without the gills that would enable him to live there! Not the cruelest joker deal by far, she knew, but it still provoked a silent snarl. Hell, even if he is amphibian—if he was an adult when the virus activated, who's to say he could hack abandoning the world he knew, friends, family, job, everything that's familiar, that gives his existence purpose and meaning, for a new world. As unknown and alien as another planet, where he'd be all alone. Could I go, if he was me?

And her thoughts turned to Dr. Tachyon, the man—and she laughed softly, bitterly at that, because Tachyon was less of a "man" in any human sense than she—responsible for the wild card. Whose people had sent it to Earth and turned humanity inside out. She wondered if she should hate the little geek for what he'd done. And yet, hadn't he spent the forty-odd years since trying to make up for that, fighting for the health and welfare of the "people" his virus had created? There were probably worse fates than working by his side.

It helped, of course, that she needed the job.

His eyes were open. Black eyes, a shark's eyes, no depth, no emotion, flat, opaque plates, bright as gleaming lacquer except that they absorbed everything they gazed upon. Looking at Cody. She shifted on her feet, figuring to stand and slip back the way she came, into the comparative safety of the next car. But when she moved, so did he. Not much, just enough to let her know he was aware of her intention. Shit. She had a gun—a service .45 she'd carried ever since the 'Nam—but it was locked in its case at the bottom of her carryall. Useless. Her shoulder blades contracted, as if she had an itch down her spine, and she crossed her wrists beneath her breasts, huddling close about herself. A vague glitter drew her eyes downward and her breath caught ever so slightly as she saw her skin glisten like the joker's. For the briefest moment, flesh and bone seemed to flow together, twisting and curling where it once was straight, tentacle instead of arm. When she looked back at the joker, he was showing teeth.

"Stop it," she hissed. "Leave me alone!"

Something wriggled beneath her blouse, an itching, tickling sensation under the armpits that set her to looking frantically about the car for a weapon.

"Damn you," she snarled, *"leave me alone!"*

A bounce and a jerk and a screech heralded their arrival at Lexington Avenue, the first stop in Manhattan, and the brakes snagged again, as they had in Queens, pitching Cody forward on hands and knees, sending her sprawling full length. The joker had anchored himself with one tentacle, was reaching for her with the others. Baring her teeth, she groped for her foot, coming up with a shoe—thankful now it had a heel—swinging as hard as she could toward the creature's face. It was like hitting sponge rubber, the flesh simply gave beneath the impact. But the joker howl-yowled in surprise and pain and rage, flinching away from her, gathering one set of tentacles protectively around its face while the other reached again for her, snagging hold even as Cody spasmed reflex-ively backward against the doors, which miraculously—a split sec-ond too late—opened. She heard a cry of rage and alarm, sensed rather than saw a pair of dark blue trousers step over her into the car, heard a sharp *thwack* as a nightstick connected with the crea-ture's arm. There was no outcry this time, but he let her go. A black, oily liquid spread across the seat beneath it, filling the car with a smell beyond anything Cody had ever imagined. A breath, she knew, would kill her and her savior both. Hands helped her up— she registered a woman's features and thought, absurdly, So young, almost a baby—a uniform as well, Transit Police, thank God, and a pair of neck chains, the one a crucifix, the other a St. Christopher medal hooked to a miniature representation of her shield. An electronic chime announced the imminent closing of the subway doors, and the woman shouldered Cody outside onto the platform, handing out her bags to her.

"You all right?" she asked, continuing after a fractional pause. "You look pretty shaken, I'll radio for some help, you just wait here or, if you can manage, head upstairs to the token booth."

She'd blocked the door with her leg so it couldn't fully close.

"What," Cody stammered, "you?"

"I'm the only cop on the train," the woman said matter-of-factly.

And she stepped back aboard.

"No," Cody yelled, lunging forward to the door even as the train started moving. *"No!"* She was screaming, staggering along the platform, trying to hold on, keep pace, as the train gathered speed; she had no chance, less strength, tripped and fell crashing to the platform, her final cry—as the taillights disappeared into the darkness—more of a sob. "No!"

A flight of filthy stairs led up from the platform. She collapsed before she'd gone halfway, back against the banister, teeth chattering, good eye staring straight ahead at the long empty station as though it was the jungle and, any second now, she expected a VC attack to come boiling her way, the classic "thousand-yard stare" that one of the paramedics—another vet—who eventually came in answer to the policewoman's radio call, instantly recognized. He asked if she was okay and she nodded, not really hearing, or caring what he said, mostly ignoring what was happening around her, hands tucked tight under her armpits, making sure the flesh beneath was still her flesh and not some changeling nightmare, while she rocked panting back and forth, back and forth, thinking of nothing save those awful doll-face lacquer eyes and what they'd almost done to her. No joker, she realized, but an ace. A monster. And, whoever he was, whatever he was, he was still loose, and still hunting. And the next woman he found might not be as lucky. And she thought of the policewoman—and her low, keening wail built up into a cry of feral rage that filled the station and turned heads and made people step smartly away from her.

Madness, she thought, not even noticing the sting of the needle as the medic shot a dose of sedative into her arm, madness!

I've become Dante, was her last awareness as oblivion claimed her . . .

. . . *and my world, my home, is Malabolge.*

◆

She knew where she was without opening her eye, hospitals have that kind of smell and emergency rooms most of all. Problem was, when she opened her eye, she didn't believe it. Two men stood over her.

"You okay, miss?" asked the one to her left.

"Everybody's favorite question," she managed to croak, thankful the rawness of her throat masked the sheer amazement that she felt.

He was a centaur, a glorious palomino who looked like he'd just leapt out of the "Pastorale" sequence of Disney's *Fantasia*. The golden coloring carried over to his human skin, which gave the impression that he had the most magnificent tan, complemented by ash-blond hair and tail. There was a boyish exuberance to his face and manner only slightly countered by his concerned expression and the surgical scrub shirt and physician's lab coat. Stitched onto the left breast pocket was the seal of the Blythe van Renssaeler Memorial Clinic, and pinned over it was his ID card.

"Dr. Finn," she finished, reading the name off his tag.

"And who are you?" was his reply.

"Cody Havero."

"D'you know what day it is?"

"Wouldn't that depend on how long I've been unconscious? It was Thursday—no." She rubbed an aching forehead. "That's wrong, isn't it? The plane landed after midnight, so I suppose it must be Friday."

"Still is," Finn said cheerfully, making a note on his chart. "No evident impairment of cognitive faculties."

"Why should there be?" she muttered, with an undertone of asperity. "I'm suffering, if anything, from shock, not a concussion."

"Now, miss . . ." he began.

"*Doctor*," she corrected.

"Yes," Finn replied, thinking she'd addressed him.

"No," she continued patiently, "*I'm* a doctor."

"Hiya, Major," the other man said from her blind side, and she rolled her head to get a better view. At first glance the joker looked normal. Most people, surprisingly, never noticed his affliction right off—even though, in a very real sense, it was as plain as the nose on his face. He had no eyes. Not simply eyeless sockets, but no sockets at all, a smooth curve of solid bone from the crown of his head to the nasal cavity. But there'd been a compensation, a nose that Jimmy Durante would have been proud of, possessing a sensitivity that would put a bloodhound to shame.

"Been an age, Sergeant," Cody acknowledged, levering herself up as he bent over to give her a rough embrace.

"Too fuckin' long, an' that's a fact."

"You two know each other, Scent?"

"Goin' on twenty, Doc," the blind joker replied. "Meet the only woman combat cutter in U.S. Army history."

"You were in Vietnam?" Finn asked her. "The Joker Brigade," he added with disgust.

"Gotta understand, Doc," Scent said to the young centaur, "there was a lotta rationalization back then. Nobody gave a rat fuck about us. Attitude was, we get killed, that's one less freak fouling the gene pool. Usual pattern, if a joker got medivac'd to an aid station, he'd hardly be there more'n a day before some REMF in razor-creased tiger stripes'd slick up from Saigon to collect him. Standard excuse was to evac him to a special joker medical facility. Made sense actually—at least, most bought it—since our regular quarters were in quarantine zone. Problem was, this 'facility' seemed to be located an hour's flight out across the South China Sea. No muss, no fuss, just a thousand-foot-high dive into a telegram home to Momma. 'Cept Cody, she didn't buy it. Man showed up on her doorstep, she told him to fuck off. Man brought some Saigon khakis to back him up . . ." Finn looked confused.

"Upper-echelon staff officers from MACV headquarters," Cody told him.

". . . damn if she didn't have a couple of network camera crews on hand doing interviews. Made sure they got pictures of the Man, made sure they had her records of the casualties. Any funny business, no way could it be kept quiet. Man backed down, did a rabbit. After that, you were a joker and you got hit, you moved heaven and earth to get to Cody's doorstep. It was like she was magic—nobody ever died on her table."

"I'm afraid, Scent, that string's gone down the drain." Along, she thought, with a lot of other things. "I don't mean to sound ungrateful, but why am I here? Maybe I'm confused about my New York geography but from what I remember of the subway map, isn't Blythe klicks from that station I was in? Aren't there closer hospitals?"

Finn spoke: "All 911 was sure of was some sort of wild-card activity at the Lex-Third Avenue station. And, I'm afraid, your reactions to the medics sort of spooked them. They figured they had a manifestation on their hands. Procedure in those cases is, everything comes to Blythe."

"You were on your way here anyway, right?" Scent chimed in.

"Lucky me," Cody agreed, but with a bite to her words. Scent chose not to take the hint.

"That's right, Major. If there was ever a right move to make, you made it. That's luck in my book."

"The train, Finn." He looked quizzically at her. "There was a transit officer," she explained, "a woman, who helped me . . ."

"Haven't heard any reports, but there's no reason why we should. I can run a check, though."

"Please, do. There was a . . . creature on the train. Looked like a joker, but . . ." She paused, shuddering at the memory. "I don't know, I keep thinking there was a sense of something. . . ." Her voice trailed off and for a moment she felt lost, trying to sort images and memories that refused to stay still, conscious only of a need to run that bordered on panic.

"Can I get out of here, please?" she asked. "And if possible, is there someplace I can tidy up before I see Dr. Tachyon?"

"Residents have a crash pad, upstairs," Scent said, not giving Finn a chance to answer, "where they grab some stray z's when they're runnin' long shifts—I'll take you."

"There really is trouble, Scent," she told him as they rode the elevator up two flights.

"Ain't that the Lord's gospel—careful," he cautioned suddenly, but Cody was already in the process of a quick and nimble two-step over a body that looked made from limp spaghetti, spilling out of its chair and partially across the hallway. "Nice move."

"That touch, at least, I haven't lost."

"If you'd been a guy, the NFL woulda been your fame an' fortune."

There was no air-conditioning—the system had been overwhelmed by the summer's murderous heat, Scent told her, and there simply wasn't money in the budget for repairs—and the atmosphere was rotten. The sky outside the windows was only beginning to hint at the approaching dawn, heaven help them once the sun actually came up. New York, she knew, didn't suffer summer gladly, and this August appeared worse than most.

"Scent, something is out there."

"A lotta shit's out there, Cody. An' it's all startin' to come down—hard."

"Shiloh."

"That's right, you were there. Yup"—he sighed—"Shiloh. Or worse. Here's the hooch. It's a mess, but that's the way you docs seem to like, I guess. . . ."

"When we're young and broke and working ninety-six hours at a stretch."

"Break my heart. Anyway, you hungry after, I know a nice diner, coupla blocks' walk, serves finest-kind breakfast."

"I'll let you know."

"Take care, Major."

"Thanks, Sergeant. This is one I owe you."

♥

Tachyon's office, surprisingly, was nothing special, standard bureaucratic box with a view of the river and the Brooklyn waterfront. One wall of bookshelves full of medical texts, a pair of computer terminals on a table underneath littered with disks. Tachyon's desk angled so he could look out the windows without turning his back on any visitor. It was an antique; she didn't know enough to name the period or style, only that it was as magnificent as the small sideboard tucked into the corner behind it. The window was wide open, covered with a screen, with piles of documents stacked haphazardly on the sill. The sky was dark and a whisper of wind stirred the papers—storm signs, a nasty one, and she reacted instinctively, stepping behind the desk to shift the material to the floor below and lever the window partially closed. Made the room that much warmer, by cutting down the admittedly minimal circulation, but at least everything in it wouldn't end up drenched. She hoped the rain would mean the end of the heat wave, but doubted it. Drought had scarred most of the country this summer, days of three-figure temperatures everywhere you went—there was talk up and down the Midwest of a return to the Depression dust bowl—and she knew firsthand what the weather had done to her beloved mountains. There'd been another report on NPR's *Morning Edition* about the Yellowstone fires, memory filling her nostrils with the acrid tang of pine smoke.

"I hope, Dr. Havero, this interview suits you as much as my office clearly does."

She jumped, taken by surprise, realizing that she'd sunk down into the chair behind the desk—automatically making herself at home—and cursing the fact that the door was to her right, her blind side. Began to stammer an apology, vetoed the thought, tried instead to pass the faux pas off with a shrug and a smile.

The voice had the natural elegance of a classic noble vampire—which made her smile easier—and the man himself was everything his office was not, cut from a mold uniquely his own. She found herself looking down at him as they sidled past each other, exchanging positions. He was a head shorter. Her left hand went out in greeting—which was when her conscious mind twigged to what her unconscious had already registered, that Tachyon's right arm ended at the wrist.

He responded with a soft left-handed handshake, the slightest of smiles acknowledging and appreciating her courtesy.

"A meeting I've been looking forward to, actually, for quite some time. Scent—I don't know if you're aware, but he's the director of our Vietnam Veterans Outreach Program—has been singing your praises lo these many years." He motioned her to take a chair. She'd seen pictures of him, of course, but on paper—and especially, the tube—it was easy to dismiss his eccentric costumes as just that, costumes, the man himself trivialized into a character from some tacky teleplay.

"But I suspect," he continued, "the anticipation is not quite mutual."

"Is it that obvious," she replied, thinking deliberately loudly, *or did you read my mind to discover it?*

In person, his appearance was no less outrageous, but far more effective. Living embodiment of an eighteenth-century aristo. Plum trousers tucked into gray suede buccaneer boots, ruffled green shirt beneath orange, double-breasted waistcoat, the effect actually enhanced by its contrast with the white hospital-issue lab coat that stood in for the burgundy frock coat hung on a corner rack.

He motioned toward the papers she'd moved. "Much appreciated," he told her, ignoring her inner and outer response. "It's often far too easy to be overwhelmed by the clutter here. As you might have guessed, I am far from the most organized of souls. And good secretaries, especially in Jokertown, are damnably hard to find."

The pieces of his face didn't fit together in any manner that might be considered classically handsome, yet the sum of the parts was undeniably attractive. The same description had often been applied to Cody. Though the end result in his case is, she thought, somewhat more delicate. A sling cradled his right arm, the stump swathed in fresh bandages, a recent wound. There'd been no hint of this in the letter he'd sent inviting her to New York. Wonder what I've missed fighting fires in the boonies? she thought. It also helped explain the fragility in his manner, she'd seen it herself too often in casualty wards. And she remembered her own reactions, coming out of anesthetic to discover her right eye gone.

"That what you want from me?"

"Hardly, given your résumé." He looked quizzically at her. "Are you always this direct?"

"Yes," she said simply.

A sudden shadow crossed the inside of his eyes and she knew somehow she'd slipped through his barriers, touched a memory as painful as her own. Her face flushed, with anger and resentment, and she didn't bother masking her exultation at this small, trivial score. Who the fuck do you think you are, cock? she snarled silently, hoping he was listening. What the hell right do you, does *anyone*, have to pick someone else's brain, goddammit, isn't anything private anymore?

"Truthfully," he continued, as though nothing untoward had happened, and Cody found herself admiring his damnable alien poise as much as she was infuriated by it, "I'd forgotten all about my letter in the press of recent events. I never expected an answer."

"Desperation has a way of overcoming even the most primal terrors."

"How clever. I only caught the one news broadcast. What exactly happened?"

She shrugged. "I shot my mouth off, got my ass shot off in return."

"Uncomfortable."

"I should introduce you to my kid, he has exactly the same opinion."

"I'd like to meet him. I have a grandson myself."

"Congratulations."

"Thank you. A true blessing, actually." From the way he spoke, the faintest coloration to his tone, she wondered if that was as true as he obviously wanted it to be.

"I'm glad for you."

"And I am still curious."

"Well"—she sighed—"after Chris was born, I packed in city life and headed for the high country. My folks left me their ranch—not really much as spreads go, nowhere near big enough to support itself, but heaven to live on—so I based myself there and hung out my shingle. Small-town GP, doing emergency surgery on the side. Figured there'd be the end of things. Until the fires.

"They're still burning. Last spring, hardly anyone knew what we were in for. Forest Service followed policy and let the lightning strikes burn uncontested. But the weather turned vicious—no rain, sun baking the woods tinder dry, winds whipping the flame front into firestorms. Alarm went out to damn near every fire-fighting outfit in the country. Indians handled the brunt of the work, about the best there are at this business.

"You ever wonder, Doc, if your virus affects the inanimate substance of the earth itself? Some of those Indians do. You value your hide, steer well clear of Apaches and the Cheyenne. They view the world as a living being, as much so as humanity itself. They see what the wild card does to people, they wonder if it can twist—even murder—the planet the same way."

"That's preposterous." He was genuinely shocked. She barely noticed. She was in the center of a broad mountain meadow with a beaten crew—most so tired they couldn't stand, much less run for their lives—staring in horror at a wall of flame two hundred meters away, where five minutes before there'd been a stand of magnificent timber.

"Maybe. Fires sure seemed alive to us. Sneaky and intelligent, and vicious as a bear trap. Forest Service brought in some joker crews to handle the scutwork cleanup in the low-intensity areas. They should have been fine. Probably, in any other fire, any other summer, they would have. I'm sure you can guess the rest."

"How bad was it?"

She met Tachyon's gaze. "Backfire caught a joker team, tore 'em up pretty badly. I was running the aid station inside Yellowstone. Seven came in still alive. All critical, badly burned, but they had a chance. We bundled 'em all into a Huey and sent it to our main receiving hospital. They turned 'em away. Said they had no bed space. Bullshit, of course, we'd transferred half their patients precisely so there *would* be room for our casualties. But they were adamant, no admittance. Three other hospitals on our list, got the same response from each. Pilot had to bring 'em back. I was running an aid station—the whole point of our existence was to get our injured into the air and out to a proper full-care facility as fast as humanly possible. I didn't have the staff, I didn't have the equipment, to cope with anything more. Took 'em two days to die.

For one, in the end, drugs didn't help. He was screaming, like a baby—this high-pitched shriek, somehow he made himself heard even over the roar of the fire—I found myself once looking around for an ax or shovel, cursing myself for not having my gun handy. I wanted to smash that poor creature's head in, just to shut him up. I lost it, totally, I think by then I was more than a little crazy myself. I found a network crew, gave 'em a live interview on morning television."

"I saw that. You were quite impassioned."

"Lot of good it did me. Hospitals had covered themselves perfectly. They hit back with loads of righteous indignation. By the time they were through, they'd made a plausible case it was *my* fault. All things considered, it wasn't the best of times to take a stand for joker rights. I'd grown up there." A softness had crept into her voice, an eerie echo of what she'd heard earlier in Tachyon's, as though neither could still quite believe what had happened to them. "I'd made that place my home, it was where I raised my son—and five minutes on the *Today* show burned it up as completely as the North Fork fire did the Gallatin Range. Forest Service"—she made a face—"shipped me out on the next chopper. Got home, discovered my attending privileges at the local hospitals had been revoked. Within a week, I started losing patients. Within a month . . .

"Sent out job applications, word got passed back that I'd been blackballed. I was a troublemaker, nobody wanted a thing to do with me."

"No one stood by you?"

"You don't know how afraid people are" *of your damned virus,* she finished silently.

There was a twist to his eyes, a small, sad smile, a flash of pain desperately masked that told Cody he knew far more than he dared let on.

"So," he said softly, finally, "you're here . . ." She filled in the rest: *because you have no choice.*

"I'm a doctor, this is a hospital. And I need the job."

"I have doctors, Cody, I don't need a doctor. I need my right arm." He made a small gesture with it, and didn't bother hiding the flash of pain in his eyes. There was a tentativeness now to his voice and manner that seemed to Cody like nothing so much as shame.

"We Takisians are so proud a species. We promote an ideal, in thought and deed and self. Deformity is cast out. Yet now, as you see, I am deformed. As unworthy in flesh to hold my name and rank as I've proved myself so eloquently in deed. Perhaps my ultimate penance for bringing the wild card to Earth."

She said nothing.

"I need someone I can trust to help me run this clinic."

"Why me?" she asked.

"Mostly . . ." He paused a moment, and she wondered whose thoughts he was collecting, his own or hers. That was what made this so damnably infuriating—not knowing whether he was inside her head or not. And then she thought of what he might see—advertently or otherwise—hard as it was for her to deal with the nasty nooks and crannies of her psyche, how much worse for him? And she had just herself to worry about; he was privy to *everyone's* secret selves. Might be a bit much, for even the most hardened voyeur. Then twisted herself back into focus, to catch what Tachyon was saying.

"It was Scent who told me about you," he said. "I am a proud man, Cody, but even I can't deny anymore my need for help. Or theirs."

She sighed, taking refuge in the view out the window. The sky was more black than blue; the storm was about to break.

"I don't know," she said finally.

"Then why did you come?"

"I thought . . ." What? she asked herself. A wayward gust filled the room, carrying a stale salt sea smell off the river, and before she was even aware she'd moved, she was on her feet, two steps toward the door, hand grabbing instinctively for the .45 tucked in the bottom of her purse.

She couldn't move. Stood like a dumbfounded statue, while Tachyon came out from behind his desk, violet eyes mixing shock and concern as he gently took the Colt from her hand, her purse from her shoulder. They went on the desk. Still frozen, she watched him pour a stiff cognac into a cut crystal snifter. Then, he released the mind lock.

She didn't fall—though she dearly wanted to—but didn't hit him, either.

She took a cautious sip; the cognac burned deliciously.

"That encounter this morning must have made quite an impression," he said quietly.

"Seems so," she agreed, trying to will her hands to stop shaking. "I gave as complete a description as I could to Dr. Finn."

"I saw. The joker you encountered isn't in our files, but that's hardly surprising." It isn't a joker, she screamed silently, don't you understand?

And said instead, as she set down the glass, "This was a mistake, Doctor, I think we both know that. I shouldn't have come here. I'm sorry."

"Actually, I think you're right. They're lepers—aces as much as jokers, though too many think their powers make them somehow immune. More and more, it seems as though every hand is turning against them. People you know suddenly become total strangers, people you trust betray you—or, worse, believe you've betrayed them. The work we do here is as much psychological as physical; we can't afford such ambivalence—and latent hostility—even on a member of the regular staff, much less my alter ego."

She started to say, "I know you'll find someone," but left the words silent in her throat, because she and he both knew they'd be a lie.

She was almost out the clinic's main foyer—painfully conscious that aside from the occasional staff member, she was the only person she saw with anything approaching a normal appearance, every so often catching a whispered curse and not-so-whispered taunt—when Scent caught up with her.

"Sorry to see you *didi mau*, Major," he said.

"Win some, lose some, Scent. We should be used to that."

"This summer—after that fuckin' convention—I feel like we're bein' fuckin' overrun. Prob'ly makin' the smart play, buggin' out while you can."

"Yeah."

"Look, that ain't why I'm here. The joker you ran into—I can't say for sure since I can't see to *make* sure, but I think they just brought it in, DOA."

"Where?"

"Morgue."

"Can you show me?"

♣

No attendants in the body shop, only a single pathologist on duty, a nat, more than willing to give full vent to his anger at the city medical bureaucracy for sending him to this gulag. He knew of Cody, figured that made them kindred spirits; they both stood up to the system and got royally screwed. She figured him for a jerk, but wasn't about to let on with him in a mood to help.

The corpse lay on the examining table and Cody was surprised to discover it no less disturbing dead than alive.

"Pretty fucking gross," the pathologist agreed.

She didn't reply at first as she continued her examination, mentally comparing the body before her with the one imprinted in her mind's eye. "Ever see anything like it?" she asked, at last.

"You kiddin'? Jeez, I hope not. B'sides, I thought each manifestation of the virus was unique."

"That's the theory," she agreed. "Any chance of a positive identification?"

"Not a fucking prayer, pardon my French. Other than the fact it's female."

"Female?" she asked sharply.

"Yeah." He shrugged. "Take a look. No tits to speak of, but what appear to be appropriate genitalia. I suppose, during the post, I can check to see if the internal plumbing matches."

"Do it." She spoke with such an automatic, offhand voice of command that he responded by writing the order down in his workbook, assuming she was senior staff. "About the ID?"

"No hands, which means no fingerprints; no way we'll get retinagrams from those eyes; and dental records . . . ?" He pointed to the sawtooth fangs filling the partially open mouth. "This is a complete physical metamorphosis—'cept, of course, bein' a joker, nothing works like it's supposed to. So you got an aquatically configured creature who can't live in water. Flippers for swimming, but no gills."

Cody looked at the thickly massive, almost elephantine flippers that were the creature's "feet."

"What can you tell me about these?" she asked.

"Whaddya mean"—he stifled a yawn—"other than what I already said?"

"Any wear and tear?"

"You can see that for yourself. Same kinda shit you'd have on your feet, you walked around barefoot. Especially in this town."

"Hasn't been doing it long, then?"

"Doubtful. Any real amount of time, they'd develop rough,

horny calluses, scar tissue from the constant pounding and abrasion. Probably compression of the legbones, as well—y'see, these really aren't feet in any sense that we mean it, they aren't designed for walking. Nah, y'ask me, Doc, this baby's right outta the box.

"And somebody sure as shit wasn't happy to see her." He pulled aside the sheet that covered the joker's torso, revealing a pair of fearful wounds. "You ever see *Jaws*," he asked, and as Cody nodded, "when I was in med school, we got some poor sumbitch, did a dance with a tiger shark. Same kinda bite structure. 'S funny." He stepped away from the table, gave the corpse a long look—and Cody revised her opinion of the man; for all his annoying behavior, he appeared to be good at his job. "If I didn't know better, I'd almost say the joker did this to herself—similar bite radius, actually a little larger, same kind of teeth structure. But no way could her mouth reach around to make those wounds."

"Maybe—twins?"

"You serious? Jeez, I hope not."

She looked at the creature's shoulder. The bite there had splintered bone and savaged the network of vessels leading out from the heart. "Cause of death?"

"Cardiac arrest, due to loss of blood, directly resultant from extreme, violent physical trauma."

"Who found her?"

"Work crew, I think. Transit. Scared 'em outta two lifetimes' growth, I hear. Shit. I do *not* understand how they get *anyone* to work down in those holes."

"Where?" Cody asked as he paused for breath.

"Got me there." He looked at his notes. "We don't have the full sheet yet, prob'ly at the precinct or en route, I only know the who 'cause the EMS crew was griping about coming here while the other ambulance got to transport the live ones to Bellevue. I guess that at least places it in Manhattan. What you got, Doc, something?"

"Not sure. Pair of tweezers."

"Here go. Looks shiny. Piece of chain, maybe, wedged into the wound. Holy shit," he exclaimed as Cody worried free both the chain and the medal it was attached to. There was almost nothing left of the miniature shield, but the St. Christopher medal was pretty much intact. Pity it hadn't protected the wearer.

"Doc, you all right? You look awful gray, want some water?"

She waved him back, one hand clenched tight into a fist, supporting her weight on the table while the other held the tweezers. Poor woman, she thought, completed the transformation barely begun with me. Not just an ace, the son of a bitch is a predator.

"Draw a blood sample. I want a test for the presence of the wild card."

"Why waste the time? Open your eyes an' take a look. She's a joker, that much is obvious."

"Humor me." She gave him a look, for additional inspiration; he got the message. "Quick as you can, please," she told him, "and send the results to Tachyon."

♠

She sat at Tachyon's desk, trying to push thoughts onto paper, mostly staring at the blank legal pad in front of her, twirling the fountain pen she'd found. Fine point, with a clear, elegant line—got the job done but with a special little flourish if you wished. Like Tachyon. She hoped Tachyon was a southpaw, or possibly ambidextrous; it would be hell retraining to use the lesser side, the writing technique would never be as fluid, each word a reminder of—how had he put it?—his "deformity."

She thought of her own loss and wondered why it hadn't crippled her. By rights, she should have been finished as a surgeon—there was no depth perception with one eye, no way to tell precisely how far away things were, yet she never had a problem. She always seemed to know where to reach, was always a split second ahead of the people around her, somehow sensing what they were going to do, where they'd be. Folks always interpreted it as luck—and so did she, to an extent, on the rare occasions when she actually thought about it.

She made a rude face and ruder noise—if it were truly luck, she should be a lot better off than she was—and started scribbling notes. According to Brad Finn, Tachyon had been summoned to the local precinct—"Fort Freak." Cody wondered if that had anything to do with the policewoman, wondered further what kind of effect her own news would have. A predator ace was bad enough, but one who went around transforming nats into jokers was everyone's worst nightmare, a return to the panicked days of last spring, when Typhoid Croyd roamed the city, and Manhattan had been placed temporarily under martial law. She'd thought of confiding in Finn—she liked the centaur—but didn't know him anywhere near well enough to trust him. The memory of what happened in Wyoming was still too raw; people she'd known had lied, those she'd trusted had turned away from her. She was determined never to be that vulnerable again. Scent, whom she'd trust with her life, was long gone home.

She considered sticking around till Tachyon's return, but found she couldn't stay still. Rain was sheeting down—bad sign, since the long breaks between lightning flash and thunder indicated the heart of the storm had yet to arrive—but the violent weather did nothing to ease the oppressive atmosphere. Quite the opposite. She prowled the office, without a clue as to why she was on edge, wary in ways she hadn't been since the 'Nam. Easy to be confused, hot rain and steamy air more common to the Mekong Delta than Manhattan. It was like this at Shiloh, in the evening twilight, when everyone knew Charley was in the jungle beyond the wire, waiting for full night before he came visiting.

She sealed her report and the evidence in a manila envelope, left it on Tachyon's desk, decided to call it quits while she hopefully was ahead.

The illusion lasted as far as the clinic's main entrance, where a laugh of genuine amusement greeted her query about the possibility of getting a taxi. The guard let her use his phone to try to call a radio cab. Most of the numbers got her a busy signal and the few companies she actually reached—after what seemed like an age on hold—hung up the moment she gave the address. A local gypsy cab pulled up, dropping off a joker. The driver was another one. But when Cody dashed to the curb, and he saw she was a nat, he gave her the finger with a hand shaped like a bird's claw and sped away, plowing though the biggest puddle at hand in the bargain, to add insult to injury.

"Fuck this," she muttered wearily, as furious with the growing joker prejudice as she was with its nat counterpart. Maybe she'd do better back in Chinatown or Little Italy. At least there she could get herself a meal; she hadn't eaten since the pathetic excuse for supper served by the airline on her flight in.

Streets were deserted, everyone with sense taking refuge under cover till the brunt of the storm passed. It was a true monsoon, water descending in an almost solid mass, overwhelming the capacity of the drains and turning most corners into ankle-deep ponds. The streets here dated back to the nineteenth century, like the buildings, cobblestone supposedly covered with asphalt. But no repairs had been made this summer, which meant that in a lot of places the asphalt had been worn down to the original pavement, which made the footing treacherous.

She thought she was going the right way, following the directions the guard had given her, but the streets didn't make sense. Most of Manhattan was laid out on a grid system, with streets running east-west and north-south. It took real effort to get lost. Not so down here. Some of the streets were more like alleys and they canted off in wild directions from the main avenues, which themselves followed the natural curve of the island. The buildings were old and looked it, mostly constructed in the last half of the last century, walk-up tenements that had never seen better days and probably weren't likely to. She smiled to herself—but only half in jest, another part of her took this perfectly seriously—and imagined the wild-card virus turning these old tenements into living beings, who played musical chairs with each other to confuse any visitors. Were the windows eyes, watching her every move, the doorways mouths? If she ducked into one to get out of the rain, would she be eaten? She scoffed, but edged out toward the middle of the street, rationalizing it by telling herself that this was the best place to flag down any cruising cab. Sumbitch would have to run her down to get by. Assuming, of course, one ever came. She'd walked more than far enough, she should have reached the periphery of Jokertown, but there wasn't a Chinese store sign in sight.

Then, on the corner, she saw a bright green globe set on a dirty green railing—she remembered that meant a subway station. *What the fuck,* she thought, and was down the steps in a flash, shaking herself like a half-drowned pup to get the worst of the wet off her before fumbling in her bag—which she'd had sense enough to wear under her slicker—for a dollar for a token. When she asked the clerk for directions, she found she was on the wrong platform. This was the downtown side, the trains here would take her under the East River to Brooklyn.

"Is there an underpass?" she asked, not terribly enthusiastic about the prospect of going back out into the storm, even if only to cross the street.

"Wouldn't matter if there was," the clerk—to Cody's surprise, another joker—replied, passing a copper token through the tiny slot. "Platform's closed, TA's doing work on those tracks."

"Wonderful."

"They're s'posed to be finished by now, that's why the work's done mostly at night so the lines and stations are open for day traffic, 'specially at rush hour, but the storm's probably got 'em backed up some. Some serious rain," he added sympathetically.

"And then some," she agreed. "So could you tell me, at least, which line am I on, I didn't see the sign outside."

"This is the F, ma'am. IND Sixth Avenue local."

Cody didn't really hear the last line, she was making a slow, careful turn toward the station, sweeping the platform the same as she would a hostile tree line. She shook her head violently, chiding herself for reacting like a baby. Jokertown may well be strange country, but she was no cherry; she knew how to handle herself, and it wasn't like this.

"How do I go uptown, then?" she asked, satisfied that—so far as she could eyeball—she was alone outside the booth.

"Take the F to Jay Street–Borough Hall, then hoof it up the stairs, over to the uptown platform. Got your choice there, miss, between the F and the A. F'll take you straight up the middle of the island, but the A makes better connections. You want a map?"

She'd mislaid the last one. "Thanks," with a smile.

"What we're here for. Got a rash or somethin'?" And when she responded with a confused look, wondering what he was talking about: "Been scratching your hand pretty hard, must itch awful bad."

She looked down, she hadn't been aware she was doing it—was the skin numb?—and she went cold, inside and out. The back of her hand glittered impossibly in the fluorescent light, with the faintest silvery cast.

She looked toward the stairs. Water was pouring down—an impressive cascade, as good as many fountains—the stream flowing past her down the slightly angled platform, through the gates, toward the tracks. She could hear other waterfalls inside, from the ventilation and maintenance grids set into the sidewalk above.

She'd been saved last time. And the policewoman had paid the price. Is that my fault? she asked herself. How could I have known? But what's the link now? And comprehension narrowed her eye. Perhaps that was the key—she was the one that got away. An ace that looks like a joker, with the power to transform people into beings like himself. No, she realized, with a flash of inspiration, not people—women! The wild-card deck deals only one of a kind, each victim is forced to live their life unique and alone. And someone as awful as that ace, he wouldn't have even a hope of normal companionship. But if his power is to make a companion . . . ? Fair enough—the lady cop was proof of that. Cody didn't have to imagine how the ace's victims felt—some awful instinct told her that she and the policewoman hadn't been the first. But if so, she thought, why hasn't anyone noticed; if there are others, what happened to them?

As she worked through all this, she began walking forward, head tracking slowly back and forth, giving her eye a clear field of everything in front of her. The turnstile sounded surprisingly loud as she passed through—everything did, her senses were operating at a peak they hadn't achieved since the war. So far as she could see, the platform was empty.

Keep putting the pieces together, she told herself, see what you build. Okay, the ace transforms women—perfectly understandable, he's alone and lonely, he wants a mate—only they don't like it. And she remembered the bite marks on the dead policewoman, and let her head loll back against the tile wall behind her. Is that it, has to be, explains why there've been no sightings—he *kills* them. She held up her hand, trying to tell herself the silver sparkles weren't flashing a fraction more brightly. She was unfinished business. Moby Dick, perhaps, to his Ahab.

Tachyon had broken down the gun when he took it away from her; she checked the clip to make sure it was full, then shoved it into the butt of her .45. She pulled the slide to chamber a round, snapped on the safety, and tucked the heavy automatic behind the small of her back, under her belt. Not the most comfortable of improvised holsters—especially given the gun's weight—but she wanted to be able to get at it in a hurry without having to fumble with her bag. The bag, though, was another problem, an encumbrance she could do without.

There was a rush of air from the tunnel, two spots of light off in the distance that slowly rocked toward her for what seemed like the longest time before suddenly exploding out of the darkness, revealing the sleek, gray-metal box shape of the subway train. As the train slowed, she peered through each window, hoping for a sight of the ace—but all the cars that passed had people in them. She dashed for the next one in line, the conductor—not wanting to spend any more time than necessary at this particular stop—closing the doors just as she snaked through. A few passengers gave her the eye, probably wondering—like the cabbie this morning, seemed to Cody like another age, another world—what she was, whether she was one of *them*. She met their gazes, same as she had after returning from the 'Nam, while moving the length of the car, automatically checking every seat. She tried the connecting door, but unlike on the train she'd ridden that morning, these were kept locked. Damn, she snarled silently, a complication she didn't need. At least, she could see through the grimy window that the next car had people in it, she could bypass it and go on to the one beyond.

She got that chance at York Street, on the fringe of Brooklyn Heights, ducking out the doors the moment they opened and sprinting fast as she could to the ones she wanted. There was the normal flow of passengers here, she had time to reach them. Problem was, her shoes—perfectly adequate for job interviews—were not cut out for this kind of work. No support, less traction. Couldn't be helped, she had to manage with what she had, wouldn't be the first time.

This car was fine, too, and the one beyond, and the ones beyond that, as the train trundled through Jay Street and then Bergen.

She was beginning to feel more than a little silly, dashing about like a madwoman, armed to the teeth, chasing a creature that could be anywhere along the subway system's hundreds of miles of tracks. There were no odds for her catching up with him—what made her think he'd be on this train, or even this line?—and if she did, she wondered wryly, would that be the best of luck, or the worst? And yet—this was where he'd made his last attack, better than nothing to go on. Why her, though? Wasn't her job, or her nature—she was neither cop nor hero. Just stubborn.

The fiery numbness had spread up her forearm. Is that a function of proximity, she asked herself, does it mean we're coming closer? Sign on the wall read CARROLL STREET. She made her move, as usual, as the doors opened, but she slipped on the rain-slick platform, bags unbalancing her enough so she couldn't recover, went down hard on one knee, pain splintering her concentration for a moment. She tried to lever herself up as she heard the door chime, called hoarsely to the conductor to wait as she tried for the nearest door, but he had his schedule to keep and they closed in her face. "Damn," she said over and over again as the train rumbled on its way, "damn damn damn damn *damn!*"

Nothing for it, she knew, but to wait for another one. There was some blood on her knee, small firebursts of pain as she gingerly put her weight on it—and a nasty tear in the already ruined panty hose—but as she lifted up to her full height, she found it would bear her weight, no problem. Thank heaven for small favors, she thought. And then she breathed the smell of a marshy shore at low tide.

Oh shit, she thought, reacting simultaneously, faster than she ever dreamed possible, starting a twisting dive that would buy her some distance and allow her to bring her gun to bear. The move was just enough to save her—the blow that should have knocked her senseless clipping the back of her skull, showering her thoughts with stars—but there was no grace to her landing, an awkward belly flop that left her sprawled on the slimy concrete. She rolled desperately sideways, managing to get off a shot—her bullet *spyanging* uselessly off the ceiling—before a massive tentacle slapped the gun from her hand, the force of the blow tumbling her off the platform and onto the track bed. As she landed, she heard a sharp clatter, her gun falling to the tracks a level below, where another line ran parallel to this one.

She pushed herself out of the muck, her mouth full of the oceanic garbage-dump stench of the ace, so thick each breath made her gag; she knew it was her he wanted, had no illusions as to what would happen then. Even if she survived, that prospect was too horrible to contemplate.

So she ran.

The track bed seemed to angle upward as it left the station, and not far away she thought she saw a glow that perhaps meant open air. Sure enough, the tunnel rose out of the ground. The rain hadn't let up, it was like running into the ultimate bathroom shower, the drops striking with such force they actually hurt. There was a wind here as well, blowing off the harbor, trying to shove her back underground. She staggered to the wall that flanked the tracks, tried to clamber over, couldn't get a decent grip, yelped as her scrabbling hand snagged one of the strands of barbed wire hung along the top.

A rumble—felt as much as heard—heralded the passage of a Manhattan-bound F on the opposite track. Her brain was totally fogged, as though she'd been drugged; the reality of the train didn't even register until it was too late for her to try to get the driver's attention. And though she waved, called, none of the passengers appeared to notice. But following the tracks as they curved along the viaduct, she dimly made out the lights of a station at its crest, the next one on the line. Not so far away, she thought, I can make it, easy. Tossed her remaining shoe, ignored the pain as stones and worse poked at her feet.

Did all right at first, no worse than a morning jog up a mountain road, wasted no effort looking over her shoulder—the ace was either there or he wasn't—better to assume the one than confirm the other. Rain tasted surprisingly sweet, for all its elemental fury, but that was the only sensation it sparked in her. She couldn't feel it strike her skin, it was as though she'd been wrapped in some impermeable membrane, mind suddenly disassociated from her body. A bellowed cry—rage and futile protest, the animal in her snared by an unbreakable trap—erupted from her gut as that awful, remembered tickling danced against the underside of her skin. The flesh she could see wasn't tanned anymore, the silver'd turned gray and oily, the arms (Illusion, she gabbled silently, dear Christ let this be my imagination) no longer quite as firm as once they'd been, seeming to flex and curve with a horrible, boneless grace. Her teeth didn't fit and every part of her body felt ready to explode, skin stretched, shrink-wrapped impossibly, unbearably taut over bones that had turned to razor blades. Each step became an effort. Her legs hadn't changed—except to acquire the same opalescent sheen as her arms—but they felt petrified. The joints wouldn't bend—at knees or hips—she had to swing her entire body to shift them. She was near the crest of the viaduct, better than six stories up, no buildings close enough to risk a jump—even if she was capable of trying. The station was her only hope.

He caught her.

With the casual roughness of someone supremely confident of his strength, he wrapped a tentacle around her neck and yanked her flat; the impact shocked her breathless, she couldn't move. He dropped heavily on her, main tentacles pinning each arm, while the secondary nests scrabbled at her blouse, popping the buttons, shredding it and the bra underneath. There was a broad concrete median separating the tracks, that's where they'd fallen—easily spotted from the station on any sort of decent day, impossible in this gale. His penis lay like a bar across her belly as he shifted position, releasing one arm so he could tear her skirt and panties out of the way. She hit him, hard as she could; all she did now was hurt her hand. She tried for his eyes but the ace was ready for her, caught her arm, forced it back down.

New voice, making itself heard inside her head, through the shrieking berserker rage, calling her name.

"Tachyon," she screamed, without knowing if she used her voice or mind or both.

Where are you? Were the words really his, or was this some psychotic trick her own mind was playing, giving her one last imaginary reed to hold on to?

There's no time, was her reply. She was boiling inside, all the elements of her self seething, bubbling, losing cohesion. He had her, the transformation was approaching critical mass; she knew that in a matter of minutes, it would be done.

Help me, then, Tachyon told her. *Open your mind, Cody, if I'm to do anything, I have to see him!*

Come, she thought. And nothing happened. No sense of trespass, or of another presence. None of the imagery she'd read of in a thousand books and comics.

But there was a glaze to the ace's eyes, and his body had gone rigid.

He's frozen, Cody, Tachyon said, *but I'm not sure how long I can hold him.*

She wriggled arms free of his tentacles, tucked her legs up as best she could, refusing this last time any of her body's protests as she forced it to move, then heaved as hard as she could. He shifted, started to stir in response—she didn't need Tachyon's frantic mental cry to know what that meant—bellowed like a weight lifter for a final effort, arms starting the ace on his way, legs doing the bulk of the work, shunting him back and sideways, he rolled sort of like a Humpty-Dumpty toy, so much weight so low on his body that he couldn't get a decent balance until he came to rest. The scene was splashed by blinding light—a train pulling out of the station, headlamps illuminating the scene—and then there was a brighter flash, sparks and flame and a shriek of agony as a flailing limb slapped the third rail. The ace bounced and spasmed and roared as electricity ripped through him—and for a moment Cody thought he might pull free and somehow escape. But she'd reckoned without the train. The engineer applied his brakes the moment he saw them, but he had too much momentum on the slope and the rain had made the rails slick, and even as it shrieked to a stop, the lead bogies crushed the creature to bloody pulp.

As the train crew scrambled to her aid, she heard the electronic *whoop* of police sirens, converging faintly from all sides—before long, the viaduct was thick with blue rain slickers, the distant platform spotlit by TV minicam news crews. She hadn't moved—didn't have the strength—she just lay in a half sprawl, on her side, staring at the smoking remains, ignoring the shocked, scandalized, fascinated stares of the passengers.

Now, there was a presence in her mind—Tachyon's thoughts with hers even as he pounded up the flights of stairs from Smith Street far below. He drew a psychic setting from the places she loved best, and was kind enough not to react when that turned out to be Firebase Shiloh, in Vietnam's central highlands. Her physical appearance was the same here as in objective reality—no idealization to her mental image of herself—but there was a relaxed, confident strength to her that gave the feeling she was a rock, to which anyone could anchor and be protected. Tachyon allowed himself to be blended into the psiscape—muttering with characteristic dismay at the ultimate lack of style embodied in military combat fatigues (the color scheme was utterly awful)—and then, slowly, gently, began to integrate Cody's mental imagery back into the real world outside. So that by the time he slipped free of Cody's awareness, she was over the shock of the moment, centered once more in mind, if not body—which, pushed far beyond its brink, promptly collapsed.

◆

She awoke in a top-floor single at Blythe—she figured that out from the view—and at first luxuriated in the simple ecstasy of being human. She flexed her fingers, watching the glow of the morning sun on her arms, and marveled that the only sheen was due to honest, human sweat.

"Sleep well?" Tachyon asked from a chair against the wall, stretching with a small groan to ease the stiffness in his back.

She answered with a smile and marveled a little at how relaxed it felt. Didn't think she had that in her anymore, shocking in retrospect to discover how deeply the tension of the past few months had left its mark. How delicious she felt to be free of it.

She started to form a question, but he answered before the thoughts had even coalesced.

"Yes, I've been here all night."

She wondered if she should be angry—obviously the mind link had left its own mark, a duality of being that might well make both their lives miserable—decided it was a pointless exercise. What was, was; what mattered was dealing with it and moving on.

"Admirable philosophy," Tachyon agreed, laughing at her sharp sigh of asperity. "Actually, though, things aren't as bad as all that. I've been monitoring you while you slept."

She couldn't help a giggle at the thought of him walking sentry, marching back and forth across the gateway to her consciousness. The image was strong enough to bring a chuckle to his lips as well.

"Making sure," he finished, "there was no residue from your encounter with Sludge."

"How'd you learn his name?"

"Any psychic contact involves entering into a degree of rapport. I can't help learning some things. In Sludge's case"—he shrugged, mixing dismissal and disgust—"the thoughts were relatively simple, desire-oriented. He was not an intellect, by any stretch of the imagination. Cunning more than intelligence. 'Sludge' was the name he chose for himself."

"He was an ace?"

"Autopsy confirmed that—analysis of his blood—just as it revealed the body in our morgue to be a nat. As near as we've been able to determine, he's been roaming the subways and other tunnels beneath the city for quite some time, preying mostly on runaways and the homeless, the underclass who'd never be missed. And none of us realized—"

"How many?"

"Victims?" He sniffed, gazing out the window—but she knew he was looking back through the ace's memories. "Impossible to know. Sludge had very little cognitive capacity. Quite a few, I suspect."

"He killed them all."

"He ate them."

They were silent a long while. Faintly, Cody heard a page over the hospital's PA system. Gritting her teeth against the possibility of pain or weakness, she levered herself to her feet. There was an IV running in her left arm; she pinched off the junction and popped the tube, then hobbled the half-dozen small and gingerly steps to Tachyon. He seemed so small before her, yet the image she remembered from her mind was as strong and resilient as she imagined herself to be. She pressed her body against his back, wrapping her arms around his shoulders, resisting the temptation to set her chin atop his head. He reached up to take her wrists in his good hand and rest his chin on them. She didn't need to see his eyes to recognize the sober, haunted expression in them. She'd seen the same in hers, too often, when she'd lost a patient that she believed could have been saved.

"A new twist," he said, allowing a faint edge of bitterness to the words, "on the old expression 'you always kill the one you love.'"

"Not to mention," Cody couldn't help responding, "'you are what you eat.'"

He laughed, a spontaneously explosive snort that caught them both by surprise, then turned somber again: "Why did you go haring off like that?"

"Impetuous broad, that's me. I gather you got my message."

"Brad Finn came over to the precinct in person. I just missed you, evidently. Captain Ellis had squad cars cruising Jokertown looking for you. We heard the report of a shot fired at Carroll Street . . .

". . . and then I heard your outcry."

"Thanks for listening."

He turned to face her. "You don't understand. In a city this size, a telepath has to maintain fairly strong shields simply to keep from being overwhelmed by the sheer volume of psychic 'noise.' I have to be attuned to a person to 'hear' them; that almost never happens after a single, casual encounter."

"Perhaps it wasn't so casual, then."

"Apparently not."

"Tachyon, whatever the reason, I'm grateful for it."

"In time—fairly short order, actually—we won't resonate on quite so common a frequency. I'll still be unusually sensitive to you, but it will take a conscious effort to scan your thoughts."

"Over what range?"

"To be honest, I've no idea. This has never happened with anyone, in quite the same way. I'm sorry."

"For what, saving my life?"

"I created that monster. Those poor women Sludge slaughtered, their deaths are on my conscience."

"Welcome to the club."

"You don't understand."

"I'm a surgeon. I spent three years as a combat cutter. I *do* understand. So what?"

"It's my responsibility."

"Fine." She deliberately took him by his maimed right arm. "*Be* responsible. You can't change the past, any more than I can resurrect the patients I've lost—or the people I've actually killed. Yeah"—she nodded—"there's blood on my hands, too, it was a *war*, it came with the territory. And if there's a hereafter, maybe I'll get to deal with it then. Who cares? It's done. But at least I've come to terms with it. Taken my terror out of the closet, where I've been denying it even existed, and hung it out in the open with the other nightmares, where I can get a good look at it, see it for what it is—and me for what I am. Doesn't mean that doesn't hurt, and won't for a long time yet to come. But it's *there*. I can deal with it. Try that yourself, might be in for a surprise."

"You're needed, Cody," he said simply.

"I'm a doctor, Tachyon, not a crutch."

He half raised his stump in its sling, then let it fall, his shoulders slump. "So you'll be going, then," he said.

"Gotta find someone to look after the ranch—couple o' guys I know in Colorado, vets, could do a fair job, give 'em a call before I fly out—spring the news on Chris, pack up the place, find a decent rack here in town." He looked at her in amazement, not altogether sure he was hearing right. "Assuming, of course"—the deliberate seriousness in her voice belied by the lopsided smile at the edge of her mouth—"we can agree on a salary."

Tachyon had the decency to cough. "I'm, ah, sure we can work something out," he hazarded.

"Let's not presume too much, shall we?" Cody said, giving the smile full rein.

She held out her hand.

And Tachyon, his own smile a match for hers, took it.

Nobody Knows Me Like My Baby

by Walton Simons

THE LEFT SIDE OF Tachyon's desk was littered with charts and paper. The right was almost bare. Jerry was trying hard not to look at the prosthetic hand, but his perverse side demanded a glance or two. Tachyon hadn't caught him at it. There was a visible hardness to the plastic that was out of place on the alien, and the color was a flesh tone or two off.

"How is your adjustment coming, Jeremiah?" Tachyon looked at Jerry and then glanced out his office window into Jokertown.

"Fine. I mean, there's rough spots here and there." Jerry smiled. Tachyon looked even more tired than usual. His already pale skin had less color and his red hair was dull and poorly kept, at least for Tachyon.

"You're sure. You seem a bit . . . withdrawn."

Jerry always felt as transparent as Chrysalis's skin when talking to Tachyon. But Chrysalis was dead. So was Jerry's pretense that life was wonderful. "Well, I just, you know, sometimes I think I don't relate well to women. They make me feel inadequate. Worse than that, they make me feel needy. I'd give my—" Jerry caught himself in time. "I just want somebody to see me the way I am and love me for it."

Tachyon nodded slowly. "Only what we all want, Jeremiah. I

suspect you are, in fact, very well loved. Perhaps you're simply unaware of it. Try to temper your patience with the knowledge that love often comes when you've tired of looking for it. As for alienation from the opposite sex, we all deal with that, too. I seem to have specialized in it myself. Of course, being from Takis, I have my own built-in excuse."

It wasn't what Jerry wanted to hear. He was tired of trying to be patient. But he hadn't expected Tachyon to turn over his little black book, either. Not that any woman could keep him from thinking about Veronica. "Sounds like good advice, I guess. Easier to say than do, though."

Sirens passed by outside. Jerry glimpsed red light flashing on the side of a building the next block over. Tachyon looked, too. Jerry had never seen the blinds closed on that window, even though the only things visible were beat-up buildings, garbage, the occasional car, and jokers. Jerry only came to Jokertown to visit the clinic once a month.

"Something else," Jerry said, trying to regain Tachyon's attention. "My power is coming back."

Tachyon looked at him for a long moment. "It never went away, Jeremiah. You were traumatized so severely that you ceased to trust it. That trust must be coming back for your shape-changing ability to be manifesting itself again. If you're pleased, then I'm pleased for you. The current political climate being what it is, you might do well to keep this to yourself. The public thinks your ace is gone. Maintaining that image is in your best interest, believe me."

"Right." Jerry could tell Tachyon was ready for him to leave. He reached in his coat pocket and pulled out a check, then placed it carefully on the left side of the desk. "Here's September's donation."

Tachyon picked up the folded-over check and clumsily opened it with his one good hand. He nodded and smiled. "This does more good than you know, Jeremiah. A few dozen more like you and the clinic might actually cover expenses."

"I'm glad to do it," Jerry said. It was true. There were so few places where he knew his money was well spent, and two thousand a month was a drop in the Strauss family bucket.

The door opened and a woman in a lab smock walked in. She had dark hair and a patch over one eye. She looked past Jerry at Tachyon. "Two more beatings," she said. Her voice was restrained, but angry. "One of them might make it. The other . . ." She rubbed her forehead.

Jerry backed away and moved around her toward the office door. Tachyon motioned him to wait.

"Jeremiah, this is our new chief of surgery here, Dr. Cody Havero. Doctor, meet a friend of the clinic." He held up the check. "And a patron as well, Jeremiah Strauss."

Cody turned and looked at him. She was very pretty, for an authority figure. Cody offered a hand and a strained smile. Jerry shook her hand and smiled back. Her grip was strong and sure. Exactly the way he imagined a doctor's hands should be.

"Nice to meet you, Mr. Strauss."

"My pleasure, Doctor." Jerry was pleased he'd called her by her title. She was both threatening and comforting, and certainly physically attractive in spite of the eye patch. He damn sure didn't want her first impression of him to be a rich, sexist jerk.

"See you next month, Jeremiah," Tachyon said. "Unless you need me for anything. If so, just give me a call."

"You'll be at Aces High next week, won't you? It's my first chance to go to one of Hiram's Wild Card Day dinners."

Tachyon sighed. "Yes, for Hiram's sake, I'll be there. Although I can't imagine it will be a very festive occasion."

Jerry nodded and backed out the door, closing it behind him. He got the impression that Tachyon wanted to be alone with Cody.

Not that Jerry blamed him. He imagined Veronica on black silk sheets, wearing an eye patch and nothing else.

Stop it, he thought. She's canceled out on you two of the last three times. Just find somebody else. Somebody you don't have to pay. How hard can it be?

"As hard as me, kid," said a Bogart voice in his head.

♥

Aces High was a smorgasbord of sight and sound. The smells of fresh bread, fine meat in wine sauces, and expensive perfume assaulted his nostrils. The people were out of the ordinary, too. But that was always the case at Hiram's Wild Card Day dinner. They'd gotten there early. Both he and Beth had wanted to see all the notables make their entrances. Kenneth hadn't been particularly happy about Jerry borrowing Beth for the evening, but refused to come with them, saying there was too much work at the office.

Jerry stood up. "Want anything in the way of an appetizer?"

Beth sighed. "No. I'll save it for the main course." She waved him away.

Jerry wandered slowly over to a large table covered with salads, pâtés, breads, and a few things he didn't recognize as food. There was a crystal mobile of the Four Aces and Tachyon over it. There were also holograms of many of the more famous aces on the walls. Jerry knew better than to look for an image of himself. He picked up a plate and eased in across from Fantasy, who had a young man on either arm. Jerry had met her on the *Stacked Deck* world tour. Although his memory of that period was fuzzy, he did recall Fantasy as one of the most obviously sexual women he'd ever seen. Tonight she was wearing a long, pearl-colored skirt and matching semitransparent top. The dark nipples on her small breasts were all Jerry could see when he looked in her direction. He hoped Beth hadn't noticed him staring at the glamorous ace. Jerry put some pasta salad on his plate and turned to get some spinach quiche.

A brown-haired man with quick eyes and an easy smile leaned in next to him. "Real men don't eat quiche. At least real men who want to impress Fantasy."

Jerry put the serving spoon back in the quiche and looked down the table at the rest of the spread. "Thanks, I guess."

The man set down his plate, which was piled high with a little of everything, and offered his hand. "Jay Ackroyd."

Jerry shook it. "Jerry Strauss." Ackroyd looked like he couldn't place the name. "I used to be the Projectionist, then I turned into the giant ape. Now, I'm just rich."

Ackroyd grinned. "Rich is plenty in this town." He reached in his pocket and pulled out a card. "If you ever need any PI work done, let me know. I could use a rich client for a change. Good luck with Fantasy if you decide to be that brave. I'd almost be afraid to get lucky with her myself."

Jerry took the card and slipped it into the jacket pocket of his tux. The room became suddenly quiet. A man walked in slowly, limping a bit. He looked fairly normal, but Jerry heard the word "joker" whispered by someone, followed shortly by the name "Pretorius." The buzz of conversation that started up had an edge of hostility. Jerry took advantage of the distraction to fill his plate, then he slipped back to his table, where Beth was still going over the menu.

Jerry hadn't seen Hiram yet, but that was no surprise. Killing Chrysalis, the Mistress of Jokertown, had kept his name in the news. The joker community had lined up against Hiram immediately. The media were being less than kind as well. The mood was ugly, and the trial hadn't even started yet. Still, it was unlikely that this Wild Card Day dinner would turn out as badly as the one two years before, when the Astronomer had crashed the party. Jerry was definitely glad to have missed that one.

A cool, unsteady breeze blew in off the terrace. Jerry set his menu to one side. Being rich and touched by the wild card had its advantages.

"I think I'm going to go with the filet mignon," he said. "How about you?"

Beth looked up, chewing her lip. She was wearing a black calf-length skirt and lavender blouse. "I see looking at Miss Tits over there has you in the mood for red meat."

"God, can't I get away with anything around you? If you were a guy, you'd look!"

Beth smiled. "I'm a woman and I still looked. Just jealous, I guess. I wish I had the body and the attitude to wear that kind of outfit." She set down the menu. "I think I'll pass on the main course and just wander over for a fruit salad. Fear of cellulite is a terrible thing. Lesser women have been broken by it, believe me."

"You have to have dessert, though."

"Well, if you insist. But don't tell Kenneth. He still has illusions of me regaining my schoolgirl figure."

"You look terrific." Jerry was about to be more specific when he saw a couple being seated a few tables away.

The man was tall and thin, with dark hair. His eyes were luminous and the air seemed to swim around him. The woman with him was wearing a red silk dress that looked spray-painted on. She was gorgeous. It was Veronica. Jerry turned his chair away from them. It obviously wasn't that Veronica didn't want to get fucked. She just didn't want to get fucked by him.

"You okay?" Beth touched his hand.

"Yeah. I was just thinking about some stuff. You know, I have to do something with my life."

"Right," she said.

He knew she wasn't fooled, but appreciated that she just let it go.

They held the ceremonies for Tachyon. Jerry was surprised the woman with him wasn't Cody. Maybe it was just a professional relationship. There were empty tables. As far as Jerry knew, that was a first for a Wild Card Day dinner. Shortly after Tachyon's arrival Hiram made his entrance. He was wearing a magnificently tailored dark blue suit, but looked thinner than when Jerry had seen him on the tour.

Hiram raised his glass and paused for a moment, waiting for his guests to follow suit. "To Jetboy," he said.

"To Jetboy," Jerry and Beth said along with all the others. They clinked glasses and drank the toast.

Jerry heard Veronica laugh. She was probably doing it just to annoy him. No. More likely she was so busy thinking about sucking her date's prick that she hadn't even noticed him.

"Thank you all for coming," Hiram continued. "I hope you all enjoy your meal, on this, our special day. May the coming year be kind to us all."

There was a smattering of applause. Hiram walked over to Tachyon's table, shook the alien's good hand, then went into the kitchen.

"Doesn't he usually float up to the ceiling or something?" Beth asked.

"Yeah. Maybe he just doesn't feel like it's appropriate. I think Hiram's a bit concerned what people are thinking of him right now," Jerry said. "The whole Chrysalis thing has to be a nightmare for him."

"Worse for her, bro. She's the one who got turned into pâté."

Jerry started to say something, but Beth interrupted. "No. You don't have to say it. I feel bad already. He seems like a very nice man. But aces aren't always good guys, you know."

"I know."

"Bush is going to win the election, and if you think things are hard on wild cards now, just wait. Wild-card chic is going to be stone-cold dead before his term is over. It could be worse than the fifties." Beth reached over and touched his face. "With your history, I just don't want you to get hurt."

Jerry smiled. He ate it up when she acted concerned over him. If only Veronica cared even half that much. "Thanks. I think I'll be okay."

Their waiter walked over. "What will you have tonight, madam?"

"I think I'll have the fruit salad," Beth said.

♣

He'd promised himself he wouldn't think about Veronica. Three nights after the party he was sitting at home. Kenneth and Beth were chewing over the implications of a Bush presidency. Dukakis's pardon of Willie Horton, a joker who'd been convicted of rape, seemed to be the final nail in the coffin. The revolving-door ad, showing homicidal jokers being spilled out into the street, had been a master stroke. The Democrats were indignant, but the ad affected the public in the desired fashion. Jerry found it all too depressing. He called up Ichiko and Veronica was available.

Jerry was sure she hadn't recognized him. He'd thought of giving himself a male-model look, but settled on a more rugged face. His hair was dark and straight; he could do that now, too. Veronica looked almost the same as before. Her white cotton dress revealed just enough to get a man's attention without telling him too much. Jerry knew what she looked like naked, but remembering wasn't enough. Not tonight. Tonight he wanted to be inside her.

Taking her to a movie was probably a mistake. If anything could tip her to who he was, that was it. Still, he wanted to see Demme's *Joker Mama* on the big screen. He was sick of video.

"A friend of mine recommended you," Jerry said. "You were at the Wild Card Day dinner with him. He said you were terrific."

"You know Croyd?"

"Slightly," Jerry said. Croyd had to be Croyd Crenson, the Sleeper.

Jerry had heard a few things about him, mostly bad. Obviously, Veronica wasn't looking for a nice guy.

On the screen a tight-knit group of jokers in human masks was holding up a bank, only to be interrupted by a duck-faced and mouse-faced duo with the same idea.

Jerry put his arm around Veronica and gave her shoulder a squeeze. She flinched. After a long moment she reached up and started stroking his hand.

She knows it's me, he thought. Her brain may not have figured it out yet, but her body knows it's me. He felt a chill, like something had gone bad inside him.

"Excuse me," he said, leaning in close. Her perfume was different from the expensive French stuff he'd bought her. "I'm not feeling well. I'd like to take you home."

Veronica looked up, surprised. Jerry pressed two hundred-dollar bills into her palm. Her hand was cold.

"For your time," Jerry said, in a voice too close to his own. "I'm sorry."

He took her by the hand and led her out of the theater. Gunshots came from the screen behind them. The lobby smelled of overly buttered popcorn and stale candy. He excused himself, went into the men's room, and vomited as quietly as possible.

She was gone when he came back out.

♠ ♥ ♦ ♣

The Tower of Gold and Amber

by Kevin Andrew Murphy

OCTOBER 1, 1988

TRUDY PIRANDELLO STEPPED OUT of the cab, absently paying the driver, and gazed up at the Golden Tower. It was large and garish, mirrored and gleaming, and very, very gold. She remembered when Bonwit Teller & Co. had stood here before, the front lit like a waterfall of jewels tumbling down from the titanic art deco maidens high above, dancing with scarves and nothing else.

But the naked ladies were gone and the ladies department store with them. Now the only shop of interest was Tiffany's, but Trudy resisted the lure of the baubles on display. She could go window shopping any day.

The doorman opened the door and Trudy went in, proceeding to the gold security desk before the equally gold elevators and producing a gold envelope from her oversized but almost empty Hermès bag—which was black and white, matching her gown, the magpie colors of a fall formal. Her dress was beaded and beautiful, if less daring than she would have liked. But it had pockets. And it was suitable given the event and, sadly, her age. Trudy was in her sixties now, and while she'd kept her figure, she'd finally given up and let her hair go white. Still, it was striking and went well with the simplicity of onyx and diamonds, especially the aigrette she wore in her curls. She forgot where she'd picked up the full parure, but it was sparkly, antique, and she loved it. She loved having a chance to show it off even more.

The security guard was a brown-scaled joker of middling height. "I'm sorry, Miss Pirandello," he said, looking like a lizard in a suit as he checked her invitation. "I'm afraid the dinner won't start until seven thirty and we won't be admitting the guests before seven o'clock."

Trudy smiled pleasantly, recognizing him. "That's alright." The lizard was Harvey Kant, one of the detectives from Fort Freak, obviously moonlighting for the evening since Midtown was far from his regular beat down in the Bowery. "I can wait." She'd dealt with him before, but she always went masked to Jokertown, as was the old custom, and cops never paid much attention to the polite and the pretty. Which suited Trudy fine.

She dropped her invitation back into her purse. The guests were the most interesting part of such an event anyway, and while it might be unfashionable, it paid to arrive early.

The next to turn up were a harried-looking father in a bespoke gray tuxedo with gray pearl and platinum studs and cuff links that matched his prematurely gray hair and a snub-nosed, freckle-faced blond girl of about eight in a pink calico pinafore, positively dancing as she dragged him forward. "C'mon, Daddy! We don't want to miss the Amber Room!"

"It'll still be there in a few minutes, Jessica," the man gasped, almost careening into the desk as he hastily produced another gold invitation.

Kant checked it. "Ah, Mr. von der Stadt. We won't be taking guests up before seven o'clock."

"I want to see the Amber Room *now*," Jessica stated flatly, glaring.

Her father was visibly sweating, even more so as the joker detective looked down and said, "Your daddy made a very generous donation to Mr. Bush's election campaign to bring you here. Are you sure you don't want to have dinner with Mr. Quayle, too? Or Mr. Towers?"

"No." The child looked equal parts disgusted and mystified. "I just want to see the Amber Room."

The lizard's expression would likely be unreadable by most, but Trudy had made a long study of human beings, jokers included. It was unlikely that Kant was a Republican or that he was being paid anything near the $10,000 minimum Duncan Towers was charging per plate—most of which would likely end up in his pocket, Towers having cannily angled that the dinner was both a fund-raiser for the Bush campaign and for the restoration of the Amber Room, his latest acquisition, with the dividing line unspecified. "I'm sorry, dear. You'll have to wait." Kant's apparent delight at hearing a slight to the Republicans warred with his disapproval at seeing a child so spoiled.

"Would you like to see my elephant?" Jessica asked sweetly, changing tactics.

"Sure." Kant smiled, revealing his lizard teeth. Jessica didn't even flinch and Kant smiled wider. It was easy to read the detective's pleasure at encountering a child, even a spoiled one, neither repelled nor even curious to see a joker.

The girl reached into the pocket of her apron, but rather than a stuffed animal, she withdrew an antique ivory cricket cage with two tiny elephants carved atop. Inside the cage was another elephant, this one the size of a hamster. It was alive. "His name's Timothy." As she said this, the elephant became slightly smaller, now just the right size for the cage. "I squinched him little."

Kant's lizard eyes went wide with horror, but Trudy only exclaimed brightly, "You're an ace!"

Jessica nodded proudly. "Can Timothy and me please go see the Amber Room?"

"Timothy and I," her father corrected automatically, then paused. "It's good you said 'please,' Jessica"—he smiled nervously—"but even aces have to wait sometimes."

"What if they're princesses?"

"Even princesses," Trudy put in, coming to his rescue. "Elephant Girl is both an ace and a princess, and I've seen her wait very patiently."

"You've met Elephant Girl?!"

"Once," Trudy admitted truthfully, "but I doubt she'd remember me." She rather hoped she didn't. "But I'll always remember her." That was true. Trudy still had a truly lovely ruby pendant she'd snatched from the Irish-Bengali princess's forehead.

"Are you an ace? Or a princess?"

"I'm not an ace," Trudy lied, "nor a princess, just a rich old lady who was there on the first Wild Card Day."

Jessica's eyes went wide. "Were you scared?"

"A little," Trudy told her, "but not as much as most people. I was a tough young lady." She glanced to the elephant. "What else have you shrunk?"

"A whole farm!" Jessica recounted happily to Kant's continued horror. "Horses, cows, pigs, chickens—everything!"

"Even the little tractors and carriages?"

"No." Jessica pouted. "I can only squinch living things. Daddy bought me a dollhouse, but it's not the same."

"Your daddy bought you a ticket to see the Amber Room, too," Trudy pointed out. "That and a wonderful ace? You're a very lucky little girl."

"You're right." Jessica spontaneously hugged her father. "I love you, Daddy!"

"I love you, too, Jessica," her father told her, then mouthed *Thank you* to Trudy, his face a mask of abject relief. Once his daughter released him, he extended his hand. "Jasper von der Stadt."

He had nice hands, soft and well cared for, with a perfect manicure and a businessman's grip. He had a gold Rolex, too. "Trudy Pirandello." She guessed Jasper was a stockbroker or something in finance, probably a widower. Trudy hoped the girl's ace wasn't to blame, but depending on timing and temperament, it very well could have been.

But this speculation was set aside for the next set of early arrivals, a loud bunch who smelled like they'd just come from cocktails. Kant checked the invitation. "Latham, Strauss, party of five?"

The leader, a distinguished man in a white tuxedo and diamond studs, had cold eyes. "Yes," he said simply. Trudy guessed he was Latham. Flanking him were a tall, unusually handsome blond man in a matching white tux and studs who could have been as young as sixteen, and a gorgeous woman in her early twenties with a Snow White complexion, a sequined green dress patterned with a cascade of maple leaves, a strand of pearls, and teardrop pearl earrings. Trudy had played arm candy enough times over the years to peg the pair as a personal assistant and protégé and a high-class call girl or aspiring trophy wife. She overheard Latham naming them as David and Diane.

Strauss, wearing a black tux with octagonal onyx studs edged with marcasite, classic deco and likely his father's, introduced himself to Kant, and named himself as Kenneth and the pretty blonde in the blue silk dress as his wife, Beth. She'd accessorized with aquamarines. Trudy approved. But the way Beth touched her necklace and then her husband's arm bespoke a recent gift, likely a birthday or anniversary, making Trudy cross the aquamarines off the list of suitable souvenirs. She was growing sentimental in her old age.

"I believe Mr. Towers is expecting us for the early viewing?" Latham mentioned.

Jessica stared at him, her mouth dropping open. "But I wanted to see the Amber Room *first*, Daddy. You promised."

"That's okay, honey," said Beth, "I think we have room for a couple more in our party. Right, St. John?" she asked Latham, pronouncing it *Sinjin*.

It was a power play of etiquette, and Latham merely nodded. Kant glanced over to where a man in a midrange suit stood near the elevators. "Sergeant Martin?" he called.

Martin was middling height and build, with dark hair, high cheekbones, and perfect teeth that he revealed with a reflexive smile. A nat. Trudy put this together with rumors she'd heard on the streets of Jokertown to conclude that this was Ernie Martin, who was either bad news or easy to work with, depending on where you stood with the law. Kant leaned close to Martin, whispering in his ear. Martin's charming smile fell as he glanced to Jessica, still proudly holding her elephant.

On the elevator ride up, Jessica held up the cricket cage so everyone could get a good look. "His name's Timothy!"

Trudy had not been invited along, but when she was young and pretty, she'd learned it was easy to add herself to a retinue, and the same trick worked when you were old and grandmotherly. But she could have been a ten-foot joker with purple spots and no one would have paid her any mind.

Once the elevator let out, she watched as Martin buttonholed Ramshead, another of the Jokertown cops Trudy knew on sight. With his gray curling ram's horns, this wasn't hard. She wondered if the whole Jokertown precinct was here. As big of an affair as this was, Towers had likely supplemented his own security with cops from all over town, then decided to put the jokers on desk and elevator duty rather than someplace where the wealthy Republicans would have to look at them over dinner.

The upper foyer had white marble columns with gilded capitals, crystal candelabras before gilt mirrors, and the overall decorator sense of a budget King Croesus, marble and gilding taking the place of true chryselephantine ivory and gold. But this was nothing compared to what lay beyond the ornate, antique, white-and-gold rococo double doors at the end of the hallway that Ramshead led them to.

The Amber Room glowed like a jewel, for a jewel it was. Amber of all colors, from pale white to deepest cherry, formed the mosaic panels bedecking the walls, true old-world eighteenth-century elegance. But mostly the room shone with the colors between—yellow, egg yolk, honey, butterscotch, and cognac—the petrified resin pieced together to form ornaments, garlands, pictures and picture frames, and even wainscoting below rondels with heraldic crests flanked by marquetry, but composed of amber instead of wood, the cracks between the pieces glittering with gold leaf.

Trudy stepped onto the lovely antique parquet floor, the traditional wooden marquetry there inlaid with tesselations and arabesques, a quadrangle of compass roses spinning out from a central circle holding a dark rosewood diamond encircled with four rosewood horseshoes overflowing with luck or at least light maple acanthus leaves. Supposedly Catherine the Great had never lost a game of cards in the Amber Room and considered it her lucky charm, though Trudy suspected this had more to do with courtiers knowing better than to smash the empress at whist than any particular luck or skill on her part.

The other lucky figures worked into the floor's mandala pattern were mostly obscured by two dozen banquet tables with settings for fourteen each, the extra chairs squeezed in at the ends and damn the fire marshal. Trudy did the math. Seating for 336 guests, pushing the room beyond fire safety to the limit of sheer physical space. Towers knew how to rake it in.

Hopefully without tragedy. Amber was highly flammable, and the walls might as well be paneled in gasoline.

But Towers was making his own luck, too, and Trudy guessed

the extra security had been hired as much for fire prevention as theft. In any case, the Great Cate's circle of horseshoes was still clearly visible in the middle of a center aisle leading to a raised dais which bore four gilded, thronelike chairs facing the main doors with a smaller amber-studded table set before them. Atop it, placed in the middle, sat a chess set of orange and lemon-yellow amber, yellow on the left, orange on the right. Trudy hoped it was just a centerpiece. The prospect of hearing Towers interview Quayle had been bad enough without having to watch them play chess, too.

The Latham-Strauss party she'd attached herself to had entered through double doors at the base of the room, the doorway decorated with a crown of gold amber spraying rays of orange amber in a sunrise pattern at an amber cornice, curlicues, fleurons, and frippery. Identical doors were on the walls to the right and the left, surmounted by gold-skinned, hunky, shirtless youths wearing bicorne hats, emerging from a veritable thicket of rococo gilded wood rocaille to give each other loving glances across the room.

A gay couple? Random eye candy? Golden boys, certainly, but too early to be Jack Braun in love with himself, unless he'd discovered time travel to go with his immortality. Castor and Pollux, maybe, twin guardians of banquet halls after that incident with Simonides?

Trudy wasn't sure, but you couldn't spend as much time as she had in museums without picking things up from the docents and you couldn't hire an Italian designer to pimp your amber firetrap back in the day without him adding propitiation to the appropriate Greco-Roman gods. Trudy thanked them for the fact that Jack was a confirmed Democrat so there was no chance of running into him here. That might get awkward.

In any case, on the far wall, between the golden twins, stood three tall arched windows with three small arched windows above them, together two stories high, looking out onto night and Central Park. The two columns between them, at the height of the smaller windows, were adorned with oil paintings of armorial bearings, or at least of cherubs trying to figure out what to do with two huge human-size shields. Below each painting, the bust of a gilded nymph surmounted a rococo mirror, framing the central window and the dais with the four thrones and the chess set.

She turned around in the horseshoe circle, getting a good look at the whole chamber. The amber panels all looked about thirteen feet tall, ranging from three to five feet wide, topped by a three-foot gilded wood entablature at the same level as the smaller windows with baroque cherubs and urns alongside fire-gilded ormolu candelabras. Below that each panel had garlands and swags of cherry amber over an oval portrait composed wholly of amber mosaic, both picture and frame, above a larger upright rectangular portrait, again of amber, with the panel around it amber mosaic as well. Here and there Trudy could see that the pattern was varied, some of the oval portraits smaller to allow space for oval mirrors below, and four of the rectangular amber mosaic portraits were inset with colorful paintings.

No, not paintings, she realized on second glance. Florentine mosaics composed of different colored gemstones. She'd need to get a closer look at those.

Busts of more gold nymphs flanked each panel, their naked breasts spilling out of golden foliage, surmounting at least two dozen tall thin mirrors with proper silver backing set at intervals about the room, reflecting the light, illuminated by smaller but no less ornate candelabras—or, actually, candle-tinted track lighting set along the edges of the ceiling alongside discreet security cameras, the lamps trained on the mirrors for reflected light, the cameras panning stealthily. A larger secondary bank of lamps and cameras ran along the strip before the windows, several of the cameras aimed at the door she'd just come through.

Trudy counted them while pretending to admire the elegant scrollwork of the gilded acanthus leaves on the white plaster ceiling, the inset vignette paintings at the four corners of the room of yet more cherubs celebrating the four seasons, and the surprisingly inclusive vision of Paradise on the central panel with what looked like Mary approving of the match of Jesus and Mary Magdalene on the middle cloud while Dionysus chomped a bunch of grapes on another and Cupid fluttered through the air and shot an arrow in the direction of a third cloud with a woman playing a mandolin and another shaking a tambourine for the denizens of Heaven. There was also an adoring cherub deliberately posed to show his butt crack, because who didn't want to see that?

Trudy looked back down, intending to take in more of the Amber Room's treasures, only to have her vision blocked by a tall man in his forties. While the cloth of his white tuxedo looked extremely expensive, the cut was awful and unflattering. His diamond studs and cuff links were so large as to be comical if they weren't real, which just made them unforgivably garish and ostentatious. Yet to say his hair and skin were shades not found in nature would be untrue—they matched some of the bright yellows and oranges of the amber—but they were shades not found in humanity unless touched by the wild card or, in his case, the bottle and the tanning booth. "Welcome to my Amber Room," proclaimed Duncan Towers. "Isn't this the greatest thing ever?"

Trudy had never encountered the real estate mogul in person, preferring a better class of establishment with more upscale clientele, but she'd seen him in newspapers and on television. That in no way compared to the reality. He gave the impression of a community theater P. T. Barnum, only more tawdry. "This thing is *huge! Big league!*" Duncan Towers's Queens accent was so thick it almost sounded like he said *bigly* as he waved expansively to the whole chamber. "But it wasn't quite big enough for my penthouse, so we added a couple panels to expand it."

He gloated like a cartoon frog, his expression beyond smug, and gestured to a new panel nearby given pride of place to the right of the windows, several spotlights making it glow. The rondel in the wainscoting displayed the Towers crest, a stylized T made to look like a medieval German tower, which was, amusingly enough, the same one his immigrant grandfather, Fritz Turm, had used on his brothel tokens. Trudy had some in her collection. But here it was done up like the crest of a noble house, lavishly rendered in bright orange amber that matched Duncan Towers's complexion.

Above that the rectangular portrait was pieced together with golden amber to create an almost photorealistic image of the Golden Tower. Trudy was certain a computer had been used for color matching. Then above that, the huge oval portrait showed the face of Duncan Towers himself, with the same smug grin, the mosaic pieced together from orange and yellow amber except for some small chips of white for his teeth and bits of the rarest blue amber for his eyes. The busty nymphs beaming down at this crime against taste were even bustier than their eighteenth-century sisters and had the faces and hairstyles of Nagel girls.

"Very nice," said Latham in a tone which implied the exact opposite.

Trudy thought everyone picked up on this except for Towers, but apparently not. "It is really nice, isn't it?" agreed J. Danforth Quayle, George Bush's vice presidential pick, his hair as yellow as blond amber, his tuxedo black. He looked like a surfer who'd got lost on the way to the beach and instead went into politics. "We were just saying that, weren't we, Marilyn?"

"Yes," agreed the horse-faced—in the nat sense—brunette beside him, using the same tone as Latham. She was wearing an amethyst gown with a lace brocade bodice with amethyst jewelry. Trudy approved, but would have no qualms about taking it.

Towers had mentioned two new panels. The Quayles were standing in front of one, an extension to the original room, an extra strip of marquetry added to the parquet floor patterned with stars and stripes. The eagle in the rondel in the wainscoting was not the Imperial Eagle of Russia but the bald eagle of the Presidential Seal of the United States. The rectangular portrait above was a picture of The White House. The two oval portraits above that were of George Herbert Walker Bush and Dan Quayle, both smiling, the exact same oval portraits used for their campaign buttons, only now huge and composed of amber.

Dan Quayle stood below his portrait, smiling the same stupid smile. Marilyn Quayle stood below Bush's smile, but she was not smiling at all and seemed to have the good grace to be slightly embarrassed.

"St. John Latham," Latham introduced himself, "of Latham, Strauss. I've been looking forward to meeting you." His eyes flicked to Marilyn Quayle, and Trudy noted the almost imperceptible nod back. Dan Quayle might be the candidate, but Latham and Marilyn Quayle would be doing most of the talking.

Trudy glanced around the room, noting various cops from other precincts, some of whom she recognized, mixed with members of Towers's building security. Ernie Martin was whispering with some in one corner, subtly pointing to Jessica. Near the entrance, Ramshead was nodding his horns in response to something just said by a moderately tall slightly balding brown-haired man in a distinctive blue-and-white unitard, complete with cape. The cape was anchored at his ankles and billowing slightly, despite it being indoors without any fans. Cyclone, the ace defender of San Francisco, was presently the leading candidate to succeed as director of SCARE, if *Aces!* magazine were to be believed. He was also the perfect ace to blow out any fires.

Ramshead shut the door and Cyclone floated over to them, his cape billowing. It looked impressive, and was doubtless meant to be intimidating, but Jessica only exclaimed delightedly, "You're an ace like me!" Cyclone's cape deflated and so did his expression. Jessica held up her elephant. "This is Timothy!"

"He's . . . cute," said Cyclone. "You're here to see the Amber Room?"

Jessica nodded excitedly.

"And so she should," agreed Duncan Towers, not even glancing into the cricket cage. "Let me give you the grand tour, sweetie. Do you know who built the Amber Room? Frederick, the King of Prussia. Like my grandpa Frederick . . ."

Towers droned on, loving the sound of his own voice, but it worked well enough for a lecture, and Trudy watched the groups separate. Latham and Strauss remained with the Quayles, Cyclone hovering around behind them literally, David figuratively, while Beth kissed her husband on the cheek and joined Towers's Amber Room tour. Diane, after a moment's hesitation, decided to do the same.

Trudy followed, collecting a glass of sparkling mineral water along the way from a waiter who'd first offered her champagne, noting as she did so who else was forgoing alcohol: the cops, of course, and Cyclone, obviously guarding the Quayles, but also, interestingly enough, Towers.

She caught up with their host in time to hear him say, "So Frederick's son gave the Amber Room to Peter the Great. Who was pretty great. Big man. Huge. Made Russia great again. Couple years later, Peter sent Frederick an ivory goblet and fifty-five giants for his collection."

"Giants?" asked Jessica. "Was he an ace?"

"Nah, they didn't have aces back then. Pete was just freaky tall and Fred was a weirdo who collected giant soldiers. Bred them like the Takisians. Had them march through his bedroom like sheep when he was trying to fall asleep."

Jessica giggled. "I count my sheep at bedtime too. It's fun."

"Everyone needs a hobby, but Fred was nuts. Pete the Great was fine. His grandson Peter? Not so much. Geeky kid, played with toy soldiers. As an adult. Hung a rat for treason for eating the paste off

one. Can you believe it? But Pete's wife, Catherine, she was German, and she was great, too. Catherine the Great. She decided Pete
had to go, so he did, and then she threw a big party in the Amber
Room. And she *loved* horses."

"I love horses, too!" exclaimed Jessica. "I've got a whole stable
full."

"So did Catherine," chuckled Towers, his eyes twinkling.

Jasper von der Stadt swilled his champagne and reached for
another glass.

Trudy followed, amused, checking out the merchandise as she
did so. The amber panels were baroque elegance with all sorts of
interesting details as you looked closer, depicting things like angels, double-headed eagles, mermen riding dolphins, soldiers supporting crowns while holding the severed heads of giants, amber
intaglios carved with lions, an intaglio landscape of a boat sailing
up to some city with a German-style cathedral, and even more glorious garlands of cherry amber carved and wreathed like laurels. But
while it would have been child's play to pop out any of the individual pieces, or even a whole mosaic, it would be a pain to piece
back together at home.

There were also the two paintings by the windows and various
ornaments of ormolu—swans, reclining muses, yet more cherubs—
which were all equally lovely, but the paintings were on panel instead of canvas and too big to fit in her purse, even if she popped
them out of the frames, and the ormolu looked heavy. Plus there
were the four Florentine mosaics. Trudy checked them all out and
realized they were on the theme of the Five Senses: *Sight, Sound,
Taste,* and lastly *Touch & Smell,* together on one panel.

Trudy rather fancied that one. It depicted two couples double-
dating with their dogs by the fountain of some castle's scenic
overlook, one man plucking roses for his lady to smell from an
architectural urn, the other couple touching each other's faces
just before they started necking, with their dogs combining both

touch and smell because one of them was sniffing the other one's butt. There was also a bust of Pan in the background. It was more than a trifle kitsch, but it was made out of jewels, and good enough for Catherine the Great was good enough for her.

But there was still no way she was getting it into her purse.

Trudy wondered if Duncan Towers had also procured Catherine the Great's erotic furniture collection. It wouldn't be on display in the Amber Room, of course—it would be in a different chamber requiring a private invitation from Towers at the very least—but she'd seen pictures and heard rumors of what had become of it after the war. If a bunch of corrupt Soviet officials were going to secretly fire sale the Amber Room and other imperialist treasures of their crumbling empire, why not throw in Cathy's kinky dick table and the armchairs with the nymphs and satyrs going down on one another?

But the Republicans couldn't waffle on about *Forces of Democracy* or *Safekeeping the Treasures of Humanity from the Horrors of War* with that like they had with the Amber Room. If a Democrat had done questionable horse trading, backroom deals, and possibly favors for the KGB in exchange for art treasures, the GOP would tar and feather him. But when one of their own did? Then that was fine, so long as the porn stayed in the back room.

As for souvenirs of the regular Bush campaign fund-raiser dinner, better choices were the two dozen amber knickknacks on display as centerpieces on the tables about the room: a crown of cherry amber on a butterscotch pillow, a fancy Russian Easter egg with an imperial eagle on top, a music box, an ornate jewelry chest, a bowl of fruit, a frothing sculpted overflowing beer stein, a pillared mantel clock, a tiny German cathedral, a tiny Russian cathedral, a beehive with bees, an owl, a model ship, a vase with roses, a Chinese foo dog, an orange tabby cat, a toad, a tortoise, a toy troika, a samovar, a carp, a bull, an apple tree, a bunch of grapes, and a statuette of three naked dancing nymphs. Trudy guessed the last were meant to represent the Three Graces, the classic classical art excuse for pinup girls. But they were all still bulky and it was almost impossible to pick just one. Fortunately Trudy had time to make her selection.

"Here," said Duncan Towers loudly from the top of the room, "let me show you my favorite piece." Trudy perked her ears and hurried over to the table where the model ship rested. It was lovingly detailed, the planks fashioned from dark brown amber, the brass fittings in opaque butterscotch, even cunningly carved little bits of rare green amber used to make the seaweed snagged on the tiny anchor and the tail of the mermaid figurehead.

In keeping with the sensibilities of her eighteenth-century origins, the mermaid was topless. In keeping with Towers's sensibilities, he fingered and fondled her breasts as he picked up the ship and brought it closer so everyone could see. "There's a secret catch here." Towers had strangely small hands for such a tall man. He fingered the mermaid lower, and more obscenely, but then a music box tune began to play *"Ach, du lieber Augustin"* or *"Did You Ever See a Lassie?"* depending on whether your frame of reference was German or Scottish. The ship began to roll this way and that way on hidden wheels, pitching around on unseen waves, the little gold amber cannons going up and down out the cannon ports, the ship occasionally spinning around completely to point in a different direction.

"Isn't this the best thing ever?" asked Towers. "It was meant as a drinking game, an old version of spin the bottle. Whomever the ship ended up pointing to had to take a drink."

The ship finished its tune and ended up pointed at Jessica von der Stadt as a little black-and-white amber Jolly Roger hidden in the crow's nest popped up to the tip of the mast. "It's a *pirate* ship!" she exclaimed in delight. "Daddy, it's just the right size for all my pets, too."

"I guess it is, pumpkin."

"Look!" Jessica opened the cricket cage and the frightened elephant ran out onto the amber deck, rushing up to the railing and
looking down the long distance to the table before letting out a
trumpet that sounded like a mouse squeak.

Duncan Towers made a similar noise.

"Pumpkin," Jasper von der Stadt told her nervously, "you should
put Timothy back. You shouldn't touch other people's toys without asking, and people will be having dinner here. What if he
poops?"

"Timothy will be good," Jessica promised and almost on cue
Timothy wasn't. "I'm sorry, Daddy."

"Tell Mr. Towers."

Jessica looked up at the real estate mogul. "I'm sorry, Mr.
Towers."

"That's okay," Towers said uneasily. "Where did you get a tiny
elephant?"

"From my ace," said Jessica, beaming. "Timothy was too big for
Santa to fit down the chimney, so Daddy took me to pick him up
and let me squinch him little." Jessica opened her cricket cage and
Jasper used his pocket square to help her coax the elephant back
inside, then wiped up the miniaturized elephant dung on the deck.
"I do it every morning for my pets before I go to school."

"They eventually grow back otherwise," Jasper explained.

"Such a wonderful power," Trudy remarked again.

Duncan Towers did not look like he found it quite so wonderful, and to be fair, neither did Jasper von der Stadt. "So," prompted
Jessica's father, "you were saying the Russians hid the Amber Room
behind wallpaper, but the Nazis found it anyway?"

"Oh yeah," said Towers, taking refuge in his spiel, "took it away
to Königsberg. Everyone thought it was bombed and burnt up with
the castle, but it wasn't. Nazis just hid it in a dungeon or wine cel-
lar or something. Then Königsberg became Kaliningrad, one thing

led to another, and with the mess in the Soviet Union now, an opportunity arose. So I took it." Towers gestured to the Amber Room. "Isn't it great?"

"It is indeed," agreed a beautiful woman, lithe and fairylike, who almost danced across the parquet floor as she came over to clutch Towers's arm and rest her head against his shoulder. She was wearing an expertly styled and fitted honey-blond wig done up in an elaborate German braided coiffure, bright gold contact lenses, amber jewelry, and an amber silk gown that looked like something Trudy had spied during Fashion Week. Trudy recognized the woman wearing it from the New York City Ballet. Asta Lenser, better known as Fantasy, was their prima ballerina and star ace, whose dancing fascinated almost every man and some women, too, making her solos the perfect time for Trudy to snatch anything that had caught her eye.

"*Fantasy!*" Trudy exclaimed in delight. This was an unexpected bonus.

The ace looked at her with a fey mien and an abstracted air that most would put down to artistic temperament, but that Trudy knew, from experience, came from being high. Fantasy's purse always contained the *best* drugs. Trudy wondered what was in the amber-beaded clutch the ace had dangling from her left wrist. "Have we met?" the ballerina asked.

"No," said Trudy, "but I have season tickets. I'm such a fan of your work."

"I am, too," said David, stepping in front of Trudy. He smelled exactly like a teenager with too much access to too much unlimited champagne. "You're the hottest woman ever. I know you've got a date now, but if you're free later . . ."

Fantasy laughed. "Young man, if you can't handle your champagne, you'll never be able to handle me." She reached for a flute on the tray of a nearby waiter and downed it in one swallow, almost giving head to the glass as she did. "Maybe in a few years." She set the glass on the tray and licked her gold lips slowly as punctuation.

David turned red in the way that only pale blonds could. Diane put a hand on his shoulder, kneading his muscles like an experienced courtesan and rolling her eyes only once she'd gotten him away from Fantasy.

Towers gloated while Fantasy fawned over him, then she said, "Oh, look, Duncan, the other guests are arriving. . . ."

Trudy glanced back. Ramshead as doorman ushering in a number of well-heeled Republicans, though not so well-heeled as Latham/Strauss, who must have paid a small fortune for the early access. Diane retreated to Latham and Beth to her husband while Trudy mingled, sipped mineral water, and checked out the jewels the new ladies were wearing, along with the gentlemen's watches, cuff links, and tux studs. Some nice pieces, but nothing she couldn't pick up at the ballet or the opera. Or Broadway.

Trudy watched Aurora swan in, star of Broadway and Hollywood, at least in the early seventies. Her star had dimmed, but her ace hadn't, the shimmering light of the aurora borealis she generated above herself making the Amber Room glitter and glow even more beautifully around her and security freak out with cries of "Pyro!"

"No," she said plaintively, sounding both mystified and hurt as she was surrounded by off-duty police officers young enough to be her sons. "My lights are cold. Harmless. I'm Aurora."

They looked back, equally mystified, until one said, "You're saying you're an ace with fire-engine red hair who isn't a pyrokinetic?"

Aurora touched her signature red-gold hair. It was still lovely, but undoubtedly touched up with dye now. "That was just a movie I was in." She bit her perfect pouting painted lips. "In the seventies . . ."

Security gave one another baffled looks. Then one said, "Wait, weren't you on *Love Boat* when I was a kid?"

Aurora nodded sadly, her diamond bracelets and choker scintillating magnificently, but as Trudy knew from sad experience, Aurora favored cubic zirconias.

Trudy moved on, accepting an hors d'oeuvre from a passing waiter, a bite of amber-tinted champagne jelly topped with crème fraîche and caviar. She hadn't figured Aurora for a Republican, but then again, she might be dating one or she was one of the entertainment biz black sheep who'd strayed to the other side of the fence. There were always some. That, or she was just desperate for publicity.

Trudy didn't much care. The drugs she'd found in Aurora's purse in the past were as worthless as her fake diamonds, nothing more interesting than headache pills and birth control. She could keep them and her lackluster career.

More and more Republicans were coming in and the room was getting crowded. Trudy paused by the little amber corner table built into the bottom right corner of the Amber Room. A tiered dish was placed on it containing amber candies, but thankfully not containing trapped ants or scorpions. Instead, the faux fossils held borage blossoms and other edible flowers. Trudy took one and sucked on it, considering, as she watched the guests stream in.

Latham had finished with his early meeting with Quayle and moved on to some Republican congressman who'd brought his bored-looking teenage son. The boy was talking with David. "Gary, huh?" said David, snagging champagne flutes for both of them.

"Yeah," said the boy, accepting the alcohol and quickly taking a transgressive sip, "but my friends call me 'Gyro.'"

Ah, youth . . . Trudy rolled her eyes and moved on, looking for something more interesting, then spied her just a bit on, over by the mosaic for *Sight*: Desiree Windermere, the best-selling romance novelist.

She looked much like she did in her dust-jacket pictures: long dark hair, pale attractive face, daringly low-cut gown, which Trudy envied her still having the youth to pull off. Desiree's dress for this evening was Renaissance-inspired, using the same color palette and basic form as the one worn by the woman with the telescope in the mosaic, the same coquelicot turban, the same sienna and russet draperies, but reinterpreted with modern twists as something suitable for an autumn formal. She'd accessorized with a full topaz parure of Renaissance design that looked authentic, a vintage Regency net reticule strung with amber beads that matched in color if not in period, and was posing for a photographer wearing a *New York Times* press pass.

Trudy stayed out of the shot, as she always tried to, considering. The topaz parure, much as she admired it, was off-limits, since Desiree's Lady Light novels were some of Trudy's favorite reads, and if nothing else, she didn't want to distract the author from delivering the next in the series. They featured Lucia Ravenswood, a beautiful young secret ace and even more secret jewel thief. Every novel she hooked up with some new young swain, usually another ace, who was inevitably revealed as a cad, a fraud, or someone who might be The One except for the fact that he dies at the end in a noble sacrifice.

Lucia's powers involved light manipulation, allowing her to dazzle foes, disguise herself with light-bending illusions, and even turn things invisible by displacing their image. Her adventures ranged from the improbable to episodes oddly reminiscent to ones in Trudy's own life, making her wonder if Desiree was just good at research or dabbled in the business herself.

Trudy wasn't the only one. "So," asked Ernie Martin, "is there a place in your next novel for a handsome police sergeant?"

"There might be." Desiree fluttered her lashes coquettishly. "But he'd have to be a villain. Would you mind?"

"A little." Ernie grinned his charming grin. "But I'm a cop. I'm used to it."

Desiree laughed lightly. "Lucia's lover for this next book will be Ilya Romanov, last heir of the Romanov dynasty, who seeks the Amber Room so he can cement his claim to the throne when the monarchy is restored. But unlike my other heroes, Ilya's not going to die. He has to marry someone of royal lineage to remain tsar, so he's going to be looking at actual princesses. One of Queen Margaret's daughters, or someone from Sweden, Spain, or the Netherlands. Maybe a princess from Takis. I'm not certain, but it will still be his tragic but noble duty. Lucia will be heartbroken, but she might be able to fall back to a dalliance with the handsome police sergeant. . . ."

"So what's Ilya's ace?" Ernie asked. "Teleporter?"

"Oh nothing so common and tawdry." Desiree waved to dismiss the thought. "Ilya's fantastically strong, which is common, yes, but he can also step through paintings, and Lucia leaves illusions behind in their place. My only plotting difficulty is I can't figure out how they can quickly unbolt the Amber Room's panels without damaging them."

Trudy sipped her mineral water rather than rolling her eyes. If Ilya were a teleporter, removing bolts would be child's play.

"We hadn't even considered the Romanovs," Ernie told Desiree softly as Trudy eavesdropped. "We know about some of the Russians wanting the Amber Room back, and the Germans, too, both East and West, since they want Nazi loot to trade for the art the Russians looted from them. But restoring the monarchy?"

"It's happened before," Desiree pointed out.

Trudy nibbled her amber candy and moved on. Word on the street was that there were all sorts of players in the game, and not just the West and East Germans and the Russians, but everyone ranging from the Poles to the Sultan of Brunei. The Amber Room was a huge political bargaining chip, and Towers was cementing his claim to it with the power of the GOP.

The room was getting extremely crowded, guests getting seats at tables because there was hardly room to stand around the edges, and Trudy wondered how many others were here casing the joint. A heist could be done at any time, and Russia, both Germanies, Poland, and who knows what other countries were undoubtedly putting together crack teams of just the right aces with the information their spies fed back, to say nothing of the international art-smuggling rings and private collectors. Trudy felt like a very small bird in a large and vicious flock, but then again, it *was* the Bush campaign fund-raiser dinner. She knew that when she bought the ticket.

But a clever magpie might still be able to fly off with a pretty bauble while the big birds fought for the prize.

She spotted an empty seat at the table with the amber pirate ship, the piece she'd decided to take home. "May I join you?" she asked Beth Strauss with as much grandmotherly sweetness as she could muster, putting a hand on the empty chair opposite her, one chair down, unfortunately next to David. It was the table at the top of the room on the right, the side closest to Towers and the orange side of the chessboard, but thankfully with her back to Towers.

"Please do," said Beth.

Trudy sat down, smiling as she glanced back to the dais behind her. Fantasy sat beside Towers, her goodie bag next to her, at the closest edge of the amber table. Even if Trudy couldn't snatch the pirate ship, the evening didn't have to be a total wash. While she made a point of never mixing business with pleasure, once she was safely back home she could indulge as she liked. Plus the goodie bag didn't have to be a consolation prize either, since both it and the pirate ship would fit in her purse.

Sitting beside Beth, on the opposite side from Kenneth Strauss, who was chatting with some young woman in a purple dress, was Jasper von der Stadt, and beside him was Jessica. Her cricket cage was on the table in front of her, though she was still guiltily eyeing the pirate ship down the table. It sat in the center between Beth and Kenneth and David and Diane. The mermaid pointed to David, who was drinking more champagne he did not need. "It's okay, Jessica," her father told her. "I'm not mad. See? Someone was willing to sit there."

"Why do you think they call it a poop deck?" Trudy told Jessica, causing her to giggle and Jasper to give Trudy a look of extreme gratitude.

The seat opposite Jessica was still empty, though the one beside her, at the foot of the table, was occupied by Cyclone, who told her, "My daughter's an ace, too."

"Really?" asked Jessica, her blue eyes going wide.

He nodded. "Her name's Mistral."

"What's her power?"

"Same as mine," Cyclone told her.

Jessica rolled her eyes as if she did not believe him, even though Trudy knew it was the truth, unlikely as it sounded. But then a man walked up to the last empty chair. "Looks like this is the wildcard corner. Mind if I join you?"

He looked to be in his twenties, tall and thin, with dark hair and glowing eyes. Reality rippled around him, like a heat shimmer in the desert, making him hard to look at. He glanced to her, then blinked. "Hey, Trudy. Been a few years."

She looked back. She'd never seen him before in her life, and with a weird joker effect like that, he wasn't someone she'd forget. Then she put two and two together. "Croyd?"

He grinned. "In the flesh." He sat down heavily and yawned. "Sorry. Been up a while, but I wanted to make this party."

Trudy signaled the waiter. "A coffee for my friend here. Espresso shots, too."

The waiter nodded while Croyd was yawning. He gave her a quick hug, then whispered in her ear, "Got anything stronger? Couldn't find my regular dealer."

"Give me a few minutes," Trudy whispered back.

Croyd was the Sleeper, and he'd been around since the first Wild Card Day. He was a damn good thief when he could keep it together, but getting him at the end of his cycle was a recipe for trouble. *Who for* depended on whether you were working with him or against him. But judging by Fantasy's goodie bag in the past, uppers and downers were practically guaranteed.

"Thanks, Trudy. You're a pal." He hugged her again. "Do me another solid? Grab an extra something for me?"

"What do you need?"

"*Anything*," Croyd whispered fiercely. "I cut a deal with the West Germans for diplomatic immunity for whatever I brought them and they think I'm this awesome ace, but my power is crap this time. I thought I'd be able to control it better if I practiced, but no dice."

"I'll try, but you'll owe me one. And fifty-fifty."

"Deal."

Trudy glanced to the other tables' centerpieces. The toad and the tortoise were the best bets, basically big amber paperweights with a nice compact shape, and the grapes were put together with gold wire so could probably be smushed. Maybe the music box if she stuffed Fantasy's evening bag into it. It would be tricky, but then again, so was she.

Trudy listened in on the conversations at the table. The young woman in purple was the daughter of the congressman Latham had been talking to earlier. He sat at the far end of the table, flanked by his wife, Mrs. Congressman, and their son, Gyro. Or Gary, as they kept calling him as he kept staring up at Fantasy with adolescent lust.

The waiter brought Croyd's coffee and the menus. The choices for dinner were themed for the progress of the Amber Room: Prussian *Jägerschnitzel mit Pfifferlingen* (veal cutlet with chanterelles) and spätzle with Königsberg flamed marzipan for dessert, Russian sturgeon coulibiac with Tula gingerbread, and American aged porterhouse with cognac-cherry demiglace reduction followed by the Golden Tower's signature towering chocolate cake, dusted with edible gold. Naturally. You were allowed to mix and match, but for $10,000, she hoped so.

Trudy opted for the coulibiac and the marzipan. It had been a while since she'd had, either. She handed the waiter her menu, then watched as the sugar bowl wandered by in front of her on its little legs. She nudged Croyd, asking softly, "That you?"

"Yeah," he whispered back. "Can bring things to life. But it's a pretty punk power. Thought I'd be able to control them, get them to sit, stay, follow me home, if you get my drift. But the things just do whatever they want. Fun to watch, though."

Trudy watched the sugar bowl continue to amble down the table, past where David was finishing yet another glass of champagne, still looking over his shoulder to lust after Fantasy. Trudy started to have a wonderful idea. A horrible idea. A wonderfully horrible and horribly wonderful idea.

But before it could fully gel, David passed out and slumped over against her. Trudy shoved him off of her, into Diane, who was a bit more sympathetic, or at least was being paid to act like it. She smoothed his hair and make soothing noises. Then she noticed Jasper von der Stadt staring past her, his mouth hanging open, his face wearing the same expression of lust as Gyro. Kenneth Strauss had the same look, too, while his wife Beth simply looked dumbfounded. Little Jessica, watching wide-eyed, started to giggle.

Trudy turned around. Fantasy had stood up and was twirling her goodie bag by its strap like a pimp twirling a watch chain, wiggling her hips just enough to count as a dance and fascinating every man in the room and a bunch of the women, too. She whipped the evening bag a couple extra times, then slung it hard, sending it flying to the end of the front row to smack Cyclone in the face.

Fantasy got up on her throne, turning around to shake her ass at the audience, then climbed onto the table, took a step down to kick aside the pieces on the amber chessboard, destroying whatever sad excuse for a chess match was in progress, then proceeded to dance right there between Duncan Towers and Dan Quayle. Marilyn Quayle looked around the room, as if hoping security would do something, only to note what Trudy had already noted earlier: Duncan Towers had not hired a single woman for the evening barring some cocktail waitresses.

All of the men were staring at her, transfixed. All of the women were staring as well . . . Trudy with incredulity. She'd seen Fantasy dance before, many times, even when a little or a lot under the influence, but whatever drugs she'd gotten this time were *really* bad. Asta Lenser wasn't even phoning it in. Her "dance," if it could be called such, looked more like a teenage boy impersonating a hooker performing a striptease.

Fantasy's gown fell to the table with all the grace of a pair of boxer shorts hitting the floor. Her panties followed. She kicked them up, twirled them briefly, then slung them at Gyro, landing them on his head. She flashed one tit, then the other, struggling with her bra like she'd never worn one before before putting it on Duncan Towers's head like a ritual headdress for a fraternity initiation. Next she pulled off her blond wig, revealing her wig cap, and twirled the wig around by its braids before depositing it on Dan Quayle's blond head. When she turned back to Towers, she mooned the audience and began the least erotic version of the bump and grind ever performed.

Trudy appraised the room. Despite the lack of terpsichorean merit, everyone was still staring. Croyd, Cyclone, and Jasper von der Stadt were all still watching openmouthed with lust. Jessica was giggling as she watched the drunk lady dance naked on a table.

Badly. None of them were paying any attention to the elephant, Timothy.

Timothy the elephant disappeared and reappeared in Trudy's hand.

She pretended she'd dropped her napkin, then reached down and placed him inside her purse. While she was at it, she glanced down under the table, spying the edge of Fantasy's evening bag where it had landed. It disappeared and reappeared inside her purse as well.

Fantasy was always great for a distraction, but she'd never been *this* good.

The naked ace raised her hands up high in the air, shaking her tits at the bank of security cameras, then reached down to grab Duncan Towers's hands as she arched over backward, still holding on to him as she grabbed her crotch and looked back at the audience, briefly making eye contact with Trudy. With one final twist of her head, she fell onto the table in a dead faint, her ass on the chessboard, her head and arms dangling backward over the edge, her legs to each side of Duncan Towers.

"Huh, what?" slurred David, coming awake.

There was some justice in the universe. The rude boy had completely missed it.

"What the hell?!" roared Duncan Towers, his bronzer smeared, his hair-sprayed helmet of blond hair now sticking straight up in the air like Struwwelpeter. He pulled out his hands and Fantasy slid off the table, falling in a heap.

Dan Quayle sat there, looking even more idiotic under the German braided wig sitting slightly askew. "Someone must have given her drugs . . . ."

"'Someone' meaning herself," Marilyn Quayle told her husband.

"Bad drugs . . ." Trudy added softly, turning around for some sense of decorum.

Diane said, "Maybe that new one, rapture. I've heard it's nasty."

David giggled drunkenly and Gyro even more, gleefully clutching Fantasy's panties until his mother exclaimed, "Gary, give those back! That poor woman!"

Ramshead collected Fantasy's panties and Fantasy as well, Towers roaring, "Get her out of here! Get her sobered up! And tell those assholes in the security room to scrub the footage now, because if one single frame leaks to the press, it's all their asses getting fired and sued!"

Ramshead nodded, and two security men spirited Fantasy away as Towers ranted further, "And you, the jackal from the Gray Lady I let in!" He pointed one small wet finger at the *New York Times* photographer in the back. "Bet you were too busy drooling to snap any pics, but breathe so much a word about this beyond 'an unscheduled dance recital' and I'll see you never set foot in any of my events again! And don't you dare give me any shit about the public's 'need to know.' All the public needs to know is that you're all a bunch of liars!" He then glanced over to the table with the amber bull as centerpiece which looked to hold the cream of Wall Street, including editors from the *Journal*. "We good, gentlemen?"

The journalists nodded as Marilyn Quayle snatched the blond braided wig off of Dan and flung it at one of the security agents who was scrabbling for the fallen chess pieces. Nervous chatter started up, men apologizing to their wives, wives accepting or demanding more, while Trudy counted on her fingers silently and waited for it. On the count of seven, Jessica von der Stadt screamed, her high-pitched little girl's scream silencing the room again as she cried *"Timothy!* My elephant! Daddy, my elephant's missing!"

"Didn't you latch the cage properly, pumpkin?" Jasper von der Stadt asked in concern.

"I did, Daddy! *I did!*" Jessica opened the cage to show him, in the process destroying the evidence of the latched cricket cage mystery. "See?"

"What the hell is it now?!" Towers roared.

"My elephant, Mr. Towers!" Jessica explained. "My elephant is missing! Help me find him! Please!"

Towers waved. "I'm sure your daddy can buy you a new one."

"No." Jessica popped to her feet, her face turning red. "There'll never be another elephant like Timothy!"

"There are plenty of elephants," Towers snapped.

"*No*," stated Jessica, "and I said *please*."

"Now Jessica, don't get angry," her father pleaded, "and Mr. Towers, please don't upset my daughter. You don't want her upset."

"I said *please*, Daddy. . . ."

"Jessica is right." Trudy rose with grandmotherly calm. "She did say 'please.' We're the party of traditional values, are we not? The Grand Old Party? I think our servers can keep the food warm while we take a few minutes to help her." She picked up her water glass and rang it with her teaspoon for attention. "Everyone, your attention, please! A little girl has lost her elephant! He's about the size of a mouse and answers to 'Timothy.' Get up carefully so you don't step on him! Remember, he's our party mascot! We don't want the press getting wind of *that*, do we? Help Jessica find her elephant! For Bush and Victory!"

"For Bush and Victory!!!" they responded.

Trudy set down her water glass and teaspoon, then picked up her purse, containing the "missing" elephant and Fantasy's evening bag. She opened that and rifled through it, finding the zippered compartment with the drugs. A badly stoppered vial of white powder spilled out, losing half its contents, but she replaced that and sorted through pillboxes until she found one with some black beauties.

"Here." She handed half to Croyd along with his water glass as he sat in his chair, still yawning, reality shimmering around him while his butter knife squirmed across the table like an inchworm. "Ration yourself."

Croyd being Croyd of course popped two immediately.

Trudy whispered in his ear, "Now follow my lead and we'll pull the heist of the century."

Croyd looked askance, so Trudy whispered her mad plan. It probably helped that he was on drugs, but Croyd was generally up for anything.

She took her purse and started hunting around the room me-thodically, looking for the "lost" elephant. While she was doing so she popped out the lenses of the security cameras in a staggered pattern so the men at the security desk couldn't just review the tapes and narrow the list of suspects.

It took quite a few minutes, and by the time Trudy was done, Jessica was well and truly distraught, sitting in her chair crying, her father alternately comforting her and begging her not to do anything rash. A few people still milled around the room looking for her elephant, but most just ignored her plight and blathered on about politics.

"Look what I found," Trudy said, presenting Jessica with her clasped hands and then teleporting Timothy to the hollow between them. She opened them. "Your party mascot."

Jessica squealed with delight. *"Thank you!"* She took Timothy in her hands, then put him in his cricket cage, latching it securely. She wiped her tears with her father's pocket square. "Where did you find him? We looked everywhere!"

"So did I," said Trudy. "Then I thought I'd look in the last place I always think to look—my purse. The poor thing must have run off the edge of the table and fallen in!"

Jessica laughed. "Oh, look at him! He's so happy he's dancing!" The elephant was indeed swaying from side to side inside his cage, waving his trunk and flapping his ears. "What's that white stuff on his nose?"

"Powdered sugar," Trudy lied. "I had a jelly donut this morning."

"Thank you," said Jasper von der Stadt. "Thank you so much." He smiled nervously. "We should probably go. We've caused enough trouble."

"Oh, nonsense," Trudy said firmly. "The Republicans are big boys and girls and you paid the same as everyone. Just go make nice with Towers and I'll stay here with Jessica." She turned to Jessica. "You want dinner, don't you, honey?"

"Yes," said Jessica. "I like schnitzel. Grandma makes it."

"See?" said Trudy. "It's settled."

Jasper nodded and went off to see Towers while Trudy remained with Jessica, sitting in Cyclone's seat while he floated up near the clouds at the top of the vault between Mary Magdalene and the mooning cherub. "You okay, honey?" Trudy asked. She felt slightly bad to have put a child through that, but only slightly. And the elephant was no worse for the wear; in fact, it was happier than it had been earlier.

"Yes, but . . ." Jessica paused, looking up at the dais where her father was apologizing to Towers while the mogul glared back, his hair fixed but his mouth pursed like he'd just eaten a rotten prune. Jessica confessed, "I want to squinch Mr. Towers, but Daddy says I shouldn't. Not ever. But he's such a big bully. . . ."

"Well, you probably shouldn't, if Daddy says not to." Trudy gestured to the amber-paneled walls around them. "Wouldn't this room make the world's most wonderful dollhouse?"

"Yes," said Jessica, "but I can only squinch living things."

"Can you keep a secret?" Trudy asked softly. "Especially if it's one that would make Mr. Towers very unhappy?"

Jessica nodded enthusiastically, so Trudy beckoned Croyd to return to his seat. "This is my old friend, Mr. Croyd. He's got a little ace himself. And I've got a secret ace of my own, one I've had a very long time. And three aces almost always wins. . . ."

♠

Dinner was nice enough for banquet food, but for the price, it ought to be, and Trudy was glad she'd ordered the coulibiac. She watched Duncan Towers up on the dais pouring ketchup on his steak. Cyclone had taken Fantasy's seat beside him, for security purposes, chatting with him and the Quayles as he ate his own steak.

Once they'd all eaten enough, Trudy set her napkin on the table, then glanced to Croyd and Jessica, and they all looked up at Duncan Towers and Dan Quayle. "We're going to make this country *great again!*" exclaimed Towers . . . and as he said the word *great* the painting above him, the one with the cherubs trying to figure out what to do with the tower shield as well as the buxom nymph-topped mirror on the pillar between the windows, quivered like they were made out of gelatin as they came loose from the wall, shrank to the size of a bookmark fluttering through the air, and disappeared.

Trudy felt them wriggling in her purse. She didn't know what effect cocaine would have on a miniaturized living armorial painting and a nymph-topped mirror, but she hoped it wasn't going to be a problem. Usually one put cocaine *on* mirrors.

Everyone inside the Amber Room noticed except the four on the dais. But Towers noticed his audience was neither looking at him nor listening to what he said, so he turned and looked, as did the other three. No one said anything until Dan Quayle decided to fill up the emptiness in the air by stating the obvious. "It disappeared!"

Yes, Dan, Trudy thought. *It did.* She watched as another panel across the room, sixteen feet high, the one with the Florentine mosaic of *Touch & Smell* she'd liked so much, quivered as it came loose from the wall and shrank. That disappeared into her purse as well.

Trudy had been the one to come up with the random pattern, with the help of Jessica. There were fifteen panels on the walls of the Amber Room. There were eleven people seated at their table that Trudy knew the names of and four more on the dais, which was an easy math problem. And Jessica, being eight, knew alphabetical order as well. Fantasy's first name was *Asta,* so the *A* panel went first, with the painting and the mirror. *B* was for *Beth.*

"Another one disappeared!" Quayle cried.

C was for *Croyd* and the panel with the mosaic for *Hearing* to the right of the main doors as they'd come in quivered, dwindled, and vanished.

It had been Croyd who'd decided that the signal would be playing it like a drinking game. The rules were simple: Any time Towers said "big," "big league," "great," "huge," or "best ever," they took another panel. Ditto when Quayle said anything stupidly obvious.

"Cyclone!" Towers barked at the ace beside him. "Do something! We've got a big problem! Big problem!"

There were four *D*s. The first two were *Dan* and *David.* Trudy had decided to skip Quayle's first initial, out of respect. Two panels, on opposite sides of the room, shivered, shrank, and shifted out of existence, at least where they were. The first of the two was the new panel with the campaign portraits of Bush and Quayle, the picture of The White House, and the Presidential Seal. The second was the panel with the mosaic of *Sight.*

Cyclone did something. He flew in the air, the sudden updraft sweeping Tower's hair back into the Struwwelpeter hairdo. The SCARE ace floated in the air like a man-size piñata, spinning around in all directions, searching the room for something out of place, the wind blowing peoples' napkins and ruffling the flower arrangements. Trudy had an urge to sing "La Cucaracha" and look for a blindfold and a baseball bat. Jessica giggled.

"Do you think this is funny, young lady?" Towers demanded.

"Please don't upset my daughter, Mr. Towers," Jasper warned him. "If you do, you'll have an even bigger problem."

"You'll have a big problem, too," Towers threatened back.

D continued with *Diane* and the next panel over, Diane sitting next to David: a relatively ordinary panel, with nothing to distinguish it except the Russian imperial eagle and a mirror. It shimmied. It shrank. It vanished.

"What the hell is going on?!" demanded Towers.

"Someone's using an ace," Quayle told him.

Three aces, actually. The final *D* was for *Duncan*. The panel at the top of the room by the windows, the other new panel, the one with the Towers crest, the Golden Tower, and Duncan Towers's own portrait, came alive. The Nagel nymphs heaved their bounteous bosoms, both turning their heads from looking at Towers's amber portrait to looking at him, then the whole panel wiggled and jiggled, dwindled and spindled, then vanished with a *pop*.

Towers stood up, looking around, then pointed to Croyd, who was sitting close to him. "You. Who are you? Your eyes . . . you're doing this."

"I am not." Croyd's eyes brightened. "I'm just a guy with glowing eyes and a weird shimmer who paid ten thousand dollars for an overcooked steak. I was told jokers were welcome in the Republican Party, or was that 'big tent' talk just a bunch of horseshit?"

"I, uh . . ." Dan Quayle faltered, looking in desperation to Marilyn.

Marilyn was no help, but Towers gestured to his security. One of them tried to grab Croyd by the arm. The Sleeper swung his arm hard, sending the moonlighting cop into the ugly bare wall where Towers's panel had been. "I'm also pretty strong, so I guess I'm an ace, too. But strong guys are a dime a dozen, so big whoop. If you're going to accuse aces, why don't you accuse the human piñata?" He pointed to Cyclone.

"I work for SCARE," Cyclone pointed out, "and I just do wind."

"You say." Croyd popped another black beauty. "But I've seen you on television. You've got a pretty sweet pad for a guy on a government salary."

"I'm from a wealthy family."

Towers looked over to a far table, the one with the amber music box and a beautiful boreal shimmer floating in the air above one guest like an accusatory beacon. "You, then." He pointed to Aurora. "Rainbow Girl or whatever the hell your name is."

The glow of the aurora borealis above her dimmed, but Aurora couldn't hide her diamonds, or at least cubic zirconias. "I just make pretty lights. They're harmless," she said plaintively, looking desperately to the wealthy men and women with her.

Trudy finally put two and two together. Of course. Aurora was trying to relaunch her career, so she was courting theater angels and investors for a new show.

"Fine." Towers looked around for someone else to accuse, only to have Jasper von der Stadt rise and stand in front of Jessica. "Don't you dare accuse my daughter, Mr. Towers."

"She shrinks things, doesn't she?"

"Not until they disappear," Jasper snapped, "and she only shrinks living things. Trust me, I've got the doll-furniture receipts to prove it."

"Maybe she discovered a new power."

Jasper von der Stadt gasped. "Have you no shame?"

Towers seemed to take this as a rhetorical question. "Well, someone's doing it. We can just wait for the police then and do blood tests to find out who's the secret ace."

"And be in violation of the Fourth Amendment," Kenneth Strauss pointed out, "not to mention the First, depending on how many in this room are Jehovah's Witnesses."

"Kenneth," warned Latham.

"No, Sinjin," Strauss shot back. "My brother is already dealing with this witch hunt, but a *child*? Mere presence of the virus proves nothing anyway."

Towers waved dismissively. "We'll get a telepath."

"Again the Fourth," Kenneth Strauss pointed out, "plus I'd object on the grounds of attorney-client privilege. Besides, would the Party really want a telepath in the room with our next vice president?"

"I hadn't even thought of that," said Dan Quayle, causing Marilyn to roll her eyes. And since G was for *Gyro,* the panel across the room, the one with the double doors to the left and Castor or Pollux and his gilded chest sticking out of the thicket of rocaille, suddenly came to life, smiling at everyone as the doors began to open. It shrank to less than nine inches high, the Gemini twin now looking like a gilded Ken doll. Then it disappeared, dollhouse doors and all.

A very surprised-looking group of waiters stood in the hall outside, looking in through the space where the doors had been.

"Great!" Towers screamed, losing his shit along with his Amber Room. "Just great!"

The two panels making up the far corner of room danced, diminished, and disappeared in quick succession, one another relatively plain panel with mirror and eagle, the other with the mosaic for *Taste,* for J was for *Jasper* and *Jessica.*

"They just keep going away," said Dan.

J was also for *St. John.* The panel right beside them, containing the double doors to the right and the other star twin and his gilded chest, quickly wiggled, squinched, and winked out of existence, doll head, doors, and all.

Through the archway lay a parlor decked out with rich eighteenth-century furnishings. Jessica, for once, beat Dan to stating the obvious. "Daddy!" she cried, pointing. "There's a table made out of giant pee-pees!"

It was, indeed, Catherine the Great's notorious dick table, supported by four huge erect phalluses spouting wooden jizz like whales. Their enormous balls doubled as breasts because they had nipples on them and the gilded round tabletop was edged with even more phalluses, the table the centerpiece of a suite with even more lewd furniture.

Gyro and David began to laugh uproariously at this sight, exactly as you'd expect from two drunken teenage boys, while Jasper von der Stadt cried, "Cover your eyes, Jessica! Cover your eyes!"

K was for *Kenneth,* Beth's husband. Jessica squirmed free of her father's hand, and the corresponding panel, another relatively plain one across the room, squiggled, squinched, and vanished as well. Trudy's purse was getting full and wiggly with sections of disassembled miniaturized living amber dollhouse, but she held the handles and kept it sandwiched between her chair and Croyd's.

"There are only three panels left," said Dan.

M was for *Marilyn,* his wife. The matching panel, the one with the other armorial painting and nymph-topped mirror, shrugged, shrank, and shifted to Trudy's purse.

"It's happening just after you say something, Dan," Marilyn realized as Towers motioned for his security to form a human wall to block the view of the erotic parlor, the charming Ernie Martin among them.

"It is?" asked Dan.

T was for *Trudy.* She took great pleasure in watching Croyd secretly animate her panel, the one with the attached corner table, and Jessica just as stealthily miniaturize it. Trudy popped it into her purse as the tiered dish of amber candies fell to the floor and shattered, scattering porcelain shards and confectionary fossils across the floor.

"Don't. Say. Anything. Dan," Marilyn ordered as everyone in the room looked at the last panel, the one at the far side of the room with the original entry doors, or at least everyone who wasn't trying to look past Towers's security, some of whom, Ernie included, were oggling Catherine the Great's naughty furniture collection.

"That's a great idea," said Towers.

V was for Vernon, as in Vernon Henry Carlysle, the legal name of Cyclone. The final panel, including the ornate crown with the spraying rays over the rococo double doors, which took on a somewhat different interpretation when compared with the fountaining phalluses in the next room, shivered and shrank, doors and all, and Trudy took even more pleasure as she popped it into her purse, which was now almost full and quite squirmy.

Trudy glanced to Croyd and Jessica. As they'd arranged, the floor followed. The beautiful parquet began to peel up at the corners like some weird wooden sea creature, then just as quickly shrank to something that looked like nothing half so much as a possessed slab of the promised Tula gingerbread lying on the bare concrete in the middle of the room between the two dozen banquet tables, pulled out from under them like a magician pulling out a rug.

Then it was in Trudy's purse, almost the last thing that would fit. Almost.

The central painting on the ceiling fell down next, wafting like the cape of a giant blanket octopus painted with clouds and a vision of Paradise as everyone in the room caught their breath, then it shrank to the size of a painted silk scarf, then it vanished into Trudy's purse, the absolute last thing her purse would hold. She snapped it shut before any of the wriggly treasures could escape.

But there were still the four inset portraits at the corners of the ceiling. One by one they popped free, shrank, and then disappeared, fluttering postage stamps appearing beneath Trudy's hand in her pocket. All except for the last, for Cyclone had gotten wise to what was going on and flew over to seize the final panel at the far corner of the room as it popped free from its frame, his billowing cape blocking both Jessica's and Trudy's sight as he caught it, struggling to keep hold of the fluttering painting as the stray corners of the artwork smacked him in the face, like trying to wrestle a rococo manta ray. Then it shrank down to the size of a fluttering postage stamp as he landed, proudly saying to Towers as he still held it, "I have—"

He said nothing more, since it had just joined the other three in Trudy's pocket.

The grand finale was fast. Trudy kept her hand in her pocket. Around the room, the amber centerpieces began to quiver: the crown, the Easter egg, the music box, the jewelry chest, the fruit bowl, the stein, the clock, the two cathedrals, the beehive, the owl, the ship, the vase, the dog, the cat, the toad, the tortoise, the troika, the samovar, the carp, the bull, the apple tree, the grapes, and the statuette of the Three Graces. All save the chess set, which had too many fiddly little bits to deal with.

The foo dog and the tabby cat turned to snarl and hiss at each other, the toad blinked its round eyes, and the carp fell over on its side, gasping. Then the two dozen amber treasures shrank one by one—all except the jewelry chest. Then, with a string of pops like a chain of soap bubbles, they disappeared, wriggling charm bracelet baubles falling into Trudy's pocket—all except for the jewelry chest again, which remained at full size, then faded out of existence like a desert mirage, with no pop and no bauble in Trudy's pocket.

But whatever had just happened, it was gone as well. All that was left was the chess set.

Duncan Towers shoved his plate with his overcooked, ketchup-drenched steak aside and dragged the chess set toward him, guarding it jealously like an orange dragon with a blond toupée. The chessmen, fashioned from orange and yellow amber, were almost camouflaged against him. "Get out," he snarled. "Get out! All of you! Especially that creepy brat and her freaky little elephant!"

A silence fell over the room, broken by Jasper von der Stadt saying, "Don't get upset, pumpkin. Please."

"No, Daddy," Jessica said, pushing past her father. "Only a big bully would send *everyone* to bed without dessert for something someone *may* have done. It's not *fair*."

"Fuck fairness," snarled Towers.

"You promised everyone the most beautiful slice of chocolate cake ever," Jessica pointed out. "I'd like my chocolate cake. All of us would. Please."

"Such a nasty little girl . . ."

"I'm not little," countered Jessica. *"You are."*

As she said that, Duncan Towers became smaller and smaller, dwindling into his clothes as an ill-fitting white tuxedo fell to the dais beneath the amber table as he screamed in progressively smaller tones, "I'm not little! Not little! Not little . . . !"

Dan Quayle got up and reached down to the pile of clothes, taking out a three-inch tall man. "Towers," he said in awe, "you're tiny."

It was still part of the rules of the game they'd set up, so Trudy teleported one of the chess rooks to her hand, one from the orange side of the board. Quayle set Towers in the empty corner, Towers now taking the place of the tower. He waved his hands in the air, raging, but was too tiny to be heard.

Jasper von der Stadt kept looking back and forth from the tiny Towers to his daughter until Kenneth Strauss interrupted. "Here's my card. You'll need legal representation. Towers has a case for assault and battery, but your daughter has an easy *mens rea* defense plus a case for intentional infliction of emotional distress."

"We're so sorry for ruining the evening," Jasper apologized.

"No we're not, Daddy," Jessica told him. "Towers was a big bully. Now he isn't."

"Yes, pumpkin," her father said. "Are you ready to go home now? Please don't be angry at anyone else, Jessica. *Please* don't be angry."

This was just the right thing to say to cause an absolute panic. Three hundred Republicans rushed the far archway toward the elevators. "Could you help me with my bag, Croyd?" Trudy asked. "It's a bit heavy."

"Sure thing." Croyd popped his last two black beauties, picked up the bag, then glanced toward the mob of security massed by the archway to Catherine the Great's erotic furniture collection. His eyes glowed brighter as he looked intensely in their direction. "Follow me. Quick," he told Trudy. They headed for the elevators, shoving his way through the bottleneck of Republicans.

Trudy dropped the chess tower into her other pocket, glancing back to Towers on the board, then to Jessica and Jasper von der Stadt. "Want to take the elevator down with me?"

"Okay," Jessica agreed happily. "C'mon, Timothy."

She skipped across the bare concrete toward the elevators, carrying her elephant in his cricket cage, while Jasper von der Stadt mouthed *Thank you* to Trudy again.

"She's a lovely child," Trudy complimented. "And such a *wonderful* ace."

Then Trudy realized why Croyd was in a hurry and security hadn't tried to grab him: They were busy with a commotion in the next room.

A chaise longue or fainting couch bowled through the line of cops. Trudy hadn't seen it in the notorious photographs, but it was definitely part of Catherine's collection. Its legs were penises. The uprights of its arms were penises. The arms themselves ended with the faces of open-mouthed nymphs or succubi that had stopped sucking the wooden woodies and were trying to suck Ernie Martin, who was lying on it, while the face of a lascivious satyr or incubus at the top of the furnishing stuck its tongue in his ear and a pair of nubile wooden legs had locked themselves around his neck. "Get it off me!" Ernie screamed. "Get this fucking thing off me!"

Jasper von der Stadt took off running, scooping up Jessica and Timothy and shoving his way through the logjam of Republicans, Trudy right behind him, the Strausses following. Trudy was afraid they wouldn't get to the elevators in time, but she'd not countenanced the power of Jessica's polite "please." They went to the head of the line and had an elevator all to themselves, the Republicans either not knowing what was behind them or still preferring to take their chances with Cathy's possessed porn rather than risk crossing Jessica von der Stadt.

On the way down, Trudy felt around in her pocket until she found the pirate ship. It had stopped squirming and was now just a tiny amber charm. She popped it to her other hand. She gave Jessica a glance, touching her finger to her lips for silence while Jasper stared at the elevator doors in front of them, listening to Kenneth Strauss's legal advice, while Beth played the dutiful wife, a supportive hand on her husband's shoulder as she nodded in agreement with what he said. Trudy stealthily showed Jessica the dollhouse-size amber pirate ship.

Jessica beamed, but said nothing, dropping it in her apron pocket with Timothy's cage, then giving Trudy a hug. Trudy tousled her hair fondly.

When the elevator doors opened they were greeted by Detective Kant. "Evening, folks. I need to ask you a few questions."

"Detective Kant," Kenneth Strauss said forcefully, "these are my clients, and what just happened with Towers and Jessica is a clear case of *mens rea*. If you want to arrest someone, arrest Towers for showing pornography to a child."

"Scary pornography," added Beth. "The footstool was chasing us."

Kant's lizard tongue flicked out. " No one's getting out of the Golden Tower until we figure out what happened. Commissioner's orders. Streets are locked down and we're searching vans to make sure the Amber Room . . . uh . . . hasn't been teleported out."

"I want to go home, Daddy," Jessica whined.

"Please don't upset my daughter," stressed Jasper von der Stadt. "Please."

"Listen," said Kant, "I'll try to expedite it as much as I can, but look, see that line there? That's the only way anyone's getting out. We're inspecting all bags and purses, too."

Trudy looked. The line he pointed to was long, at least fifty people, with Croyd at one end of it holding her purse, yawning as he waited for her. At the other end of the line was Ramshead and a knot of other cops, along with a police consultant who was tall, thin, and Russian-looking, with a pencil-fine mustache, someone you wouldn't give a second glance except for the mirror shades he was wearing. At night. Which he didn't need. Not just because Trudy knew he didn't have any eyes behind them (though he didn't) but because Sascha Starfin, the former bartender from the old Crystal Palace, was also a skimmer telepath, so he could see what those around him were seeing while reading their surface thoughts.

The best plan for dealing with a telepath was avoiding them. Barring that? Slipping them hallucinogens or taking some yourself. But Trudy had already put Jessica through enough. She didn't want to contemplate what she might do, tripping on the contents of Fantasy's goodie bag. Jasper tugged Jessica along, getting in line along with the Strausses while Trudy tried to come up with a plan. If she ever had to confess all her capers, she'd prefer to do it at the end of a long life, when the cops couldn't do anything but be impressed. Now? *What would Lucia Ravenswood do?*

Desiree Windermere was at the front of the line. "This?" asked the romance novelist, opening her Regency reticule and withdrawing a hardback book. "It's an advance copy of my latest, *Lady Light and the Heart of Hope.*"

Ramshead nodded his horns at the bodice ripper, but Sascha said, "No it's not—that's Catherine the Great's jewelry box!"

The mirage dissolved, the hardback resuming its proper appearance of an amber chest. Trudy had read the novels, so she knew what was coming next. Desiree Windermere raised one hand in a dramatic gesture and a blinding burst of light sprang forth.

Ramshead and the other cops were dazzled, but it is hard to blind someone when they didn't have eyes. Trudy watched Sascha Starfin struggling with empty air, Desiree Windermere standing a few feet away also struggling with empty air, one of Lady Light's other tricks in the novels being displacing her image. The trick didn't work very well with a blind telepath. . . .

But Trudy had a trick as well. She used the momentary distraction to step over to the wall, pop the glass from the fire alarm, pull it, then pop the glass back in.

Desiree Windermere could take a hint. Just as soon as the alarm sounded, huge flames and belching black smoke erupted in the far reaches of the atrium, just like they had in *Lady Light and the Burning Heart of Desire* when Lucia had pulled the same ruse with her light illusions to escape the palace in Monaco.

Trudy grabbed Croyd and her bag, sprinting for the door while crying, "Fire! Fire!" She wasn't the only one. Jasper and Jessica and Beth and Kenneth followed hard on their heels, as did over a hundred wealthy Republicans. The fire alarm completely drowned out Sascha's feeble cries that it was an illusion, while Ramshead and the other cops still staggered around blind. Residents and restaurant goers and Republicans belched forth from the Golden Tower in a panicked mob, bowling over the sawhorses the police had set up.

Jasper had picked up Jessica, who was wailing, "Daddy, I want to go home!"

"I'll get you there, pumpkin."

They ran down East Fifty-fifth Street a couple blocks, Croyd yawning and starting to stagger. "I'm sorry," he apologized, "I'm just so tired."

Trudy popped a spare black beauty into her hand. "Here." She knew Croyd from before.

"You're a pal, Trude. . . ."

"Don't mention it." She spotted an empty cab. "My friend needs to get to the West German Consulate."

"The cops—" the cabbie protested. He shut up as she pressed a few hundred into his hand. "West German Consulate, yes, ma'am."

Trudy got Croyd and the Amber Room packed in the back, then slipped him the last of Fantasy's black beauties. She watched as the cab took off, then spotted a police car moving to intercept. Then the left wheels fell off the cop car, the hub caps and lug nuts reappearing in the garbage can beside her.

She hurried to catch up with the Strausses and von der Stadts. "Just throwing away some gum," she explained.

"Did you leave your purse in the cab?" asked Beth.

"Blast it, yes!" Trudy exclaimed. "Oh well, just means I get to shop for another."

"Is your friend going to be okay?" asked Kenneth. "They're doing an absolute witch hunt for wild cards right now."

"He should be fine. He's a survivor."

"Where did Mr. Croyd go?" asked Jessica.

"He was very tired. He'd been up a long time and needed to get some shut-eye."

"Will he be able to play with us again?" Jessica asked. "Maybe set up a dollhouse?"

"Maybe sometime," Trudy said, "but right now he really needs his sleep."

She wondered how much the West Germans were going to pay Croyd and how much of that she would actually see. But she shouldn't be greedy. She had four paintings, almost two dozen lovely amber treasures to pack a curio cabinet, *and* a keepsake for her shadow box.

She patted the chess tower in her pocket. Such a lovely memento.

"I don't know how to thank you," Jasper told her. "You've been such a help. Our town house isn't far from here. After I get Jessica to bed, would you like to stay for drinks?"

"Sure," said Trudy, then she glanced up to Jessica and winked. "We nasty girls need to stick together."

Jessica giggled.

Horses

by Lewis Shiner

THE WOMAN ON THE other side of the coffee table had a blond crewcut and wire-rimmed glasses. She was around forty. No makeup, a man's gray sportcoat over a white T-shirt, loose draw-string pants. Dyke, had been Veronica's first impression, and so far nothing had changed her mind.

"Things are just a little out of control right now," Veronica said. "It's not my fault. I need a little time."

The woman's name was Hannah Jorde. She sighed and said, "I'm so sick of hearing the same old shit." She put her glasses on the table and rubbed her eyes. "You're an addict, Veronica. I would have known that in two seconds, even if Ichiko hadn't told me. You've got every symptom in the book." She put her glasses back on. "I'm going to get you in a program. Methadone. It'll make you feel better, and keep you alive, but you'll still be an addict. Only you'll be addicted to methadone instead of heroin."

Veronica said, "I can quit—"

"Please," Hannah said. "Don't say it. Don't make me listen to it. I just want to tell you a couple of things, and I want you to think about them. That's all we can get done this first time anyway."

"Fine," Veronica said. She put her hands under her thighs because they had started to shake a little.

"You're an addict because you don't want to deal with what's going on inside you. You're not just killing yourself, you're already dead." She let the words hang for a second and then said, "What is it you do for Ichiko?"

"I'm a—" She stopped herself before she could say "geisha," Fortunato's approved term. "I'm a prostitute."

Suddenly Hannah smiled. She could be pretty, Veronica thought, if she made a little effort. The right clothes, makeup. A wig for that awful haircut. What a waste. "Good," Hannah said. "The truth, for once. Thank you for that." She filled out a slip of paper and handed it across. "Start your methadone and I'll see you tomorrow."

◆

A van with a loudspeaker passed her on Seventh Avenue. The recorded message reminded her that it was Election Day and she should exercise her constitutional freedom. Doubtless paid for by the Democrats. Everyone expected a landslide for Bush after the Democrats' disaster in Atlanta.

A man leaned out of the van and said, "Hey, baby, did you vote today?" She showed him the manicure on her right middle finger. That went for the American political system, too. What kind of freedom was it when the only people you could vote for were politicians?

She got in line outside the methadone clinic, pulling her coat tighter around her. It was embarrassment as much as cold. She didn't know which was worse, to be surrounded by so many junkies or to be taken for one of them. They mostly seemed to be black women and white boys with long greasy hair.

At least, she thought, she was still on the street. Ichiko had given her three choices: check into a detox center, see Hannah, or look for another job.

Her turn came and the woman at the window handed her a paper cup. The methadone was mixed in a sweet orange-flavored drink. Veronica drank it down and crumpled the cup. The black hooker behind her teetered up to the window on impossibly high heels and said, "Weeee, law, give me that Jesus jizz."

Veronica threw the cup on the street and looked at her watch. Time enough to get uptown to Bergdorf's before her dinner date.

♥

She should have guessed from the name he'd used to make the dinner reservation: Herman Gregg. But she didn't figure it out till she got to the table.

"Holy shit," Veronica said. The subdued light of the restaurant was enough, even for Veronica, to know the face. "Senator Hartmann," she said.

He smiled weakly. "Not senator anymore. I'm just an ordinary citizen again. But you can see why I didn't want to be alone tonight. You know what they say about politics and strange bedfellows."

"No," Veronica said. "What do they say?"

Hartmann shrugged and put the menu down. "How hungry are you?"

"I don't care. If you just want to go upstairs, that's fine." He'd already told her he had a room upstairs at the Hyatt. "Don't feel like you have to buy me dinner, like this is a real date or anything."

"Somehow this isn't quite what I expected. I'd heard so much about Fortunato and his extraordinary women."

"Yeah, well, Fortunato's gone. Things have fallen off a bit. If you're not happy, you don't have to go through with it."

"I'm not complaining. I guess you're more human than I expected. I kind of like that."

Veronica stood up. "Shall we?"

He was very quiet in the elevator, didn't touch her or anything. Just one hand on the elbow as they got out, to point her toward the room. Once inside, he locked the door and turned the TV on.

"We don't need that, do we?" Veronica asked.

"I have to know," Hartmann said. He took his jacket off and folded it over a chair, then untied his shoes and put them neatly underneath. He loosened his tie and sat on the end of the bed, his tiredness visible in the curve of his spine. "I have to know just how bad it is."

When Veronica came out of the bathroom in her bra and panties, he was in the same position. Bush was running almost two to one ahead of Dukakis and Jackson. Concession speeches were expected momentarily. She helped Hartmann off with the rest of his clothes, put a condom on him, and got him under the covers.

He didn't want anything fancy, just got right down to business. As he rocked against her, the election returns continued in a steady stream: "Texas now shows Bush with a staggering fifty-eight percent of the vote, and that's with thirty-seven percent of the precincts reporting." Hartmann's spasm happened quickly and left him on the edge of tears. Veronica stroked the small of his back, where the sweat had just broken, and made soothing noises. Just as he rolled off her, one of the TV reporters said his name and he sat up guiltily.

"Many of us must be asking ourselves the same question tonight," the reporter went on. "Could Gregg Hartmann have beaten Vice President Bush? It was just two and a half months ago that Hartmann withdrew from the race after his loss of composure at the Democratic National Convention in Atlanta. That convention will long be remembered, not only for its bloodshed, but as a turning point in the nation's attitude toward victims of the wild-card virus."

She carried the used condom into the bathroom, knotted it, wrapped it in toilet paper, and threw it away. The odor of sperm almost gagged her. She sat on the edge of the tub and washed herself and then brushed her teeth, over and over, telling herself she didn't need a shot, not yet.

It was after two when Hartmann turned the TV off. Bush was a joke, Hartmann told her. His campaigning against drugs was sheerest hypocrisy, given what his CIA had done in Central America. His cabinet officers would never live up to his claims of ethics, and his "kinder, gentler" America would have no room for aces or jokers.

The wild-card issue meant little to Veronica. Fortunato, the man who had brought her in off the streets, was an ace. Her mother had been one of Fortunato's geishas and had meant for Veronica to have a college education and a real career. But Veronica had turned tricks anyway. The money was easy and it was easy as well to think of herself that way, as a whore. Together Miranda and Fortunato had decided that if she was going to sell her body, she might as well do it right. Fortunato had brought her back to his apartment and tried, unsuccessfully, to make her into one of his ideal women. She loved him in the way that people loved something sweet and not entirely of this world.

Because of Fortunato she'd met—and had sex with—other aces and jokers. None of them had seemed quite real to her, either. There weren't even that many of them, not compared to unwed mothers or the homeless or old people, not enough to deserve all the attention they got. And it wasn't like it was a disease that other people could catch, like AIDS or something.

That thought gave her a chill. For a while the wild card *had* been contagious, and her sometime boyfriend Croyd Crenson had been spreading it. She'd been exposed to him but fortunately nothing had happened. She didn't want to think about it.

Eventually Hartmann fell asleep, the soft flesh of his stomach shaking with muffled snores. Veronica lay awake, counting all the many, many things she didn't want to think about.

♣

She didn't sleep even when she got back to Ichiko's, around dawn. This time it was the idea of seeing Hannah again that kept her turning from side to side, chills moving up through her from her stomach.

She got up around noon and made a breakfast she couldn't eat. Ichiko walked her out to the cab or she might not have made it. Even then she tried to tell the cabbie to stop, to let her out, but she couldn't find her voice. It was like being back in convent school, being sent to the principal, the oldest, scariest nun in the world.

She walked up the stairs and into Hannah's office. She couldn't feel her legs. She sat in the middle of Hannah's square, gray couch. Today Hannah wore jeans and a man's dress shirt and a cardigan with interwoven gold thread. Veronica couldn't take her eyes off the sparkles of gold.

"Did you have a chance to think?" Hannah asked her.

Veronica shrugged. "I've been busy. I don't spend a lot of time thinking."

"Okay, let's start with that. Tell me about the things you do."

Without meaning to, Veronica found herself talking about Hartmann. Hannah kept asking for details. What did he look like naked? What exactly was the taste in her mouth afterward? She sounded like she was only mildly curious. What was it like when his penis was inside her?

"I don't know," Veronica said. "It didn't feel like anything."

"What do you mean? He was inside you, but you couldn't feel it? Did you have to ask him if he was in yet?"

Veronica started to laugh, and then she was crying. She didn't know how it happened. It seemed to be somebody else. "I didn't want him there," she said. Who was that talking? "I didn't want him in me. I wanted him to leave me alone." Her whole body shook with sobs. "This is ridiculous," she said. "Why am I crying? What's happening to me?"

Hannah moved over next to her and wrapped her arms around her. She smelled like Dial soap. Veronica buried her head in the golden fibers of her sweater, felt the softness of the breast underneath. Everything gave way then and she cried until she ran out of tears, until she felt like a wrung-out sponge.

♠

Standing in line, Veronica tapped her foot nervously on the sidewalk. One of the long-haired boys behind her sang a song about shooting up in a low, monotonous voice. "You know I couldn't find my mainline," he sang. He didn't seem aware he was doing it.

Veronica wanted the methadone, wanted it badly. What do they put in that stuff? she thought, and stopped herself before the laughter turned into the other thing again.

She put her hand into her purse and held on to a folded piece of paper with Hannah's phone number on it.

♦

Veronica came in on a blast of cold air and stood for a second, rubbing her hands together.

"Flowers for you," Melanie said. She had a Russian-language textbook open while she watched the phones. Melanie was new. She still believed in Fortunato's program, that they were geishas not hookers, that men actually cared how many languages they spoke and whether or not they could discuss postmodernist critical theory. When she finished her telephone shift, she would be off to cooking class or elocution lessons. Then, that night, she would spread her legs for a man who only cared that she had lots of red-blond hair and big boobs.

"Jerry again?" Veronica asked. She threw her coat on the couch and collapsed.

"I don't see what you have against him. He's sweet."

"I don't have anything against him. I just don't have anything *for* him, either. He's a nobody."

"A nobody with a ton of money, who thinks the sun rises and sets on you. Anyway, I've got him down for you tonight, from ten o'clock on."

"Tonight?" The walls seemed to close in around her. She couldn't breathe. "I can't."

"You have a date you didn't put on the computer?" Ichiko had bought a Macintosh over the summer and had computerized everything. The girls were responsible for keeping their own schedules current, and if one of them screwed up they all got yelled at.

"No, I . . . I'm sick."

"He's already paid and everything."

"Call him back. Will you? I have to go upstairs."

She staggered up to her room and got in bed with her clothes on, doubled up, clutching a pillow to her stomach. From there she watched the street outside turn dark and the headlights of the cars sweep past. Liz, her chubby gray cat, climbed onto the peak of her hip and began to knead the covers, purring loudly. "Please shut up," Veronica said.

Liz was another reminder of Fortunato. She had been Veronica's to start with, though she hadn't cared that much about her. Then Fortunato had formed some kind of bond with the cat. Liz used to follow him around his apartment, crying, and would get into his lap whenever he sat down. When Fortunato left for Japan, it seemed like the cat was all Veronica had left of him.

Finally the cat settled down and started to snore softly. Veronica couldn't relax, and soon she was trembling. It wasn't like the shaking that came when she needed a shot. That part of her was quiet. This was something else. She wondered if it was the methadone, some bizarre allergy. The longer it went on, the more out of touch she became. She couldn't stop shaking. Was she dying?

She fumbled the phone off the hook and dialed Hannah's number. "It's Veronica," she said. "Something's wrong."

"I know that," Hannah said. "Why don't you come over?"

"Come over?"

"To my apartment."

"I don't know if I can make it. I feel so weird."

"Of course you can. Stand up."

Veronica stood up. Somehow it was all right.

"Are you standing?"

"Yes," Veronica said.

"Good. Write down this address."

A few minutes later Veronica was in a cab. She looked down at her legs, saw her wool-knit A-line skirt wrinkled beyond hope. She got a mirror out of her purse and looked at her smudged eyeliner and bloodshot eyes. "I can't help it," she said out loud, and the words almost started the flood of tears again.

She knew she was on the edge of something. She didn't have the strength to keep herself from being pulled into it, but she could feel the depth of the chasm in the pit of her stomach.

Hannah lived on the third floor of a building on Park Avenue South that had escaped remodeling. The varnish was worn off the center of the stairs and the landings were raw concrete. Hannah met her at the door of her apartment. "You made it," she said. She seemed relieved and happy to see her.

Veronica could only nod. The apartment was two rooms and a kitchen. There was almost no furniture, only tatami mats and pillows, and an expensive stereo with huge speakers that sat in the middle of the floor. Japanese pen-and-ink drawings hung in cheap Plexiglas frames on the wall. The Asian simplicity of it reminded her of the apartment she'd shared with Fortunato.

"Settle down anywhere," Hannah said. "I'll bring you some tea."

The music on the stereo was instrumental, one of those New Age things. It was an acoustic guitar in a weird tuning over lots of percussion. Like the rest of the room, like Hannah herself, it suggested a serenity that Veronica couldn't feel. Hannah brought her tea in a small, thick cup with no handle. The tea was green and vaguely sweet.

Hannah sat cross-legged on the couch next to her. "You look like you haven't been sleeping."

"I'm all knotted up inside. Maybe it's the methadone."

"It's not the methadone. It's three years of feelings trying to get out."

"Is it cold in here?"

Hannah touched her hand. The shaking got worse. "No," Hannah said. "It's not the methadone and it's not the temperature. It's just you." And then she leaned forward slowly and kissed Veronica on the lips.

It was gentle but not sisterly, warm but not demanding. Veronica shivered and held herself, feeling like she was fighting to keep from drowning. "You're confusing me. . . ."

"You were already confused. When was the last time you enjoyed making love? When was the last time you lay next to somebody and got comfort out of it? When was the last time you thought you deserved to be happy? You don't have to answer me. I already know."

She stood up and took Veronica's hand. Veronica followed her, not to the bedroom, like she expected, but to the bath. Hannah started the water running and undressed her, carefully, not touching her more than she had to. The room began to fill with steam. "Get in," Hannah said, and Veronica got in the tub. The hot water stung her, made her face flush. "Your body is still very beautiful," Hannah said. "You've been careful with the needle."

Veronica nodded. The hot water stopped her shaking and helped her relax. She felt drugged. Had there been something in the tea?

Hannah took her own clothes off and put her glasses on the edge of the sink. She was a little heavy in the waist, and her stomach curved without jeans to hold it in. Her underclothes left red lines around her waist and under her breasts. Still, she seemed beautiful to Veronica, her pale nipples, the discreet tangle of hair between her legs. Veronica found herself about to reach one hand out to touch Hannah's body, then stopped herself, ashamed and confused.

Hannah poured oil into the tub. It foamed and colored the air with the heavy green smell of wildflowers. Then she knelt beside the tub and kissed Veronica again. Veronica's mouth opened, against her will, and she tasted the mint tea on Hannah's breath. "What are you doing to me?" she whispered.

"Seducing you," Hannah said. "If I do anything that scares you or you don't feel comfortable with, just say so." She put her hands on Veronica's cheeks, then slowly ran them down her neck and shoulders. Veronica leaned back against the tub, eyes closed, her breathing coming raggedly. Hannah's small, soft hands moved to her breasts. "Oh," Veronica said. She was melting. Her entire body was liquid. She couldn't tell where it ended and the bathwater began.

This time when Hannah kissed her she leaned into it and put both arms around her.

By the time Hannah helped her into bed Veronica had no will of her own. She had no strength, no intelligence, only sensation. Hannah was slow and gentle and unafraid. She knew where to touch her and how much pressure to use. The first climax was the most intense Veronica had ever felt. It had been so long she barely recognized the feeling. There were others. They blurred into a continuum of pleasure.

And at the end of it came sleep.

♥

Sunlight woke her. Her eyes opened and saw dark green sheets. The rest of it came back and she sat up quickly, holding the sheet against her. Hannah lay on her side, watching.

"What did you do to me? What was in that tea?"

"Nothing," Hannah said. "What happened was that we made love."

"This is too weird. I have to get out of here." She looked around the room for her clothes, reluctant to get out of bed naked with Hannah there.

"Wait," Hannah said. There was a stillness about her that Veronica found inescapable. "I know what's wrong with you. I'm an alcoholic. I was drunk for ten years and now I've been sober for six. I was married to a man that I hated, and I hated him just because I didn't want to have sex with him. It wasn't his fault, it was the way I am. Only nobody could tell me that was the reason."

"What's that got to do with me? Are you saying I'm queer?" There was a towel on the floor next to her. She wrapped herself in it and looked in the bathroom. Her clothes were folded neatly on the floor.

"Maybe you're not gay." Hannah raised her voice just enough for Veronica to hear her. "Though I believe you are. That doesn't matter. You hate yourself for what you're doing with your body. It makes you feel helpless. And helplessness is what addiction is all about."

Veronica buttoned her rumpled silk blouse and brushed at the creases in her skirt. "I got to go."

"I've got three o'clock set aside for you. If you want to talk some more."

"Just talk? Or do you fuck all your patients?"

There was a short, hurt silence. "You're the first. I suppose I should feel like I've pissed away all my ethics, but I don't."

Veronica opened the door. "I'll think about it," she said. Then she belted on her coat and ran down the stairs.

♣

Jerry was waiting for her when she got back to the brownstone.

"Melanie said you were sick," he said. "I wanted to see if I could help."

"No, Jerry. It's sweet of you and all, but no."

"Where were you? Did you go out on another date?"

Veronica shook her head. "I've been to the doctor, that's all."

Jerry looked her up and down, obviously made the decision not to call her out. He sat on the sofa and looked at the flowers he'd sent her the day before, still on the desk by the phone, the card unopened. "I'm wasting my time, aren't I?"

"Jerry. What do you want me to say? You shouldn't have fallen in love with a hooker. I mean, what were you thinking about? Did you think I was available on a Rent-to-Own plan?" She sat down next to him, touched his face. "You're a sweet kid, Jerry. Women should go nuts for you. Real women. That's what you deserve. Not some half-breed Puerto Rican junkie hooker."

Junkie, she thought. She'd actually said it.

"You're the one I want," Jerry said, looking at the floor.

"You don't even know me. You've got no idea. You're trying to catch up on twenty years overnight, and you see me as some kind of shortcut. Nothing happens that fast. Give yourself some time."

"Can I see you tonight?"

"No. Not tonight." She paused, got up her nerve. "Not ever. Not anymore."

"*Why?* I *love* you."

"You don't know what love is. You don't know what you're

talking about. You've got some kind of stupid romantic ideas from all those movies you watch and they don't have anything to do with real life. I can't stand it. I don't want to be the only thing propping up this make-believe world of yours. I'm not strong enough."

She stood up.

"Veronica, please!"

She couldn't look at him. His face was all twisted, like he was trying not to cry. "I'm sorry, Jerry," she said. "You'll find somebody. You'll see." She ran upstairs.

♠

It wasn't even noon, but she was wide-awake, her head clear. It made her nervous to feel as good as she did. She showered and put on jeans and a sweater and went downtown for her methadone. Okay, she thought, standing in line, feeling the November sun warm her hair. You can admit you're a junkie. You can admit you're tired of turning tricks. What does that leave you?

All the girls had savings accounts in Ichiko's name. Half their earnings went into the fund every month, carefully monitored by the new computer. If Veronica gave up the Life, she could collect the money. It would keep her alive for at least a couple of years. Then what? Find some poor sap like Jerry and settle down to have kids?

She got to the head of the line. A boy in a white lab coat behind the window glanced at her card and gave her the dose. She drank it and threw the cup at an overflowing trash can. It wasn't enough. It wasn't enough not to hurt, not to have the need. Heroin was more than that, more than an end to pain. It was the rush, the joy, the way the cool fire went through her like God's love.

She took a battered list of phone numbers out of her purse and started dialing. Twice she left messages on phone machines and the third time she got lucky. "Croyd?" she said.

"Himself. Where are you, darlin'?" His words ended with muffled clicks. She hadn't seen him in three months. He'd obviously slept, and woken in a distorted body. That was okay. Veronica could see past the surface.

"Chelsea," she said. "Want to get high?"

◆

He was near the East River, in the waterfront apartment where she'd first spent the night with him, two years before. That was Wild Card Day, when the Astronomer had killed Caroline, and Fortunato had left for Japan.

When she was high, those memories never bothered her.

Croyd answered the door and Veronica stood and stared at him for a long moment. "I'd kiss you," Croyd said, "but I'm afraid I might hurt you."

"That's okay, I'll pass." The clicking she'd heard on the phone came when he shut his beak at the end of a word. He was over seven feet tall and covered with feathers. A thin membrane linked his arms to his sides. "Can you fly?"

He shook his head. "Too heavy. Shame, isn't it? I can glide a little, dive out of a second-story window. So it's not a complete loss."

His eyes were shiny black and the wrinkled feathers above them gave him a look of fierce intelligence. "I may be wasting my time," she said.

The beak opened into a smile. "The wings may not be functional, but the rest of me is."

Veronica shook her head. "I'm in trouble, Croyd. Have you got any coke?"

They sat at his kitchen table, a slab of pine with cigarette burns and peeling varnish. Veronica did two lines then passed the straw to Croyd. He snorted his into the small black holes at the base of his beak. Veronica wiped the mirror down with her index finger and rubbed it into her gums. "Better," she said.

"You sure you don't want to finish this conversation in bed?"

She shook her head. "I need a friend right now. Weird shit is happening to me. I can't get a handle." She told him about Hannah, about nearly throwing up after her last "date."

Croyd listened intently. At least he looked intent. When she finished he said, "It's probably stupid for me to say this. I mean, this is not in my best interest. But you can't go against what you feel. You need to see this woman again, in the light of day, and make up your mind about her. Maybe you are gay. So what? Do you really care what a bunch of square assholes think about your sex life?"

"I feel like I'm fourteen," Veronica said. "All these emotional roller coasters. I can't keep up."

"You want my advice, don't even try. Let it happen. And if you get in trouble, you can call me." It sounded like they were finished, but Croyd hesitated, like there was something else he had to say. "There's nothing else happened, right? I mean, no . . . no symptoms."

He was talking about that whole Typhoid Croyd business. She shook her head. "No. No sudden ace powers, no flippers on the ends of my legs. I don't think it did anything to me at all."

"It's just—I feel responsible, that's all."

"Don't worry about it."

He walked her to the door and she hugged him tight, despite the peculiar acid smell of his feathers. His hands rested flat against her back. "I have to be careful," he said. "If I bend my fingers too much, these claws come out." He showed her the claws. There was a light of pleasure in his eyes when he looked at them.

"So long, Croyd," she said. "Thanks for everything."

♥

She got to Hannah's office just before four. "I'm late," she said.

Hannah held the door for her. "It doesn't matter. There's nobody else scheduled for this afternoon." Then she said, "I'm glad you came."

Veronica was giddy from cocaine and nerves and couldn't sit down. Hannah took her usual position, in the chair across the table from the couch.

"How's the methadone working out?" Hannah asked.

"Fine," Veronica said. "It's great." She walked behind the couch, turned around, leaned into the back of it. "No, it's not great. It's not enough. I still want to get high. I need it."

"Why?"

"*Why?* What a stupid fucking question. Because I like to feel good. Because when you're high, you don't care about wading through all the world's shit—"

"What shit?" Hannah said. "What shit are you living in that you didn't put yourself into? You've got everything backward. You think you can control your drug habit and you can't control your life. It's the other way around, you just don't know it. You have no control over heroin. It owns you. They call it horse, but it's really riding *you*. That's step one of what they call the Twelve-Step Plan. You have to admit you are powerless to control your addiction. And then, later on, you can learn to take responsibility for the rest of your life. As in 'the ability to respond.' Not blame, not control, but responsibility. Something you can live with."

Veronica shook her head. "That's all easy for you to say. But I don't have any kind of life. My mother is a washed-up whore who's pimping *me* now. I never knew who my father was, and I don't think my mother did, either. I got no brothers or sisters to turn to. I learned all that shit Fortunato taught us, but it's not a college diploma. It's not going to get me a soft job someplace. Look at the odds. I'm going to end up like the kids I went to school with. Fat and old, either divorced or married to a husband that beats me up on weekends." It was hard to believe. She'd actually talked herself right out of her cocaine high.

"So what is it you want?"

"Escape. I want a good-looking man with a fast car and a lot of money to come and take me away someplace."

"And then what?"

"Then we live happily ever after."

"That's bullshit, Veronica. You know better than that. If all you want is some man, you could have had plenty. What's the difference whether you're dependent on a drug or dependent on a man? There isn't any, and you know it."

Veronica thought of Jerry, who would take her away if she would only let him. "Why do you care what happens to me?"

Hannah walked over to the window and looked out at the street. "When you walked in here I saw myself, six years ago. There's a fire in you. A heat. Sexual, emotional, spiritual. It's been too much for you, all your life. You had to use heroin to keep it from eating you up." She turned and looked Veronica in the eyes. "I want that fire. I want all you have. The two of us, together, burning until we burn each other up."

Veronica could not get her breath. She stood up, feeling the fabric of her sweater move against her tight, aching nipples. She walked to the door and locked it. The pressure of her jeans between her legs was maddening. She kicked off her shoes and pulled the sweater over her head.

"Show me," she said.

♣

At fifteen she'd been in love with an eighteen-year-old *pachuco*, had fucked him at every possible opportunity, in the backseat of his car, in the park, once in the stairwell of her high school. It was always quick and brutal, and afterward she went home to her empty room. There she could think about the boy and make herself come with her fingers, the way she could never come when he was inside her.

Since then she'd had sex with hundreds of men. None of them had made her come either, not even Fortunato, and as for love, she'd convinced herself it was just another lie.

Hannah changed all of that. They made love five or six times a day. It was all so equal. For everything of Hannah's there was something of Veronica's. Afterward they slept in each other's arms. Under Hannah's gentle hands and tongue, Veronica found a responsiveness she didn't think was possible, not for anyone.

"Women don't come from having men inside them," Hannah told her. "I've read in books that we're supposed to, I've heard there are women who do. But I've never talked to one of them. Every woman I've ever talked to needs something more."

"More," Veronica said. "I want more."

She only left Hannah's apartment long enough to score her daily methadone. She wore Hannah's clothes, when she bothered to wear clothes at all. She did what Croyd had told her to. She stopped fighting and immersed herself in sensation: the smell and feel and taste of Hannah's body, the exotic foods and teas that Hannah prepared for her, the long nights of physical and emotional intimacy where nothing was forbidden.

Almost nothing, anyway. Veronica found herself talking for hours about her childhood, the terrors of Catholic school, the tangled genealogy of her aunts and uncles and cousins, the hypocrisy of Catholic sexuality in which teenaged girls routinely gave blow jobs but recoiled in horror from the thought of losing their sacred virginity.

It was Hannah that held back. She talked about her childhood, her ex-husband, her parents. She was an imaginative and enthusiastic lover, afraid of nothing. She had Veronica reading about addiction and feminism and Marxism and vegetarianism and everything else that was a part of her life. But she never explained the transition, the years between her drunken marriage and her sober counseling job.

There were hints. She had been part of some kind of radical feminist group. She never mentioned the name. "They believed in a lot of things I wasn't comfortable with," was all she would say.

"What sort of things?"

"Things that might appeal to somebody who was still full of anger and bitterness. Things you have to outgrow if you're going to get anywhere."

Veronica assumed she was talking about violence. Bombing or assassination or something else illegal. And because Hannah didn't want to talk about it, Veronica left it alone.

Veronica was the first to say "I love you."

It was dawn. They lay side by side, their hands between each other's legs, lips just touching. The pleasure was so strong that the words came out without her quite meaning them to. Hannah held her tightly and said, "It scares me when you say that. People use the word 'love' on each other like a weapon. I don't want that to happen to us."

"I love you anyway. Whatever you say. Whether you like it or not."

Hannah pulled far enough away to look into her eyes. "I love you, too."

"I want to kick the methadone. I want to get clean."

"Okay."

"I mean now. Starting today."

"It'll be ugly. I can get you drugs to help, but it's going to tear you apart. Are you sure you're ready for that?"

"It's what I want."

"Give it one more week. We need to get out a little, get you back into the world. If you still want to do it next week, then we'll try it."

♠

That afternoon they went to a movie together. They held hands like teenagers. At dinner afterward, over Chinese food, Hannah said, "I think you should bring some of your things over. Clothes and things. You know. And your cat."

"You mean move in."

"I guess that's what I'm saying."

"I think I would like to do that," Veronica said. She dabbed at her eyes with her napkin. They both pretended not to see the tears. "What do I tell Ichiko?"

"I don't know. What do you think?"

"You're going into counselor mode again."

Hannah shrugged.

"I guess I tell her I'm moving out. That I'm through. I think she's probably figured that out already."

♦

In fact Ichiko had. "I hope you will be very happy," she said. She hugged Veronica. "I can see already that you are. Here's a little money to make things easier." The amount on the check was larger than Veronica had any reason to expect. "Your trust fund, plus a little extra from me."

"I don't know. . . ."

"Take it," Ichiko said. "Times are changing. I don't feel so good about this business, the way I used to. I look around, I see all this hatred. They hate jokers and aces. When I first came to this country, they hated me for being Japanese. Fortunato's father had to hide us during the Pacific War so they wouldn't put us into camps. People afraid of each other, hurting each other. My geishas don't help that anymore. When a man uses a woman, it doesn't make him a better man. Any more than having black people for slaves made white people better. In the end they only come to hate each other."

"What are you saying? Are you going to close down the business?"

Ichiko shrugged. "It's something I think about, more and more. There is all this pressure on me, these gangsters and big-money men wanting to take over the business. If I close down, they will go away and leave me alone. I have enough money. Who cares about money anyway?" She pushed the check toward Veronica again, and this time Veronica took it. "You go and be happy and find love where you can."

Veronica went upstairs and finished packing. Eventually she knew she couldn't put it off any longer and knocked on the door of her mother's room.

Miranda had heard most of it from Ichiko, and what she hadn't heard she'd figured out for herself. She took Veronica's hands and held them both for a long time without saying anything. Finally she said, "You know I don't care that you're in love with a woman and not a man. You know I'm happy you're giving up . . . the Life. I never wanted that for you in the first place." She sighed. "Just be careful, darling, please. You've only known this woman for what, not even two weeks?"

Veronica pulled her hands away and stood up. "Mother, for God's sake."

"I'm not trying to rain on your parade—"

"Yes, you are. That's exactly what you're trying to do."

"I'm just saying you don't know her very well. I want this to work out for you, really I do, but it may not, and—"

"Save it," Veronica said. "I don't want to hear it. Just once, be happy that I'm happy. And if you can't, then keep your mouth shut about it." She walked out and slammed the door and took her things down to the cab where Hannah waited.

♥

On the ride home, with Liz huddled nervously on her lap, Veronica started to shake.

"Are you okay?" Hannah asked her. "Did you get your methadone today?"

"I took it," Veronica said. "It's not that." Though the symptoms were much the same. She felt clammy and her bowels were knotted up. "I'm scared, that's all."

Hannah put her arms around her. "Scared? What are you afraid of?"

"I have my whole life in front of me. It's just out there, waiting. I don't know what to do with it."

"You live it," Hannah said. "That's all. One day at a time."

♣

The next afternoon they walked down Fifth Avenue, looking in the windows. Veronica stopped in front of a blue-sequined strapless gown in the window of Sak's. "God," she said. "How gorgeous."

Hannah took her arm and led her away, smiling. "And how politically incorrect. That's just a harness men put you in. Come on. Let's get this money of yours in the bank before it turns to fairy dust or something."

They walked down to the Chase Manhattan and went in. There was a single line, marked off with red velvet ropes, for the Paying and Receiving tellers. Veronica stepped up to the back of the line, already six people long, and two more moved in behind her.

"I'm going to walk around," Hannah said. "I hate lines. They make me claustrophobic."

There was a nervousness in Hannah's eyes Veronica had never seen before. She remembered what her mother had said, realized how little, in fact, she knew this woman she was in love with. "You're not kidding, are you?"

"No," she said, her smile flickering like a bad fluorescent bulb. "I'm not." She stepped over the velvet rope and wandered off into the open part of the lobby. Veronica couldn't help noticing a good-looking blond kid a few feet away from her, filling out some kind of form at the service counter. Hannah saw him, too, and turned for a second look.

Veronica felt a stab of jealousy. The kid was in his late teens, dressed in expensive khaki pants, loafers, and a V-necked sweater with nothing underneath. He had a long black coat draped casually over one arm. His hair fell over his ears and collar and he had the start of a five-o'clock shadow. There was an effortless sexuality about him that was obvious to everyone around him.

Hannah smiled and shook her head. It looked like she was smiling at herself rather than the kid. She started to walk away. The man in line behind Veronica cleared his throat noisily. Veronica looked up, saw the line had moved, took up the slack. She looked back at Hannah just in time to see her stagger.

"Hannah . . . ?" Veronica said.

Hannah caught her balance and took a couple of hesitant steps. It was like her shoes had heels that were too high for her. But Hannah never wore high heels. She turned and looked at Veronica.

Her eyes were wrong. There was something crazy in them, and in the way she smiled. Veronica looked at the long line that stretched out behind her. She didn't want to lose her place, but if something was really wrong . . .

Suddenly Hannah began to run.

It was clumsy and slow, but it took the security guard by surprise. Hannah had the gun out of his holster and pointed at his head before he knew what was happening.

"Hannah!" Veronica screamed.

The gun kicked in Hannah's hand. The shot boomed off the marble walls and the room went silent for a long second afterward. The bullet threw the guard against the wall, his face collapsed around the black hole in his cheek. He left a long red smear against the pale stone of the wall as he slumped to the floor.

Veronica tried to jump the velvet rope and caught her foot. Hannah turned toward her as she fell and fired again, the bullet howling over Veronica's head. The silence gave way to screams and shouts of panic. An alarm went off, barely audible over the rest of the noise. The customers, most of them men in dark suits, ran for the doors. Hannah spun around to watch, a hideous joy on her face.

Veronica got her legs under her and ran at Hannah. Guards converged from all over the building, guns out. One of them shouted at Veronica, something like, "Hey, lady, stay down!" Another guard fired a shot over Hannah's head and Hannah fired back at him, twice.

By then Veronica was in the air.

She tackled Hannah around the waist and they slid across the polished floor. The gun came loose and skittered away. With the strength of absolute fear she pinned Hannah's arms above her head. "It's me, goddammit!" Veronica yelled. "What's wrong with you?"

Across the lobby a body hit the floor.

It was the blond kid in the sweater. He seemed stunned, paralyzed, as if he'd had a stroke. His face was distorted with terror and something else, some kind of alien presence. He started to raise one hand to his face, then jerked forward like a fumbled puppet.

And then, just as the guards swarmed over them, Veronica saw the light come back into Hannah's eyes. Her mouth moved, but no sound came out. Two pairs of hands pulled Veronica away. Two more bank guards and an NYPD cop shoved gun barrels into Hannah's face, screaming at her not to move. In seconds they had her in handcuffs and out the door.

Veronica tried to get loose and the guards tightened their hold. She strained to find the blond kid in the crowd.

He was gone.

They took her to the precinct station in a squad car. At first they just wanted her story, over and over. Veronica told them she and Hannah were roommates, told them about the heroin, about the check she'd been taking to the bank. When they asked her what happened there, she told them she didn't know. "It wasn't Hannah," she said.

"We've got a dozen witnesses that say it was."

"I mean, it wasn't her inside her body. It was like she was . . . I don't know. Possessed."

"Possessed? The devil made her do it?"

"I don't *know*."

She told the story again and again, until the words lost all meaning.

Then a cop in a suit came out of the darkness and said, "What do you know about a bunch that calls itself WORSE?"

"I never heard of them. Can I have a glass of water?"

"In a minute. Can you tell me what the initials stand for?"

"I told you, I never—"

"Women's Organization to Reach Sexual Equality. Now does it ring a bell?"

"No, I—"

"Last year there was a riot outside an abortion clinic. These people from WORSE sent five protesters and a cop to the hospital."

"Good for them," Veronica said.

"The cop died. Now do you think it's funny? There's at least seven incidents in the last year where these women have provoked violence in the streets. One of the people they've got it in for is your old employer. Fortunato."

"What's that got to do with Hannah?"

"Not much. She's only the president."

"What? That's impossible."

"I guess you know everything about her, right? How long did you say you've known her? Ten days?"

"She said she had nothing to do with those people anymore."

"You just said you'd never heard of WORSE."

"She never mentioned the name. She said she used to be part of some radical organization, but she didn't agree with their methods. She said it was over a long time ago."

A little man with pattern baldness and glasses said, "She's clean, Lou. She's telling the truth." The man was a low-grade ace, the weakest sort of telepath. The cops had ten or fifteen on staff to use as lie detectors.

"To hell with it, then," the man in the suit said. "We're cutting you loose. But I don't want you away from a phone where I can find you for more than an hour at a time. You got that?"

"I want to see her," Veronica said.

"Forget it. Her lawyer's there. That's all she gets."

"Who's her lawyer?"

The man in the suit sighed. "Bud?"

One of the cops looked through the file. "Lawyer's name is Mundy." He whistled. "From Latham, Strauss. Hot stuff."

"Now get out of here," the man in the suit said.

Two uniformed cops gave her a ride home, then followed her inside. They had a warrant, signed and sealed. She sat on the floor and watched them as they took the apartment apart. One of them found the sexual toys in the drawer by the bed. He held up the wooden ben wa balls for his partner to see, then looked over at Veronica.

"Fuck you," Veronica said, blushing, close to tears. "Leave that stuff alone."

The cop shrugged and put the balls away. Finally they left. Veronica had watched them carefully. There was nothing in the apartment, not a single piece of evidence, to connect Hannah to WORSE.

As soon as they were gone, she called Latham, Strauss. The answering service took her number. She hung up and moved restlessly through the house, putting the Plexiglas-framed drawings back on the walls, refolding clothes and putting them in the drawers, wiping down the cabinets.

The phone rang.

"Veronica? This is Dyan Mundy."

"Thank God."

"I was about to call you when I got your message. Hannah asked me to. She wanted you to know she's okay, they haven't hurt her." The woman's voice exuded confidence, control, a kind of artificial warmth. Veronica visualized chin-length blond hair, gold rings, three strands of pearls. "There's no way I can get you in to see her just now. She understands that, and sends you her love."

Tears ran down Veronica's cheeks. "What happened? Did she say what happened?"

"She tried to explain, but frankly, her story doesn't make much sense. She apparently had some kind of out-of-body experience. She felt this shock and disorientation and then she was suddenly off to the side somewhere. Watched herself shoot the guard as if from a great distance. I don't know how well that's going to play in court. Do you know if she's ever been treated for an emotional disturbance? Is there any history of it in her family?"

"There's nothing the matter with Hannah," Veronica said. "Somebody else was in her body when the guard was killed. It wasn't Hannah."

"That's what she said."

"What about the blond kid?"

"What blond kid?"

"When Hannah got . . . taken over, or whatever it was, there was this blond kid. He just keeled over, like a zombie. Then at the end Hannah was back in her own body and I couldn't find the kid anywhere."

"I don't understand. What are you trying to make out of this?"

"I don't *know*. But I think that kid was involved somehow."

A long pause. "Veronica, I know you're upset. But you have to trust me. She's in the hands of the best law firm in the city. If anybody can save her, we can."

♠

She couldn't sleep. She thought of Hannah alone in a damp and stinking cell, claustrophobic, terrified out of her mind. Nothing Veronica could do would convince the police—or even Hannah's lawyer—of what she knew to be the truth. Something that wasn't Hannah had pulled the trigger.

She called all of Croyd's numbers, with no luck. Jerry would gladly help, but what could he do? His brother's law firm was already on the case. And what good were lawyers against an entire bank lobby full of eyewitnesses?

Hannah's smell was still in the sheets. It made Veronica crazy with longing. It was like a heroin habit, tearing up her guts. She couldn't lie there any longer. She put on running shoes and went out onto the street.

It was nine o'clock on a Friday night. The life of the city went on without her, as it always did. She drifted toward the light and noise of Broadway, hating the faces she saw around her, wanting to throw herself into the river of yellow cabs and pound on them and scream until the world stopped what it was doing and came to help. New York was the best city in the world to be happy in, and the worst if you were desperate. It towered over the helpless, sped by them in clouds of monoxide. It shoved past them on the street without apology, and left its garbage all around them to wade through.

Life meant nothing without Hannah. Without Hannah she would end up back on the needle, would find herself giving blow jobs on car seats for ten dollars a pop. Anything would be better.

That was when she saw the gun.

It was inside the glass display case of a pawnshop, just visible behind the guitars and stereos in the window. It was chrome-plated and heavy and spoke the word "power" to her.

She went inside. The man behind the counter was fifty going on twenty-two. Veronica had had too many tricks just like him. His hairpiece wasn't even the same color as the fringe around his ears. His polyester shirt was green, with horses on it, ten years out of fashion. It was unbuttoned to show his chest hair and gold chains.

"How much is that pistol?" Veronica asked him.

"Now, what would a sweet little number such as yourself want with a big, nasty Smith and Wesson .38?" He crossed his arms over his chest and leaned back against the wall behind the counter. On the TV over his shoulder, two football teams smashed into each other.

"I'm not in the mood for bullshit, pal. How much is the gun?"

The man shook his head, smiling. "I see it all the time. Sweet little thing gets a little upset with her sugar daddy, maybe catches him with his hand in the wrong cookie jar, and suddenly she's got to blow him away. This is what television has done to modern society. Everybody wants to blow everybody else away."

"Look, pal—"

The man leaned forward. "No, *you* look. The law says I'm responsible for what I sell. I don't like your looks, I don't have to sell you shit." He straightened up and his voice softened. "So why don't you be a good little girl and run along home to Papa?"

In that moment Veronica saw her entire life as one humiliation after another, all at the hands of men, all of whom felt they were privileged to decide her destiny. From the father who never acknowledged her, to Fortunato who told her how to dress and how to smile, to Jerry who expected her to love him just because he loved her, to the countless men who'd used her and walked away. She was sick of it. For once she wished she had Fortunato's power, could reach out with her mind and crush this pompous, ugly little man to jelly.

The fluorescent lights overhead flickered. It should have distracted her, but instead she felt connected. The lights flashed with the rhythm of her breathing and she knew she was the cause. She felt the power flowing through the wires, flowing out of the grid and into her mind. The wild card. Croyd. It was happening. The picture on the TV rolled, then turned to snow. The second hand on the big electric clock next to it stopped, then swung back and forth like a pendulum, keeping time with the flashing lights. The man started to turn toward the TV and then went pale. He sat down slowly, his arms crossing tighter, as if he were cold. Sweat beaded his face.

"Are you hurt?" she asked him.

"I don't know." His voice was weak, and higher than it had been.

She hadn't crippled him, apparently. Beyond that she didn't care. "Give me the gun."

"I . . . I don't know if I can."

"Do it!"

He got onto his hands and knees, fumbled a key into the lock, slid the back of the display case open. He had to use both hands to lift the gun onto the counter. Veronica reached for it, then realized what she'd done. Why did she need a gun?

She ran into the street, waving for a cab.

◆

She got as far as the holding tank on nerve alone. The beefy, red-haired guard outside the lockup refused to let her any farther and

Veronica tried to do to him what she'd done in the pawnshop. Nothing happened.

She felt a surge of panic. She had no idea what the power was or how it worked. What if she couldn't use it again right away? What if she needed something that had been in the pawnshop as a catalyst?

"Lady, I told you, this is a restricted area. Now, are you going to get out of here or do I got to call somebody?"

Panic turned to helplessness, helplessness to anger. What good was this power if she couldn't use it to help Hannah? And with the anger it came. The lights flickered and the music from a TV inside the lockup dissolved in static. Suddenly she could hear the prisoners screaming. The man staggered, leaned forward to support himself on his desk. "Jesus Christ," the man said. "Jesus Christ."

"Where's the keys?"

"What'd you do to me, lady? I can't lift my fuckin' arms."

"The keys."

The man slumped into his chair, unsnapped the keys from his belt, and slid them across the desk. Behind Veronica a man's voice said, "Charlie?"

Veronica concentrated on the voice without turning around and heard the man slump to the floor. The third key she tried fit a control panel next to the steel lockup door. A motor wheezed and the door bucked but didn't open. She realized she was still disrupting the electricity and forced herself to relax.

The door slid back. There were four cells inside. Three of them held drunks and addicts and derelicts. In the fourth were four black prostitutes, and Hannah. All of them but Hannah were screaming for help.

Hannah hung from a pipe in the ceiling by her trousers. Her face was swollen and purple and her tongue stuck straight out of her slack mouth. Her eyes bulged. A patch of hair had been ripped out by the zipper in her pants and a drop of dried blood still clung to her scalp.

Veronica threw herself at the bars, her screams lost in the voices around her. She felt the keys tugged out of her hand and one of the hookers opened the cell from inside. Veronica ran to Hannah and held her with one arm around her waist, the other hand tugging at the knotted pant leg around her neck.

She refused to think. Not yet. Not while there was still something left to try. She laid Hannah's body out on the sticky gray floor of the cell. She pushed the swollen tongue aside and dug vomit out of Hannah's throat with her fingers. She blew air into her lungs until she lost all breath herself.

One of the prostitutes had stayed behind. She looked at Veronica and said, "She a wild woman before she die. Bitch went completely crazy. Never saw anything like it. We couldn't get near to her."

Veronica nodded.

"I tried to stop her, but there weren't no way. Girl was crazy, that's all."

"Thank you," Veronica said.

Then the cell was full of police, guns drawn, and there was nothing she could do but raise her hands and go along with them.

♥

She waited until she was alone with two detectives before she used her power again. She left the two of them barely conscious on the floor of the interrogation room and walked out into the night.

The street was headlights and horns honking, blaring jam boxes and shouting voices, all of it too bright, too loud, too overwhelming. Inside her it was the same. Her mind would not shut up. Hannah was her life, the only thing that mattered. If Hannah was dead, how could she still be alive?

The thought was white-hot, too painful to touch. Better, she thought, to just think of herself as already dead. She watched a bus roar past her and wondered what it would feel like to go under its wheels.

Then she remembered the look on Hannah's face as she lay on the floor of the bank, as her consciousness came back into her. She remembered the prostitute in the cell. Crazy, wild woman, the prostitute had said.

Someone had done this to Hannah. Somewhere in the city there was someone who knew what had happened, and why.

Not dead, Veronica thought. Hannah is dead, and I'm not. Someone knows why.

It turned into a refrain, a mantra. It brought her back to Hannah's apartment, took her inside. She lay down in Hannah's bed and held one of Hannah's shirts to her face and breathed the smell. Liz crawled up onto the bed next to her and started to purr. Together they lay there and waited to see if the sun would ever rise.

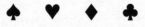

Mr. Nobody Goes to Town

by Walton Simons

JERRY PUSHED THE INTERCOM button and stared up at the closed-circuit TV. A cold wind whipped at him, stinging his face and ears. Overeating at Thanksgiving dinner hadn't given him much in the way of winter fat. But it was only early December, he could keep working on it.

"Who is it?" said a polite female voice over the intercom.

Jerry recognized Ichiko. "Jerry Strauss. I'd like to come up and talk to you about Veronica. Or, at least, get warm."

There was a buzz and the automatic door bolt clicked open. Jerry pushed his way in and walked into the sitting room, rubbing his hands. A woman sat on the low couch. She was tall, with long brown hair, distant eyes, and soft features. She stared past Jerry toward the street. Jerry walked to the door of Ichiko's office and knocked.

"Come in."

Jerry slipped in and sat down in the chair opposite Ichiko's desk. The office was more high tech than Jerry had expected. There was a computer on her credenza and a bank of TV screens showing the outside of the building and the sitting room. Jerry had only seen the one camera; the rest must be hidden. Ichiko was wearing a dark blue dress. Her eyes looked tired, but she managed a smile.

"Thanks for seeing me," Jerry said. "I was just wondering if you had any idea how I could find Veronica, or even contact her."

Ichiko shook her head. "She moved all her belongings out a few weeks ago. She didn't tell me about her future plans."

"Do you have any ideas at all?"

"No." Ichiko pressed her fingertips together. "Really. Would you like to try someone else as a companion?"

"No. I don't know how I got into this situation in the first place. It's not really like me. Veronica was special, I guess."

"All women are special. Men as well, I suppose." Ichiko stood. "I'm sorry I've been unable to help you, Mr. Strauss."

"It was just a shot," Jerry said, standing and taking a step toward the door.

Ichiko looked up at the monitors. A red light was flashing under one of them. Two young Asian men were staring up at the screen. One of them pulled out a can of spray paint. He held it up to the camera. The screen went dark.

"Damn," Ichiko said. She pushed the intercom to the sitting room. "Diane, get in here now."

Jerry heard footfalls outside and the door swung open, almost hitting him. The young woman shut the door behind her. Her already pale complexion had gone white. "They're at the outside door," she said. "Two Egrets."

"What's going on?" Jerry backed away from the door and stood behind the desk with Ichiko and Diane.

"Immaculate Egrets. Street thugs," Ichiko said. "We've refused to pay them protection money. I used to be able to threaten them with the return of my son, but it's been so long."

"Fortunato?" Jerry asked.

"No, Santa Claus." Diane's voice was trembling, but she managed a quick stare that made Jerry feel like a six-year-old.

Jerry looked at Ichiko's desktop. There was a picture of Fortunato. He picked it up and sat in the chair, studying the photograph.

"What are you doing?" Ichiko's voice was calm and curious.

"The best I can," said Jerry. "Either one of you got a mirror?"

Diane fumbled in her purse and handed him a compact. Jerry stared into it and started changing his features and skin tone.

"Jesus," said Diane. "No wonder Veronica was spooked by you."

Jerry ignored the comment and handed her back the compact. He turned to Ichiko. "How do I look?"

"A little more forehead," she said.

There was a pounding at the office door, then laughter.

"Diane, let them in," Jerry said, trying to force authority into his voice.

The girl opened the door and stood back. The two Egrets walked into the room like foxes entering the henhouse. They saw Jerry and stopped.

"What do you want?" Jerry said.

"Pay up," said the larger of the two kids. He took a step forward. Jerry stood up slowly. He could only make himself a little taller, but he'd pushed the limits.

"Get out, scum." Jerry folded his arms into what he hoped was a mystical-looking position. "Get out, or I'll turn you into something like this."

Jerry let his facial features go completely. He let his jaw sag and rolled out a huge, blue tongue. He flattened his nose and elongated his ears. Flaps of skin from his forehead began to melt over his brow.

The Egrets ran, bouncing off each other in the office doorway. A gun popped loose and skidded across the floor. Jerry walked around the desk and picked it up. It was cold, blue, and heavy. He tucked it into his coat.

"They might be waiting for me outside," he explained.

"Your face," Diane said, wincing. "Fix it or something."

Jerry closed his eyes and let his body image take his face back to normal.

"You have done me a great service," Ichiko said. "If you truly wish to find Veronica, a group called WORSE may be hiding her. However, I suggest you hire a professional to take up the chase. They're dangerous women from what I hear."

Jerry nodded. "Thanks." He stared at Diane. She looked away. Scaring her was more fun than he wanted to admit. He blew her a kiss and walked slowly out of the office and into the cold streets.

♣

Ackroyd sat behind the cluttered desk, a manila folder conspicuous in the center. His right eye was slightly swollen and dark. "Want a drink?" he asked as Jerry sat down. "It's all part of the service."

The old metal chair creaked as Jerry settled into it. "No. Oh, well. Don't want to be a bad guest."

Ackroyd opened a drawer and pulled out a glass and bottle of scotch. He wiped out the glass with a tissue. "Straight up all right?"

"Sure. A little week-before-Christmas cheer can't hurt." Jerry needed it for his nerves. The folder was pretty thick. Maybe there was a lot more to know about Veronica than he suspected. "Not going to indulge yourself?"

Ackroyd shrugged. "I've got a bit of a headache today."

"I noticed your eye. I hope you didn't get it while you were working, you know, doing what I asked." Jerry picked up the glass and took a larger-than-normal swallow.

"Jokertown's getting tougher and tougher. Mostly nats stirring up trouble. It's kind of open season on wild cards nowadays." He opened up the folder. "Which brings us to your little lady Veronica."

"She's not exactly my lady." Jerry wasn't sure what Veronica was to him anymore, whether he really cared or she was just a lingering obsession.

"Whatever. To start where you lost track of her, she got involved with a woman named Hannah, who just happened to be involved in a rad-fem group."

"WORSE," Jerry said.

"Real good." Ackroyd stroked his chin. "You kept that to yourself. It'll help if you tell me everything you know from now on. Anyhow, whether there was anything sexual between Hannah and Veronica isn't clear. You heard about the bank murder not long back?"

"I think so. Woman shot a guard to death or something, then killed herself in jail." Jerry pictured Veronica with another woman, then took another stinging mouthful of scotch.

"That was Hannah. Veronica broke into the precinct and found the body. Apparently, she has the power to make men sick. I've known a few women like that myself. Anyway, that's how she got past all the cops. After that she went to ground. Rumor is that Hannah's buddies are hiding her out. I could try to infiltrate WORSE, but I don't think I'd get past the physical. Did you ever feel sick around her?"

"Not the way you're meaning it." Jerry exhaled slowly. "If she had some kind of ace, she never used it on me."

"Just curious." Ackroyd gingerly fingered the mouse under his eye. "An interesting sidebar to this. There's a rumor that Hannah was possessed or something when she shot the guard. Could be nothing. Could be an ace power."

"Then maybe Hannah didn't really commit suicide." The scotch was kicking in and Jerry was fighting off the image of Veronica's head between her lover's legs.

"Hard to say. I'll keep my ear to the ground." Ackroyd picked up the bottle. "Cash customers get a second shot if they want it."

"No thanks. Keep looking for Veronica." Jerry straightened his shoulders. "I think I'll look into Hannah's murder myself. Who's the officer in charge of the investigation?"

"Lieutenant King, homicide. Don't get in his way." Ackroyd cocked his head to one side. "I like you. Why don't you leave the detective work to me? I'm a trained professional. Years of rigorous study in detective school. Well, weeks anyway. I know my way around. You—"

"This is something I really want to do. I found out about WORSE, you know." Jerry felt focused for the first time in weeks. It might be real purpose and it might be just the scotch. "How tall is King?"

"Just under six feet." Ackroyd gave Jerry a long, slow look. "I know a little about your history. This may or may not apply to you, but it's not a good time to be a public wild card."

"Mine doesn't play anymore, Mr. Ackroyd. If you do know my history, you should be aware of that."

"Whatever you say. I'll let you know if I turn up anything on Veronica." Ackroyd smiled, his mouth hard and small. "And be careful."

♠

The office wasn't exactly what Jerry had anticipated. The cream wallpaper and walnut wainscoting were an unexpected relief in the otherwise deprived depths of Jokertown. Pretorius was an unusual lawyer, though. Successful, too, or Hiram Worchester wouldn't have hired him.

"Mr. Strauss. Thank you for coming." Pretorius extended a large hand. Jerry shook it and sat down. Pretorius ran a hand through his white hair and leaned back in the chair. "As you know I've been hired to defend Hiram Worchester. Since you were on the world tour with him, I thought we might use you as a character witness."

"Well, I can't say that I know Mr. Worchester very well. I was having problems myself then, you know. Dr. Tachyon had just gotten me out of my ape body. The people who knew him said Hiram was acting in a very strange manner, especially in Japan. That's kind of secondhand information, though." Jerry extended his palms. "The few occasions I've seen Hiram since, he's been very courteous and decent. I don't know if that's any help to you."

"Hard to say. You build a case in little ways, sometimes. We might need your testimony, and we might not." Pretorius pushed his wire-rim spectacles up the bridge of his nose. "Are you planning on taking any sort of vacation or business trip in the near future?"

"No," Jerry said. "Not as far as I know."

Pretorius nodded. "Good. I appreciate your time. We'll contact you if the need arises."

"Just out of curiosity, how are you going to plead? My brother's a lawyer," Jerry explained, "he'd be disappointed if I didn't at least ask."

"Well, in the interest of professional courtesy, I'll tell you that we're pleading not guilty." Pretorius took a deep breath. "Diminished capacity. Not an argument I care for much, but this is a unique case." He snorted laughter. "Of course, they all say that."

"Thanks. Let me know if you need me." Jerry stood and headed for the door. He didn't want Pretorius to walk him. He'd heard about the leg. "And good luck."

Pretorius stayed behind the desk. "Thank you, Mr. Strauss. We are most certainly going to need it."

◆

Jerry leaned against the railing and stared west at Ellis Island. The Staten Island Ferry was one of the few things that hadn't changed in the time he'd been an ape. Kenneth stood silent behind him, his collar turned up against the chilling breeze that ran across the water, churning the surface into whitecaps.

"Winter already," Jerry said.

"Yeah. I suspect it's going to be a hard one."

"Got your shopping all done?" Jerry asked.

"I still have a little wrapping left to do. You?"

"Believe it or not, I actually got it done." Jerry held his gloved palms to his face and blew into them, trying to warm his nose. "I hope Beth likes what I got her. I didn't really know what to get the woman who already has everything."

Kenneth made a face Jerry couldn't quite read. It didn't look happy. "I'm sure whatever you got her will be fine," he said, still staring at the water.

Jerry waited a long moment before speaking again. "Did it bother you that Mom and Dad made such a fuss over me?"

Kenneth turned and looked into Jerry's eyes. "I hated you for it. At the time. They just never had much use for me, but they died trying to get you back."

"Oh." Jerry looked away.

"It's not that way now. You didn't cause them to ignore me. They chose to. I was afraid to hate them, so I hated you instead. I was into hate when I was younger. Self-righteous anger gives such an uncluttered perspective of the world. Makes life simple. I guess we need that when we're young." Kenneth put his hand on Jerry's shoulder. "But believe me, I'm tremendously happy to have you back. You make us feel more like a family."

Jerry shrugged. "If you'd wanted a kid, you'd have had one, I figure. Now you're saddled with me. I'm supposed to be your older brother and I feel like such a burden."

Kenneth raised an eyebrow. "You know better than to fish for compliments with a lawyer, even if he is your brother. But in the interest of your constant need for reassurance, I'll confess that you're a welcome addition to the household." He paused. "And Beth loves you very much."

Jerry wished Kenneth seemed as glad to say it as he himself was to hear it. "Thanks. She's really great. I don't know what I'd do without her."

"That makes two of us."

Jerry leaned in. "I'm not sure she knows that."

"I think she does. Work is important to me. But Beth is always at the center. I found that out when she left me a few years back." Kenneth exhaled slowly, his breath condensing into mist. "I thought I was tough. I learned otherwise. No, I don't think we have any misunderstandings in that area anymore."

"Speaking of work, how is that going?" Jerry felt a twinge of nausea.

Kenneth paused. "It's not what I expected when I was in law school. There's more compromises than you might expect. I defend big-money clients. Justice is purchased at least as often as it's served, but we do what we can within the system. Fifteen years ago I might have been representing the joker squatters over there." He pointed. The ferry was at the point of its nearest approach to Ellis Island.

Jerry didn't think Kenneth wanted to talk about his work. He almost never did. "God, I feel like garbage all of a sudden." His stomach was knotting worse than before.

Kenneth put a hand over his mouth. "Me, too. I hope it's not the flu. Christmas is no time to be sick."

"Amen to that, brother," Jerry said. "Let's find a place to sit down."

♥

Jerry swallowed hard. He wasn't sure he could pull this one off. He hadn't figured on Lieutenant King being black. Changing his skin color and hair texture was no problem, but inside he knew he was still pure whitebread. That was going to be hard to hide.

King always took a long lunch on Thursday. Jerry would have at least half an hour before the man he was impersonating came back. He bit his lip and walked into the room.

Everyone he could see snapped to look at him. Many were reading books or newspapers, which they immediately put down or hid away. The office clattered to life with the sound of fingers on keyboards and paper shuffling. People were afraid of King. That was good. Jerry could use that. A short young man wearing glasses walked up to him quickly.

"You're back early, sir," the young man said. "Anything up?"

"You have to ask?" Jerry managed to sound tough. He tried to relax enough to enjoy his own ability to intimidate. "Get me the file on Hannah Jorde."

The man jerked his head back like someone had shoved a bee up his nose. "But . . ."

"Do it now. I'll be in my office." Jerry turned away, his hands shaking slightly. Ackroyd had reluctantly given him the layout of the room and Jerry headed over to King's office. The door was closed. Jerry turned the knob. It was locked.

Jerry's stomach went cold and he sagged against the solid oak door. Shit, he thought, what now? He fumbled in his pocket for his own keys and got them out, then pressed the end of his finger against the lock. He made the flesh and bone softer and began to push them inside. It felt like the bone was going to tear through the skin at the tip of his finger, but he shoved it in further. He hardened up a bit and turned his hand. The lock clicked. Jerry softened up and withdrew his aching misshapen finger, then quickly re-formed it to its original shape. He opened the door.

The office didn't look big enough to belong to a lieutenant. Jerry sat behind the desk and looked it over. There was a stack of paperwork, a few files, and a gold pen-and-pencil set for fifteen years of service to the force. Jerry leaned back in the massive rolling chair. The young man walked in, set down the file, and gave him an expectant look. "Will that be all, sir?"

Jerry nodded. "Close the door on your way out. And no calls."

"Yes, sir." The man slipped out and closed the door quietly behind him.

The file was about twenty pages or so thick. There was a transcript of Hannah's interrogation, which Jerry only skimmed. She'd said someone traded bodies with her long enough to kill the guard, and the police didn't buy it. Neither side backed off during the conversation, but Hannah didn't sound hysterical or near suicide. Not to Jerry anyway. He flipped quickly past the photos of her dead body. Even alive, she wouldn't have been that pretty. He couldn't figure out why Veronica would have slept with her. At the end of the file was a composite drawing labeled "possible suspect." The young man's features looked familiar, but Jerry couldn't place him for a moment or two. Then it clicked.

"David too-fucking-good-to-be-true. St. John Latham's boy wonder," he said softly.

Maybe there was a God, and Jerry was getting a late Christmas present.

♣

The street was cold, windy, and poorly lit. Jerry pushed his gloved hands into the pockets of his leather bomber jacket as far as they would go. He needed something to occupy his time. Kenneth and Beth had been cuddling on the couch, and he didn't particularly feel like watching foreplay. He figured following David was likely to be anything but boring. Besides, if he had something to do with Hannah's murder, Jerry could find him out and look like a hero. Jerry had started out the evening as a pretty boy, figuring David would be hanging out with the beautiful people. There weren't many that fit that description in Jokertown, and that was where they were now. Jerry had bought a beat-up hat off a hatchet-faced joker to hide his nat features.

David was about thirty yards ahead of him on the other side of the street. Jerry didn't want to get too close. Not yet, anyway. The police-sketch resemblance to David was probably a coincidence. Then again, anything could happen, especially in Jokertown after hours.

David slowed his pace and stopped in front of an alley mouth, turning to look inside. He paused a second, then went in. Jerry cut across the street. A gust of wind whipped a *Jokertown Cry* up off the pavement and into his face. Jerry pulled it away and trotted into the alley. He heard footfalls ahead. David's, he figured. He could also hear muted laughter and what sounded like a scream.

Jerry's mouth went dry. This wasn't really how he'd planned to spend the evening. An Adonis like David should be out picking up gorgeous girls, or boys at least. Jerry took a deep breath, chilling his throat, then walked in.

Jerry saw the light when he stepped around the dumpster. David was just stepping inside. Jerry walked up slowly, trying to appear casually interested. The entrance looked like it had been stuck onto the garbage-stained bricks of the alley wall. A joker stood at the door, looking silently at him. He wore a black silk garment that fully covered his shapeless body. His smiling face was peculiarly stiff.

Jerry tried to step past and get inside. The joker grabbed him by the shoulders and pivoted him around.

"No," the joker said softly. "This is a private club."

Jerry turned to give an indignant look, but there was another scream from inside. He took a step back and wandered off down the alley. Jerry looked at the dumpster as he walked past it. A torn-up gray coat stuck out slightly from inside. Jerry laughed to himself. He was rich and not used to being kept out of any place. He tucked his bomber jacket carefully under some of the less repulsive garbage and pulled out the coat. He shrugged it on and winced.

In Jokertown, even frozen garbage stank. Jerry uglied himself up by enlarging his ears and nose and giving himself fleshy whiskers all over his face. No way that sack-of-potatoes doorman would recognize him now.

Jerry shortened one of his legs and loped down the alley toward the club entrance.

He was almost inside when the doorman started tittering and pulled him back out. Jerry's deformed jaw dropped.

"You didn't really think a few cosmetic alterations would get you in, did you?" The doorman waved him off. "As I said, our clientele is very special."

Jerkoff asshole, Jerry thought, then wondered if the joker could read his mind. He trotted back down the dumpster to retrieve his jacket and headed home.

♠

The phone message from Ackroyd was brief.

"I figure you already know this, but Hannah was supposed to be defended by one Dyan Mundy of Latham, Strauss. Nothing new on Veronica. Somebody more crass would mention money, but I know you're good for it. Still . . ."

Jerry had been out trying to pick up a waitress at his favorite seafood restaurant. Her lack of positive response had prompted him to have several shots of whiskey before starting on his flounder. He'd put on a pot of coffee when he got home and had downed half of it before heading to the law office.

He'd seen Dyan Mundy a few times and pretty much stayed out of her way. She was easily six feet tall, built like an Eastern European athlete, and had her brown hair slicked back. A pair of glasses and a no-nonsense attitude completed her ensemble. She was between meetings when Jerry got to the office. Her desk was uncluttered. There was a picture of her family on one corner. She was as large as her husband and two children combined. A row of dying plants sat on the windowsill.

"What can I do for you, Mr. Strauss?" She seemed somewhat nonplussed at his request to see her.

"It's about the Hannah Jorde case," Jerry said. "I understand you were her attorney—briefly, of course."

Dyan leaned back in her chair and tapped her fingertips together. "I suppose there's no harm in telling you what little I know. She was arraigned on a charge of first-degree murder. I spoke to her briefly about the case. She was very confused, but lucid. Completely committed to this body-switching story. Her suicide surprised me. It seemed inconsistent with her overall attitude. I guess you can never predict those things."

Jerry nodded. "You saw her alone?"

"Yes. No. David came along at Mr. Latham's request. But he got sick just before we got to her cell and had to leave."

There was a sharp knock at the door. It opened before Dyan could say anything. Latham stepped in and closed the door behind him.

"Ms. Mundy, even an attorney of your limited experience knows better than to discuss a case in such a casual manner. I suspect Mr. Strauss is doing nothing more than gathering gossip for party chatter." He stared hard at Jerry. "I'm sure Ms. Mundy has business to attend to and would appreciate your leaving."

Jerry stood. "I'm sorry if I created any kind of problem." He brushed quickly past Latham, who closed the door behind him. Latham's voice sounded like a buzz saw cutting into soft wood. It was going to be a long afternoon for Dyan Mundy.

♠ ♥ ♦ ♣

Snow Dragon

by William F. Wu

. . . **AND** *THIS* **WAS** for her father and *this* was for her brothers if she has 'em, and *this* was for her mother, and *this and this* was for her Nordic grandfathers . . .

Underneath Ben Choy, on the squeaking narrow bed and rumpled sheets, the large, round tits of the cute white girl jiggled rhythmically. Her pale blond hair was splayed out over the sweat-stained pillowcase, her eyes now squinted shut against the glaring bare lightbulb overhead as her breath came faster. Outside the little room, down the hall, someone flushed the community toilet.

. . . And *this* was for every one of her white relatives, and *this* was for the KKK, and *this* was for Leo Barnett, and *this* was for the father of every white girl he had ever liked. *This* was his revenge against all of *them.* And *this* and *this* and *this.*

◆

Later, his breath regained, Ben sat up between Sally Swenson's spread legs. He turned sideways to lean back against the peeling yellow paint of the thin interior wall, one of her legs under his lower back. Then he extended his own legs under her other knee, to hang over the edge of the bed. The sheet had fallen to the floor.

She roused herself enough to prop his two pillows under her head and looked at him with big, guileless blue eyes.

"Is it always this hot in here?" she asked. "Even this time of year?"

"Yeah." Ben glanced at the one window in the room. On the outside surface, misshapen ice rippled the glow from the street-lights below. On the inside, a mist of condensed moisture had been streaked by drips running down the wooden sill.

He turned to look at her. A sheen of sweat still covered her heart-shaped face and she smiled slightly, uncertainly, as he looked at her. She had liked what he had just done to her. That was for her father, too, whoever he was.

"Don't you pay a lot more for the heat?"

"No." He swung the pendant on his neck chain back to the front, from where it had slipped over his shoulder. It was an old Chinese coin his grandfather had sent him, held by the chain strung through the square hole in its center.

"Is it included with the room?"

"Yeah." Idly, Ben slid a hand up her inner thigh to twirl her blond pubic hair around one finger. A real blonde. "It's a cramped, disgusting little room, but the landlord pays the heat. The radia-tor is hard to control, so I'd rather have it too hot than freeze to death."

"Makes sense to me."

He studied the skin over her pelvis and upper thighs. She was so white that she didn't have even the slightest hint of an old tan. Maybe she couldn't tan at all.

"What's downstairs? It was dark when we came in."

"Grocery store." And she didn't seem to mind lying there talk-ing while still spread wide open. She was really white. And cleanly, purely pink.

"A Chinese grocery store?"

"Sure." He shrugged. "You can get anything there, really."

"Do you mind my asking questions?"

"No."

"Doesn't this room bother you? I mean, it's so small. You don't even have a phone, do you?"

"I hang out in the Twisted Dragon. Anybody wants me, they come there. Or call. I just sleep here."

"Or screw girls here." She giggled playfully, quivering her tits.

"Yeah." He had picked her up a few hours ago in the Twisted Dragon. She had wandered in alone, wide-eyed and curious, her vulnerability plain to see. Among the street toughs and jokers, this slightly chubby and very attractive nat had turned most of the heads in the place—but Ben was under no illusion that she was very bright.

Another victim. Ben, do you simply hate all women? Or just yourself, even more?

Ben clenched his teeth against his sister Vivian's accusation. It seemed to echo in his mind. She had made it many times.

"I've never been to Chinatown before," Sally said shyly.

"Or Jokertown."

She shook her head tightly, with a self-conscious smile, her big eyes glowing.

"And you want someone to show you around." Ben gave her a cynical smile.

Her face was pink now, too.

You like them dumb and helpless, don't you? Vivian had said that plenty of times, too. *Not to mention the impressive bra size.*

"I want a drink." Ben pushed Sally's outside leg away and got up. Even the aged hardwood floor was fairly warm. He picked through the clothes he had scattered earlier and found his underwear. It was the Munsingwear brand, with the pouch in the front. He began to dress.

Ben put on a black turtleneck over a gray thermal shirt and blue jeans and black boots. As an afterthought he added a light blue sweater. Once he was dressed, he pulled a small piece of white paper wrapped in a wad of tissue out of his pants pocket.

It was an intricately folded sculpture, one he had been practicing more often lately, representing a Chinese dragon. Satisfied that it was in good condition, he stashed it again and picked up a brush from the little table that had come with the room. He paused when he saw her looking at him. She hadn't moved.

"Do you want me to go with you?" she asked.

"Don't care." He turned away to face the small mirror standing on the table and brushed his hair back into place.

"Do you want me to stay here?"

"Don't care."

"Can I sleep here tonight?"

"Don't care."

He tossed down the brush and shrugged into his padded brown stressed-leather jacket. JETBOY STYLE! the poster for the jacket had said. Fadeout's money had paid for it after a recent job.

"Why do you wear those baggy pants?" She giggled again.

Ben's jaw tightened. "I'm going down to the Twisted Dragon."

Stung, she watched him, only her blue eyes moving as he stomped to the door.

He knew his lack of interest hurt her more than any rejection would have; he didn't care about that, either. Nothing of value was in the room for her to take. He left the door standing open without looking back.

♥

Ben paused just inside the door of the Twisted Dragon to brush snow off his shoulders and to shuck his leather jacket. The snowfall outside was gentle and the breeze not too cold, really, but he was so used to his overly heated room that the night seemed colder than it was. Anyhow, the twinkling, colorful Christmas lights over the stores and other decorations in their darkened windows had put him in a bad mood. It was a white people's holiday that had nothing to do with his heritage.

I like Christmas, anyway. Vivian always answered his objections the same way, every year.

Even in the Twisted Dragon, a tape of instrumental versions of Christmas carols was playing faintly in the background. A two-foot green plastic Christmas tree on one end of the bar blinked red and green lights. He started down the aisle away from it.

"Hey, Dragon."

Ben turned again.

"You know Christian? He wants to see you." Dave Yang, a short, stocky Immaculate Egret with a frequent but forced smile had come down the aisle behind Ben and now jerked his thumb back over his shoulder.

Ben studied the phony smile carefully. Then he glanced at the tall British mercenary with pale blond hair who was lounging on a bar stool. He faced this way with a smirk as he leaned back against the bar. Christian was a new player in the Shadow Fist organization.

"I met him once; that's all." Tingling with tension, Ben followed Dave back up to the bar and eyed Christian without a word.

"And what do you drink, Mr. Dragon?" Christian raised an eyebrow.

"Bailey's on ice." Ben did not relax.

The bartender nodded and turned to get it.

"A sweet tooth, eh?" Christian laughed, crinkling his lean, weathered features. "The mercs I know would call that a lady's drink, but no fear. You require a new twist on the old joke: 'What does a man drink, who can turn into a tiger or dragon or any other animal at will? Answer: Anything he wants to.'"

Ben clenched his jaw. Under the smooth words, the Britisher's tone was taunting.

"So," Christian continued. "Have you reversed your name Chinese-style? Is it Mr. Dragon or Mr. Lazy?"

"What did you want to see me about?" Ben demanded.

"And they say we Brits have no sense of humor. Ah, well." Christian sipped his drink, then turned to the Immaculate Egret as he swirled the ice in his scotch and water. The bottle of Glenlivet was on the bar behind him. "What are you drinking? Plum wine or some such?"

"Bourbon and water," said Dave, grinning again. "You buying?"

"One Beam's Choice and water," said Christian over his shoulder. He did not bother to make sure the bartender heard him. "You mustn't be so vague, or people will hand you cheap goods. Now, then." His tone hardened. "Leave us."

Without taking his eyes off Christian, Ben saw that the Immaculate Egret walked away without a word. He hated to see the arrogant white man assume that kind of power here in Chinatown. Christian had all these Immaculate Egrets, members of a Chinatown street gang, doing his bidding without question. Still, the move told Ben how much power Christian had here. He would not be a man to cross in a room full of Immaculate Egrets.

"Sit down, Dragon. We have business."

Ben hesitated. Since joining the Shadow Fist organization, he had taken all his orders from Fadeout. He had never worked for anyone else.

"You have heard, haven't you, that I am an authoritative member of the umbrella organization that runs this part of town?"

Ben's jaw tightened again. Christian might be drawing him away from Fadeout or this might be some kind of loyalty test Fadeout had set up. For that matter, with Fadeout's ace ability to turn invisible, he could be sitting undetected on the damn bar right now observing Ben's every move.

Ben shrugged elaborately and sat down, patting the pocket with his paper sculpture and Cub Scout knife out of nervous habit. He would have to watch himself very carefully.

Christian spun his stool and set down his glass, hunched confidentially over the bar. "I want you to take a package out to Ellis Island. You are not to report this message or this instruction to *anyone at all*. Understood?"

Ben nodded, staring at the bar in front of him. He understood; whether or not he would obey was another matter. When the bartender brought his drink, he left it untouched.

"And you will get it from the Demon Princes."

Ben looked at him in surprise. "You're doing business with a joker street gang?"

"They hit a Shadow Fist courier this afternoon and took our package."

"So you want me to clean up your mess."

"Indeed." Christian snickered and ran a callused hand through his pale blond hair. "Our Immaculate friends think of themselves as tough, but they are really just a well-armed adolescent mob. I'm told the Demon Princes are the largest and meanest independent gang in Jokertown."

"That's right." Ben knew they allowed only jokers in their gang and were led by a guy named Lucifer. They were involved in petty crime and small protection rackets, but had a code of no violence against jokers.

"Our amateur commandos can probably take them, but one never knows. You do it instead."

"What kind of package am I looking for?"

"A padded manila envelope with blue powder in plastic bags inside." He gestured with his hands, indicating a size that would just fit into the patch pockets of Ben's jacket.

It was probably the new designer drug called rapture, Ben guessed.

A drug runner, Vivian's voice said disgustedly.

"Where are the Demon Princes?"

"Your problem, mate."

"How do I get to the island?"

"Am I your mum? Make like a birdie and fly, for all I care. Or swim like a fish, but mind the pollution."

Ben's stomach tightened at the man's sneering tone, but he said nothing.

"You haven't touched your drink."

"Have we finished business?"

"That we have."

Ben shrugged and took a swallow. He tried to think of something to say; if he could draw Christian out, he might learn more about where he stood. However, he couldn't think of anything.

The big problem was that he didn't know exactly how powerful Christian really was. He certainly didn't doubt that the man was a major player in the Shadow Fist organization. Of course, no one could force Ben to follow his orders tonight, but he had no idea what the consequences would be if he refused.

Christian seemed to have all the Immaculate Egrets here now jumping to do his bidding; if he decided to eliminate Ben, he seemed to have plenty of soldiers to pull it off. On the other hand, the courier job sounded nasty, too. Finally he decided that he would definitely be better off doing the job and keeping an eye on the newcomer in the future. At least, it was the better of two bad options.

"I must confess to a certain fascination with your name," said Christian. "Picked it yourself, I assume?"

"Yeah. I took it from a guy out of Chinese literature. He was a thief, but sort of a good guy."

"Ah! A kind of yellow Robin Hood."

Ben smiled slightly. Some knowledge of his heritage was one

of his few sources of pride. Even most of the Chinatown people around him didn't know the origin of his nickname.

If only you lived up to the original Lazy Dragon, Vivian said with a sneer in his mind. *You don't deserve your name.*

"Enough chitchat." Christian drained his glass and set it down with a decisive *clunk*. Without another word, he got up and sauntered into the back, toward the storerooms and kitchen.

Ben wouldn't learn anything more from Christian tonight. He took one more gulp of his drink and slid off the stool, moving to the restroom. His face and throat were warm with the liqueur.

Inside, he took the small oblong piece of soap from the dirty sink and wrapped it in toilet paper. Then he stuck it into another pants pocket. Supplied with potential reinforcement, he returned to the bar to pull his jacket on again.

More than a few of the Immaculate Egrets glanced up at him from their booths and tables, but no one moved or spoke. Ben knew from their studied reserve that they were aware he was doing Christian's bidding. He had no idea if they approved or not.

If not, they might express their opinion with Uzis sometime later tonight.

♣

Ben stepped outside and drew in the sharp, cold air as he glanced around. Only a few people were in sight, all of them down the street toward other Jokertown nightspots. The snow was falling softly in big, wet flakes. A light film of white snow covered the sidewalk and street, darkened by occasional footsteps and the streaks of tire tracks.

The snow on the sidewalk just outside the Twisted Dragon was stamped to water by many feet, but one very large pair of footprints was accompanied by the twin tracks of a small two-wheeled cart.

The Walrus, who had his newsstand over on Hester and the Bowery, was making his nightly rounds of Jokertown bars, hawking papers and magazines. He wasn't far ahead, by the look of the tracks, and he often stopped to talk affably with his customers.

Ben hurried after him.

No one can save you from yourself, Ben. Vivian's voice had thankfully been out of his mind while he had been measuring Leslie Christian. Now it came back with a reminder no less condescending than Christian himself. His sister had never approved of anything he did.

"Shut up," he muttered out loud as he walked down the deserted sidewalk.

Ben was in a vise; he had no question about that. Fadeout, for whom he had been a top aide for some time now, was on one side. The other side remained a mystery.

Get out, Ben. Get out of this life right now. Just run for it. They'll never know what happened to you. Vivian had said that more than a few times, too.

"I'm no coward," Ben muttered aloud. It came out in more of a whine than he had intended.

It's not cowardice. It's the smart thing to do.

Ben gritted his teeth and tried to shut out the voice as he walked faster. He failed.

If Fadeout is testing your loyalty, then he represents both sides and you'll pass the test by reporting this mission to him right away.

"Obviously," Ben growled under his breath.

If Christian is testing your loyalty to Fadeout for someone else, or for his own purposes, you flunk the test by reporting to Fadeout.

Ben hurried faster; he was almost running now from the insistent voice.

Then again, someone might have decided to take you out completely by sending you on an impossible mission, or a setup of some kind.

The mission could be suicide . . . reporting to Fadeout could be suicide; so could not reporting it.

Fadeout could be watching right now.

Suddenly panicked, Ben whirled and looked around. Fadeout could turn invisible, but he couldn't avoid leaving footprints in the snow. None had followed Ben out of the Twisted Dragon.

The sound of Vivian's giggle echoed in his mind.

"Shut up!" he shouted aloud to the empty street. Angry at himself now, Ben spun again and strode fast through the falling snow. Nobody was going to scare him off. He would eat Demon Princes for a late-night snack.

He finally spied the Walrus at Chatham Square, waddling out of the offices of the *Jokertown Cry*. As always, he was in shirt sleeves, a rotund figure of oily blue-black flesh barely more than five feet tall. Tonight he wore a red Hawaiian shirt with orange, blue, and green birds of paradise all over it and he pulled his little wire cart behind him toward Ernie's.

Get out while you can, Ben. If you die, I die, too.

Ignoring Vivian's voice in his mind, Ben jogged carefully after the Walrus in the snow. He didn't know him well, but they had spoken a few times. The Walrus was an endless font of jokes and gossip; everyone, including Ben, liked him.

"Hi," Ben said breathlessly as he slowed down to fall in step alongside the Walrus. The Walrus knew him only as a frequent patron of the Twisted Dragon, in his human form.

"'Evening, Ben," said the Walrus, looking at him from under a battered porkpie hat. Tufts of stiff red hair stuck out from under it. Twin tusks curved down around his mouth. "I sold all my Chinese papers back at the Twisted Dragon. May I interest you in something else?"

"Forget it; I can't read Chinese, anyway. But, uh, I need to find some Demon Princes."

"Mmm, well. They aren't exactly customers of mine. I don't know as how they read. No, sir."

"Come on, Walrus. You hear everything."

"An urgent matter, eh? You're running around on a snowy night like this, during the holidays and all."

"Look, I don't have a lot of money. Right now, that is. But my time always comes."

"I'm just a talkative cuss making rounds. No money necessary." The Walrus nodded pleasantly. "But I don't know that I can help you, Benjamin."

Ben shrugged, trying hard to come up with something he could trade.

"I see the Twisted Dragon has a new regular," said the Walrus airily, looking up at the swirling snow. "English, by his accent."

That was what he wanted. Ben hesitated; talking about the Shadow Fist Society was never a good idea. Then he decided to take the risk—he was in serious trouble anyhow, and wasn't even sure just how bad it was. "Leslie Christian. Highly placed, just moved right in. Word is he tells stories of being a merc all over the world."

"And I hear a note of disapproval."

Ben shrugged.

"I tried selling papers tonight at Hairy's Kitchen. Business was bad, though. Most of the patrons were illiterate, I think."

No, Ben. You don't owe Christian anything.

"Thanks, Walrus." Ben grinned and spun in a little twist of snow. As the Walrus continued to pull his little cart down the sidewalk, Ben jogged the other way.

Ben, stop. I'll stop you. Somehow, someway, I'll stop you. If not tonight, someday. Stop ruining our life and our home!

Ben had heard it all before. He jogged on down the cold streets. For now, at least, the voice stopped.

Outside Hairy's Kitchen, Ben slowed down to let some pedestrians go by and then looked in the big picture window. Eight

Demon Princes were lounging around a big round table at the back. Lucifer himself wasn't there; the guy in charge had a head that looked like it was covered with purple grapes, except for dark circles for his eyes and mouth, and he wore an expensive black leather jacket. Next to him, a companion with a flattened fish head like that of a flounder stuffed pizza into his mouth with hands shaped like split, mitten-shaped fins.

Empty plates were piled up on the table. The joker gang members were laughing and poking fun at each other. Their weapons, AK-47s, Uzis, and AR-15s, were casually slung around the backs of their chairs.

The rest of the place was deserted. Even Hairy and his help had retreated to the kitchen. The Demon Princes had been bragging, and no one, including them, doubted that a response was due from the Shadow Fists.

Without backup, negotiation was out of the question for Ben.

On missions for Fadeout, he had always had protection for his comatose body. Now he was on his own. Ben walked briskly around the corner into an alley and took the folded paper dragon out of his pants pocket.

In the alley, he stopped next to a dumpster with an open lid. There he unwrapped the dragon carefully; finding it in good condition, he dropped it to the layer of snow. Then he grabbed the top of the dumpster and jumped to get one leg over it. With a rolling motion, he fell gently into a foul-smelling pile of cardboard, newspaper, and garbage. Only the cold made the stench bearable.

Be careful, at least, Vivian said reluctantly.

Ben wriggled around until he was lying on his back in a reasonably comfortable position. Then he closed his eyes and concentrated on the folded paper lying outside the dumpster.

In a second, he could feel himself growing.

As the folded paper became massive reptilian flesh and organs and scales, Ben looked out with the dragon's eyes at the mouth of the alley. Ben walked his forty-foot-long, four-footed, wingless body forward on short legs. No one saw him cross the cold, broken pavement toward the sidewalk.

When he turned the corner of the building, pedestrians on the sidewalk suddenly scattered into the street. Even the most hardened denizens of Jokertown didn't want to cross him. Ben's clawed feet could not work a door latch, so he coiled himself outside the door.

Through the glass, he saw grapehead suddenly rise half out of his chair, pointing at him. Ben shot forward, smashing his massive head through the door; as he raced down the aisle inside the restaurant, the door snagged on the thickest part of his neck and ripped from the wall. In front of him, the Demon Princes grabbed their assault rifles and fired as they dove for cover.

Ben felt line after line of bullets tear into him, but the size and speed of his dragon body carried him forward, crashing into the table. The remains of the door hung around his neck like a collar. He snapped twice at the stunned jokers in a blood fury, biting one in half each time. More bullets ripped into him, but now the Demon Princes were running for the door, firing wildly.

He struck after them like a giant rattlesnake and bit the legs off grapehead, leaving stumps that spurted jets of blood over the smashed table. Then he darted forward again and snapped the fish head off that joker's neck. As he spat out the head, he heard heavy footsteps thumping through the doorway.

As pain dulled his vision, Ben saw the remaining Demon Princes scramble past a large figure cloaked in a black velvet cape and hood. The intruder, gigantic for a human but much smaller than Ben's dragon, wore a fencing mask under the black hood and marched forward angrily.

It was the joker known as the Oddity, in its winter attire.

Ben had never met it before, but he knew the approach of an enemy when he saw it. He clawed his body around to face his adversary. Pain shot throughout his long torso. His coordination was off and his body slow to respond. Though his cold-blooded reptilian constitution was tough, the bullets had torn flesh away from the bone up and down his body and he could no longer move properly.

"This is *Jokertown*," the Oddity intoned fiercely, in the harshest of its three voices. "You have no business here, ace. Not even with a street gang."

Ben could see the shapes moving and shifting underneath the black velvet cloak. The Oddity had once been three people who were now fused together and whose parts were forever mixing and matching in painful motion. He tried to talk back, but only hissed and growled in his dragon throat.

"Is that you, Lazy Dragon?" The Oddity lumbered toward Ben and reached out with one heavy, muscular white arm and one slender, feminine arm—both its hands were masculine but artistic and sensitive. "I've heard rumors about you on the street. But whoever you are—you need to learn to leave jokers alone."

Ben gathered himself and struck forward again, snapping his jaws. He missed the Oddity, who threw its arms around Ben's clamped jaws and squeezed like an alligator wrestler. The arm that had been soft and smooth was slowly gaining in weight and thickness; soon both its arms would be heavy and muscular. One hand had started to become feminine. Ben tried to wrench his jaws open again, but they were held fast.

Now Ben rolled, thrashing wildly; the tables and chairs shattered around him. What was left of the door broke and fell from his neck. Glasses, mugs, and dishes tinkled to shards. The Oddity was flung loose, its own great body adding to the destruction in a swirl of black velvet stained with the shiny blood of Demon Princes and Ben himself.

Anxiously, watching the Oddity, Ben struggled to untwist his long body. His short legs scrabbled helplessly for a moment on the debris as he tried to stand. To one side, the Oddity had lumbered to its feet and was clumsily advancing through the smashed furniture.

The Oddity reached out with its arms again just as Ben felt his claws gain some traction. He opened his jaws and darted downward to the Oddity's legs, but his failing neck muscles were slow and crooked. As Ben's teeth clacked hard on empty air, the Oddity again caught his mouth shut in an iron embrace.

Ben's dragon body was slowly dying. His vision was a blur as he squirmed and convulsed to buck the Oddity off his face, but his movements were even more painful now and less in control. The Oddity continued to ride him, even when they slammed into a wall, smashing the wall-board and splintering the support beams.

With a sudden searingly hurtful convulsion of his entire length, Ben flipped his long tail around and knocked the Oddity's ankles out from under it. The Oddity crashed onto its back, releasing Ben, and crunched broken dishes and glasses even further. Ben opened his jaws again and snapped wildly, getting no more than a mouthful of black velvet.

Shaking free of the cloth, Ben scratched again for a brace under his feet and tried one more time to slash the Oddity's torso with his fangs. He was slow and clumsy now, disoriented and frustrated by his inability to move his huge body the way he wanted. The Oddity again wrapped up his long snout in arms that were slick and shiny with sweat and blood. This time it was the Oddity who pushed off the floor with one massive leg, rolling to one side.

Ben felt a thrill of fear as he was flipped onto his back by brute strength; the lights spun above him in streaks. Suddenly the Oddity got new purchase against the floor and heaved to one side, the fencing mask an expressionless mock before one of Ben's eyes as the Oddity's arms twisted Ben's dragon neck. He heard a loud snap—

. . . and found himself lying in the cold dumpster outside, surrounded by trash and garbage.

Ben did not dare attract the Oddity's attention now. The bar of soap he had taken from the Twisted Dragon had not been carved; if the Oddity or anyone else came after him, he had no protection. He waited, listening.

The night had turned much colder. The snow fell heavily in fine white flakes that came swirling endlessly out of the night sky on a wind growing harsher as he lay there. Occasionally a car swished through the slush on the street, but the slush was hardening to ice. Everyone was quiet in the presence of slaughter.

From the sound of voices murmuring cautiously, he knew that a small crowd had gathered outside the door of Hairy's Kitchen. From the footsteps and the shift in the voices, he knew when the Oddity had made its way out of the wrecked establishment and wandered down the street to the depths of Jokertown. Ben climbed out of the dumpster, dropped to the ground, and peered around the corner.

The crowd was already breaking up. Now that Ben's dragon was again a scrap of paper and the Oddity gone, the spectacle had ended.

Glancing about alertly for Demon Princes, he slipped through the shattered doorway and hurried past the wreckage in the aisle to the remains of the table where they had been carousing. So far, Hairy and his staff were still holed up in the back or maybe off the premises completely. He could not help seeing some of the remains of the jokers he had so easily torn apart a few minutes before.

Ben stepped over a bloodred chunk of human flesh and felt a sudden gag in his throat. He stifled it, looking away. In the heat of the struggle, in dragon form, he had fought desperately, biting and slashing Demon Princes with abandon. He had felt different, somehow, at the time. The fight had been necessary, and as a dragon, he had fought the way a dragon must.

Now it was hard to believe he was the same person, inside, as the one who had slaughtered these people so quickly and easily.

It was you, all right, Vivian said with quiet anger.

Ben had killed before in his animal forms and would do so again. In most cases he had never faced the remains in human form afterward. Now, however, the bloodshed sickened him. It just hadn't seemed the same a few moments ago.

He clenched his human jaws this time and forced himself to keep searching.

Ben couldn't be sure the package was here; one of the Demon Princes might have had it on him or they might have stashed it earlier this evening. It might have been carried by one who got away. As he looked around, gusts of cold wind blew through the restaurant, rattling dishes and debris and sending napkins flying. After a moment of picking pointlessly through the pieces of furniture and broken dishes, he turned to the torso of the grape-headed joker.

Ben winced and tried to look only at the shiny black leather jacket, adorned with fancy zippers and silver studs, not at the stumps of the joker's legs or the spray of blood all around him. Quickly he patted down the joker and felt a bulge in a large zippered pocket. Gagging from the smell of blood, he retched once.

You have no right to be sick at this, Vivian said accusingly. *You caused it.*

Ben called up enough saliva to spit and wiped his hand on his sleeve. Then he unzipped the pocket. Holding his breath against the bloody stench, he pulled out a small padded manila envelope.

A siren wailed in the distance, coming closer. That was fast for the Jokertown Precinct. Still, even Fort Freak had to respond when someone made a mess this loud and public.

Ben had to be sure. He pulled open the flap of the envelope and looked inside. The envelope was stretched to its limit by plastic bags jammed with blue powder, sealed by cellophane tape. It was rapture, a designer drug from the labs of Quinn the Eskimo—a Shadow Fist product that was sheer poison.

A drug runner, Vivian said, sneering with hatred and contempt.

He closed the flap, secured the envelope in one of the big patch pockets on his leather jacket, and walked briskly out of Hairy's Kitchen into the worsening storm.

♠

Ben had forgotten about Sally Swenson until he was walking down the filthy hallway to his door. Hoping she had changed her mind and left, he unlocked the door and slipped inside the stifling heat of the room. By the slant of light from the door, he could see her blond hair still splayed out on the pillow much as it had been when he had left. In the heat, though, she had kicked off the sheet, which lay rumpled at the foot of the bed. She was breathing slowly and deeply.

"Sally." He reached down to wake her and then stopped. Overall, she had seemed harmless enough, and he expected to be back well before dawn. The last thing he needed now was a hassle with her.

He turned on the lamp and set the door carefully so that it was in the jamb but not latched. The door was warped and the irregular shape helped hold it in place. Then he set the knob to lock. Tonight he would have to do without the dead bolt.

You can still get out of this, Vivian said quietly, hopelessly.

"Hope this works," he muttered to himself, ignoring her voice. He took the manila envelope out of his jacket and put it on the floor. Then he undressed, before he began to sweat in the warmth. When he was naked, he took out his Cub Scout knife and the bar of soap he had taken from the Twisted Dragon.

He paused. A cold-blooded creature like a dragon was too vulnerable on a winter night like this. He needed a creature that could tolerate the weather, cross the water to Ellis Island either by air or water, and still hang on to the package. It also had to be a creature that could intimidate the unknown persons he would meet; that was a given on a mission like this.

"Now, then," he whispered, mostly just to hear a friendly voice. He got to work. When he had finished, he set his soap carving in the middle of the floor and slipped into bed next to Sally. She did not stir. He pulled up the sheet, closed his eyes, and concentrated on his carving of a polar bear.

In a few seconds, Ben stood up on all fours, raising an ursine body of considerable bulk under a heavy layer of white fur. He took the doorknob gently in his teeth and walked backward, pulling the door all the way open. Wondering if he could actually get out of the room, he picked up the manila envelope gently in his mouth. Then he squeezed his furry weight through the doorway with effort. He heard the aged wood crack as he pushed free into the hallway.

The hall was almost too narrow for him to turn, but he managed. He dropped the drug packet for a moment and pulled the doorknob until he heard the latch snap into place. Satisfied that his human body was as safe as it could be, he picked up the package and padded downstairs.

The streets were even colder and more blustery than before. Fine snowflakes fell fast, swept by the gusts of wind. The snowfall had become a blizzard that had nearly cleared the sidewalks of lower Manhattan. Even so, Ben was completely comfortable in this body.

A polar bear was not the strangest sight most people had ever seen in or near Jokertown. As Ben padded along Canal Street at a soft jog through the whipping snow, the few pedestrians still hurrying for shelter gave him a wide berth, but that was all the reaction he got. Right now, his biggest worry was some street punk with a powerful gun who would shoot him on impulse.

Finally, Ben thought to himself as he reached the Lexington Avenue subway. He hurried down the steps, out of the harrowing wind. At the bottom, he trotted past the token booth and hopped over the turnstile.

A cop standing to one side put a hand on his sidearm, but it was only a defensive move. Ben trotted to the platform, scattering a small crowd of people who gasped in surprise. He glanced them over, saw no one reaching for a gun, and relaxed.

"It's *real*," one lady whimpered. "Somebody call the cops. *Damn*, I hate these subways nowadays."

"Bet it's an ace," said an older man.

"Looks more like a joker," snickered a teenaged boy.

"Quiet; he'll hear you," hissed the first lady.

"I knew it was cold out, but this is ridiculous," said another man. "Say, what's he got in his mouth?"

"*You* ask him," said the teenager.

Ben ignored them. When the train stopped and the doors opened, a small knot of people froze in place, staring at him. Then they hurried to exit from other doors and Ben boarded.

He had to sit down in the center of the aisle just inside the doors; even so, he blocked the way. No one else entered his car, and several of those already there suddenly got out at this stop after all, through other doors. The rest simply stared impassively at him.

Ben was relieved when the train began to move. At each stop on the way to the southern tip of Manhattan, he glared out as soon as the doors opened. The people on the platform all flinched and either found another car or decided not to ride the subway tonight at all. Not very many people were out at this hour, on a night like this.

Finally, at Battery Park, he stepped off the train and hurried away. He knew he was too long to fit through the exit turnstile, however, and had to leave by jumping the entryway again. Then he trotted up the steps and back out into the storm.

In the park itself, Ben leaned into the icy, gusting snowfall as he trotted toward the water. He figured this was as close to Ellis Island as he could get on land, since a passenger ferry stopped here during the day between trips to Liberty Island and Caven Point, New Jersey. The bitterly cold wind off the Hudson River where it opened into the Upper Bay blew into his face, and he knew he had chosen well. The heavy fur and layer of fat insulated him just fine.

Now for the fun part, he thought to himself. He set the manila envelope down in the snow and picked it up again, this time completely enclosed in his mouth.

Ben inhaled deeply through his nose and plunged into the freezing waters. He was relieved to find that he was still comfortable. In fact, he could swim just fine, paddling with all four legs and holding his eyes and nose above the surface.

Behind him, the lights of Manhattan glowed with spectral white beauty through the blizzard. He didn't lift his head to look forward toward New Jersey and the various islands, fearing that he would need all his energy to swim the distance to Ellis Island. He only focused on the lights of Ellis Island itself. The waves splashed against his face, making it hard to see, but he was able to blow out any water that got in his nose.

The polar-bear body was powerful and suited to a long swim in frigid waves. He just kept paddling through the darkness. Though he couldn't judge the distance very well, he was pleasantly surprised that he wasn't tiring.

Suddenly, however, he felt a tremendous desire to give up, to turn around. It surprised him; he fought it, focusing his eyes on the lights ahead. The very water seemed thicker, the waves stronger, the wind harder.

Maybe he was getting tired, after all. He tried to guess how far he had to go. It might have been several hundred yards, but suddenly it looked like more. He forced himself to keep swimming.

It's farther to go back now anyway, he told himself. Actually, he didn't really feel tired at all. He just felt a compulsion to turn around and swim away.

Leslie Christian wouldn't think much of that.

Ben churned his legs in the water, harder and harder.

Suddenly a wave of fear swept over him, making his stomach muscles clench. It came without thought or logic; he felt a primal panic rising in him, lifting the ursine hackles on the back of his neck and shoulders. He kept swimming, but his legs were reluctant, weakening with dread.

Another crest of fear rose in him, and he stopped swimming. His huge body bobbed in the tossing waves, held aloft by his fur and layer of fat. Ellis Island, no more than a light or two in the distance, filled him with revulsion. As he looked at it through the blizzard, the island grew blurry and seemed to shift even farther away from him.

Ben blinked a splash of water out of his eyes, trying to focus. Even the falling snow ahead of him seemed to turn oddly in his vision. He was disoriented, scared, and wanted to go home.

He forced his legs to start kicking again, in a dog paddle. Instead of turning, though, he paddled straight ahead. He concentrated on his legs, just to keep them moving. The island, the fear and dread of the unknown he would meet there, and this strange panic that had struck him were still present, but he ignored them. Two legs at a time, pushing against the water, filled his mind. That was all: one, two; one, two.

Ben kept swimming.

The trip seemed to take forever. At last, however, he entered a cone of bright light and dared to look up. It was a single powerful lamp on one of the buildings; others near it were burned out. Ellis Island was a rectangle, with a ferry slip in one long side that created a horseshoe shape. The island was smaller than he had expected, maybe less than two city blocks.

Now that he knew he was going to make it, he slowed down, looking for signs of life. Only certain windows illuminated from inside suggested anyone was here, but in this weather that was no surprise. He paddled into the ferry slip, still looking around, and finally reached up to the dock with his front legs and pulled himself out of the water.

On an impulse, he shook himself, spraying icy water in all directions.

As he got his bearings, he became aware of an unpleasant smell.

It reminded him of garbage barges, but the smell was more varied, and worse. Fortunately, the hard wind was blowing it away from the island.

He squinted his bear's eyes into the rush of snow against his face. The main building was maybe six stories' worth of brick and limestone trim, considerably longer than a football field from left to right as he faced it. At each corner, copper-domed observation towers stood another forty feet higher than the roof against the storm. The building had an old look, as though it was from the turn of the century, but Ben was no student of architecture.

An eerie feeling of being watched from behind ticked the back of his neck. He turned to look as his hackles rose, but nothing was behind him except the water. The sensation persisted and he looked up, to see only the heavy snowfall swirling down at him.

A movement in the shadows to his left caught his eye. He turned, tensing. Someone took a wary step forward.

"What do you want?" a woman's voice demanded.

Ben hadn't expected anyone to be outside here. Also, he couldn't talk as a bear. He only watched as the speaker came forward another step. She walked upright, at least six feet tall. Her face was that of a ferret: black nose, wedge-shaped head with round ears, and a black mask around her eyes over buff fur. Her fur shifted toward silver on her abdomen. Most notably, two-inch fangs curved downward from her mouth.

"Careful, Mustelina," said a young man's voice. "I never saw him before."

Ben looked at him. He was a strange bushy bundle of average height for a man, steely gray in color.

"Shut up, Brillo," said Mustelina. "A joker's a joker. What's your name?"

Ben shook his head and tried to shrug, still watching them suspiciously. At least he understood what Mustelina was doing out here; she was made for this weather, nearly as much as he was.

She probably handled the blazing, humid New York summers better than he would in this form. Brillo, too, was apparently warm enough out here.

"What if he's not a joker?" Brillo yelled harshly against the wind. "What if he's a real polar bear?"

"Oh, get off it, will you?" She took another step toward Ben. The wind rippled her white fur. "Can't you talk at all?"

Ben carefully swayed his head from side to side in a definitive gesture that Brillo could not deny. Then he inclined his head toward the main doors of the big building. His mouth was still clamped shut.

"Bloat better meet him," said Mustelina firmly. "Come on." She walked along the ferry slip toward the main doors with a springy, prancing step, her head bent against the wind.

Ben padded after her, keeping an eye on Brillo. Brillo stayed away from him, though, as they both approached the entrance.

As Ben drew closer to the building, he looked up at the huge triple-arched doors that reached up into the second story. Over them, snow lay on some kind of concrete birds flanking an insignia in relief. Thousands of people could be in a building this size.

"Bloat runs things here," said Mustelina as she pulled open the heavy door.

An incredible stench hit Ben's sensitive ursine nose. He forced himself to walk inside, his stomach rebelling. Mustelina and Brillo followed him.

Ben blinked in the light of the huge room, which had apparently been a lobby at one time. Then he stopped in surprise as the door slammed shut behind him. He was staring face-to-face with the most repulsive joker he had ever seen.

Bloat was monstrous in size, a gross mountain of flesh maybe fifty feet wide and eight feet high. His head and neck looked normal enough at the top and his shoulders and arms were ordinary, but they stuck out uselessly from the incredible mass of his body. Five inlet pipes of some kind jabbed into his body. The stench originated with a resinous black sludge that had accumulated around him on the floor.

Several jokers were hanging around, of all shapes. Some were nearly lost in the shadows at the edges of the big room. At this hour, most of them were probably asleep. Those who were here turned to look with suspicion and hostility at Ben.

"Bloat," said Mustelina, with a fervent awe in her voice. "This joker just swam all the way out here to join us and climbed out of the water. He can't even talk."

"Really?" Bloat's voice was a thin squeak. "Another guest? Welcome, my friend." Bloat peered down at him from his greater height. His expression revealed a leering suspicion his voice had not conveyed.

Ben nodded his bear's head in greeting, feeling a tingle of alarm. He really didn't know much about this place at all.

Mustelina had said Bloat ran the show here, but Ben wished Leslie Christian had told him exactly who should receive the drug packet. And if he had to defend himself, he would have to drop the packet in order to bite anybody.

"He's no joker!" Bloat shrieked. "He's an ace of some kind!" Suddenly he glowered sternly at Ben. "You're no glamour boy, though, are you?"

Ben froze, his pulse racing, wondering how Bloat knew all this. Maybe the rapture was for him, after all.

"That's right," Bloat shouted gleefully. "That packet's for me! Hand it over!"

Ben tensed, looking up at Bloat's face, suddenly realizing that the huge joker was reading his thoughts.

The jokers around them turned expectant, their hostile eyes fixed on Ben. Ben shuffled around to keep them all in his vision. From what he could see, he could defend himself, but a fight wouldn't help him complete his mission.

"Watch him," Bloat warned in his high voice. "Don't let him get away."

"May I?" a commanding male voice asked. A youngster strode out of the shadows with a springy step. He was slender and vibrant, bristling with energy—maybe seventeen years old, dressed in jeans and an oversized purple turtleneck sweater. A short, dark-haired teenage girl stood behind him.

Ben looked from him to Bloat and back.

"Oh, all right, David," Bloat said with exaggerated indulgence. "Make sure. But I've already read his mind, so I know. So there."

David pranced right up to Ben. He grinned with large, even teeth in a handsome face that needed a shave. His blond hair was shaggy and one shock of it fell into his face over bloodshot, watery eyes. He held out one hand.

Ben hesitated, studying David's confident, self-mocking smile. Without the power of speech, surrounded by unknown jokers, he saw little choice of action. He opened his mouth and let the envelope slide forward a little, smelling beer on David's breath as he did so.

He heard shuffling feet and nervous, high-pitched laughter high above him. As David, still grinning, edged forward carefully and took the package, Ben looked up and saw an observation gallery at the third-floor level over the main floor. The people up there were only shadows.

"Ugh," said David, laughing too hard. "Polar-bear saliva."

At first no one laughed. Then Bloat's high giggle pierced the air and the jokers laughed along with him.

David was no joker, though. Neither was the girl behind him.

"So you don't know who he is," Bloat gloated at Ben. "Well . . . I'm not going to tell you!" He laughed again at his own cleverness.

Ben glanced at the door. His chances of running were negligible. His paws couldn't even work the doorknob.

David drew out a packet of the blue powder. He tore a hole in the plastic with the tip of his little finger and then stared at the tiny blue stain on his skin with a sudden fascination.

"Well, David?" Bloat squeaked impatiently.

"That's the stuff, all right," David said softly. "Rapture." He grinned crookedly at his finger and then looked up at Bloat with glowing eyes. "Let's just say I wanted to make sure we get credit for the rent we pay."

"David," Bloat whined. "I don't cheat my friends." He looked around and spotted a tall, slender woman cowering in the shadows. "Giggle, you cutie. This is the one I promised you. Give her some, David."

Giggle crept forward carefully. She wore loose, bulky winter clothes and soft shoes, but as she moved, she laughed quietly. Yet the expression on her face was one of torture and anguish.

"Everything tickles her," Mustelina said softly to Ben. "Even the feel of clothes on her body and the floor when she walks. Every sensation makes her laugh, but she hates it."

"It's called rapture," said David, holding out the packet. "It activates on contact with the skin . . . and it's strongest locally."

Giggle ventured forward slowly and stuck an index finger into the hole in the plastic. She drew it out and looked at it. First she smiled shyly. Then she snatched the packet out of his hands, giggling helplessly at her touch on the plastic. She poured the powder into her palm and smeared it on her face and neck. Gasps and laughter rose up on all sides.

"It's Bloat's," said David warily. "And very expensive."

Bloat laughed in shrieking delight, however, entertained by the spectacle as Giggle dropped the packet on the floor and stripped off her bulky sweater and the blue T-shirt under it. She knelt and began desperately rubbing the rapture all over her bare arms, shoulders, breasts, and stomach.

"You won't stop feeling tickled," said David. He leered at her obvious pleasure, idly rubbing the blue stain on his finger with his thumb. "But you'll love it now."

As everyone watched Giggle, Ben glanced around carefully. He couldn't get out without help.

Giggle had stripped naked and was squatting on the floor, smearing rapture on her thighs. She giggled at the sensation, but no longer looked tortured. Now her face had a dreamy glow.

Ben watched her in a kind of detached horror. Rapture was a nasty drug and she was drenched in it. Still, he was in too tight a spot to worry about some stranger.

Bloat was laughing louder than ever and his joker followers imitated him. David watched Giggle with rapturous enjoyment. The young woman who had entered behind him was now standing alongside him, looking at Giggle with wistful amusement in her pretty blue eyes.

"David," she said softly, twisting a finger around one of her black curls of hair. "Who's the polar bear?"

"You got me, Sarah," said David, his eyes still glowing at Giggle.

"I want to jump him," said Sarah. "I wonder what rapture feels like to a bear."

Ben's ursine ears caught her words even through the riot of other voices. No one else had heard her.

Ben backed away a step, wondering what she meant. If she just wanted a ride, Ben could do that. If she meant sex, she was really crazy. Ben looked around quickly, sure that he was physically stronger than anyone he could see. That told him nothing about what ace abilities might be present here.

Giggle was dancing, naked and smeared with blue, inside a circle of jokers. They were clapping in rhythmic unison, still laughing and shouting encouragement as the rest of the packet of rapture was passed around. Bloat hooted and laughed and wiggled his stubby appendages helplessly.

Suddenly Giggle spotted Ben. Swaying from side to side and giggling, she pranced toward him, her smile white inside her blue face. The circle around her parted, still clapping, and she came to Ben, still dancing and twirling.

The circle re-formed to surround both of them. Someone started a chant to go with the rhythmic clapping: "Bear! Bear! Bear!" Giggle laughed and grabbed Ben's ears, dancing from side to side.

David and Sarah were now in the front of the circle, still within Ben's hearing. The blond youth studied Ben with his watery, bloodshot eyes. Then he put his arm around Sarah and shrugged. "Go ahead, for all I care,"

Ben tensed, watching Sarah, ready to leap forward to attack or to dodge away, as necessary.

She didn't move. Suddenly a force struck Ben's mind, sending him reeling—shoving him out of the polar bear. In his vision, the swaying blue shape of Giggle rippled and blurred. The clapping and chant of "Bear!" overwhelmed him.

Disoriented, he pushed back, growling almost without meaning to. He was hot now beneath his fur and fat inside this place and he did not understand what the force was. The room suddenly seemed to tilt as the mysterious force pushed him away from the sight, hearing, and tactile feeling of the bear.

Ben was lost in a blur of closing darkness, just barely able to make out Sarah seeming to grow larger in his mind. Panicked, unable to hang on to the bear, he focused his concentration on his human body back in Chinatown. He pictured his room, his bed, his nude body in the bed next to Sally. He concentrated harder and finally, belatedly, spun dizzily back into familiar darkness.

◆

Vivian felt Ben's confusion. She had been sleeping in the dark room, grateful for the rare solitude, but her mind came awake suddenly. Ben's mind, disoriented and not present, was no longer controlling their body. The feeling was intuitive, but reliable.

Vivian's mind came instantly awake. She eagerly hurried to blink their eyelids, move their arms and legs, to make them hers, not theirs—or his. She came awake, took control of their body, and felt the change once again.

It didn't hurt at first, exactly, but her adrenaline flowed into her bloodstream and the shifting of blood from the change caused throbbing in her head, her chest, and her pelvis. Her bones ached as their shape and size altered, her pelvis growing and her shoulders and rib cage narrowing. Her head and face hurt sharply as their shape changed. She felt some of the sensation of an elevator dropping suddenly or a roller coaster suddenly starting a steep downgrade.

The shifting of soft tissue was less intense, but it rippled and moved on her chest, between her legs, on her face, through all of her muscles. Then the physical changes stopped and left her breathing hard on the bed in Ben's room. She opened her eyes. The layer of ice on the window softened the glow of light from outside.

Carefully, as she always did after changing from rider to driver in their body, she slid one hand to her chest. Her breasts were small but certainly female. At the same time, her other hand moved between her legs, where she found what she expected. She was Vivian, as Ben still called her from childhood—or Tienyu, as she called herself now.

She cleared her throat softly. It was her voice.

She could feel Ben's presence now, too. He had probably been killed in his animal, she guessed, and his mind was reeling from the surprise. That's what would have caused him to lose control of their body momentarily.

For an indefinite period, however, he would now be riding in their body while she did what she wanted. Like she had done as a rider, he could communicate conscious, direct thoughts to her, but they could not read each other's minds unless the message was deliberate and willful on the part of the sender.

Right now Ben apparently had nothing to say.

Next to her, Sally stirred languorously and turned on her side toward Vivian. Vivian remained motionless, not wanting to wake her. Sally's hand eased across her waist, however, in a casual caress and slid down between her legs.

Vivian tensed, then gently moved to get out of bed, away from Sally's hand. She was hoping Sally was still mostly asleep. However, as Vivian sat up and put her feet on the floor, Sally raised up on one elbow.

"Who are you?" she said sleepily. "Where's Ben?"

Vivian got up and moved away from the bed. "I'm Ben's sister. Ben's gone."

"Gone? Jeez, why didn't—hey, what were you doing in bed with me?"

For a moment Vivian stood uncertainly in the steamy room, naked except for the coin on her neck chain. She toyed nervously with it. Then she switched on the lamp.

Sally flinched, squinting in the sudden light, and pushed herself up into a sitting position.

"Get out," said Vivian.

"What? Come on, Ben said he didn't care if I spent the night. What time is it, anyway?"

"I said get out." Vivian glanced around for Sally's clothes and snatched up her big flesh-toned bra, stiff with its underwire. "Here." She threw it at Sally.

Sally pulled it away from her face, fumbling for something to say and not thinking of anything.

Then, as Sally began putting it on, Vivian picked up Ben's pouched briefs and looked at them, making a mental note to buy something that would fit better tomorrow. At least he had kept to their basic bargain; the jeans were baggy on him, but would fit snugly around her pelvis. The thermal undershirt, turtleneck, and heavy winter socks, of course, were gender neutral, and she had never bothered to own a bra. Ben's boots were always a little loose on her, but not much; their feet only altered a little during the change and the socks made up some of the difference.

Sally's face was bright red and taut with anger, but she had nothing to say. Once her bra was on, she kicked away the sheet and stood up, turning her back to Vivian as she finished getting dressed.

Tomorrow morning Vivian would find the building manager, pretending to know nothing of Ben's whereabouts. She would play the role of Ben's worried sister and take over the rent. From what she remembered when Ben first took the room, the manager wouldn't care if she lived there as long as the rent came on time.

Bundled up in her scarf and winter coat, Sally glanced back over her shoulder. "Thank you for being so considerate," she snapped. "If I don't get killed out there at this hour, I'll freeze to death." She yanked open the door and stomped out, her blond hair swirling.

Vivian suppressed a twinge of guilt. If Sally was old enough to get picked up in the Twisted Dragon, she was old enough to get home at night. As Vivian closed the door and locked it, she grudgingly decided she couldn't blame her brother too much. Sally did look very nice and, of course, she had been willing.

"Say good-bye, Ben," she taunted in a whisper.

Good-bye, Ben muttered sourly in her mind.

♠   ♥   ♦   ♣

Nobody Knows the Trouble I've Seen

by Walton Simons

THE COURTROOM WAS JAMMED with people. There seemed to be almost as many reporters as had been at Bush's inauguration two weeks before. The rest were friends, or enemies, of Hiram's, or just the idly curious. There were no jokers in the room, Pretorius being a notable exception. Kenneth had managed to get Jerry a seat.

"All rise."

The judge walked in and the noisy courtroom grew silent. The old magistrate made her way to the bench and sat down slowly.

The judge cleared her throat. "In the case of the *People of the State of New York* v. *Hiram Worchester*, I understand that the prosecution has seen fit to reduce the charge to involuntary manslaughter. Is that correct?"

The prosecutor rose. "Yes, your honor."

"And how does the defense plead?" the judge asked.

Pretorius arose. "Guilty, your honor."

"A plea bargain, as anticipated," Kenneth said, above the muttering of the courtroom crowd.

"Mr. Worchester," the judge said, "please rise."

Hiram complied, standing as straight as his size would allow.

"Given your stature in the community and the unusual circumstances involved in this case, I see no real benefit to yourself or society in imprisoning you. Therefore, I sentence you to five years probation. Any use of your wild-card ability during that time will constitute a violation of your probation. An individual with your unique gift should be ashamed that it was used to take another life. Society has grown tired of such foolishness. Hopefully, in the future you will be a positive example for us all. If not, you will find the court unsympathetic."

Hiram nodded weakly and wiped his brow. Pretorius stood and put his arm around him.

The heavy wooden doors slammed open at the back of the room. A four-armed joker man pushed his way inside. "Murderer. You're nothing but a rich murderer."

Two officers grabbed the joker, pushed him to the floor, and cuffed him.

"We're going to get you, Worchester," the joker screamed as they dragged him from the room. "We're going to see you dead, just like Chrysalis."

"Jesus." Jerry nudged Kenneth. "Chrysalis is dead and it was an accident. Don't they know that? Hiram was crazy. He's suffered enough."

"Possibly," Kenneth said. "Though the people who cared about Chrysalis might disagree with you. As they say, it depends on whose ox is getting gored."

Pretorius and Hiram began pushing their way through the crowd toward the doorway. Reporters clustered around them like sperm on an unfertilized egg.

"I wouldn't want to be in Jokertown tonight," Kenneth said.

"No kidding," Jerry said.

♥

David Butler was driving a beat-up old Chevy. That was weird enough. Jerry hadn't intended to end up in Jokertown and certainly wasn't happy about it. Neither was his cabbie. He'd decided this was a good time to check up on David again. Jerry had tailed him a couple of times since losing him at the peculiar club, and had wound up bored to death. Once he'd even ended up at the opera.

They passed a building with a big red heart painted on the wall. Valentine's Day was less than three weeks away and the only person he wanted to give flowers or candy to was Beth. That would just piss Kenneth off. Not that anything had been said along those lines, but he'd detected a touch of resentment from his brother every now and then. That was the least of his worries now. He was tailing a possible murderer through Jokertown in an off-the-meter cab. Besides, it was beginning to snow.

He'd almost decided to give up and tell the driver to take him home when a car at the far end of the street exploded into fire. David's car skidded to a stop, straddling the curb. Jerry's driver slammed on his brakes and crashed into a light post. Steam began hissing from under the car's hood. Debris from the flaming car clattered onto the cab. A large group of jokers poured out of a side street. Several of them noticed the cars and pointed.

"Holy shit," Jerry said. "Get us the hell out of here."

The cabbie turned the key. There was a brief clicking sound, then nothing. "She's shot. We'll have to run for it."

Jerry clambered out of the car. David had abandoned the Chevy and was ducking down a side street. The group of jokers was moving toward them. Jerry couldn't understand what they were saying, but from the tone it wasn't friendly. He sprinted after David. A knot of jokers moved to cut him off, but Jerry turned the corner a good ten yards ahead.

He began to change. Jerry thickened his brow ridge and lumped up his skull a bit. He put ugly knots on the backs of his knuckles. It wasn't much, but should keep him from being taken for a nat.

David, still running, turned and saw Jerry and the pursuing jokers. David stepped it up and began to put some distance between them. Jerry gritted his teeth and ran harder. The cold air stung his throat and chest, and he had to be careful to keep his Italian leather shoes from slipping on the ice-slicked pavement. The snow began to thicken and swirl in the wind.

There were screams up ahead. David rounded a corner and disappeared from view. Jerry kicked hard after him with the last of his strength. He slipped down as he turned the corner and found himself at the edge of a crowd. There were at least two or three hundred jokers jamming the street. Several cars were on fire, casting a flickering glow against the surrounding buildings. A large, overstuffed dummy was being thrown around and torn at. Worchester in effigy, no doubt.

Jerry couldn't see David, but there was an open alley mouth nearby. Jerry walked over and slipped into the alley. It was empty. At least as far as he could tell. A few feet down there was a door hanging halfway off its hinges. Jerry pushed it open and stepped inside. He waited a few moments for his eyes to adjust, but still couldn't make out much. He stepped out of the dimly lit doorway and strained to hear any movement inside the room, but there was only a faint dripping noise. After a few long moments, Jerry turned back to the door and was about to push it open when a group of nats walked past. There were five of them, two boys and three girls. They were young, barely twenty, if that. One of the women had spiky dark hair, the other was shaved bald. They were flanking the blond boy who was obviously their leader. David.

The crowd of jokers roared. Jerry peered over the kids and saw the mob part. A nine-foot-tall joker with green skin moved toward the center of the mob. It was Troll, and perched on his shoulders was Tachyon. There were a few angry shouts, but most of the jokers got quiet.

Jerry heard a growling noise behind him. He turned and saw a pair of green eyes staring at him. They were too far apart to belong to a house cat. Jerry lengthened and pointed his own teeth. If there was a fight, he wanted to have some kind of weapon. One of his fangs cut painfully into his lower lip.

"Listen, my friends," Tachyon shouted. Jerry could barely make out the words, but calling the jokers his friends was being a little presumptuous after what had happened with Hartmann in Atlanta. "I understand your anger, but this is not the answer. The fires you're starting here will only burn down your own homes and kill your own people. Hiram Worchester is not your enemy. Ignorance and blind prejudice are the true foes every joker must face. And the only way to defeat them is through decency and dignity."

"Let's have some fun," David whispered.

"Go back to your homes now," Tachyon continued. "Set an example for everyone, whether they're jokers, nats, or aces." Tachyon raised his arms in a pleading manner. David's two girls grasped him tightly by the shoulders and his body shuddered.

Troll laughed. He picked Tachyon up by the back of his lab jacket and let him dangle, feet kicking. The crowd began to yell.

"Troll," Tachyon screamed. "What are you doing?"

Troll tossed Tachyon cartwheeling into the mass of jokers. Tachyon landed amid a tangle of bodies. Jerry could see him struggling to get back up.

"Let's build a fire the Fatman can see all the way up at Aces High," Troll shouted. The crowd howled its approval and fists punched the air.

Jerry heard another growl behind him, closer this time. He took a deep breath and bolted from the door, slamming into David and the two girls, knocking all three of them out into the street. Troll saw the commotion at the edge of the crowd and looked directly at them, his face showing panic. The giant joker swayed for a moment, then collapsed.

The girl with the spiked hair helped David up. "Let's get the fuck out of here."

Jerry rolled over and saw the bald girl standing over him. She raised her leg to kick him in the face. Jerry twisted out of the way and took the blow on his shoulder, then bit through her blue jeans into her calf. The girl screamed and tore away from him, then turned and limped after her retreating friends. Jerry spat the taste of blood from his mouth and struggled to his feet. Jokers were running everywhere. The fires were spreading. Troll wobbled into a standing position and moved toward Tachyon, who was still shielding himself with mind-controlled jokers. Troll cut his way through to the Takisian and gently lifted Tachyon up onto his shoulders. Tachyon gave him a questioning look, then motioned him to get moving. Troll shouldered his way back through the dispersing crowd. The clinic was only a few blocks away. Jerry figured it was the safest place to be and began plowing through the jokers after Troll.

Jerry heard sirens from several different directions, all getting closer. He bounced his way to the edge of the mob and onto the sidewalk just as a police car swung into view. A bullet slammed into the brick wall behind him, spraying him with tiny rock fragments. Jerry didn't know who'd fired the shot and didn't want to find out. He dodged down a side street and headed for the clinic.

♣

Blaise made Jerry nervous, scared him even. The red-haired boy stayed at the window for half an hour, watching the rioting with a smile on his face. Sirens, both police and ambulance, had been passing by all night. Once, Blaise turned to Jerry and said, "Fire and blood. So much of it. So beautiful." Other than that particular twisted observation, he'd seemed to regard Jerry as invisible. Jerry sat there in silence, folding and unfolding his check.

It was 2:00 A.M. before Tachyon got back to his office. The right side of his face was bruised and puffy and his good arm was in a sling. "You should have waited, Jeremiah," he said as he collapsed into his chair. "On a night like this, money is less of a concern."

"It's not about money." Jerry handed the check over. "But I might as well give it to you anyway. I was doing something else down here. How is Troll, by the way?"

"Confused and embarrassed. He doesn't remember throwing me. I went into his mind and there's simply a blank spot during that period. Like he was blacked out." Tachyon touched the purple skin above his eye and winced. "The timing for such an incident couldn't have been worse."

"Could we talk alone for a few minutes?" Jerry looked over at Blaise.

Blaise glanced hatefully at Jerry, then looked at Tachyon, who was pointing to the door. The younger Takisian stood his ground for a moment, then stalked out of the room.

Tachyon sighed. "Now, what is it you want to discuss?"

"What happened to Troll was no accident. He wasn't in his own body when it threw you. Somebody else was. You've heard the reports about people having their bodies switched with someone else? There was a bank robbery—"

"Yes," Tachyon interrupted. "We have a mother and daughter in our psychiatric ward who claim their minds were somehow switched by a third party. Do you believe that's what happened to Troll?"

"I know it," Jerry said. "And I think I know who's behind it, too."

"Who?" Tachyon snapped out of his exhausted state.

"David Butler. He works at my brother's law firm, Latham, Strauss." Jerry leaned forward in his chair. "I've been tailing him off and on, and he was at the riot tonight with some of his friends."

Tachyon sighed and nodded. "A year ago I might have been tempted to intervene myself, but I've seen the folly of that. I think our best course is to turn Mr. Butler in to the authorities. You're not making any of this up?"

"Of course not," Jerry said. "I don't go around accusing people of being criminals unless I'm sure of it. My brother's a lawyer."

Tachyon pushed the intercom button on his phone. "Could you get me Lieutenant Maseryk?"

Jerry wasn't sure this was such a good idea, but Tachyon seemed sold on it. What kind of prison could hold David anyway?

♠

Jerry was sitting on the couch outside his brother's office. Presumably, he was there to have lunch with Kenneth. But he was really there to see the look on David's face when the police came for him. He'd made Tachyon find out for him where and when the arrest would be made. It was a small price to pay for the information he'd provided. Seeing the young Adonis arrested would provide him with some much-needed satisfaction.

He was thumbing through a copy of *Aces*. There was a paragraph on him in the "Where Are They Now?" section. They'd also printed a picture of Jerry as the giant ape with the word "retired" underneath. Little did they know.

The doors opened and two detectives walked in. At least Jerry assumed that was who they were.

"Could you ask David Butler to come out and see us?" the older of the two asked while flashing a badge. "It's an official matter."

The secretary made a quick call and David appeared moments later. He stopped short and frowned when he saw the policemen, then recovered.

"David Butler?"

"Yes, how can I help you?"

"We'd like to ask you some questions." The policemen walked up to him. "If that's all right with you?"

"Certainly," David said stiffly. He turned to the secretary. "Tell Mr. Latham I may be out all afternoon."

"Of course," she said.

"Shall we go?" David asked.

The detectives stood on either side of David and walked him from the room.

Jerry sighed. He'd hoped that David would react a little more, not that he'd expected him to break down and confess. But a little whimpering would have been nice. Hopefully, that would come later. Jerry was only sorry he wouldn't be there to see it.

♦

He was asleep when the phone rang. Jerry picked it up and yawned into the receiver. "Sorry, hello."

"Jeremiah." It was Tachyon. His voice was somber. "I'm afraid I have some bad news."

Jerry sat up. "Not too bad, I hope. I'm not sure I'd be up for that."

"David has escaped."

"What?" Jerry yelled without meaning to. "How did it happen?"

"The police were interrogating him and getting nowhere, so they decided to call in a skimmer, someone who can pick up surface thoughts." Tachyon paused. "David panicked and switched bodies with one of the officers. He made the man knock out his partner, then returned to his own body. The officer blacked out from the shock. Then, apparently, David just walked out. No one has seen him since."

"Great, Doc." Jerry didn't want to sound angry, but he was. "Thanks for calling."

"I'm sorry, Jeremiah. I did what I thought was best."

"I know. Good-bye." Jerry hung up and flipped through his

Rolodex for Jay Ackroyd's number. Maybe Jay could get a lead. If not, it was out of Jerry's hands.

♥

Jerry sat on the couch in his projection room, massaging his crotch. He'd watched the first half of *Jokertown,* but had stopped when Nicholson got his nose slit. It was just too damn depressing. He'd popped in a porn video, but it wasn't doing much for his morale, either. He had another porn movie, *Jokers and Blondes*, but that might be a little weird for his taste.

He turned off the TV and sighed. He'd had a couple of shots of whiskey and his brain felt as soft as his penis was hard. He thought of Kenneth and Beth upstairs, probably fucking like weasels. "Enjoy yourselves. Don't think of poor, old Jerry. Have an orgasm for me."

He'd considered sneaking up to their bedroom door and listening on several occasions, but had never actually done it. Maybe tonight would be the night. He got his feet under him, wandered into the living room and up the stairs. He stopped at the top and steadied himself on the banister. Beth was probably a great fuck. It would be consistent with her character. She was great at everything else. He took a step toward their bedroom door.

No, he thought, you're not that far gone yet. It's none of your damn business. Shame on you.

Jerry turned and headed for the upstairs bathroom. He quickly stripped and turned on the shower. The water was cold, like the air outside, but it didn't seem to help.

♠ ♥ ♦ ♣

Nowadays Clancy Can't Even Sing

by Victor Milán

THE TALL MAN OPENED his mouth and said, "Beware. There is danger here."

Mark Meadows swayed like a radio mast in a high wind, sat down on the hood of a black stretch limo parked in front of the store to wait the dizziness out. It had been a woman's voice, tinted with Asian accent like ginger flakes.

The slim, blond twelve-year-old girl with him watched him closely, concerned but not afraid. She'd seen these spells before.

He looked up and down the block. Fitz-James O'Brien Street was about the same as always. This fringe of the Village had grown rougher the last few years. But so had the world. And people left him pretty much alone.

He had friends.

You guys are getting pretty restless, he thought. He felt furtive stirrings in the back of his brain, but no more words came unbidden.

Deciding her father was all right, the girl began to swing pendulumlike on her father's arm, chanting, "We're home, Daddy, we're home." Her voice was that of a four-year-old. The rest of her was twelve.

He gazed down at her. A rush of love suffused him like a hit of windowpane. He pulled her close, hugged her, and stood.

"Yeah, Sprout. Home." He opened the door beneath the smiling hand-painted sun and the legend COSMIC PUMPKIN—FOOD FOR BODY, MIND & SPIRIT.

Inside was cool and almost dark. It used to be sunny in here on spring days like this, but that was when there was still plate glass in the windows instead of plywood sheets. The sound system was on, tuned by one of his clerks to one of those New Age easy-listening stations popular with people who spend their evenings watching *Koyaanisqatsi* on remote-programmable VCRs. A little thin for even Mark's blood, but at the moment better than the usual fare: Bonnie Raitt, something recent with a soft ska beat.

Good business for midafternoon, he thought, with the reflex twinge of guilt he got any time he had such commercial thoughts. A small guy with a fleshy, pointy nose and a silklike jacket with a strip-club logo on the back was haunting the glass-top counter that displayed the dope paraphernalia the Pumpkin was carrying until the inevitable Crusading DA finally got around to cracking down. He seemed to be thinking of hitting on one of Mark's stumpy, brush-cut clerks, who was sweeping the floor behind the deli counter with muttering bad grace and shooting him hate looks. She gave Mark one, too, when she noticed him. He was a man; this was all *his* fault.

A handful of even less descript types sat at tables hunched over racing forms and steaming cups of Red Zinger tea. A tall dark-haired woman stood at the comic rack with her back to him, looking at a reprint of an early Freak Brothers classic. The DA was after those, too.

Mark put a hand back around to where his long blond hair, more ash now than straw, was gathered into a blue elastic tie. It was too tight, and pulled at random patches of his scalp like doll hands. Nineteen years this spring he'd been wearing his hair long, and he still hadn't gotten the hang of tying back a ponytail.

Absently he noticed that the woman was well dressed to be grazing the undergrounds. Usually the customers in pricey threads scrupulously confined their attentions to his sprouts-and-tofu cuisine.

His daughter chirped, "Auntie Brenda," and went running back to give the clerk a hug. The tall man smiled ruefully. *He* could never tell his clerks apart. They both thought he was a weed, anyway.

Then the well-dressed woman turned and looked at him with violet eyes and said, quietly, "Mark."

It felt as if one of the youthful football jocks who had been the curse of his adolescence had just chop-blocked his pelvis out from under his spine.

"Sunflower," he managed to say through a throat gone as pliable as an airshaft.

He heard the squeak-scruff of his daughter's sneakers on stained linoleum behind him. A moment of silence hung in the air, stretching gradually, agonizingly, like a taffy strand. Then Sprout boiled past and threw herself at the woman, hugging her with all the strength of her thin arms.

"*Mommy.*"

The rat-faced man slid out of the booth and walked up to Mark. He had wet-looking black eyes and a mustache that looked as if it had been carelessly dabbed on in mascara. Mark blinked at him, very carefully, as if his eyes were fragile and might break.

The smaller man thrust a packet of papers into his hand. "See you in court, buppie," he said, and sidled out the door.

Mark stared down at the papers. Freewheeling, his mind registered official-looking seals and the phrase "determine custody of their daughter, Sprout."

And the other customers came boiling up from their checkered cheesecloth tables as if tied to the same string, stuck big black cameras in Mark's face, and blasted him back into the door with their strobes.

His vision full of big swarming balloons of light, Mark staggered into the little bathroom and threw up in the toilet beneath the Jimi Hendrix poster. Fortunately the poster was laminated.

♣

Kimberly Anne slid into the limousine by feel, watching the Pumpkin's front door with bruised-looking eyes. Around the fringes of the plywood she could see the photographers' flashguns spluttering like an arc welder.

"Poor Mark," she whispered. She turned with mascara beginning to melt down one cheek.

"Is it really necessary to put him through all this?"

The backseat's other occupant regarded her with eyes as pale and dispassionate as a shark's. "It is," he said, "if you want your daughter back."

She stared at fingers knotted in her lap. "More than anything," she said, just audibly.

"Then you must be ready to pay the price, Mrs. Gooding."

♠

"My advice to you, Dr. Meadows," Dr. Pretorius said, leaning back and cracking the knuckles of his big, callused hands, "is to go underground."

Mark stared at the lawyer's hands. They didn't seem to fit with the rest of him, which was a pretty unorthodox picture to start with. You didn't expect hands like that on a lawyer, even a long-haired one, especially not resting above a gold watch-chain catenary on the vest of a thousand-dollar charcoal-gray suit. They jarred. Just like finding the cream wallpaper and walnut-wainscoted elegance of Pretorius's office in a second-floor walk-up in what the tabloids liked to call the festering depths of Jokertown. Or like the strange tang like pus-filled bandages that seemed to stick in the back of Mark's nose.

Mark couldn't evade the issue any longer. "I beg your pardon?" he said, blinking furiously. Behind his chair Sprout hummed to herself as she studied the array of insects mounted under glass on the walls.

"You heard me. If you want to hold on to your little girl, the best advice I can give you as a lawyer is to go underground."

"I don't understand."

"'Oh, my God,'" Pretorius quoted, "'you're from the sixties.' Doesn't ring any bells? You didn't see that movie they made out of W. P. Kinsella's autobiography? No, of course not; chewing up a blotter and sitting through a revival of *2001* three times is more your speed in movies."

He sighed. "Are you telling me you don't know what 'going underground' means? You know—Huey Newton, Patty Hearst, all those fabulous names of yesteryear."

Mark glanced nervously back at his daughter, who had her nose pressed to the glass over some kind of bug that looked like a ten-inch twig. Mark had never realized before just how nervous insects made him.

"I know what it means, man. I just don't know—" He raised his own hands, which in the somewhat stark light began to look to him like specimens escaped from Pretorius's cases, to try to draw communication out of himself, out of the air, whatever. Outside of one area of life he had never been much good at getting ideas across.

Pretorius nodded briskly. "You don't know if I'm serious, right? I am. Dead serious."

He let his hand drop forward onto his desk, onto the copy of the *Post* Jube had given Mark. "Do you have any idea who you're dealing with here?"

A blunt finger was tapping Kimberly Anne's face where it peered over Sprout's shoulder. "That's my ex–old lady," Mark said. "She used to call herself Sunflower."

"She's calling herself Mrs. Gooding now. I gather she married the senior partner at her brokerage firm."

He stared almost accusingly at Mark. "And do you know whom she's retained? St. John Latham."

He spoke the name like a curse. Sprout came up and insinuated her hand into her daddy's. He reached awkwardly across himself to put his free arm around her.

"What's so special about this Latham dude?"

"He's the best. And he's a total bastard."

"That's, like, why I came to you. You're supposed to be pretty good yourself. If you'll help me, why should I think about running?"

Pretorius's mouth seemed to heat-shrink to his teeth. "Flattery is always appreciated, no matter how beside the point."

He leaned forward. "Understand, Doctor: these are the eighties. Don't you hate that phrase? I thought nothing was ever going to be as nauseous as the cant we had back in the days when Weathermen weren't fat boys who got miffed at Bryant Gumbel on the morning show. Oh, well, wrong again, Pretorius." He cocked his head like a big bird. "Dr. Meadows, you claim to be an ace?"

Mark flushed. "Well, I . . ."

"Does the name 'Captain Trips' suggest anything?"

"I—that is—yes." Mark looked at his hands. "It's supposed to be a secret."

"Cap'n Trips is a fixture in Jokertown and on the New York ace scene. And does he ever wear a mask?"

"Well . . . no."

"Indeed. So we have a fairly visible but apparently minor ace, whose, ahem, 'secret identity' is a man who follows a rather divergent lifestyle in a day when 'the nail that stands out must be hammered down' is the dominant social wisdom. St. John Latham is a man who will do anything to win. *Anything*. Do you see how you might be, how you say, *vulnerable?*"

Mark covered his face with his hands. "I just can't . . . I mean, Sunflower wouldn't do anything like that to me. We, we're like *comrades*. I knew her at Berkeley, man. The Kent State protests—you remember that?" His confusion came out in a gush of reproach, accusation almost.

He expected Pretorius to bark at him. Instead the attorney nodded his splendid silver head. The perfection of his ponytail filled Mark with jealous awe.

"I remember. I still walk with a limp, thanks to a National Guardsman's bayonet in my hip—among other reasons."

Pretorius sat back and gazed at the ceiling. "A radical in '70. An executive in '89. If you knew how anything but uncommon that story is. At least she's not with the DEA. And while we're on that subject, I have formed the impression you don't say no to recreational chemistry."

"It doesn't hurt anybody, man."

"No. Ain't nobody's business but your own; couldn't agree more. Being a Jew in Nuremberg in the thirties didn't hurt anybody, either."

He squeezed his eyes shut and shook his head. "Doctor, you are a big, soft, inflated Bozo the Clown doll in the climate of today, and Mr. St. John Motherfucking Latham is going to knock you all over the courtroom. So I say to you, *Run, baby, run*. Or be prepared for a sea change in your life."

Mark made a helpless gesture, started to stand. "One more thing," Pretorius said.

Mark stopped. Pretorius looked to Sprout. She was a shy child, except with those close to her, and the lawyer had an intimidating way—he intimidated her dad, anyway. But she faced Pretorius, solemn and unflinching.

"The question that needs to be asked is, what do *you* want, Sprout?" Pretorius said. "Do you want to live with your mommy, or stay with your father?"

"I—I'll abide by her wishes, man," Mark said. It was the hardest thing he'd ever said.

She looked from Pretorius to Mark and back. "I miss my mommy," she said in that precise, childish voice. Mark felt his skeleton begin to collapse within him.

"But I want to stay with my daddy."

Pretorius nodded gravely. "Then we'll do what we can to see that you do. But what that will be"—he looked at Mark—"is up to your father."

◆

Seven o'clock turned up on schedule. Susan—he was fairly sure it was Susan—marched to the front door to flip over the sign to SORRY-WE'RE CLOSED just as a woman materialized and pushed at the door from outside.

Susan resisted, glaring. Mark came around the counter wiping his hands on his apron and felt his stomach do a slow roll.

"It's okay," he managed to croak. "She can come in."

Susan turned her glare on Mark. "I'm off now, buster."

Mark shrugged helplessly. The woman stepped agilely inside. She was tall and striking in a black skirt suit with padded shoulders and a deep purple blouse. Her eyes had grown more violet over the years. The blouse turned them huge and glowing.

"This is personal, not business," she said to Susan. "We'll be fine."

"If you're sure you'll be okay alone with *him*," Susan sniffed. She launched a last glower at Mark and clumped out into the Village dusk.

She turned, Kimberly, and was in Mark's arms. He damned near collapsed. He stood there a moment with his arms sort of dangling stiffly past her like a mannequin's. Then he hugged her with adolescent fervor. Her body melted against his, fleetingly, and then she turned and was out of his arms like smoke.

"You seem to be doing well for yourself," she said, gesturing at the shop.

"Uh, yeah. Thanks." He pulled a chair back from a table. "Here, sit down."

She smiled and accepted. He went around behind the counter and busied himself. She lit a cigarette and looked at him. He didn't point out the LUNGS IN USE—NO SMOKING, PLEASE sign on the wall behind her.

She wasn't as willowy as she had been back in the Bay days. Nor was she blowsy from booze and depression as she had been when their marriage hit the rocks and she self-destructed at the first custody hearing, back in '81. Full-figured was what he thought they called it, glancing back as he waited for water to boil, though he had it in mind that had become a euphemism for "fat." She wasn't; voluptuous might have put it better. Whatever, she wore forty well.

. . . Not that it mattered, not really. He was still as desperately in love with her as he'd been the first time he saw her, thirty years and more ago, tricycling down their southern California tract-home block.

The lights were low, just a visual buzz of fluorescents above the deli counter. Mark lit candles and a sandalwood stick. The Windham Hill mob was history. The tape machine played real music. *Their* music.

He brought an earthenware pot and two matching mugs on a tray. He almost tipped the assembly onto the floor, slopping fragrant herbal tea on the red-and-white-checkered tablecloth as he transferred the pot to the table. Kimberly sat and watched him with a smile that held no mockery.

He spilled only a little of the pale amber liquid as he poured and handed her a mug. She sipped. Her face lit.

"Celestial Seasonings and old Bonnie Raitt." She smiled. "How sweet of you to remember."

"How could I forget?" he mumbled into the steam rising from his mug.

A rustle of beaded curtain, and they looked up to see Sprout standing in the gloom at the back of the store. "Daddy, I'm hungry—" she began. Then she saw Kimberly and came flying forward again.

Kimberly cradled her, telling her, "Baby, baby, it's all right, Mommy's here." Mark sat, absently stroking his daughter's long smooth hair, feeling excluded.

At last Sprout relinquished her hold on Sunflower's neck and slid down to sit cross-legged on the scuffed linoleum, pressed up against her mother's black-stockinged shins. Kimberly petted her.

"I don't want to take her away from you, Mark."

Mark's vision swirled. His eyes stung. His tongue knotted. "Why—why are you doing this, then? You said I was doing well."

"That's different. That's *money*." She gestured around the shop. "Do you really think this is any way for a little girl to grow up? Surrounded by smut and hash pipes?"

"She's all right," he said sullenly. "She's happy. Aren't you honey?"

Wide-eyed solemn, Sprout nodded. Kimberly shook her head.

"Mark, these are the eighties. You're a dropout, a druggie. How can you expect to raise a daughter, let alone one as . . . special as our Sprout is?"

Mark froze with his hand reaching for the pocket of his faded denim jacket—the one that held his pouch and papers, not the one with the Grateful Dead patch. It came to him how great the gulf between them had become.

"The way I've been doing," he said. "One day at a time."

"Oh, Mark," she said, rising. "You sound like an AA meeting."

The tape had segued to Buffalo Springfield. Kimberly hugged Sprout, came around the table to him.

"Families should be together," she said huskily in his ear. "Oh, Mark, I wish—"

"What? What do you wish?"

But she was gone, leaving him and her last words hanging in a breath of Chanel No. 5.

♥

The stuffed animals sat in a rapt semicircle on the bed and in shelf tiers along the walls. The light of one dim bulb glittered in attentive plastic eyes as the girl spoke. Mark watched from the doorway. She had not pulled the madras-print cloth to, indicating she didn't want full privacy.

She spoke in a low voice, leaning forward. He could never make out what she said at times like this; it seemed to him that the length of her sentences, the pitch of her voice even, were somehow more adult than anything she managed in the world outside her tiny converted-closet bedroom, in the presence of anyone but the Pobbles and Thumpers and teddy bears. But if he tried to intrude, to come close to catch the sense of what she was saying, she clammed up. It was one area of her life Sprout excluded him from, however desperately he wanted to share it.

He turned away, padded barefoot past the dark cubicle where he had his own mattress on the floor to the lab that took up most of the apartment above the Pumpkin.

Red-eye pilot lights threw little hard shards of illumination that ricocheted fitfully among surfaces of glass and mechanism. Mark felt his way to a pad in the corner beneath a periodic table and a poster for Destiny's gig at the Fillmore in 1970's long-lost spring and sat. The smell of cannabis smoke and the layers of paint it had sunk into enfolded him like arms. His cheeks had become wet without his being aware.

He pushed a cabinet on casters away from the wall, untoggled the fiberboard rear panel. The compartment hidden inside contained racks of vials of various colored powders: blue, orange, yellow, gray, black, and silver that swirled together without mixing. He stared at them, ran a finger along them like a stick along a picket fence.

A long time ago a skinny kid with a crew cut and highwater pants, who had just dropped LSD for the first time ever, had stumbled into an alleyway in horror, fleeing a People's Park confrontation between National Guardsmen and students in the dark angry days that followed Kent State. Moments later a glowing beautiful youth emerged: an ace for the Revolution. Together with Tom Douglas, the Lizard King and doomed lead singer for Destiny, he had stood off the Guard and the Establishment ace Hardhat, and saved the day. Then he partied the night away, with help from the kids, Tom Douglas, and a beautiful young activist called Sunflower. He called himself the Radical.

In the morning the Radical disappeared. He was never seen again. And a certain nerd biochem student stumbled back out of the alley with a head full of the strangest memory fragments.

Becoming the Radical again—if he'd ever really *been* the Radical—had become Mark's Holy Grail. He had failed in that quest. The brightly colored powders were what he had found instead. Not what he was looking for—but a means to acceptance all the same. To having, at least for one hour, a dose, what a long-dead Egyptian scribe once prayed for as "effective personality."

He felt stirrings down around the back of his skull, like the voices of children on a distant playground. He pushed them back down, away. From below the racks he took a bong with a cracked, smoke-stained stack. Right now he needed chemical sanctuary of a more conventional kind.

♣

He soared upward from the roof, upward from the smog and squalor into blue morning sky that darkened around him as he rose. The Village dwindled, was subsumed into the cement scab of Manhattan, became a finger poking a blue ribbon between Long Island and the Jersey shore, was lost in swirls of cloud. Clouds hid the shit-brown garbage bloom from the bay into the Atlantic: a blessing in his present mood.

He rose higher, feeling the air chill and attenuate around him until it was gone, and he floated in blackness, with nothing between him and the hot healing eye of the sun.

He stretched, feeling his body fill with the wild energy of the sun, the lifegiver. He was Starshine; he needed no air, no food. Only sunlight. It hit him like a drug—though he knew the rush of cocaine and sizzle of crystal meth only at one remove and unwillingly, through the experiences of Mark Meadows.

From the Olympian height of orbit you could barely see what a splendid job man was doing of fouling his own nest. He ached to spread the word, the warning, to help the world to its senses with his poems and songs. But the moments of freedom were too few, too few. . . .

He felt the pressure of other voices within, dragging him back to Earth, in thought if not yet in body. Meadows had a problem, and he knew that this brief liberation was Mark's way of consulting him. As he would the others.

Changes are due in your life, Mark Meadows, *he thought. But what might those changes be? If he himself could do no more, he wished Meadows at least would involve himself more in the world, take a stand. He wished Mark would give up his habits of drug abuse—though he couldn't escape irony there, since if Mark went completely straight, it would be in effect the end of him, of Starshine in his golden body stocking, floating up above the world so high.*

He gazed off around the molten-silver limb of the world. A gigantic oil spill was fouling the coast of Alaska; for all his powers, what could he do? What could he do to halt acid rain, or the destruction of the Amazon rain forest?

That last he'd even tried, had flown to Brazil on wings of light, begun destroying bulldozers and work camps with his energy beams, putting the workmen to flight, burning the rotor off a Gazelle gunship that had tried to drive him away—though begrudgingly he had caught it before it crashed, and eased it to a soft landing on a sandbar. Unworthy as they were, he didn't want the crew's deaths weighing down his soul.

He had gotten so engrossed in his mission, in fact, that he'd overstayed his hour, stranding Mark in a smoldering patch of devastation in the middle of the Amazon basin with a whole regiment of the Brazilian army closing in and mightily pissed off. Even with his other friends to call on, Mark had some bad moments getting back to the States. He'd been so miffed he hadn't summoned Starshine for six months afterward.

It did no good, of course. The Brazilian government borrowed more money from the World Bank and bought more and bigger earth-raping machines. The destruction went on with barely a hiccup.

The truth is, the world doesn't need more aces, he thought. It doesn't need us at all. We can't do anything real.

He looked into the sun. Its roaring song of life and light blinded him, suffused him. But for all his exaltation, he was a mote—a spark, quickly consumed.

And he knew that he had come to his truth.

♠

Dr. Pretorius leaned back in his swivel chair and crossed hands over his hard paunch. His suit was white today. He looked like a hip Colonel Sanders.

"So, Dr. Meadows, do you have a decision for me?"

Mark nodded, started to speak. A door opened behind Pretorius and the words stuck tight in Mark's throat.

A woman had slipped silently into the room—a girl, maybe; she looked more like a special effect than a human. She was five and a half feet tall, inhumanly slim, and blue—blue green, actually, gleaming in the same shade as the dyes used in blue ice. The room temperature, already cool, had dropped perceptibly.

"You haven't met my ward, have you? Dr. Meadows, let me present Ice Blue Sibyl."

She looked at him. At least she turned her face toward him. Whatever she was made of looked hard as glass, but seemed constantly, subtly to be shifting. Her features seemed high-cheekboned and forward thrusting, though it was hard to be sure. Her body was attenuated as a mannequin's and almost as sexless; though she appeared to be nude, the tiny breasts showed no nipples, nor did she display genitalia. Still, there was some alien, elflike quality to her, something that caused a stirring in Mark's crotch as she looked at him with her blue-glass stare.

She turned her face to Pretorius, tipped it attentively. Mark got the impression that some communication passed between them. The lawyer nodded. Sibyl turned and walked to the door with sinuous inhuman grace. She stopped, gave Mark a last glance, vanished.

Pretorius was looking at him. "You've decided?"

Mark reached out and hugged his daughter to him. "Yeah, man. There's only one thing I can do."

◆

"Hello? Is anyone here?" Dr. Tachyon stepped cautiously through the open door. Today he wore an eighteenth-century peach coat over a pale pink shirt with lace spraying out the front of a mauve waistcoat. His breeches were deep purple satin, caught at the knee with gold rosettes. His stockings were lilac, his shoes gold. Instead of an artificial hand, he wore a lace cozy on his stump, with a red rose sprouting from it.

Amazement stopped him cold. The Pumpkin was gutted. Tables were overturned, the counter torn up, the magazine racks lying on their backs, the psychedelic-era posters gone from the walls. Somewhere music played.

"Burning Sky! What's happened here? Mark! *Mark!*"

Through a doorway at the back that looked curiously naked without the beaded curtain that had always hung there stepped a remarkable figure. It wore torn khaki pants, a black Queensrÿche T-shirt stretched to the bursting point across a disproportionately huge chest. With a narrow head and finely sculpted, almost elfin features set on an inhumanly squat body, the newcomer looked the way pretty-boy movie martial-artist Jean Claude Van Damme would if they put him in a hydraulic press and mashed him down a foot or so.

He stopped and turned a cool smile on Tachyon. "So. The little prince." His English had a curious, almost Eastern European accent. Just like Tachyon's.

"What have you done to Mark?" Tachyon hissed. His flesh hand inched back toward the little H&K nine-millimeter tucked in a waistband holster inside the back of his breeches.

The other put fist to palm and flexed. Cloth tore. "Served loyally and without stint, as befits a Morakh."

Being destroyed as an abomination befits a Morakh, Tachyon thought. He was about to say so when an equally outlandish apparition loomed up behind the creature. This one had a gray sleeveless sweatshirt and paint-splashed dungarees hung on a frame like a street sign and graying blond hair clipped skull close. He seemed to consist all of nose, Adam's apple, and elbows.

"Doc! How are you, man?" the scarecrow said.

Tachyon squinted at him. "Who the hell are you?"

The other blinked and looked as if he were about to cry. "It's me, man. Mark."

Tachyon goggled. A blond rocket in cutoffs shot out the door, hit the Morakh in the middle of his broad back, scaled him like a monkey, and seated itself with slim bare legs straddling his rhinoceros neck.

"Uncle Tachy!" Sprout chirped. "Uncle Dirk is giving me a piggy-back ride."

"Indeed." Ignoring the Morakh's scowl, Tach stepped close to kiss the girl on her proffered cheek.

Durg at-Morakh was the strongest non-ace on Earth: no Golden Boy or Harlem Hammer, but far stronger than any normal human. He was not human; he was Takisian—a Morakh, a gene-engineered fighting machine created by the Vayawand, bitter enemies of Tachyon's House Ilkazam. He had come to Earth with Tachyon's cousin Zabb, a foe of a more intimate nature.

Now he served Mark, having been defeated in unarmed combat by Mark's "friend" Moonchild. He and Tachyon tolerated each other for Mark's sake.

Tachyon gripped his old friend by the biceps. "Mark, man, what has happened to you?"

Mark grimaced. Tachyon realized he had never seen his chin before.

"It's this court thing," Mark said, glancing at his daughter. "They start taking depositions soon. Dr. Pretorius said I needed to, like, straighten up my image."

Taking his cue, Durg patted Sprout's shins and said, "Let us go for a walk, little mistress." They went out into the sunlight on Fitz-James.

"'Dr. Pretorius,'" Tachyon repeated with distaste. The two regarded each other like a pair of dogs who claim the same turf. "He thinks you should then give in, change the way you live—the way you wear your hair?"

Mark shrugged helplessly. "He says if I challenge the system, I'll lose."

"Perhaps if you had a more competent lawyer."

"Everybody says he's the best. The legal version of, like, you."

"Well." Tach fingered his narrow chin. "I admit I've no cause to believe that your 'justice' is aptly named. What are you doing to your store?"

"Pretorius says if I go in as a head-shop owner I'll get blown out of the water. So I'm selling off the paraphernalia and letting Jube take the comix as a lot. I'm making the Pumpkin into more a New Age place. Gonna call it a 'Wellness Center' or something."

Tachyon winced.

"Yeah, man, I know. But it's, like, the eighties."

"Indeed."

Mark turned and went into the back, where he had boxes of refuse piled to go into the dumpster in the alley. Tachyon followed.

"What music is this?" he asked, gesturing to a tape player with a coat-hanger antenna.

"Old Buffalo Springfield. 'Nowadays Clancy Can't Even Sing.'" He dabbed a fingertip at a corner of his eye. "Always has made me cry, darn it."

"I understand." Tach plucked a silken handkerchief from the sleeve of his stump and dabbed at the sweat that daintily beaded his eyebrows. "So Pretorius thinks changing your lifestyle at this late date will impress the court? It seems a childishly obvious expedient."

"Appearances count for a lot in court, he says. See, the judge decided to hold open hearings at the end, not just take depositions and briefs like they usually do in custody cases. And Doc Pretorius says Sun—Kimberly's attorney's trying to get the press in, and they'll play it up big, the ace thing and all. *You* know how popular we are now. So this image thing, it's like, if a biker gets busted for murder or something, they shave off his beard and put a suit on him for trial."

"But you are not on trial."

"Dr. P. says I am."

"Hmm. Who is the judge?"

"Justice Mary Conower." He bent, picked up a box, and brightened. "She's supposed to be a liberal; she was, like, a big Dukakis supporter. She won't let all these ace haters trash me. Will she?"

"I remember her from the campaign. Last fall I'd have said you were correct. Now . . . I'm not so sure. It seems we have few friends on any side."

"Maybe that's why Dr. P. told me to go underground instead of doing the court thing. But I always thought being a liberal meant you believed in people's rights and stuff."

"A lot of us thought that, once." Something stuffed in a box caught Tach's eye. He stooped like a hawk.

"Mark, no!" he exclaimed, brandishing a crumpled purple top hat.

Mark stood holding the box and avoiding his eyes. "I had to straighten up. Stop doing drugs. Pretorius said they'd ream me out royally if I didn't. Might even go to the DA and get me busted."

"Your Sunflower would do this to you?"

"Her attorney would. Dude named Latham. They call him, like, Sturgeon or something."

"'Sinjin.' Yes. He would do that. He would do anything." He held up the hat. "But this?"

The tears were streaming freely down Mark's shorn cheeks now. "I decided on my own, man. After the vials I got now are all used up, I'm not making any more. There's just too much risk, and I gotta keep Sprout. No matter what."

"So Captain Trips—"

"Has hung it up, man."

♥

"Have you ever used drugs, Dr. Meadows?"

With effort Mark pulled his consciousness back to the deposition room. The oak paneling seemed to be pressing him like a Salem witch. His attention was showing a tendency to spin around inside his skull.

"Uh. Back in the sixties," he told St. John Latham. Pretorius opposed conceding even that much. But this new Mark, the one emerging from a cannabis pupa into the chill of century's end, thought that would be a little much.

"Not since?"

"No."

"What about tobacco?"

He rubbed his eyes. He was getting a headache. "I quit smoking in '78, man."

"And alcohol?"

"I drink wine, sometimes. Not too often."

"You eat chocolate?"

"Yes."

"You're a biochemist. It surprises me you aren't aware these are all drugs; addictive ones, in fact."

"I do know." Very subdued.

"Ah. What about aspirin? Yes? Penicillin? Antihistamines?"

"Yeah. I'm, uh, allergic to penicillin."

"So. You do still use drugs. Even addictive drugs. Though you just now denied doing it."

"I didn't know that's what you meant."

"What other drugs do you use that you claim you don't?"

Mark glanced to Pretorius. The lawyer shrugged.

"None, man. I mean, uh, none."

♣

When they got back to the Village from Latham's office, Mark could tell Sprout was tired and footsore, simply because she wasn't bouncing around in the usual happy-puppy way she had when she was out somewhere with Daddy. She wore a lightweight dress and flats, and her long straight blond hair was tied in a ponytail to keep it off her neck. Mark fingered his own nape, which still felt naked in the sticky-hot spring-afternoon breeze, rich with polynucleic aromatic hydrocarbons.

A couple of kids in bicycling caps and lycra shorts clumped by on the other side of the street. They watched Sprout with overt interest. She was just falling into adolescence, still skinny as a car antenna. But she had an ingenue face, startlingly pretty. The kind to attract attention.

Reflexively he tugged her closer. *I'm turning into an uptight old man*, he thought, and tugged again at the loosened white collar of his shirt. His neck felt rope-burned by the tie now wadded in the pocket of his gray suit coat.

The light of the falling sun shattered like glass on windshields and shop windows and filled his eyes with sharp fragments. Even in this backwater street the noise of nearby traffic was like a rocker-arm engine pounding in his skull, and each honk of a horn threatened to pop his eyes like a steel needle.

For years Mark had lived in a haze of marijuana smoke. He dabbled in other drugs, but that was more in the nature of biochemical experimentation with himself as subject—such as had called up the Radical, and subsequently his "friends." Grass was his drug of choice. Way back in those strange days of the late sixties—early seventies, actually, but the sixties didn't end until Nixon did—it seemed a perfect solace to someone who had come to terms with the fact that he was doomed to disappoint everyone who expected anything of him. Especially himself.

Now he was emerging from the cushioning fog. Off the weed, the world was a *lot more surreal* place to be.

Someone stepped from the doorway of the Pumpkin, features obscured by the broad straw brim of a hat. Mark's hand moved to the inside pocket of his coat, where he kept a set of his dwindling supply of vials.

Sprout lunged forward with arms outspread. The figure knelt, embraced her, and then violet eyes were looking up at him from beneath the hat brim.

"Mark," Kimberly said. "I had to see you."

♠

The ball bounced across the patchy grass of Central Park as though it were bopping out the lyrics to a sixties cigarette-commercial jingle. Sprout pursued it, skipping and chirping happily.

"What does your old man think of all this?" Mark asked, lying on his elbows on the beach towel Kimberly had brought along with the ball.

"About what?" she asked him. She wasn't showing her agency game face this afternoon. In an impressionistic cotton blouse and blue jeans that looked as if they'd been worn after she bought them instead of before, knees drawn up to support her chin and hair hanging in a braid down her back, she looked so much like the Sunflower of old he could barely breathe.

He wanted to say, "about the trial," but he also wanted to say, "about you seeing me," but the two kind of jostled against each other and got jammed up like fat men trying to go through a men's room door at the same time, and so he just made vaguely circular gestures in the air and said, "About, uh, this."

"He's in Japan on business. T. Boone Pickens is trying to open up the country to American businesses. Cornelius is one of his advisers." She seemed to speak with unaccustomed crispness, but then he'd never been good at telling that kind of thing. It had been one of their problems. One of many.

He was trying to think of something to say when Sunflower—no, *Kimberly*—clutched his arm. "Mark, look—"

Their daughter had followed the bouncing ball into the middle of a large blanket and the Puerto Rican family that occupied it, almost bowling over a stout woman in lime-green shorts. A short, wiry man with tattoos all over his arm jumped up and started expostulating. Half a dozen children gathered around, including a boy about Sprout's own age with a switchblade face.

"Mark, aren't you going to do something?"

He looked at her, puzzled. "What, man? She's okay."

"But those . . . people. That is, Sprout ran into them, they're justifiably upset—"

He laughed. "Look."

The Puerto Ricans were laughing, too. The fat woman hugged Sprout. The tough kid smiled and tossed her the ball. She turned and came racing back up the slope toward her parents, graceful and clumsy as a week-old foal.

"See? She gets along pretty well with people, even if . . ." The sentence ran down uncompleted, as they usually did on that subject.

Kimberly still looked skeptical. Mark shrugged, then by reflex touched the pocket of the denim jacket he wore despite the heat.

Maybe he did rely on the implicit promise of his "friends" too much. He'd have to go cold turkey from that, too, one of these days. He wasn't calling up the personae too often. Occasionally he felt the peevish pressure in his brain like heckling from the back of an old auditorium, though he had explained to his "friends" what he had to do and thought most of them accepted it. But eventually the powders would be gone.

As it was, Pretorius would kill him if he knew he still had any of them. Pretorius thought a raid was a real possibility, and the vials contained a wider variety of proscribed substances than a DEA agent was liable to resell in a year.

But what am I supposed to do? Pour them down the drain? That felt like murder.

Then Sprout's arms horseshoed his skinny neck and they went over, all three of them, in a laughing, tickling tangle, and for a moment it was almost like real life.

◆

The Parade of Liars, as Pretorius called the succession of expert witnesses he and Latham took turns deposing, trudged on from spring into summer. The Twenty-eighth Army taught the students in Gate of Heavenly Peace Square what the old dragon Mao had told them so often: where political power springs from. Nur al-Allah fanatics attacked a joker-rights rally in London's Hyde Park with bottles and brickbats, winning praise from Muslim leaders throughout the West. "Secular law must yield to the laws of God," a noted Palestine-born Princeton professor announced, "and these creatures are an abomination in the eyes of Allah."

A skinhead beat a joker to death with a baseball bat. The media swelled with indignation. When it turned out that the chief of staff of the House Democratic Steering and Policy Committee had tried the same thing back in '73, liberals called it "a meanness out there, a feeding frenzy" when people took him to task for it. After all, he had helped to pass some very *caring* legislation, and anyway the bitch survived.

Kimberly flitted in and out of Mark's life like a moth. Every time he thought he could catch hold of her, she eluded him. She seldom kept a date two times running. But she never stayed away long.

The hearings began.

♥

Pretorius turned up precious few character witnesses for Mark. Dr. Tachyon, of course, and Jube the news dealer; Doughboy, the retarded joker ace, broke down and sobbed mountainously as he recounted how Mark and his friends had saved him from being convicted of murder—and, incidentally, saved the planet from the Swarm. His testimony was corroborated by laconic Lieutenant Pilar Arrupe of Homicide South, who chewed a toothpick in place of her customary cigarillo. Pretorius wanted to bring on reporter Sara Morgenstern, but she had dropped from sight after the nightmare of last year's Atlanta convention.

No aces testified on Mark's behalf. The Aces High crowd was laying low these days. Besides, most of them seemed embarrassed by Cap'n Trips and his plight.

He just wasn't an eighties kind of guy.

♣

"Dr. Meadows, are you an ace?"

"Yes."

"And would you mind describing the nature of your powers?"

"Yes."

"What do you mean by that?"

"I mean, I, uh—I would mind."

"Your honor, I ask that the court take notice of the witness's lack of cooperation."

"*Your honor—*"

"Dr. Pretorius, you needn't gesticulate. You and Mr. Latham may approach the bench."

♠

Pretorius always thought the rooms of the New Family Court on Franklin and Lafayette had all the human warmth of a dentist's waiting room. The too-bright fluorescents hurt his eyes.

The media were back in force, he noted with displeasure as he gimped to the bench. After the publicity that attended Mark's getting served, the press had lost interest; lots of nothing visible had happened for a while.

"Dr. Meadows is refusing to answer a vital question, your honor," Latham said.

"He can't be compelled to answer. *Indiana v. Mr. Miraculous*, 1964. Fifth Amendment protections against self-incrimination apply."

With blue eyes and blond hair worn in a pageboy cut, Judge Mary Conower looked more *pretty* than anything else—ingenue, belying her reputation as a hard-ass. A slight dry tautness to her skin gave her the appearance of a cheerleader gone sour on life.

"This isn't a criminal trial, Doctor," she said.

Pretorius bit down hard on several possible responses. He was getting kind of old to pull another night in the Tombs for contempt.

"Then I object on the grounds that the line of questioning is irrelevant."

Conower raised an eyebrow at Latham. "That seems valid."

"Mrs. Gooding contends that the fact of her former husband's acehood constitutes a threat to the welfare of her daughter," Latham said.

"That's absurd!" Pretorius exclaimed.

"We intend to demonstrate that it is not at all absurd, your honor."

"Very well," Conower said. "You may attempt to so demonstrate. But the court will not compel Dr. Meadows to describe his powers."

◆

Latham stood a moment before Mark, staring holes in him with reptile eyes. In the audience someone coughed.

"You have friends who are aces, Dr. Meadows?"

Mark glanced at Sprout, busy drawing doodles on one of Pretorius's legal pads, at Kimberly, who was dressed like the centerfold in *Forbes* and wouldn't meet his eye. Finally he looked to Pretorius, who sighed and nodded.

"Yes."

Latham nodded slowly, as if this was Big News. Mark could feel the press begin to rustle around out there like snakes waking up among leaves. They sensed he was getting set up; *he* sensed he was getting set up. He glanced at Pretorius again. Pretorius gave him a drop-'em-and-spread-'em shrug.

"It's been suggested that you play a sort of Jimmy Olsen role to several of New York's most powerful aces. Is that a fair assessment?"

Mark tried to keep his eyes from sidling to Pretorius yet again. He didn't want Conower to think he was shifty-eyed. This justice trip was a lot more complicated than he ever thought.

. . . It came to him he had no idea how to answer the question. Other than, *No, more of a Clark Kent role*, which he badly did not want to say. He turned red and stuttered.

"Would it be fair," Latham continued, with a fractional smile to let Mark know he had him right where he wanted him, "to say that you are on intimate terms with certain aces, including one who variously styles himself Jumpin' Jack Flash and JJ Flash?"

"Um . . . yes."

"Briefly describe Mr. Flash's powers for us, if you will. Come, there's no reason to be coy; they're not exactly a secret."

Mark hadn't been being coy. Latham's smug unfairness didn't make it easy to answer.

"Ah, he, ah—he flies. And he, like—I mean, he shoots fire from his hands."

Plasma, schmuck, a voice said in the back of his skull. *I just pretend it's fire. Jesus, you're making a royal screw-up out of this.*

He looked around, terrified he had spoken aloud. But the mob showed blank expectant faces, and Latham was turning back from his table with a manila folder in his hands.

"I'd like to call the court's attention," Latham said, "to this photographic evidence of the damage done by just such a fire-shooting ace."

In the crowd somebody gasped; someone else retched. Latham pivoted like a bullfighter. Mark felt his stomach do a slow roll at the sight of the eight-by-ten photo he held in his hand. Judging from the skirt and Mary Janes, it had been a girl not much older than Sprout.

But from the waist up it was a blackened, shriveled effigy with a hideous grin.

♥

Pretorius's cane tip cracked like a rifle. "Your honor, I object in the strongest possible terms! What the hell does counsel think he's doing with this horror show?"

"Presenting my case," Latham said evenly.

"Preposterous. Your honor, this picture is of a victim of the ace the press dubbed Fireball, a psychopath apprehended by Mistral this spring in Cincinnati. Whatever his relationship to Mark Meadows, JJ Flash had no more to do with it than you or I or Jetboy. To show it here is irrelevant and prejudicial."

"Do you suggest I might be swayed by evidence not germane to this case?" Conower asked silkily.

"I suggest that Mr. Latham is attempting to try his case in the press. This is rank sensationalism."

Conower frowned. "Mr. Latham?"

Latham spread his hands as if surprised. "What am I to do, your honor? My opponent avers that ace powers are harmless. I demonstrate the contrary."

"I aver no such damn fool thing."

"Perhaps he would put it, *Ace powers don't kill people*—people *kill people*. I intend to demonstrate that the destructive potential of these powers is too enormous to be dismissed with a flip syllogism."

Pretorius grinned. "I have to hand it to you, St. John. You are stone death walking to straw men."

He shifted weight to the cane from his bad leg and turned to the judge. "Mr. Latham is trying to drag in atrocities with no connection to JJ Flash other than that they were committed by an ace with fire-related powers. And even if Flash were involved, to indict Dr. Meadows on that account smacks of guilt by association."

"If Dr. Meadows commonly associated with known members of the Medellin Cartel," Latham said ingenuously, "would your honor say that fact lacked relevance to his suitability as a parent?"

Conower squeezed her mouth till her lips disappeared. "Very well, Mr. Latham. You may present your case. And may I remind you, Dr. Pretorius, that *I'm* the one charged with evaluating the evidence?"

♣

Mark felt more exposed and humiliated than he ever had in his life. This was *worse* than one of those balls-out-on-Broadway dreams. All his life he'd shunned attention, in his own persona at least. Now all these strangers were looking at him and Sprout and thinking about those awful pictures.

Pretorius turned away from the bench. His eyebrows bristled over blue-hot eyes. Latham approached the witness stand with a look like an Inquisitor with a fresh-lit torch.

Kimberly was studying her fingernails. Mark looked at Sprout. Seeming to sense his attention, she looked up into his eyes and smiled.

He wanted to die.

♠

"We need to do more, Mrs. Gooding," St. John Latham said.

"Such as what? You seem to be doing a marvelous job of emasculating my ex-husband as it is."

Latham stood. She sat on the couch, to the extent *sitting* was possible on a chrome-framed Scandinavian slab. It was more a matter of trying not to slide off onto the black marble floor. If the lawyer noticed the bitter sarcasm in her voice—as if she and Mark were on one side and he on the other—he didn't acknowledge it.

"Dr. Pretorius is a chronic romantic, and his notions of human nature and interactions downright quaint. Nonetheless, he is not a *total* fool. He is cunning, and he knows the law. And you are not without your vulnerable points."

She threw her cigarette half-smoked into her drink and set the tumbler down on the irregular glass coffee table with a clink. "Such as?"

"Such as your breakdown in court during the first custody hearing. It lost the case for you then. It cannot help you now."

The two exterior walls that met at one corner of the Goodings' living room were glass. Kimberly gazed out over Manhattan and thought about how much the view reminded her of a black velvet painting. Apartments with panoramic views like this one always came off better in the movies, somehow.

"I was under a lot of stress."

"As are you now. It is not inconceivable that Pretorius might try to reduce you to another such breakdown on the stand."

She looked at him. "Is that what you'd do in his place?"

He said nothing.

She lit another cigarette and blew smoke toward him. "Okay. What did you have in mind?"

"A concrete demonstration of your husband's ace powers. Or solid evidence of the actual nature of the connection between him and Flash and Moonchild and the rest, if he is no more than a Jimmy Olsen figure."

Her eyes narrowed. "What are you saying?"

"If your former husband loves your daughter as much as he claims, a perceived threat to her would certainly lead him to employ any powers he might have."

She went white, tensed as if she were about to leap up and attack him. Then she settled back and elaborately studied her manicure.

"I shouldn't be surprised that you're a bastard, Mr. Latham," she said. "After all, that's why I hired you. But it occurs to me—"

She lowered her hand and gave him a smile, poisonous and V-shaped. "It occurs to me that you're insane. You want me to use my daughter for *bait*?"

He didn't flinch. Didn't even flicker.

"I said *perceived* threat, Mrs. Gooding. I am talking about a set-piece—a stratagem. There would be no real risk."

Showing as little emotion as he, she picked up her glass and threw it hard at his head. He shifted his weight. The glass sailed past to shatter against the window. In New York, people who live in glass houses have to have stoneproof walls; it's in the building code.

"I'm paying you to win this in court, you son of a bitch. Not to play games with my daughter's life."

He showed her the ghost of a smile. "What do you think the law is but playing games with people's lives?"

"Get out," she said. "Get out of my house."

"Certainly." Calm. Always calm. Infuriating, impermeable, ir-resistible. "Anything the client desires. But reflect on this: Not even I can get your daughter for you if you don't want her badly enough to sacrifice."

◆

Sprout clung tightly to her parents' hands. "Mommy and Daddy, be nice to each other," she said solemnly. "In that court place, everybody always sounds mad all the time. It makes me afraid."

She clouded up and started to sniffle. "I'm afraid they'll take me away from you."

Her mother hugged her, hard. "Honey, we'll always be with you." A hooded look to Mark. "One of us will. Always."

Sprout let Kimberly lower her onto the mattress among the stuffed toys and gazed up with wide eyes. "Promise?"

"Promise," her mother said.

"Yeah," Mark said around an obstruction in his throat. "One of us will always be around. We can promise you that much."

♥

Kimberly sipped Chianti from her jelly jar. "Your room looks so naked without all the psychedelia." Candlelight struck half-moon amethyst highlights off her eyes. "I mean, who'd imagine you without that huge poster of Tom Marion over your bed?"

He smiled ruefully. "The worst part is this futon I got in place of my old mattress. It's like nothing at all sometimes. I wake up with sore patches on my knees and elbows from the floor."

Kimberly drank wine and sighed. Mark tried hard not to think about the way her breasts rode up inside the thin cotton blouse. He'd been alone too long.

"Oh, Mark, what happened to us?"

He shook his head. His eyes grew misty. Way back and down, he felt derisive sounds coming out of Flash and Cosmic Traveler, sitting like hecklers in the cheap seats of his mind. It was rare enough they agreed on anything. He felt wordless care and concern from Moonchild, nothing at all from Aquarius. Starshine was vaguely disapproving. He was probably afraid Mark was going to have fun. It wasn't socially conscious.

She moistened her lips. "I know St. John is being awfully hard on you. I wish it didn't have to be this way."

He looked at her with eyes that felt as if they had no moisture in them, parched by each random breath of air. It was strange, considering how close he was to tears.

Would it do me any good to beg? he wondered.

Oh, please, the Traveler said.

She settled back on his pillow. Even in the eighties a man got to have a pillow. For a moment she half lay that way, one leg cocked, her hair hanging in her eyes and around her shoulders with just a little bit of perm kink still in it. He thought she'd never looked so beautiful. Not even when she was carrying Sprout and they were both breaking their necks to make believe that everything was going to work out.

She sighed again. "All my life I've had this feeling of shapelessness," she began.

Mark's mouth said, "Oh, baby, don't talk that way, you're *beautiful*," before he could stop it. Flash and Traveler hooted and twirled noisemakers. Even Moonchild winced.

Kimberly ignored him. "It's like I've always been searching for landmarks to define myself by: jocks, radicals." A smile. "You."

She smoothed her hair back and let her head drop toward one shoulder. "Does any of this make any sense?"

Mark made earnest noises. She smiled and shook her head.

"After we split I spent a few years in heavy therapy. I guess you knew about that, huh? Then one day I decided it was time to try something new, just completely different from anything I'd done before. I did the furthest-out thing I could think of: set out to become a by-God businesswoman, a real hard-charging lady entrepreneur. Entrepreneuse. Whatever. Is that strange, or what?"

She laughed. "And I did, Mark, I did it. I do it. Racquetball and power lunches. I even have a muscular male bimbo for a secretary, even if he is gay. You can't *imagine* what this is costing me in lost time, aside from dear St. John's astronomical fees."

Mark looked away and felt selfish for reflexively thinking of what all this was costing *him*, and not at all in terms of money.

"Then I met Cornelius. He's really a wonderful man. I'm sure you'd like him if you got to know him. Only you and he are . . . worlds apart."

She poured them both more wine. "Domestic little creature, aren't I? I'm starting to have the horrible suspicion that no matter how liberated I think I am, my gut notion's Norman Rockwell. You know, all those *Saturday Evening Post* covers when we were kids— don't make faces like that, I know it's silly. But I want to capture that *feel*."

She leaned toward him. He ached to stroke her hair. "Anything you want is fine. I want you to be happy."

She smiled at him, sidelong. "You really mean that, don't you? In spite of what's going on."

He wanted to say—well, everything. But the words tried to come so fast they jammed tight in his throat.

She brought her face close to his. Her mass of hair shadowed both their faces.

"Remember that guy I went with in high school? The big guy, blond, captain of the football team?"

Mark winced at long-remembered pain. "Yeah."

She laughed softly. "About three weeks after he broke your nose, he broke mine." She set the jelly glass down beside the futon and kissed him lightly on the lips.

"Funny how things turn out sometimes, huh?"

His lips were numb and stinging all at once, as if somebody had punched him in the mouth. She slipped her hand behind his head, drew his face to hers. Almost he hung back. Then their mouths touched again, and her tongue slid between his lips, teased across his teeth. He grabbed her like a drowning man and clung, with his hands, his lips, his soul.

In her sleep, in her room, Sprout cried out.

They were both on their feet at once. Mark just beat Kimberly through the door of his microscopic bedroom.

Lying on her own lumpy mattress, Sprout murmured to herself, hugged her Pooh-bear closer to herself, and rolled over and back deeper into sleep. Mark and Kimberly watched her for a moment, not speaking, barely breathing.

Kimberly disengaged, went and sat on the futon. Mark practically melted beside her, reaching for her. She was tense, unyielding.

"I'm sorry," she said without looking at him. "It won't work. Don't you see? I've tried this. I can't go back."

"But we can be together. I'd do anything for you—for Sprout. We can be, like, a family again."

She glanced at him over her shoulder. Her eyes gleamed with tears. "Oh, Mark. It can't be. You're too much the free spirit."

"What's wrong with freedom?"

"Responsibility took its place."

"But I can be what you want! I'll do anything for you. I can help give you shape, if that's what you need."

Smiling sadly, she shook her head. She stood up, faced him, took his face in her hands. "Oh, Mark," she said, and kissed him lightly but chastely on the lips, "I do love you. But really, it's all you can do to get up feet-first in the morning."

She was gone. Mark lurched to his feet, but her Reeboks were already doing a muted Ginger Baker number down the stairs. He hung there in the door frame, heart pounding. He could feel it especially in the scrotum; his belly and inner thighs ached and trembled with frustrated tension.

He had almost forgotten what the blue balls felt like.

This shit, JJ Flash said, *has got to stop.*

♣

"Dr. Pretorius, what do you mean by appearing in my court like this?"

"You mean this, your honor?" He gestured at his right leg. The immaculately tailored trousers ended at the knee. The limb below was black and green and warted like a frog's. Yellow pus oozed from a dozen lesions. Judge Conover's nose wrinkled at the smell.

"This is *my* wild card. It makes me a joker—except the condition is spreading upward by degrees, and when it reaches my torso, it will kill me. So I suppose it also qualifies as a Black Queen, albeit slow."

"It's disgusting. Do you intend to make mockery of this court?"

"I intend to display only what exists, your honor. Be it the physical disfigurement of a joker or the emotional and mental disfigurement of bigots who would condemn people for having drawn a wild card."

"I am tempted to find you in contempt."

"You can't make it stick," he said affably. "Jokers may not be enjoined from public display of their traits, unless these conflict with indecent-exposure laws. That's state *and* federal law; would you like citations?"

Her cheeks pinched her nose. "No. I know the law."

He turned to Kimberly, who sat in the box as if she'd just been carved from a block of ice.

"Mrs. Gooding, you've been to court before to get custody of Sprout. What happened the first time?"

Anger flared in her eyes. He let himself show a slight smile.

"You know perfectly well what happened," she said crisply.

"Please tell the court anyway." He let her see him glance toward the press-packed courtroom. He and Mark had awakened to head-lines screaming TRIPS CUSTODY CASE LAWYER EQUATES ACES, DRUG LORDS and ACE POWERS KILL, ATTORNEY SAYS. He wanted her and Latham to know he intended to share the joy.

There was also an article that said President Bush, after specifi-cally pledging not to do so during his campaign, was considering calling for a revival of the old Ace Registration Acts. Didn't have anything to do with this, of course. Just another sign of the times.

She folded her hands before her. "I was under an enormous amount of stress at the time. There was our daughter's condition, and marriage to Mark was not precisely easy on me."

Touché, he thought, *not that it'll do you any good.*

"So what happened?"

"I broke down on the stand."

"Went to pieces is more like it, wouldn't you say?"

Her mouth tightened to a razor cut. "I was ill at the time. I'm not ashamed of that, why should I be? I've had treatment."

"Indeed. And how else have circumstances changed from that time?"

"Well—" She glanced at Mark, who as usual was gazing at her like a blond basset pup. "My life has become much more stable. I've found a career, and a marvelous husband."

"So you would say that you can offer a far more stable home environment to Sprout than you could before?"

She looked at him, surprised and wary. "Why, yes."

He expected Latham to object right then, on GPs, just to break the rhythm of questioning even or maybe especially if he didn't know where it was headed. *You aren't infallible after all, are you, motherfucker?*

"So you are saying that now you are a suitable parent because you're richer? What you're saying, then, is that rich people make better parents than poor ones?"

That pulled Latham's string. He actually jumped to his feet and raised his voice when he objected.

Conower was pounding her gavel to restore order. She was going to sustain, no doubt about it. But he'd seen the flicker in her eyes. He'd gotten the point home. Punched her liberal-guilt button with his customary sledgehammer subtlety.

Christ, I hate myself sometimes.

♠

After lunch break Pretorius asked, "Have you ever used illegal drugs, Mrs. Gooding?"

"Yes." She was forthright, meeting his eyes, not trying to evade an allegation she knew he could prove. "A long, long time ago. It was in the wind." A half smile. "We weren't as wise back then."

Nicely done. "And did you ever try LSD-25?"

A pause, then, "Yes."

"Did you use it frequently?"

"That depends on your definition."

"I'll trust your judgment, Mrs. Gooding."

She dropped her eyes. "It was the sixties. It was the thing to do. We were experimenting, trying to liberate our consciousness as well as our bodies."

"And did you ever stop to consider the genetic damage such ex-perimentation might be doing?" He let it ring: "Did you not con-sider the welfare of your future children, Mrs. Gooding?"

The courtroom blew up again.

◆

After Conower called recess Mark was waiting for Pretorius, kind of hopping up and down without leaving his horrible chair, ergo-nomically designed to conform perfectly to the mass man but to fit no individual. He looked as if his ears were made of iron and had been stuck in a microwave.

"What was all that bullshit *about*?" he hissed at Pretorius. "Acid isn't a proven teratogen. Not like, like alcohol."

"Alcohol isn't the issue. They haven't gotten around to repro-hibiting it yet, at least not in time for the morning editions. Latham wants to make an issue of drugs. So we'll give him drugs good and hard."

For a moment Mark could only sputter in outrage. "Wuh-what about the truth?" he finally managed to get out.

"Truth." Pretorius laughed, a low, sour sound. "You're in a court of law, son. Truth is not the issue here."

He sighed and sat. "Never believe that the days of trial by com-bat are over. Trials are still duels. It's just that the champions wised up and rewrote the rules. Now we fight with writs and precedents instead of maces, and instead of risking our own lives, all we risk is our clients' money. Or lives or freedom."

He rested both hands on the gargoyle-head knob of his cane. "You don't like what I'm doing. Son, I don't either. But I take my role as your champion seriously. If I have to wallow in shit to win your case for you, that's what I do.

"These are witch-hunt times. You want to challenge that essen-tial fact; hell, so do I. But if that's all I do, you lose your daughter.

That's why they call it the *system*, Mark. Because like it or not, it's the way things work. Defy it too openly, it grinds you up and spits you out."

♥

Mark and Kimberly had a date for that night, Friday. She didn't keep it. He wasn't surprised. He didn't even blame her. He felt dirtied by the way Pretorius had treated her, ashamed.

What was worst in his own mind was that he hadn't stopped him.

Saturday the guilty depression got to be too much. Mark closed the Wellness Center early. There was something he had to do. A matter of voices in his head.

♣

The small man stood with one red Adidas on the roof parapet, looking at the stop-and-go Third World traffic of Jokertown a dozen stories below. He wore a red jogging suit over an orange T-shirt. His face was narrow, foxlike, with a sharp prominent nose and a sardonic bend to the eyebrows. Russet hair blew like flames in the stinking breeze.

He held a hand out before him. A jet of flame spurted from the forefinger tip. It became a ball, jumped from one finger to the next. He rolled the hand palm up. The flame swelled to baseball size, settled in the palm. For a moment it burned there, pallid in the sunlight, while he stared at it, as if fascinated. Then with a roar it shot into the high haze on a gusher of fire that seemed to spring from his palm.

He watched the flame dissipate. Then he drew a deep breath, let it sigh out through a lopsided grin.

"About fucking time," he said, and stepped into space.

He let himself fall about fifteen feet, far enough to see a startled face flash by in a window. Then he straightened his body and put his arms out before him like a swimmer in a racing dive and took off flying. No point freaking the citizenry *too* much. The poor schmucks in J-town had enough on their plates already.

He flew north, toward the park, thinking *Mark's really put his foot in it this time.* At least the poor fool hadn't quite had the nuts to make a clean break with the past. Didn't have a cold enough core to pour out his remaining vials of powder and see his other selves swirl away down the drain.

Thank God. It was chafing enough, the half-life he and the others led, like spectators at the back of an old and cavernous movie house where the film kept breaking. He hated that he only existed on sufferance, only knew his own body, his own flesh, the feel of flight and the wind in his hair, in sixty-minute increments. For a man as full of life as he, that was hell.

Hell was a cold place, for him. The life that roared inside him, he expressed as flame.

A helicopter vaulted off a building top to his left. He angled toward it. When he was a thousand yards away, he kicked in some flame, went streaking for it like a SAM. He threw himself into a corkscrew, drawing a spiral of orange fire into which the chopper flew.

It was a traffic chopper. The crew knew him; the announcer grinned and waved while his assistant pointed a live-action minicam at him.

JJ Flash, superstar. He grinned and waved. The pilot's face was as white as a brother's ever gets. He obviously hadn't run into Jumpin' Jack before.

That was fine, too. Flash had a certain amount of mean in him, that needed some harmless outlet.

. . . About then he realized where he was heading. He smiled again, wolfishly. His subconscious knew what it was doing.

♠

Kimberly Ann Cordayne Meadows Gooding looked up from her magazine. A man was floating outside the glass corner of her penthouse, tapping with one finger. She gasped. Her hand reached up to twitch her indigo robe a little more closed over the sheer lilac negligee.

He made urgent gestures for her to open the window. She bit her lip, shook her head.

"It doesn't open," she said.

"Fuck," his mouth said soundlessly. He pushed away about six feet, rolled out his hand palm up, as if introducing his next guest on late-night TV. Orange fire jetted out and splashed against the window.

Kimberly recoiled. Almost she screamed. Almost.

The window wavered, melted in a rough oval. A breath of warm diesel-perfumed wind washed in. The man in red stepped through.

"Sorry about the window," he said. "I'll pay for it. I had to talk to you."

"My husband's a rich man," she said. Her voice caught, like a hand running over silk.

"I'm JJ Flash."

"I know who you are. I've seen you on *Peregrine's Perch*."

Without asking, he dropped onto a merciless white chair. "Yeah. And you've seen those pictures your fuck lawyer flashed around. Some poor teenybopper pan-fried by a psycho in a town I've never even been to."

She glanced at the window. The wind was blowing her hair. "Maybe Mr. Latham's the one you should be visiting."

"No. You're the one I want. Why are you jacking Mark Meadows around?"

She leapt up. "How dare you speak to me like that!"

He laughed. "Can the indignation, babe. All your life . . . as long as you've known him, it's been the same. You tantalize and glide away. He's a putz in a lot of ways, but he deserves better."

He tipped his head sideways and looked more like a fox than ever. "Or are you just setting the boy up?"

For a moment her eyebrows formed fine arches of fury above eyes that had gone meltwater pale. Then she stood and spun, walked a few steps away. He watched the way her full buttocks moved the heavy cloth of the robe.

"He must tell you a lot about himself," she said tartly.

A grin came across Flash's face. He held up crossed fingers. "We're like this." The grin hardened, set. "Answer the question, babe."

She stood by the melt-edged hole. "Do you think it's easy for me?"

"From where I sit," he said, "it looks like the easiest thing in the world."

"I love Mark. Really," she said in a clotted voice. "He is the kindest man I've ever known."

"Or the biggest schmuck. Because you equate *kind* with *weak*, don't you?" He was on his feet now, in her face.

Weeping, she started to spin away. He caught her by the shoulder and made her face him. Small flames danced around his fist.

"Too many women," he said, "are afraid of themselves. They buy the old Judeo-Christian rap that they're innately wicked, tainted. So they look for a man to abuse them. Give them the punishment they deserve. Like that jock who busted Mark's beak and then yours. Is that your gig, Ms. Kimberly Perfect?"

She gasped. Smoke wisped up around the curve of one nostril, and suddenly her gown flashed into flame.

Kimberly shrieked, tried to run. Flash held her. His free hand tangled the burning synthetic, pulling with surprising strength. Robe and gown tore away.

She slumped to the floor, sobbing in terror. Flash methodically wadded the burning garment, almost seeming to wash his hands with it. The fire diminished, went out. He tossed the half-molten mass in the corner and knelt beside her.

She clung to him. For a moment he held her, absently stroking her hair. Then he pushed her away.

"Let's see what kind of shape you're in, while I can still do you some good."

Ignoring her attempts to marshal belated modesty and indignation, he looked her over. She seemed unharmed, except for a reddening glare of burn stretching from her left shoulder to breast. He laid a hand over the angry patch, began to run it down.

She tried to jerk back. "Just what the hell do you think you're doing?"

"Drawing the energy out," he said, preoccupied. "It's like hitting a minor burn with a piece of ice. If I get to it quickly enough, there's no harm done."

She looked at him. "I thought fire was your element," she said from somewhere down in her throat.

"It is." He cupped her breast. Where his hand had passed, the skin was white, unmarked. "Just a little parlor trick."

"You're a dangerous man to be around, Mr. Flash."

His thumb stroked her nipple. She gasped, stiffened. The nipple rose. Her eyes held his. Her lips were moist.

"I'm not an eighties kind of guy," he said huskily, "any more than Mark is. He's a gentle flake from the sixties.

"And I'm a bastard for the nineties."

She grabbed the back of his neck and pulled his head down.

◆

In an alley behind an elegant Park Avenue high rise Mark Meadows sat with his knees up around his prominent ears.

How long has it been, that I've dreamed of that? Of holding her, feeling her, tasting her, seeing the way her eyes go dark and then pale, the way she tosses her hair and clutches and moans . . . .

He felt two-timed. He felt like a voyeur. He felt like a fool.

He put his face in his spider hands and cried.

♥

That night Mark sat up and killed a bottle of wine. Sprout played with her Tinkertoy set. Kimberly never came.

Eventually Mark got down on the new white linoleum he and Durg had laid and helped Sprout build an airplane with a propeller that really spun. It never got off the ground.

♣

"I'll do it," she said.

He looked at her the way a cobra looks at you through the glass in the zoo. Without interest, without sign of even seeing.

"Do what, Mrs. Gooding?"

"What—whatever you ask me to. To make sure I keep her."

She stood there, her whole body clenched, holding a breath inside until it threatened to burst her rib cage. Just daring him to ask what caused her change of heart.

He didn't give her the satisfaction. He just nodded. And she found herself hating his certainty as desperately as she needed it.

♠

Sunday the front doorbell rang just as the sun was checking out. Mark came and stared through the replacement glass for a long moment before unlocking the door.

She had a flushed, bright-eyed, breathless quality, as though there was frost in the air. She wore a loose dark smock over blue jeans tonight.

"Feel like a walk?" she asked.

"You mean, after what happened the other day? You can still, like, talk to me?"

She recoiled a fraction of an inch. Then she went to the toes of her fashionable low-top boots and kissed his cheek, "Of course I can, Mark. What happens in court ought to stay there. Let's go."

◆

Afterward he never could remember what they talked about. All he could remember was feeling that, despite it all, she might *really be coming back this time.*

Then they turned a corner and stopped. A pair of NYPD motorcycles were drawn across the street. Down the block a building waved flags of flame against the night. Fire trucks were drawn up in front, arcing jets of water into the blaze. As he watched, one pulsed once spastically and died.

He drifted forward, pulling away from Kimberly's hand that clutched his sleeve. He felt the flames on his face. At the far end of the block a knot of skinheads cheered and jeered. One was just darting back into their midst, pursued by a fireman clumsy in his big boots. In horror Mark realized the skin had just slashed a hose.

"What's happening, man?" he asked a bystander.

"Somebody torched an old apartment. Chink family on the third floor was trying to start some kind of tailor shop." He spat on the sidewalk. "Slopes got it coming, you ask me. Tryin' to mess with our rent control, sneak the place into bein' commercial property. They in it with the landlord, that's for sure."

A line of cops crowded the skins, pushing them back. Mark ran forward. Sprout screamed, "Daddy!", broke Kimberly's grip, and lunged after him. Kimberly followed, trying to grab her arm.

An ambulance was parked this side of the blaze. Beside it cops were trying to keep back an Asian family. A man and woman were wrestling with the officers and firemen who hemmed them in, howling and windmilling painfully thin arms. A man in an asbestos suit was hanging on the end of a ladder; a truck was trying to bring him into position to get inside a window, but huge bellows of flames kept lashing out at him, driving him back despite his protective clothing.

Several other men in inferno suits stood in a puddle on the street with helmets off. "You gotta get *in* there," a florid-faced man with a chief's badge on his helmet yelled. "There's still a little girl inside."

"It's suicide. Fucking roof's going."

Mark was fumbling in his Dead patch pocket. Kimberly caught up with Sprout a few feet away.

"Mark! What's happening?"

He shook his head, unheeding. Black and silver—no. Yellow: useless. Gray, worse than. In his haste he discarded them. His lives fell in glittering arcs to shatter on the asphalt.

"Mark, what—what in God's name are you doing?"

The last two. One blue—and, thank God, an orange. He stuck the blue vial back in his pocket. Then he tossed the orange one's contents down his throat.

Kimberly saw him stagger back. And then he *changed*. The familiar gawky outlines blurred, shifted, condensed.

A different man stood there, with film-star looks, a Jewish nose, a devil's grin. And a red sweatsuit, worn over an orange T-shirt.

JJ Flash tipped a one-finger salute to Kimberly. "Later, toots. Take care of the kid."

He launched himself into the sky.

♥

The man on the ladder said a couple of Hail Marys and prepared to jump through the window. He was going to his death. But that was better than hearing the little girl in there crying every time he closed his eyes for the rest of his life.

He jumped. Something grabbed the back of his protective hood, bought him up short, and hung him on the end of the ladder.

"Just trying to save you from yourself, pal," said the man hovering next to him in midair. "Better leave this one to the professionals."

"Jumpin' Jack Flash!" the fireman gasped.

The ace put a finger beside his nose. "It's a gas-gas-gas," he said, and darted into the heart of the fire.

♣

JJ Flash was on fire.

But his flesh didn't blacken and crackle, his eyeballs didn't melt. His blow-dried hair wasn't even mussed. In the midst of hell, he was in heaven.

P. J. O'Rourke heaven, in fact—the fire felt like sitting in a Jacuzzi with a couple of lines up each nostril and a teenage girl by your side eeling out of her string bikini and getting ready to audition as a sword-swallower for Barnum & Bailey. This was *fine*.

Best of all, he could still hear the little girl crying. "Where are you, honey?" he yelled. She didn't seem to hear, just kept bawling, but that was enough. He went down a short hallway wallpapered in big batts of flame, gave a wall a jolt so hot the inferno around him seemed tepid. It went away in a puff of yellow incandescence.

She was sitting in about the only square yard of the whole fucking building that wasn't on fire, a little girl in pigtails and smoldering pj's with Yodas all over them. He walked up to her, knelt, and smiled.

The roof fell in.

♠

Even the firemen gasped when they heard the thunderous series of cracks and saw a fresh spray of sparks shoot up through the column of smoke. Sprout screamed, *"Daddy!"* and threw herself forward.

A Puerto Rican cop in a riot helmet grabbed her arm. "Hold on, little lady," he said. "Your daddy'll be fine." The wet lines on his cheeks made a liar of him.

♦

JJ Flash lay on his side with the little girl beneath him and an elephant on top. He moved, felt the raw ends of ribs grate against each other.

The girl was still alive, sheltered by his body. A miracle she hadn't seared her lungs. He looked up. There was still more building to fall on him, and while the flame couldn't harm him, a structural member could damn well snuff his lights. And there was only so long before the little girl breathed in the flames that were crowding around like teenyboppers at a Bon Jovi concert.

"As Archbishop Hooper said," he grunted, "'*More fire.*' " Hugging the girl to him, he reared up. The flame rushed in with a joyous greedy roar. He thrust his arm down its throat.

♥

It wasn't fire that almost nailed the poor son of a bitch working his futile hose from the end of the ladder. It was a jet of incandescent gas and vaporized cement and steel, bright as the sun and a couple degrees cooler. For a heartbeat the inferno died back to a few stray flickers.

A man flew out of the hole the jet had made. Flames wreathed his body and the little girl he hugged against him. They were absorbed into his body as he landed lightly next to the frantic family.

"Here you go, ma'am," JJ Flash said, handing the girl to her mother. "Better let the medics look her over before you hug her too tight."

He turned away before they could try hugging *him*, scanning the crowd for Sprout. All Mark's personae shared his overriding imperative love for her; they couldn't help it. Plus he just plain liked the kid.

♣

"*Madre de Dios*," the Puerto Rican cop said, staring at Flash.

Kimberly Gooding reeled away. Her mind was spinning. Unraveling as it went.

And then she saw him. Standing at the end of the block, immaculate in his camel-hair coat. He caught her eye and nodded.

For the first time since she'd known him, St. John Latham was showing something like emotion. He was showing ... . triumph.

She knew, then, what she had been a party to.

Kimberly put her hands to her cheeks and dug in, slowly and deliberately, until the nails drew blood from just beneath her eyes.

♠

"Mr. Latham," Judge Conower asked gravely, "where is your client?"

"She has been released to the custody of a private mental-health clinic."

"And her condition?"

Latham paused just a sliver of a second. "She is in a fragile state, your honor."

"Indeed. Mr. Latham, Dr. Pretorius, kindly step forward."

The house was packed today, and Pretorius was expending lots of effort not to have hackneyed thoughts about bread and circuses. He glanced aside at Mark, who sat beside him wearing a lightweight buff blazer over the bandages wrapped around his upper body. JJ Flash or Mark A. Meadows, his ribs were cracked just the same. Mark only had eyes for his daughter, sitting at the table in the center between the opposing camps, directly facing the bench.

"This court is compelled to find that Ms. Gooding is clearly too unstable to be entrusted with custody of Sprout Meadows."

Pretorius caught his breath. Could it be—

"On the other hand," the judge said, turning to him, "your client is in fact an ace—perhaps several aces, whose names have been linked to extremely risky and irresponsible behavior. Moreover, he seems still—and in spite of his sworn testimony—to be a user of dangerous drugs, if the preliminary tests conducted on the vials recovered from the street at the site of last night's fire are any indication. In fact, at the close of these proceedings, Dr. Meadows will be remanded to the custody of the Drug Enforcement Agency.

"With these facts in view I cannot in conscience award him custody of the girl, either. Therefore I declare Sprout Meadows to be a ward of the state, and remand her to a juvenile home until arrangements can be made for a foster family."

Pretorius slammed down his cane. "This is monstrous! Have you asked the girl what she wants? *Have you?*"

"Of course not," Conower said. "We are acting on the advice of a qualified expert in children's welfare. You could hardly expect us to consult a minor in matters this important, even if the minor in question were not . . . special."

Sprout leapt to her feet. "Daddy! *Daddy, don't let them take me away!*"

With a wordless bellow Mark jumped onto the table. Bailiffs with sweat moons under their arms were on him like weasels, pulling him back down. A couple of men in suits stepped off from the rear wall and began making their way purposefully through the crowded courtroom.

Mark managed to get a hand inside his blazer. It came out with something, darted to his mouth.

"Stop him!" the judge screamed. "Cyanide!"

Another bailiff threw his bulky body across the table at him. And *through* him, into the front row, scattering TV cameras and onlookers and a portable spotlight array. The two bailiffs who had been wrestling with Mark fell against one another and rolled back to the floor.

In Mark's place a glowing blue man stood atop the table. He wore a black hooded cloak; stars seemed to glow within its folds. He shot the court the finger, wrapped the cloak about him, and sank with all deliberation through the table and the floor.

◆

Dr. Pretorius thumped the bottle of Laiphroaig down on the table and measured by eye how much of it he'd killed at a shot. About a quarter, he thought; about right. He passed the bottle across the desk to Mark.

"We fucked up," he announced as Mark's prominent Adam's apple worked up and down.

"No, Doc," Mark said breathlessly, wiping his lips with the back of his hand. "It wasn't your fault."

"Bullshit. I told you to run; I should have stuck to my guns. Now you're on the run without the girl . . . sorry; shouldn't have reminded you."

Mark shook his head. "It's not like you did remind me," he said quietly.

Pretorius sighed. "You know what we did, Mark? We compromised. You cut your hair. I went against the wishes of a client because I thought it was for his own good. An aging hippie and an old libertarian: we sell out and for what? To screw the pooch."

He took off his glasses and rubbed his eyes. The door opened and Ice Blue Sibyl came in to massage his shoulders with her blue-ice fingers.

"What will you do now, Mark?" he asked.

Mark gazed out the window at the darkness that lay over Jokertown. "I have to get her back," he said. "But I don't know how."

"I'll help, Mark. Anything I can do. Even if I have to go underground myself." He grabbed a pinch of belly. "I'm getting flabby. Spiritually as well as physically. Might do me good to go on the run. And in this kinder, gentler America, I suspect it's what I'll have to do, soon or late."

But Mark said nothing. Just stared out the window.

Somewhere out there, beyond the open wound of Jokertown, his daughter was crying.

♠   ♥   ♦   ♣

You're Nobody Till Somebody Loves You

by Walton Simons

ACES HIGH WAS AS close to deserted as Jerry had ever seen it. Two-thirds of the tables were empty, and there was nobody whom Jerry recognized as a celebrity. There was an aura of tense quietness, almost expectancy, about the place. Hiram was nowhere to be seen. Luckily, it didn't affect Jerry's appetite.

Jerry had eaten the shrimp and other goodies out of his salad and was ready to move on to his steak. Jay Ackroyd, whom Jerry had paid off, was happily chewing away at his lamb, occasionally pausing to wipe a drop of gravy from the corner of his mouth with a silk napkin.

"You're not still stuck on Veronica, are you?" Ackroyd asked.

"Nope. I'm giving up destructive women for Lent. Hopefully, it's a habit I won't get into again." Jerry sliced into his steak. It was deliciously pink and oozed juice. He stared at it a moment, then set down his knife and fork and took a large swallow of wine. "Besides, I don't care about her anymore." He'd been practicing the lie for weeks. "Now, about our other friend?"

"Right." Ackroyd pulled a file from his briefcase and handed it over to Jerry. "Here's everything I could find on Mr. David Butler. It's mostly background. He's rich, well schooled, good family, good future. He has a wild streak, but most rich kids do. Lots of club-bing, probably bisexual. But this *is* New York."

Jerry took the file and flipped through it. "Don't know where he is now, though?"

"Nope." Ackroyd chewed and swallowed. "You seem to special-ize in people that disappear, don't you?"

"I guess." Jerry didn't bother to try to hide his disappointment. If he hadn't let Tachyon talk him into going to the police, Jerry might have nailed David himself. "Any hunches?"

"There's something going on at Ellis Island. Gangs of kids, some dangerous jokers, maybe even an ace hiding out there. They call it the 'Rox.' Only teenagers could come up with a name like that. Probably as safe a place as any for a kid wanted by the law. Cops don't go out there anymore." Jay grabbed a waitress as she walked past. "See if Hiram will visit with us, will you? Tell him it's Jay. If not, well, let me know when you get off." He gave her a wink and slipped her a ten.

"You're acting like a man who's just been paid," Jerry said.

"I always act this way," Jay said. "You seem a little down. Bet-ter cheer up or I'll start telling you my knock-knock jokes."

"Sorry. Normally, I'm better company than this. Must be the weather," Jerry said. It was partly true. The late-winter sky had been gray for days on end. Sunshine always made the world feel nicer. Without it, even the good things left a little to be desired. "Is that all?"

"Of course not. There's weeks of work in that file," Ackroyd said. "One very important fact that came out is that for several of the 'jumper' incidents, David Butler had a well-substantiated alibi."

"Which means?"

Ackroyd paused a second, as if waiting for Jerry to answer his own question. "There's more than one of them. And nobody knows how many more there might be."

"Just great," Jerry said. "That's all the world needs."

"Something else bothering you?" Ackroyd rubbed his chin. Jerry was silent. "Knock, knock."

"All right. Things are tense at home. I live with my brother and sister-in-law, you know. And Kenneth seems to resent me for spending time with his wife, even though he's usually too busy to pay her much attention." Jerry shrugged. "It's not like she's interested in me. I doubt she'd date me if I were the last man on Earth."

Ackroyd sat quietly for a moment. "Hopefully, the sun will start shining again soon. In the meantime, you might want to consider moving into your own place. Might defuse the situation. Just a thought."

"Right." Jerry looked away. Hiram stepped out of his office and wove his way through the tables toward them. His charcoal suit, as always, was exquisitely tailored, but the man inside looked worse for wear. There were deep lines in his face, especially around the eyes.

"Hiram," Jay said, "sit down with us. Have dessert and an after-dinner drink. We're boring the hell out of each other."

Hiram smiled weakly and looked around, his head moving in a quick, jerky manner. "Thank you, really, but no. There's so much to catch up on, with all the other business that's been going on." He paused. "And, well, it might not be a good idea to be seen with me now. Guilt by association, you know."

"We're not worried," Jay said. "In fact—"

There was a thunderous noise from the kitchen and fire leapt out from the doorway. Jerry was knocked from his chair and into the next table. His elbow smashed into one of the table legs, shooting pain up his arm. Smoke churned into the dining area.

Jerry dragged himself into a standing position. Jay and Hiram were already making their way toward the kitchen. Customers, those that could, were picking themselves up and pushing out of the restaurant. The injured were moaning or screaming. Jerry heard the sound of fire extinguishers from the kitchen.

"Hit the exhaust fans," Hiram directed. He pushed his way into the kitchen. Jay was right behind him.

Jerry followed slowly, coughing from the heavy smoke. He walked across the restaurant and stuck his head into the kitchen. One of the swinging doors had been torn from its hinges. Hiram was kneeling next to someone, lifting their head.

"I'm sorry," Hiram said. "I'm so sorry."

Jay pulled his friend up. "Hiram, call Tachyon. Tell him we have several severely injured people coming his way. Do it now."

Hiram nodded and walked out of the kitchen. Jerry stepped back. He could see the pain and anger in Hiram's eyes. It made his self-pity over Veronica seem selfish. Jerry stepped into the kitchen.

"Anything I can do?" he asked Jay.

"Not unless you're a doctor." Jay pointed his finger. There was a pop. A moaning man vanished. There were two more pops. Jay knelt down next to the final body in the room and shook his head. "It's too late for this one."

"If those other people make it, it'll be because of you," Jerry said.

"More because of Tachyon," Jay said, wiping his eyes. "But you have to do as much as you can. There's no excuse for doing less."

"Nope," Jerry said, thinking of David. "No excuse at all."

♥

He could have asked Kenneth to bring home David's file, but that would have tipped his brother about Jerry's suspicions. Besides, the file was probably in St. John's office. Latham, Strauss was very selective about who it hired; hopefully there would be some clue as to David's whereabouts. It could be a starting point, anyway.

The door to Latham's office had been tougher than Lieutenant King's and his finger bone had poked painfully out through the skin. Jerry kissed a salty-tasting drop of blood off his fingertip and went inside. He turned on the desk lamp. The fluorescent bulb crackled to life and greenish light covered the desk. He looked about the dimly lit office. It was oppressively neat and boring. No plants, no personal photographs, no clutter, nothing to give it any semblance of life. Jerry tried the desk drawers, but they were locked. He figured what he wanted would be in the file cabinet anyway, but the key to it was likely in the desk.

Jerry crossed the room to the file cabinet. He blew on his hands. The heat was turned way down and even double-paned glass let some cold air seep in. The drawers were locked here, too. Jerry didn't want to tear up his fingers, but it looked like the only way he was going to get anywhere.

He heard a noise outside and froze. He'd known this was a possibility, but had trusted to luck that it wouldn't happen. After a moment's hesitation he changed his looks to mimic Latham's. Cold and impersonal, he thought, trying to make everything go dead inside him. He took a deep breath, turned off the lamp, and headed for the door. If it was anyone but Latham, he'd be okay.

She met him at the door. She was wearing a tight blue off-the-shoulder designer dress. Her carefully combed hair hung past her shoulders. She smelled as beautiful and expensive as she looked. After an instant Jerry recognized her. Fantasy, or Asta Lenser, and she was definitely no dog. Much closer to Myrna Loy, in fact.

He interrupted the silence with a cough. "How can I help you?"

She sighed. Jerry thought he smelled wine on her breath. Her eyes were so dilated he couldn't tell what color they were. "Just looking for company. Rumor has it that you're, shall we say, more accessible to the temptations of the flesh these days."

Jerry tried not to act excited. Not only was he not going to get caught, he was likely going to get laid. Kenneth and Beth had seen Asta naked at a fund-raiser, of all things. Now, with luck, it was his turn. Still, he had to play it cool, or she'd know he wasn't the genuine Latham. "That might be possible. Using my residence is out of the question, though."

She twined her fingers in his necktie, gracefully pirouetted, and pulled him toward the office door. "I love it when nasty rumors turn out to be true."

♣

Her penthouse was huge, with high ceilings and expensive modern decor. There was less black and silver on a sports car lot than in her living room. She dimmed the lights and kicked off her shoes.

"Let's see now, counselor. Bedroom number one, two, or three for you?" Fantasy put a finger to her red lips for a moment. "No. Don't tell me. Bedroom number three. My instincts are never wrong."

"I'm sure that will be satisfactory." Jerry was having trouble maintaining his Latham act. He wanted to get to the sex so he wouldn't have to talk anymore.

Fantasy half walked and half danced to the bedroom doorway, then lifted her chin and stepped inside.

Jerry struggled out of his coat and tossed it on the nearest chair, then followed. She was standing next to the large brass bed, pulling her dress off over her head. All she had on underneath was a pair of tie-on black satin panties. She undid them with dramatic flair and let them drop to the floor, then did a slow half turn so he could see her from behind.

Jerry just stared. Her body was flawless, at least no imperfections showed up in the dimmed light. She was small-breasted, but he preferred that. "You're very admirably proportioned."

She walked over to him and began unbuttoning his shirt. "You know, if Kien finds out about this, we're both in for hell on earth."

"Really?" Jerry didn't know who Kien was and frankly didn't

care. It would be Latham's problem if they were found out. Right now he was deciding what size to make his penis. Asta undid his belt and began slipping his pants down. He quickly decided on a *Penthouse Forum* model.

She cracked a pill under his nose as they sat down, naked on the bed. Jerry's head jerked back. His nose stung for a second, then everything was fine. "Actually, Kien wouldn't do anything to you right now. He's too interested in your teen groupies."

Jerry figured this might have something to do with David, so he filed the information away for future use. She put her mouth on his. He was buzzing with pleasure and didn't want to do anything but fuck. She opened her mouth and worked her tongue over and around his. Jerry lay down and pulled her with him, running his hands over her soft flesh. He couldn't feel any imperfections, either.

Her kisses were intense and aggressive. She ran her fingers across his chest and abdomen, sometimes touching him delicately with the tips and sometimes digging in slightly with her nails. She reached down between his legs and traced the underside of his penis with her fingernails. In spite of its size, Jerry had no trouble getting it up. He ran his fingers through her pubic hair, twisting it lightly here and there.

She pinched the tip of his penis, almost hard enough to hurt him.

"Jesus," he said.

"Why counselor, I didn't know you were a religious man." She pulled his hand away and kissed it. "You have a nice, light touch, but I've got something a little more intimate in mind. Any objections?" Silence. "I'm ready to call my first witness."

Asta straddled him, facing his feet, and lowered herself onto his mouth. Her scent overpowered the expensive perfume she'd doubtless dabbed on her inner thighs. He ran his tongue up and down, separating her already moist labia. He decided to put his tongue into her as far as he could; given his power, that was all the way.

Fantasy gasped, then looked down at him. It was the most sincerely hedonistic expression he'd ever seen.

"I know a lawyer's greatest weapon is his mouth," she said, "but I wasn't aware just how dangerous it was."

"A lawyer's greatest weapon is his desire not to lose," Jerry said. Whatever she'd popped under his nose was kicking in, and he felt powerful and in control.

"Here's to the winners," Asta said, tossing her hair back and lowering herself back onto his mouth.

Jerry whipped his tongue lightly across her, then pointed it and pushed in again. Fantasy breathed heavily for several moments then leaned forward, taking him into her mouth. Pleasure spread through him. Veronica had plenty of oral technique, but not the enthusiasm Asta had shown with only a few strokes. Jerry exhaled slowly and put his tongue on autopilot. She made a muffled laugh. This had to be as good as it got.

♠

He was two-thirds of the way through both *The Big Sleep* and his bottle of peppermint schnapps when he heard a knock on the door.

"Come in," he said, pausing the VCR.

Beth sat down next to him and looked disapprovingly at the bottle.

"I'm depressed, so I'm drinking," Jerry explained. "It's a time-honored tradition."

"What are you depressed about?"

Jerry thought a moment, then told her everything. Told her about Veronica, and the return of his wild-card ability, his night with Fantasy. He left out his suspicions about David. She'd probably just write it off as jealousy.

Beth sat there the entire time with her hand on her chin.

"You know what's funny," Jerry said. "The sex with Asta was the best I've ever had, maybe the best I'll ever have, and it just depressed me. You know why? Because it wasn't for me. It was for Latham and I was just a stand-in. Nobody would ever want to fuck me like that."

"Maybe. Maybe not." Beth shook her head. "Does it make that big a difference?"

"Hell, yes. What's the measure of success nowadays? For a man it's how much money you make and how many women want to ball your brains out. I'm already rich, so the only area I can make good is with women."

"Jesus, Jerry, you don't have to buy into that crap. You're the one who decides what is or isn't a useful and happy life. Don't let Madison Avenue or anyone else tell you."

Jerry leaned away from her. "That's easy for you to say. You're married and happy. You've got what you want."

"Yes, because I know what I want and I worked hard to get it. Nobody did it for me."

"So, I'm just lazy. That's it." Jerry turned back to the TV.

"You're not just lazy, you're an emotional six-year-old. You don't see anyone's feelings or needs but your own. And you'll never get along with women as long as they're just something you do to make yourself feel more adequate." Beth paused. "It makes me wonder how you feel about me."

"I'm wondering about it right now, too." Jerry turned and looked at her. He could see the hurt in her eyes. The line was crossed, he might as well get his money's worth. "I trusted you with all my secrets, and all you can do is criticize. Why don't you just leave me alone. Go off and suck Kenneth's dick."

Beth stood slowly, left the room, and closed the door quietly behind her.

"I'm sorry," Jerry said, when he was sure she couldn't possibly hear. He took another slug of schnapps from the bottle. Bogart wouldn't have handled it this way. "Jesus, on top of everything else, I'm turning into an asshole."

He unpaused the VCR. He hoped Bogey and Baby would tell him otherwise, but they only had eyes for each other.

◆

Jerry carried a stack of boxes to the van. The air was cold and damp. Easter was just around the corner. Jerry thought of celebrating by biting the heads off chocolate bunnies. Misery loved company. He glanced up at the second-story window to Kenneth and Beth's bedroom. Beth looked down at him for a moment, then turned away. The finality of the gesture was crushing. Jerry felt like something inside him just died.

Kenneth walked out carrying a pair of suitcases. He set them carefully in the back of the van and closed the doors.

"This isn't really what you want to do," Kenneth said. "Cut your losses. Apologize to her and she'll meet you halfway. Trust me, I'm speaking from experience."

Jerry stared hard at Kenneth. "You know. My main reason for leaving is that both of you think I'm too stupid to handle my own life. That gets a little tiring after a while."

"Dumb, and proud of it. That's you," Kenneth said, turning away angrily. "Do what you have to do."

Jerry got in the van and turned the key. The engine sputtered to life. They'd be sorry soon enough. He'd already figured out how to make sure of that.

♠   ♥   ◆   ♣

A Broken Thread in a Dark Room

by Carrie Vaughn

JOANN COULDN'T GUESS WHAT kind of flowers Billy Ray might like. In fact, she couldn't imagine him in a room with a vase of roses or artistically drooping tulips at all. So when she visited him in the hospital, she carried a cactus, a spiny lump with a wilting yellow flower on the top, nested in a terra-cotta pot. It seemed to suit him, and he'd be less likely to kill it than something that required more attention.

"Good afternoon, Agent Ray," she announced from the doorway, giving her a moment to survey the room and take in Ray's condition before approaching. She adjusted her hood over her short-cropped black hair and arranged her cloak around herself. Black on the inside, reflective silver out, the cloak enveloped her, making sure her power was insulated and reducing her chances of hurting someone by accident. Today she wore street clothes, a plain blouse and trousers, rather than her enveloping black uniform. But she kept the leather gloves on, again, reducing any chance of stray contact.

Her ace power: she absorbed energy—all energy. She could even feel a soft charge coming off the cactus, a hum of life force, and made sure to keep hold of the pot, not touching the plant. If she touched it, she might kill it. She kept some distance between her and Ray's bed.

The black-haired, pale man was normally fit, powerful. Now, he appeared gaunt. Shifting in bed, he glared a moment, grunted something that she took to be a greeting, and went back to flipping channels on the TV mounted to the wall—with his left hand. His right hand rested on top of the sheet over his chest. Five fingers present, fully regrown after he'd had half his hand cut off. The new digits were thin, pink. Weak and unused. No calluses.

All in all, he looked pretty good, given what had happened in Atlanta at the Democratic National Convention. He'd been opened like a fish, stem to stern, his guts poured out and half his jaw sliced off. But the wild card virus had made Ray a stubborn SOB. Something might kill him someday, but it wasn't going to be a punk like Mackie Messer. Somehow, doctors had stitched him back together, and his superhuman healing was doing the rest. His longest recovery stretch yet. Guy must have been going bonkers.

After this round, his face was going to look even weirder. His jaw had mostly grown back, but right now it looked like someone had taken a woodworking plane up the left side of his face, and the skin was pink and flaking. But that snarl was recognizably Billy.

She couldn't see under the sheet to judge how the rest of him was doing. He was lying unusually still. Like his muscles still weren't working right. Her stomach got queasy thinking of it, so she stopped.

Some kind of talking-heads news program was playing, rehashing yet again the recently finished presidential election, including some clips of Senator Hartmann's speeches. She wished Ray wouldn't do this to himself.

"Please tell me you haven't been watching video of what happened to you," she said.

"Naw. Too grosh for teefee," he said flatly, in a tone that suggested annoyance. The words came out mushy through his half-healed jaw.

"I brought you this." She set the cactus on the rollaway tray that also held a bottle of water with a straw and a plate of mashed potatoes. Easier to eat when you only had half a mouth, she supposed. He also had a recent issue of *Time*, which featured a cover photo of Hartmann, his arm raised over his face, fleeing the camera.

"Huh," he muttered. "Scheerful."

"It reminded me of you." He didn't tell her to leave, so she pulled a chair from the wall over and sat, wrapping her cloak around her. He didn't look like he'd had many visitors. No cards, no flowers. Just that lumpy cactus. She nodded at the magazine. "Catching up?"

"You know where he wentsh? Whatsh he'sh doing?"

"Who, Senator Hartmann?" He glared even harder. Obviously Senator Hartmann. "Laying low, I suppose."

"Shaved the man'sh life. Never even shent me a card." Now, he looked sad. Hangdog, like. She didn't know what to say. *Nobody'd* heard from Hartmann after that debacle.

"I'm sorry. Sorry this happened."

"Sh'okay. Sho what'sh wrong with you?" he asked.

"How do you know something's wrong?" She tried to sound casual.

"You got that look. You're not really here, you're tshinking aboutsh sometshing elshe."

She hadn't intended on unloading on Ray. He really didn't need unloading on at the moment. He was proud of his healing abilities but he still looked half-gutted. Even his rib cage looked wrong, sunken under the sheet. But then—she'd come here at all because he was the one person who might get it. She sighed. "I just got out of a meeting at SCARE."

He chuckled, an odd, watery sound. "Sho is Shyclone in charge yet or no?"

"He's still gunning for it, but he, ah, had an incident a little while back at a Republican fund-raiser. He's trying to keep his head down." A roomful of rich donors, mixed with wild-card antics and a major art theft, right from under his nose? Oh yeah, Cyclone didn't want anyone talking about that one.

Ray chuckled again. "That oughta be good. Tshink you can get me the report?"

"He's trying to bury it. But he might still get the head of the agency just because he knows which asses to kiss."

"And you are all about trutsh, justish, and all that shit."

"You know, you might think about going for management someday," she suggested, and wasn't even joking. Ray knew what targets to gun for. And they weren't getting any younger. She was in her thirties now. Been at SCARE and the Justice Department for almost a decade. Ray was right there with her. Fieldwork might have been fun, but career advancement only went so far. Did Ray realize that, or was he just in this to beat people up? "I bet you'd spend less time in hospitals."

"I like hospitalsh." Then he frowned. "No, I don't. Sho what'd the guy do now?"

"Let's just say I got the short straw."

"No wait, let me guessh, there washn't actually any drawing of shtrawsh. You volunteered becaushe you alwaysh volunteer for the shit no one else wantsh to do."

She raised her hands in a show of surrender. "You got me. Except Cyclone doesn't even want me doing this job because it's not, and I quote, 'up to our standard of visible public service.' Unquote."

His grunt was smug. "Shyclone's a dick."

"He has an idiosyncratic set of priorities." Like how many column inches of mentions he could get in the *New York Times*, how many times *Aces!* put him on the cover . . .

"So what's the gig?"

"Trouble in New York."

"Shome ace bank thief the FBI needs help on? A new joker gang running over the local copsh?"

"National Park Service requested help on an investigation into some stray animal deaths."

He stared. "Joann, we shtop assassins. We foil international conshpiracies. We're not park rangersh. We're not dog catchersh."

She raised a brow. "So you agree with Cyclone?"

"No, it'sh jusht—"

"We assist federal agencies in wild cards—related incidents. And this sounds weird enough, I think it warrants attention."

"Well all right then. Have fun with that."

"It's gotta be done."

"If you shay sho. At least you're not likely to see combat. Tell Shmokey the Bear I shaid hi."

Joann stood, the fabric of her cloak rustling around her. "You're looking a lot better, Ray. I'm not just saying that."

"Yesh you are. I gotta get out of here. I'm shick of thish. Take me with you."

"You should relax while you can."

His grunt might have been anything, agreement, frustration, or maybe just some noise in his healing gut. She waved, and he went back to flipping TV channels.

♥

Joann's meeting with her contact at the Park Service was for mid-morning, and she arrived a few minutes early, not sure she'd be able to easily find the spot. She had an address in Midtown. She wasn't expecting the building at that address to itself be a national monument, a colonial-era neoclassical building with a wide staircase, a row of columns, and a statue of George Washington out front. Reading the various informational signs and plaques, she learned that this had been the first capitol building for the brand-new United States, and was where Washington's inauguration had taken place. And she ended up being late to the meeting.

Inside, she took a couple of wrong turns, enduring stares after her formidably cloaked form. She was a tall black woman, powerfully built, and one of the few aces who went around in something like a costume. She was used to the stares. Really, she was grateful—if people didn't know what to think of her, they kept their distance.

The basement of the impressive building had been converted to more typical government offices, with standard-issue tile flooring and familiar flickering fluorescent lights. She finally came to the door with the correct plastic nameplate. It was standing open, so Joann went in. The office might have had a little more whimsy than the typical run-down government office—a cheerful Smokey Bear poster admonishing viewers to prevent forest fires, even though they were in the middle of Manhattan; a calendar picture showing a beautiful landscape of mountains; a bunch more pictures pinned to a corkboard, what looked like the previous months from the same calendar showing oceanside cliffs, a desert at sunset, and geese on a lake. Several desks were piled with folders and paperwork, ancient telephones, a not-so-ancient computer, and a tree stand with a single ranger hat on it.

Joann looked around for some kind of receptionist, a front desk where she should check in. Didn't find one. The open space and clutter was democratic, without hierarchy.

At a desk in a corner, a dark-haired Hispanic woman was talking on the phone, mostly offering affirmatives. She looked up at Joann and smiled. "Can you hold just a minute? Thanks." She set the handset down. "Hi, you must be Agent Jefferson from SCARE."

"Ah. That obvious?"

A short, vibrant woman in a colorful blouse and plain slacks, she gestured, encompassing Joann's flowing cape and enveloping

hood. "A little. I'm Maria Fuentes, assistant to the park superin-
tendent." She strode forward, held out her hand for shaking, and,
as she always did, Joann drew back, just a little.

"I'm sorry, I can't touch anyone. But it's very nice to meet you."
She nodded her head, shifting the hood.

Maria blanched, but recovered quickly and nodded. Professional, she didn't even ask Joann to explain her power—or worse,
demonstrate. "Would you like some coffee? That pot's pretty
fresh." She pointed to a coffee station, a one-pot coffee maker next
to a stack of Styrofoam cups and packets of sugar and powdered
creamer. "I just need to finish up this phone call, it should only
take a minute. I hope that's okay."

"Go ahead," Joann answered, and wandered around the rest of
the office, looking.

Fuentes retrieved the phone. "Okay, so we're out of park
maps . . . I know that delivery was supposed to come in . . . yes,
that's fine. Go ahead and get photocopies made, I'll authorize the
reimbursement as long as you don't go over thirty bucks. . . ."

Joann tried to imagine Cyclone handling that kind of call, that
kind of day-to-day business. Couldn't, at all. On the next wall, she
scanned a pair of prints pinned to the bulletin board. Simplified
architectural drawings, evocative watercolors showing pleasant
walkways lined with perfect trees in a lovely park, surrounding an
antique edifice of red brick, some hulking nineteenth-century mu-
nicipal building with rows of arched windows and fanciful, self-
important towers topped with rounded copper cupolas, green with
age. Joann felt like she should have recognized it, but didn't.

The phone clicked back into its cradle. "Sorry about that. Thanks
for waiting."

"What's this?" Joann asked as Fuentes joined her by the drawings.

"Plans," Maria said wistfully. "Once-upon-a-time plans. Ellis
Island belonged to the Park Service until last year. We'd been

making plans for years for turning it into a National Monument, converting the main building into an immigration museum. We were just a couple of years out from implementation. But nothing like that's ever going to happen now. Not with everything that's happening over there. Now, no one wants the place."

"I've heard a lot of rumors, that squatters and drug dealers have taken it over?"

"It's all coming out in bits and pieces, that's part of the problem. Local law enforcement won't claim jurisdiction. The DEA, ATF, the NSA, and they all refer us to the FBI, who won't get involved without concrete evidence that federal laws have been broken—"

"And since the only people affected are jokers and drug dealers, they're all saying it's not their problem."

Maria shrugged. "Classic bureaucratic wall."

Thinking of Cyclone and his framed *Aces!* covers, Joann smiled. "No one wants to do the scut work."

"I see you understand. Which I'm guessing is why you're here and not someone else?"

"Got it in one. Really, I'm happy to help where I can. Is your problem connected with what's happening out at Ellis Island?"

"No, at least I don't think so. Frankly, I don't know what's going on. Nobody does."

"Can you tell me exactly what's wrong? Something about stray animals? Did I get that right?"

She pursed her lips. "It'll be easier if I show you. We'll have to take a ride to animal control; I hope you don't mind."

Joann arched her brow, her interest piqued.

♣

Fuentes drove them in a Park Service car to a nearby animal control office.

She pulled into an alley between two tall brick buildings and park by a loading dock, right next to a sign that declared NO PARK-ING.

"It's okay," the official explained cheerfully. "Government business."

Joann reflected a moment on the perks of driving a government car in Manhattan.

Fuentes had been through here enough that the uniformed officer at the front desk waved her through to a back room. The man stared at Joann as she walked by, as if he didn't live in Manhattan and had never seen a costumed ace before. She did make a striking figure in her cloak, dark skin, and her unwavering demeanor.

This wasn't a pound, with lots of cages holding forlorn dogs and cats waiting for adoption. Or that was in a different part of the building. Not that Joann could ever cuddle with a puppy or take home a kitten. Rather, this was a base of operations for the officers who answered calls and did the grunt work. Somewhere, a handful of dogs were barking. The sound echoed down the tiled hallway, from behind one of the many closed doors.

Fuentes opened one of the doors and led her inside. The temperature dropped, and the barking faded. This looked like a morgue. A couple of steel exam tables occupied the middle of the room, but they were half sized, able to hold a large dog but nothing much bigger. Tables and cupboards lined the walls, storing medical equipment, test tubes, microscopes, jars of cotton swabs. A row of steel freezer doors, about the right size to slide a body bag into them. The unpleasant odor of old disinfectant lingered. In the middle of the tile floor was a drain.

"They mostly do rabies testing and other exams here," Fuentes explained. "But this . . . this is different. Here, you might want these." Fuentes offered latex gloves and a surgical mask from a drawer by the freezer. Because she didn't want to expose her own leather gloves to whatever was about to happen, Joann traded them out for the latex and tied on the mask.

The ranger opened the locker, slid out a tray, and stood back.

Lying on the tray was the body of a dog. At least Joann thought it was a dog, some kind of black lab mix. Really, though, it was only the skin of the dog, deflated, as if its skeleton and innards had been sucked out, its eye sockets exploded. If she'd seen a picture of it she might have thought it was rubber, some kind of prop or joke, which was likely why Fuentes brought her here to see it in person. She never would have believed it otherwise.

Wincing, Joann dared to touch it, to prod at a limp paw and lift a fold of structureless skin. A dead dog, she could touch all she wanted and not worry about draining its energy.

"We've found bodies like this in Battery Park as well as a number of other locations along the shore, dozens of them," Fuentes explained. "Almost every day for six weeks now, we've found these . . . these skins. And nobody can tell me if it's dangerous. Parks and rec doesn't want to investigate—but somebody has to, right? Animal control's never seen anything like it."

"Are there any puncture wounds? Any kind of mark from a weapon?" Joann searched, lifting up limbs, cringing at the unnatural way the skin drooped and folded.

"Nothing. It's like their insides just vanished." Fuentes opened other drawers, drew out other trays. All of them held deflated bodies of common city creatures. Dogs, cats, a couple of squirrels.

"Is that a raccoon?" Joann asked of a round, whiskered lump of fur. The distinctive striped tail was the only part she recognized.

"Yes," Fuentes said. "Just about everything that walks on four legs in the city has been killed like this."

"And you think it's wild-card related," Joann said, unable to mask her skepticism.

"What else could it be? It's just so . . . *weird*."

That was the problem. With the wild card on hand to explain anything remotely *weird,* anything the least bit out of the ordinary was instantly some crazy ace or joker on the loose. Joann wasn't convinced.

"You've checked for diseases? Maybe some kind of predator?"

Clearly frustrated, Fuentes sighed, planting a hand on her hip. "We've been over everything. The pathologist has done tests on all the bodies. None of them has wounds. And because it's just a bunch of animals, nobody higher up the chain will do anything about it. The police have their hands full with a million other problems. I can't even get the CDC to look at the case. You—you're the first person who's taken this even a little seriously. *Something's* happening on the south end of Manhattan, and I—I don't know what else to do."

And Lady Black, Joann Jefferson, was the savior of last resort. Assuming she could actually save anything. That there was even anyone to save. She frowned at the sad collection of evidence Fuentes had presented her, a dozen desiccated, barely recognizable lumps of fur. Individually, they didn't even rate as tragedies. Just one of millions of small victims in the city. All of them together? Yes, there was a mystery. Joann just wasn't sure she was qualified to figure it out.

"Right. Where was the most recent one of these found?"

♠

After even just half an hour in the freezer at the animal control office, Joann wanted a shower, and something to get that musty, rotten-fur smell out of her nose. Instead, she was back in the car with Fuentes, navigating noon traffic.

"All the bodies were found in the morning?" she asked. "This is happening at night?"

"Yes," Fuentes said. "From the very southern end of Battery Park all the way up to Jokertown. All on the shore. It's a pattern, but I can't figure out what it means."

"And there haven't been any human corpses?"

"No."

Obviously not. If boneless human corpses started turning up this would get kicked way above her pay grade. Examiners hadn't found any pathogen. The bodies turned up at random. Joann would say they'd been hunted. That something along this stretch was hunting, at night. Some kind of predator. But what predator killed and left unmarred skin behind?

They stopped at a stretch of riverside warehouses and piers, at the edge of a greenway bounded by trees. Moving north was parkland, with baseball fields and jogging paths. Fuentes was right to be worried about the people who frequented the area. They were near residential neighborhoods. A lot of kids around here. This was the southern edge of Jokertown.

Joann scanned the area, formulating a plan. This was okay. She could handle this. If something—whatever it was—was out here hunting, she could find it.

"I'll look around and get back to you with what I find."

"Just like that?" Fuentes asked. "By yourself?"

Joann lifted her chin and smiled. "I told you I'd help and I will. Trust me."

◆

Joann returned to the spot after midnight. Most of the city showed no sign of resting, but here, a bubble of calm created its own reality, separate from one of the largest cities on earth. Along the park, the trees seemed sparse, but they absorbed sound, blocked the usual city racket. The lawn muffled her steps. Even this small pocket of nature felt self-contained. The quiet extended to the warehouse area, the pavement and handful of piers along the river. She could hear the sound of water lapping, a gentle splashing against wood and concrete that was almost soothing. Distant orange streetlight cast it all in a dull glow.

Her cloak disguised her. She pulled it close, edging back her hood to increase her field of vision. Listened. A muttering voice drifted from under a tree. A figure bundled in a coat pulled a child's wagon, piled high with belongings, down a sidewalk. A collection of homeless people, settling in for the night. Joann wondered if any of them had seen anything, if they'd even been interviewed about what was happening. Maybe one of them would talk to her.

She walked, keeping watch, listening for the footfalls and scratching of the animals that were this killer's victims. Ha, a highly trained and motivated government agent, and she was tracking down stray dogs on the Lower East Side. Maybe Cyclone was right.

A series of streetlights lined the water, but most were broken or burned out. Some lights on a distant pier offered the only scrap of illumination, orange spots rippling on the ink-black water of the East River. Several hours passed, and nothing happened. A couple of cats got into a terrible hissing match, swatting at each other and screaming until one fled across the empty street and into an alley. The victor stayed with its back arched, watching the retreat, until stalking off with a flagpole-straight tail back to shadows. Nothing attacked the cats. Nothing even seemed to be out and about watching, like she was.

Sunrise over the river was lovely. The first silvery light faded to a pale orange then gray, coming on so slowly she didn't notice when the sun finally rose, painting drops of gold across the water.

She'd do this one more night, and if she didn't find anything she'd suggest to Fuentes that she either increase the security presence in the area or install some kind of security camera system. Though she suspected Fuentes would tell her they didn't have the budget for it. In the end, if it was only cats and dogs getting killed, no one would make this a priority. But Joann understood the concern: Was it only a matter of time before a horrific, deflated human skin was discovered?

She caught a cab back to her hotel. The driver didn't talk but kept looking at her in the rearview mirror, and gripped the steering wheel more tightly than he was probably used to. Joann wasn't telepathic but she could guess what he was thinking: was she an ace or some crazy person just trying to look like one? Was she going to cause trouble, and if so how bad was it going to be? She told him to keep the change, handing over cash and making sure their hands didn't touch. The guy didn't even suggest that a woman shouldn't be walking alone at the crack of dawn.

♥

The next night went pretty much like the one before, right down to the same voice muttering under the same set of branches as a street person settled in for the night. She walked a different route, trekking farther among the docks along the river, away from the park, keeping her eyes open for critters—or their corpses. She found a dead rat, but the bite marks and blood covering it were no mystery.

She was about to turn around, head back to the park, and end her patrol when something splashed in the water off a nearby pier. Her mind spun off possible scenarios: A person or animal had fallen in from the concrete wall, or had climbed out from the harbor. Giant fish? Fabled sewer alligator? Joann had heard stories of a were-alligator ace living in Manhattan's sewers, but had never gotten confirmation. She crouched, kept to the shadows, and watched, because the splashing wasn't over, one disturbance and done. It kept going, the water churning, growing more turbulent. She crept closer to the edge, trying to get a better look. A phosphorescence appeared under the water, coming closer until it broke the surface, a final burst churning around it, and what emerged was the strangest joker Joann had ever seen.

The body was a sphere, translucent. She could only tell it was a body at all by the small, squashed face perched on the top. White-skinned, human eyes and mouth set in a workmanlike expression. The body was a rubbery membrane bulging out some eight feet across. It resembled a stomach, and Joann's own gut lurched thinking that if she looked closely, she might see something unpleasant digesting inside it.

Skimming forward on the water's surface, propelled by what appeared to be hundreds of cilia, the joker reached the shore, docking there like a ship. A whispered voice sounded ahead, and footsteps padded on the sidewalk. A pair of figures, hunched over and glancing furtively around them, scurried toward the floating joker.

Joann kept her dark cloak around her and remained still, watching, spying.

The two newcomers were jokers as well, more conventionally disfigured, if one could use those words together. They were human-shaped, but moved strangely. In the dark, Joann couldn't tell exactly what they looked like. One of the pair had paper grocery bags, stuffed full, cradled in each arm. After a whispered conference, this one handed the bags over to the floating globe. Well, sort of handed them over. Joann couldn't think of how else to put it, as the person pressed the bag against the membrane of the body—and it went *through*. Like seeing the action of a cell wall magnified. Then the two jokers followed, each of them putting their hands against the body, then pushing until the skin—was it skin or something else?—parted to let them through, then immediately sealed shut behind them.

Right then, another person charged down the street, straight for the pier. "Don't go! Take me with you! Please, take me with you!" A young white kid, scrawny, with stringy hair and a couple days' worth of thin beard, he was wearing a dingy green army jacket two sizes too big, torn jeans, and falling-apart sneakers.

She could still see the joker's passengers through the translucent flesh. They reacted to this newcomer, looking back at him, up at the joker's face, out at the water. Anxious, like crooks in a getaway car. The joker himself had settled in the river a little with the extra weight. As soon as the skin had sealed, the cilia below whirled into action, and the joker drifted away from the shore.

"Back off!" the joker muttered as the gap between them and the dock widened. The passengers within settled, clearly relieved.

For a moment, the scrawny kid looked like he might jump at the joker, a last-ditch effort to catch the ride. The joker's odd face showed expression—lips scrunched in anger, eyes glaring. The kid wasn't welcome, and Joann imagined if he jumped, trying to stow away, he'd just slide off that weird bulbous body and end up in the East River.

But he didn't jump. He collapsed at the edge of the pier, crying. Twenty or so feet out, the joker sank under the surface, leaving behind a faint glow that was swallowed by the water.

"Please!" the kid begged one more time, pleading at the last glowing ripple.

Eventually he stumbled unsteadily to his feet, wiped his face with a corner of his jacket, and trudged back the way he'd come.

Based on the way the kid had beelined for the pier, and the joker's reaction, Joann guessed this wasn't the first time this scene had played out.

This was certainly a mystery, but not the one she'd come to solve. She'd ask around. Maybe the police knew what was going on here. She'd read what little she could find on what was happening out at Ellis Island and surrounding areas. It was hard learning anything cohesive at all. A few reporters had written stories that ended up on page ten or so of the *Times,* a few police reports had been issued, a couple more from the Coast Guard. None of the various agencies seemed to have talked to one another. Jurisdiction wasn't clear cut, and everyone seemed to be hoping someone else would take the lead, make a decision. Was this strange interaction connected to all that?

No wonder Fuentes couldn't get anyone to look into this problem of dead vermin. Far too much was happening here. And this all seemed like exactly the thing SCARE ought to be investigating. Not that she'd be able to convince Carlyle of that.

Officially, as far as Joann knew, the strange submersible joker and its passengers weren't breaking any laws. Trespassing, maybe. Loitering after dark? Should the floating joker be required to have a boating license? A taxi license, for carrying passengers? She might pass along those angles to someone looking for some leverage. In the meantime, right now, she didn't see anything for her to do. Make a note, pass it along—

The aquatic joker was long gone and Joann was on her way back to the park and to some more populated area where she could find a cab when a scream echoed. She froze. Pulled back her hood to hear better. In a second, the sound registered—it wasn't a human scream that echoed off the water and in her ears. That was a cat, a high-pitched yowl, instantly cut off.

The sound had come from the edge of trees separating the park from the piers and warehouses, and she ran. This was what she'd been searching for.

Anyone might disregard the scream as a couple of stray cats having it out. But instead of more hissing and yowling, the pattering of fleeing paws, what she heard next was an incongruous slurping. Low, wet—disturbing. She approached carefully, not wanting to startle whatever was hiding there. If she could just *see*—

She found him. The scrawny kid from the edge of the water, only now he held the limp body of a cat to his face and seemed to be devouring it, vampirelike. He wasn't biting, wasn't chewing. But the fur and skin deflated as the animal's insides somehow vanished. And the kid looked for all the world like he was trying to get the last bit of soda out with a straw. Without leaving a wound on it, he was sucking the innards, bones and guts and all, out of the cat.

Well, that was a mystery solved. Sort of.

He dropped the animal and tilted his head back, his eyes half-lidded, as if he was drunk. He must have had some kind of power to gain sustenance by absorbing his prey, via some kind of osmosis. Was it compulsory? Was he driven to this, or was it a choice? The best way she knew to find out was to ask.

"Hey," she said softly, and his eyes went round, and his whole body tensed to run. She expected this and quickly added, "It's okay, I just want to talk. You're not in trouble."

She also expected that he wouldn't listen to this, and he tore through branches and kicked up dirt, fleeing her. She'd already pulled off her glove, and reached out to grab him. All she needed was a foot.

She thought this was going to be an easy catch, that he'd be weak, wobbly, like he was at the pier. A street kid who must have been starving, he had so little meat on him. But she miscalculated—he'd just fed, and whatever he'd done to that cat was how he got his strength. Now, he was powerful. He kicked away from her and ran fast, through the trees and into the park.

She gave chase. She didn't need to catch him, not really. All she had to do was touch him.

The layout of the park hemmed him in. He didn't have a straight path to the street, where he could vanish into nighttime traffic. He sprinted across the lawn, looking for a sidewalk, a way out. Putting on a burst of speed, she lunged at him, slapped her hand against his back—*pulled*. A spark of power surged up her arm, and her body reached out for more, waiting to suck it all in, down to the last bit. She yanked back and wrapped her cloak around her, insulating herself. She hoped she hadn't taken too much. This was a balancing act. She didn't like using her power like this. If she touched

someone, if she guessed wrong about how hard to grip and when to
let go—well, she'd just have to be right.

The kid cried out, stumbled. Kept going a couple more steps,
then fell to his knees, gasping for breath. "What . . . what . . ."

"I did that," she said, crouching to his level. "I can do more."

"What— Who—"

"I just want to ask you a few questions. Is that okay?"

"What did you do to me?" He moved slowly, like an old man.

"I took away some of your energy. That's what I do."

He sat back on his ass and started crying. Sloppy, wet, snot dripping out of his nose. His hands hung in the air like he didn't know
what to do with them, like he didn't have enough energy left to
wipe his own face.

"I'm sorry!" he sobbed, once he was able to finally make words.
"I can't help it, I don't want to do it, I try not to do it, but I . . . I
can't stop, I have to do it, nothing else works, I can't keep anything down—"

"Whoa, slow down. What's the matter? What do you mean, you
can't stop?"

"I can't eat real food! I can only . . . I can only do *that*! You saw!"

"That's how you eat? You have to eat like that?"

"I try to stop and I *can't*!"

She could piece together his story: kid turned his card, and it
did something to him. Nothing visible at first, but in fact his whole
digestive system had been rewired. Instead of eating food, he now
had to feed on live prey, as some kind of vampire of internal organs and skeletons. No doubt there was some kind of fascinating
physiological explanation, like cellular osmosis. But a thing like
that was enough to ruin a life. He was kicked out of the house,
maybe he ran away. He was trying to make do, and failing. He looked
to be maybe sixteen, seventeen, and he seemed to be in the process
of hitting bottom. Stuck on the edges of the city, feeding off strays
and rodents.

"Have you asked anyone for help?" she asked. "Have you been to the Jokertown Clinic? They specialize in cases like yours."

"Why . . . why would they help me?"

"Because that's what they do. You should go see them. Explain what's been happening. It's just up the road."

"So . . . you're not here to . . . arrest me? Or something?"

Or something. Joann wondered what he'd been expecting, really. After she swooped in on him like some ace avenger? Of course the kid was freaked out.

"No, I just wanted to figure out what was happening to the stray animals around here. And now I did. You've been freaking out the park rangers."

The kid actually laughed a little, an exhausted, stuttering noise. "I didn't mean to make trouble. I just didn't know what to do."

"Do you want me to call the clinic for you? Or take you over there?"

He turned his gaze to her, wide-eyed and pleading. "Would you really do that?"

"Yes. Come on." The conventional, socially polite thing to do would be to reach out and help him up. Instead, she stepped back, giving him room. Because she couldn't reach out, not physically. He seemed confused a moment, waiting a beat for that hand he could grab. Slowly, he managed it on his own. "What's your name?" she asked.

"V-Vlad."

Skeptical, she asked, "Really?"

He shook his head. "That's what everyone calls me."

"Everyone who?"

"Street people. Jokers. Stuff."

"Okay. Vlad. People call me Lady Black. Or Joann, if you'd like. Tell me one more thing: What happened at the water? That joker who looks like a bubble—"

The kid shut down. His expression went tight, like a switch had been flipped. He wasn't supposed to talk about this. This was dark stuff, and he was in on it. Or wanted to be. Joann changed her tack. She wished she had a way of appearing less scary. Hard to do, with the cloak and hood. Well, she always did like a challenge.

"Hey, it's okay. I already said you're not in trouble. I'm just trying to understand." She hoped she sounded soothing. Maternal, even. No idea if she pulled it off. "Let's take a walk to the clinic, and we don't have to talk about anything anymore."

That last was to keep him from charging off, and it worked. He scuffed his feet, but he stayed, arms tightly crossed, folded in on himself. Joann picked a jogging trail that led out of the park, found a sidewalk—one lit with streetlamps, even—and gestured Vlad to come with her. For a time, they traveled in silence. A nice evening stroll. She glanced at him a time or two, but he stayed with her. Looked less and less like he was going to bolt.

Vlad finally spoke. "That's Charon. He takes people to the Rox—"

"That's Ellis Island, right?"

He shook his head adamantly. "Not anymore. Now it's the Rox."

"And Charon takes people there."

"You can't get in without him. But . . . but . . . he won't take me! Because I'm not . . . I'm not a joker. He says I'm not. But I am! At least, I feel like one."

Her heart sank a little because she knew exactly what he was talking about. She couldn't make physical contact with another living being. She was forever isolated behind her cloak, trapped by her power. Wasn't that a kind of deformity? Just like having a completely altered digestive system? Even if it wasn't visible on the outside.

Vlad scrubbed his face again, wiping tears before they started, and scowled. "I just want to go with them. They won't take me! I can't go. I don't belong."

He wasn't a joker. Not physically. He didn't look like he belonged. So they left him on the shore. Rejected by the rejected.

♣

Vlad looked even more scrawny and forlorn under the bright lights outside the clinic's emergency entrance. Washed out, his face was tense. They both stood for a moment, wincing against the stark contrast to the nighttime world. Joann felt the energy of it tingle across her skin, and drew her cloak more tightly around her, insulating herself.

"Ready for this?" she asked him.

"No. But I guess we've come this far."

The emergency department was spare, clinical. Rows of plastic chairs, a small front desk. Doors leading to other parts of the hospital. Joann—Lady Black—drew attention. Those nearby turned and stared, and their movement attracted others, until the whole room paused to look. She wasn't so famous that most people would instantly recognize her—not like Peregrine or Cyclone or Jack Braun. But she was clearly *someone*. She ignored them all and drew Vlad to the front desk. He was cringing under all the stares.

She had spent much of the walk figuring out how she was going to explain this—not sure Vlad would be up for telling his own story—but was saved when a short, urgent, and strikingly red-haired man came through the nearby doorway. Dr. Tachyon looked up, his expression brightening.

"Lady Black! How lovely it is to see you, how are you these days?"

She and Dr. Tachyon had met during the World Health Organization tour a year or so back. A lot had happened since then. *A lot.* Her gaze drifted to his right hand—prosthetic now. His natural one had been destroyed by the same attacker who gutted Billy Ray. It was good to see the man on his feet and working.

"I didn't expect to find you on duty, Doctor," Joann said.

He made one of his expansive movements, arms raised, his good hand lifted, imploring the heavens. "This is the only place I feel useful. Can't sleep, might as well work."

This hadn't been his first all-nighter recently, judging by the shadows under his eyes.

"Take care of yourself. This place needs you."

"Sometimes I wonder," he muttered. "Well, what have you brought us?"

"Doctor, meet Vlad. He's . . . well. He's an interesting case."

"Oh?" Tachyon's sudden focus was wholly professional and intensely curious. Somehow, Vlad cringed even more tightly into himself.

"It's okay," Joann murmured. "You can trust him."

Meeting Tachyon was a stroke of luck. His interest piqued, they got into an exam room right away, no waiting, and Joann lingered nearby while Vlad explained, haltingly, anxiously, about his feeding his urges. Tachyon produced a stethoscope and patiently asked to examine the kid, who nodded furtively. For all his faults and foibles, Tachyon was a good doctor, and he was able to draw Vlad out.

"I'd like to get some X-rays, if you're amenable," he asked, and Vlad nodded, a bit more openly this time. "Will you excuse us for just a moment?"

The doctor nodded at Joann, and they stepped into the corridor.

"Well?" she asked.

"I've no idea what the virus did to him. Just when I think I've seen everything, all the horrors—" He shook his head. "There are legal issues as well. He isn't eighteen, is he? Any idea where is parents are?"

"No, I just met him a couple hours ago. I wanted to get him here before the police picked him up."

"Ah. Yes."

"I don't know what can be done for him. But you guys have counselors, social workers, some insight into this sort of thing. Maybe you can help him settle in a little better."

Tachyon blew a breath out. "I don't know how much we can really do. But we'll try."

"Thank you."

"You have but to call."

♠

Joann felt like she'd actually done some good. Maybe helped one person, solved a problem for another. Cyclone would have said it wasn't flashy enough. Wouldn't make the front page. He'd be writing up a press release and trying to spin it as some great ace victory. Yeah, right, sneaking around in the middle of the night, making sure stray cats weren't killed and some wild-card kid didn't get ground up on the streets. Real flashy. But she was happy with the night's work.

Back at her hotel, she managed a few hours of sleep, and stopped by Federal Hall to see Maria Fuentes around lunchtime. She was working at her desk, the paperwork in a different configuration than it had been the day before. It hadn't seemed to decrease at all.

"I don't think you'll have any more problems with dead animals," she said, after greeting her.

"You found what was happening?" Fuentes asked, standing from her desk, her expression alight. "You stopped it?"

"I think so."

"So what was it?"

She didn't want Vlad to face charges. Kid had enough to worry about. "Will you just trust me when I say it's taken care of?"

"You're the only one who believed that anything was even wrong. If you tell me it's over, and it won't happen again—well, that's the end of it." Her smile was so earnest. "Thank you, Agent Jefferson."

"Call me Joann."

"All right, I will. And I'm not sure there's anything I could ever do for you all over at SCARE, but—"

"I'll call, definitely," Joann said.

◆

She took the train back to DC that evening, happy to be home, settled, and on to the next task. Maybe Cyclone wanted the razzle-dazzle, but Joann would be happy with a record of actually *helping* people, particularly wild-card victims. The way people had been there to help her, when her card turned.

A family story went that right before the Civil War, her great-great-great-grandmother escaped from a plantation in Georgia, was guided to freedom by Harriet Tubman herself, and then went on to help other fugitives by providing food and shelter on their stops heading north. There was almost no way to verify the story, whether Joann's ancestor really had met the famous woman. Escaped slaves changed their names, vanished into new communities. The Underground Railroad didn't exactly keep records. But it was a great story, and her father had delighted in showing Joann storybooks about Tubman and telling her, over and over, "There's what a hero looks like. Heroes help people, and we can all be heroes if we try."

Sometimes, Joann felt like a fool for believing that.

The next morning, just exactly as she was arriving at the SCARE offices, the department secretary held up a slip of paper.

"Agent Jefferson, you just missed a call."

"Oh?" She took the slip, even as Terri explained.

"A park ranger in New York, I think? Marie Fuentes? She wouldn't say what was wrong but she sounded upset."

Frowning, Joann sat at an empty desk and picked up the phone. "Hello, Marie?"

Fuentes's urgent voice answered. "Joann, it's happened again. Another one. Whatever's doing this is back, or there's something else . . . I don't know what to do! I thought you said this was over!"

Joann rubbed her forehead. "Wait. What happened?"

The woman's sigh was tense, frustrated. "Another animal. A ranger found it on morning rounds. Same place. Does that mean there's more than one thing doing this?"

"Not necessarily. At least . . . give me a couple of hours, I'm going to make some calls. I'll come back to New York today if I need to. We'll take care of this, don't worry."

"It's really hard not to." All the woman's relief from the day before had vanished. Whatever trust Joann had earned was gone.

"I know. Hold tight, I'll call you when I have more information. Thanks for letting me know."

She hung up the phone, looked up the number for the Jokertown Clinic—it was in all the SCARE Rolodexes—and called.

"Blythe van Renssaeler Memorial Clinic, how may I direct your call?"

"Is Dr. Tachyon in?"

"I'm sorry, he's not avail—"

"Tell him it's Lady Black. He'll talk to me."

"I'm not sure—"

"Lady Black from the Special Committee on Ace Resources and Endeavors."

A pause followed, and then a cool, "If you'll hold for just a moment, please."

Joann waited. She waited long enough that she was wrangling her next set of arguments and persuasions when the line clicked back on.

"Yes?" came Tachyon's harried, overworked voice.

"Joann Jefferson here. I'm calling about Vlad, I got word he's back on the street?"

He groaned. "Oh, dear. I'm so sorry. What a tragedy, what an awful tragedy."

"Doctor, what happened?"

"I'm sorry, we couldn't hold him. He wouldn't stay."

"Why not?" She didn't mean for her voice to sound so accusatory, but she was losing patience.

"I don't know, why does a frightened teenager ever do anything? He was in a closed room with too many people and he got scared. He wouldn't let us admit him, even though we have programs to pay for treatment for people like him— I don't know, I simply don't."

"You couldn't hold him on some kind of mental health grounds, for his own good?"

"Technically, he's not sick. He's definitely not contagious, and we couldn't keep him on psychiatric grounds. Apart from some depression and anxiety, which frankly are quite to be expected in someone his age who's homeless, he's fine."

"Except that he's homeless and depressed."

"Well, yes. We gave him information for some shelters and youth programs. But, well. He didn't seem interested. He just wanted to leave. We're not a prison here. Well, not usually."

It wasn't that Vlad didn't want to stay there, Joann realized. The kid wanted to go someplace else. When it was clear the clinic couldn't cure him, but merely give him coping strategies, he left. "Because he wanted to go to the Rox," she stated.

"I'm hearing more and more about that place. What is going on there?"

"I'd like to find out."

"Please, if you meet the young man again and can convince him to return—"

"I'll do what I can. Thanks, Doctor."

She hung up, and noticed Terri watching her from across her own desk. "What's that all about?"

Joann smiled grimly. "I guess I'm going back to New York."

♥

She intended to track down Vlad on that stretch of the East River as soon as she could, and talk to him. If he would listen. Convince him that fleeing to the squatters on Ellis Island wasn't the answer. She wasn't quite sure how she was going to do that. She hoped that when he saw her, that he'd understand that she cared. That she wanted to help. Maybe that was naive. Well, she didn't lose anything by trying.

She wasn't expecting to find Maria Fuentes waiting for her, parked in exactly the spot she was when she'd first taken Joann to the area. Well after dark, the woman looked out of place in her neat pantsuit and sensible low-heeled pumps. She didn't even have a sidearm. Did park rangers even carry sidearms?

"Ms. Fuentes," Joann said evenly. "Hello."

"You going to tell me what's going on now? What am I looking for?"

"I think it might be best if you weren't here, at least not for tonight."

"I deserve to know what's happening here. How dangerous is this, really? This is my jurisdiction, my call."

That was debatable. In fact, half a dozen jurisdictions could argue over this corner of land. And depending on the perspective, they'd all be right. "It's my jurisdiction because I was the only one willing to come down here and deal with it. Can you please let me finish what I started?"

"I want to stay. I need to stay and see for myself."

Joann blew out a breath. "Okay. Fine. But be careful."

The sun was setting over Manhattan, and pale orange street-lights, the ones that weren't broken, came on. Fuentes drew out a flashlight, started scanning the trees along the edge of the park.

"Put that away, please," Joann told her.

"Why?"

"Because you'll scare him off. We just need to wait."

Fuentes frowned, skeptical. But she shut off the light. Joann walked the same circuit she had before, to see if anything had changed over the last couple of days. Nothing had. The site still felt forgotten, with lurkers in the shadows. A haven for people who didn't want to be found. All Joann had to do was put herself in the middle of it. Glancing furtively around her, Fuentes stuck close. Too close, really. Joann's skin prickled at her presence.

"You still haven't told me what we're looking for," Fuentes whispered.

"You'll see him soon enough. If he decides to show up."

"Who?"

Truthfully, she wasn't sure which one of the two, Charon or Vlad, she was waiting for. The latter wouldn't reveal himself without the former appearing at the pier. So she had to hope for them both to appear. She had no guarantee that either one would.

"We might be waiting a long time," Joann said, sighing.

♣

Hours passed. Fuentes eventually went back to her car. She was going to try to nap and asked Joann to come wake her if anything happened. The ace had no intention of doing so.

Joann walked her patrol. Her cloak rippled around her as she hugged herself. The night felt damp. The hazy sky, tinged orange by city lights and pollution, didn't offer signs of rain, but the air smelled like incoming weather. If rain started, she'd pack this in and try looking for Vlad another night. He wasn't likely to hurt himself.

Probably wasn't going to hurt anyone else. But she wanted him to get help. He needed help. If he would just let someone help him . . .

The temperature seemed to drop, even as she waited.

And why would Vlad even come back here? Because he was waiting for Charon, the joker ferryman. The last six weeks he'd stalked up and down along the edge of Manhattan, searching for the right place, hunting as he went until he found where Charon docked. He was trying to get to Ellis Island. So Joann waited to intercept him. He wasn't going to leave this spot.

And there, finally. A glow on the water. It might have been something natural, bioluminescent, if it didn't move so steadily, unerringly to the pier. Even knowing what to expect, the weirdness of Charon's shape and movement came as much of a shock as it had before. How was the man even alive? He had to have organs in there somewhere. Then again, maybe not.

She wondered: would the joker talk to her? Would he be able to tell her if he'd seen Vlad? Stepping quietly, she moved closer to the pier, keeping her hood down and cloak close, to help disguise her.

This time, Charon was delivering passengers to the mainland, not picking them up. A couple of kids, about Vlad's age, nested at the bottom of the bubble. As soon as the joker touched land, they squeezed out, hands creating splits in the skin as they pushed through. Like insects breaking out of chrysalises.

Joann stayed back. Didn't interfere. The two kids, punk-looking, with interesting haircuts they might have done themselves without a mirror, and torn-up hand-me-down army surplus clothes and boots, raced off. They didn't see her lurking nearby, ran right past her, on to whatever quest they were bound on.

Before Charon could flee, she approached, pushing back her hood and calling, "Hey, can I talk to you?"

Charon's furtive eyes blinked at her, then looked past her, and

Joann turned to see a hunched, scrawny figure race forward. So intent on the floating joker, he didn't seem to notice Joann at all. He had a mission.

Vlad, his hands grasping in front of him, fingers stiffly bent like claws, stumbled out on the pier. "Let me in. *Let me in.*" The words became a growl.

Charon's eyes went wide, what there was of his head leaning back. The cilia under his body vibrated rapidly—anxiously, even— and the joker drifted back from the pier.

Yelling, Vlad burst into a run and jumped at the joker. Landed on him, meeting Charon's gaze and snarling as his fingers dug into the swollen, translucent skin. But the joker's body didn't split to let him in. Charon splashed in the water, half-rolling and sinking as the cilia struggled to maintain balance.

"Vlad, stop!" Joann dashed onto the pier.

Charon was never going to help him. He seemed to have complete control over who entered his body and who didn't, and he wasn't going to allow Vlad. The kid seemed to know it, too, and he was finished asking. His hands clenched, gripping harder. Charon hissed, maybe in pain, maybe only in annoyance, and started to sink—he could just drown Vlad.

But Vlad opened his mouth and suckered it, lampreylike, to the joker's skin, the rounded slope of what might have been his shoulder, if he had arms. He lunged in, as if he could burrow into the other's body, and his mouth worked, sucking. A physiological change came over him—a protuberance emerging from Vlad's mouth, visible through Charon's translucent skin. Charon groaned, and his eyes rolled back.

Now a crime was being committed. This was assault.

"Vlad, back off!" But the kid was lost in a haze of rage and hunger, his strange power driving him on. He was only focused on his target.

Charon flailed in a panic, which translated to lurching and splashing, as if he were a great fish caught on a line, fighting at the water's surface. Joann had to stop this; she wasn't sure how.

With little time to think, she acted. Lady Black unhooked the collar of her cloak. Swept it off her shoulders, dropped it to the ground. Everywhere, energy surged, reaching toward her. Her nerves crackled with it; her skin glowed. Even yards away, streetlights flickered on and off, going dark. More, she could draw more to her, she could draw all of it. . . .

Rolling, Charon lurched toward the edge of the pier. Vlad's back faced her now. Leaning as far forward as she dared, she reached. She grabbed Vlad. And then her power *reached*. All he was flowed toward her, into her. His back arced in pain; he screamed. But he let go, and she yanked him back to dry land.

Still his energy poured into her. Her skin flushed with power, her blood rushing—she could take in so much more. His body grew cold, his muscles wrenched tight, rigid with shock. She smelled of brimstone.

Head swimming, vertiginous with energy that tingled on her skin—she imagined she could see sparks snapping around her body—she let go. Forced herself to scramble away from him, to break that flow of power. To starve herself of what her own wild card demanded. She was in control, not the virus. Backing off, she found her cloak and swept it around her. Insulated herself, and the power stilled. The flow of energy ceased. She took several slow breaths while the thrumming in her nerves subsided. Her mind cleared.

Now, she was able to look at what she'd done.

Charon had come to rest against the pier. His body slumped over the concrete and even seemed a little deflated. A line of blood dripped from a puckered wound near his head.

"Are you hurt?" Joann approached. "Can I help?"

He looked around, dazed. As he righted himself, he straightened, coming back to full buoyancy, bobbing on the water. In a soft, croaking voice he said, "You need to get out of here. None of this is your business."

"I'm trying to help—"

"Word of advice: don't." Charon scowled at her. The mass of cilia pushed off from the wall, and he sank with the barest churning of water, until he was gone. Leaving her with the other person she'd tried to save.

Vlad lay on the pier. His eyes were shut, he wasn't moving. Joann wanted to touch him. To feel for a pulse, to squeeze his hand or smooth back his hair. She couldn't do any of those things. Her power reached, drawing energy, every scrap of it, wherever it could find it.

It found nothing from Vlad.

She knelt by him, still catching her breath, her mind racing, wondering what else she could have done, what she should have done differently. His mouth hung open slightly. Nothing seemed different about it, nothing to suggest why he had to feed like he did. He seemed perfectly normal. She didn't touch him. She didn't want to touch anything, and so sat quietly, hugging her cloak around her.

"What was that?" a nearby voice cried out in shock. "What did you do?"

Marie Fuentes was at the foot of the pier, on her knees, hands over her mouth, staring in horror. She'd seen the whole thing, and had probably gotten knocked back by some of Joann's power. The whole warehouse area up to the park was dark now, and the water of the river was black, opaque. Nothing reflected off it. The waterfront felt like a cave.

"What are you?" Fuentes demanded again, shrieking.

A killer, Joann thought. She met Fuentes's gaze and said evenly, "I stopped him. That's my power. That's what I do." She stepped forward, intending to confer without raising her voice. To ask Fuentes what should be done about all this. She didn't get very far.

"Get away from me. Don't come near me." Fuentes stumbled to her feet, backed away. Her gaze locked on Joann, unable to look away from the horror she was. Right up until she turned and ran.

So, on top of everything else, Joann wasn't going to be able to ask her for a ride out of there.

♠

Joann didn't have to call the police. As she suspected, Fuentes did it for her, and about twenty minutes after she left, sirens and flashing red and blue lights flooded the street along the pier. Joann was waiting for them, sitting cross-legged, holding her SCARE badge straight up while a dozen flashlights panned over her. There was a lot of shouting, a lot of guns out and pointed at her, which should have made her nervous or angry—or both, reasonably. But all she had to do was push back her hood and she could drop them all.

"Federal agent! Justice Department!" she called tiredly, multiple times, until the cops stopped shouting at her to put her hands up, even though they were already up. Yeah, there was a good chance she might have been shot. But this was wild-card Manhattan and she was wearing a mysterious cape. They finally gave her a break and let her explain.

It looked like the Jokertown precinct had responded to the call. The lead detective, wearing a suit and overcoat, leaning against a squad car and talking into a radio, had a pair of ram's horns spiraling off the sides of his head. The half-dozen officers who'd responded to the call all seemed nonchalant to her eyes. Like, this was Jokertown, they found bodies all the time. Just a street kid. Joann had to work to keep her mouth shut. Eventually, the horned detective—his name badge said "Storgman"—came over and told her this was clearly a case of self-defense. There'd be some paperwork. Likely an autopsy. "Call Dr. Tachyon before you do that autopsy," Joann said. "Or whoever's the pathologist these days over at the

Jokertown Clinic. The kid's a wild-card victim." Storgman made a quick note. His partner shrugged and turned away, and Joann despaired that any of her requests would be heeded.

She called Fuentes a half a dozen times over the next couple of days. Was shunted to an answering machine every single time.

She wrote her own report, making it as detailed and objective as she could. Described how she came to investigate the case, the involvement of the Park Service, her discovery of Vlad and what he was doing. Trying to justify her own use of force against him, but without conviction. She also suggested that the activities of Charon and his passengers, and their link to Ellis Island, should be investigated. Didn't have any confidence that they would be. But at least it was on paper now. Anyone who did decide to investigate—or who wondered why Joann hadn't done more—would have an answer, in black and white, filed in triplicate and made available to the public, per government regulation.

She had become a good bureaucrat, at least.

◆

First thing she saw in the hospital room, even before glancing to the bed to make sure Ray was there and his normal surly self, was the cactus in the terra-cotta pot she'd brought a couple weeks before. The pot had been moved to a windowsill, and the fat spiny plant had shriveled and turned yellow, desiccated to a skeleton of its former self. The flower was a brown, flaking spot at its base. The thing had died, horribly. And she hadn't done it.

"Ray, what did you do to it!"

He looked to where she stared with such horror. "What? Oh. That. I'm not sure. It just . . . it just did that. . . ." His jaw looked almost back to normal, or at least as normal as it was ever going to be, though a puckered welt across his cheek was still healing. Made him look like he was wearing half a mask. His speech sounded clear.

"It's a cactus! How did you murder a cactus?"

"I don't know, okay! I gave it plenty of water—"

Joann managed not to put her hand on her forehead and groan. She invited herself to sit in the chair by the bed. "And how are you feeling today, Agent Ray?"

He was sitting up, dressed in cotton pj's, one leg hanging over the edge, foot tapping the air. "Ready to go back to work. Tell Cyclone you saw me, and that I'm ready to work."

Joann crossed her arms and glared. "How far are you running?"

"I'm . . . I'm running."

"Treadmill? You been outside yet?"

"My abs still aren't quite where they need to be—"

"Billy . . ."

"What are you, my mom?"

She glared, and he scowled, which twisted the scars in a new pattern and made him look particularly mean. But he had a dejected look in his eyes that made staying mad at him impossible.

"One of these days you're going to face something you can't bounce back from. Just . . . take it easy, okay?"

"I am. I will." He sat back, studied her. Actually looked at her, which made her squirm a little.

"What's happened with that thing in New York?" he asked, which surprised her even more. Her hood was up, her face mostly hidden, like always. Something in the slope of her shoulders must have indicated her mood. She hadn't been able to stop thinking about that case.

"I killed someone. Just a kid, really. He needed help, and I tried, but . . ." She shrugged. Crossed her arms. Didn't want to talk about it, but also kind of did.

So she told him the whole story, right up to where she decided to use her power. She realized that she'd known she was probably going to kill him. She did it anyway. And if she had to do it over, she wouldn't change anything. But she still mourned.

She sighed. "He was hurting someone. I'm not sure he even meant to. But . . . I had to stop him."

"Yeah, you did."

"I couldn't think of another way."

"You did what you had to," he said, with a confidence she didn't share.

"I just wish . . . hard to feel like an ace when I can't control my power. When it just *happens*."

"I've noticed a thing," he said. "We don't call ourselves aces, jokers, whatever. It's other people who call us that. They decide, not us. That kid—was he a joker or an ace? I mean, a power like that—he could have made a hell of an assassin—"

"Billy—"

"You know what I mean. Eh, in the end, it doesn't matter. Just what we do with it."

That sounded almost wise.

"What about that other guy?" he asked. "The guy you *did* save?"

"Charon?" She had saved him, she supposed. The guy almost even thanked her for it. In her experience, when underworld types told you to stay the hell out, it meant they sort of liked you.

"Yeah. What's his story?"

She shrugged. "I don't know. He's a ferryman. He's got some kind of connection to Ellis Island."

"And what's going on with *that*?"

"I don't know. But . . . I can't get past the feeling that this is all going to blow up into some giant, bloody mess."

"Well. Just as long as it waits a few more weeks till I'm back on my feet. I'll fix that problem."

He grinned his crooked grin, and she wasn't comforted.

♠ ♥ ♦ ♣

"Nobody's Fool"

by Walton Simons

THE EARLY-DAWN LIGHT FILTERED through the mist over the water. Jerry sat at the powerboat's wheel, trying to figure out how to start it. The gun he'd gotten from the Immaculate Egret was in his pocket. He'd done his best to clean it. It wouldn't do to have it explode in his hand.

David was on Ellis Island, the Rox. Jerry was willing to stake his life on that. He'd head out to the island and gun David down, die a hero's death. There was a note in his apartment explaining everything. He hoped that Beth was the one to find it.

Jerry started the engine. Fumes boiled up from the boat's stern. Jerry cast off the lines and carefully backed out of the slip. He'd rented the boat. No point in buying one, since it was going to be a one-way trip. Once he was clear of the dock, Jerry stopped backing the engines and started moving forward. He spun the wheel and pushed the throttle. The eighteen-foot boat bounced out through the waves toward Ellis Island. Cold spray stung his face. Jerry wished he'd taken some Dramamine. His stomach was in less than great shape. But it usually acted up when he was scared. Still, facing David had to be easier than facing Beth. At least with David he had a chance of winning.

A tug passed by in front of him. Jerry took its wake at high speed and bounced out of his seat. He hit his mouth on the dash and split his lip.

"Shit," he said. "Can't I get anything to go right?" He pointed the nose of the craft toward Ellis Island and pushed the throttle all the way forward.

About a half mile away, his stomach knotted up and he felt his breakfast at the back of his throat. Jerry bent over and put one hand to his mouth. His brain flashed sparks. The sky above seemed to change color, from blue to green to purple. Jerry felt like iron hammers were pounding his flesh. He felt a cold spasm in his gut and fell over, the wheel spinning out of his grasp. White noise hissed in his ears. He stretched his arm out toward the throttle and pulled it back, then blacked out.

There was a harbor patrol boat next to his when he came to. A man in a yellow poncho was chafing his wrists. Jerry sat up slowly, his ears ringing.

"You all right?" the man in the poncho asked.

"I've been better, but I'll live." Jerry slowly sat up and looked over his shoulder. He'd drifted away from Ellis Island.

"You were headed to Ellis? That place is a rat's nest now." The man shook his head. "Are you crazy?"

"No. Just enthusiastic." If the man caught his reference to *King Kong,* he didn't comment on it.

"Want a tow back in?"

"Yeah, thanks," Jerry said. "If you don't mind."

This had obviously been a bad idea, but hindsight was always twenty/twenty.

♥

Jerry's instincts told him to stake out Latham's penthouse. There was no particular logic to it, but a good detective always trusted his guts. At least, that was what he'd read and seen in the movies. For once, he'd been right.

A car pulled up right before midnight and a young man got out. Jerry recognized him in an instant. David had an arrogance to his walk that didn't change even when he was being hunted. Latham met him at the door. They hugged, and then St. John talked while David listened and nodded. The conversation was brief. Jerry couldn't be sure, but he thought they actually kissed lightly before David trotted back down the steps to the car.

Jerry tailed David to Central Park. He knew it was dangerous to walk in the park at night. Even back before he'd turned into a giant ape, that was a bad idea. David was about twenty yards ahead of him and walking fast.

On the other side of a wooded hill was the Central Park Zoo, where he'd been the feature attraction for over twenty years. Maybe as a giant ape he'd have been able to take David with no trouble. As it was, he'd have to rely on his ability with his stolen gun and a little luck.

A cool wind stirred the hair on the back of his neck, tickling it. He'd made himself look tough by giving his facial disguise a few scars. Jerry knew he could die doing this, but at this point there just wasn't anything else in his life. If he could cash it in trying to make a positive difference in the world, maybe people wouldn't remember him too badly. Beth, especially.

David stepped off the path and up into the trees. Jerry walked forward slowly, staring at the shadows for some hint of movement. When he reached the point where David had disappeared, Jerry paused, then moved quietly into the trees. He headed off the path at a right angle, putting his feet down carefully to avoid making much noise. An empty beer can glinted in the moonlight not far ahead. Jerry took a few more steps and found himself at the edge of a tiny clearing. He reached inside his coat to make sure the gun was still there. An arm caught him from behind and pushed hard against his windpipe, and he felt a forearm against the back of his neck, Jerry felt a hand yank the gun from his shoulder holster. He sucked hard at the air, but hardly any made it to his lungs.

"What have we here?" David asked, stepping into view. Jerry recognized him by his voice. There wasn't much light to see by, and his vision was blurring.

Jerry tried to gasp out an answer, but could only manage a choked hiss.

"Let's sink him in the pond," a young female voice said.

"That may not be necessary, Molly," David said. He leaned in close to Jerry. "We're going to let you go for a second and you're going to tell me why you were following me." David held up the gun. "With this, no less."

The arms came loose from either side of Jerry's neck and he fell to his knees, gasping. A simple lie would probably be best. Not that it would matter. "I . . . just wanted your . . . money."

Several of the kids laughed. David shook his head. "You were going to rob me? What a piece of shit you are. You have no idea who you're dealing with, little man." David's voice was cold, yet he looked strangely beautiful in the pale light. Jerry figured it was the last face he'd ever see.

"Do him," said a husky female voice from behind. "I'll snap his neck if you don't want it to look suspicious."

A long, quiet moment passed. "I think not," David said. "He truly is beneath us, and I can't see much entertainment value." David grabbed Jerry's face. "Look at me, thief. Remember my face. I'm going to be famous soon. People everywhere are going to be afraid of me. It's only your insignificance which saved you. Find a hole and pull if in after you. If any of us ever sees you again, you're dead. Understand?"

Jerry nodded. He felt sick. Maybe they were just setting him up and were going to kill him anyway.

David popped the clip from Jerry's gun and tossed it into the trees, then smashed the handle of the gun into Jerry's head. Jerry collapsed to the ground, his forehead banging with pain.

"Here's your gun back, thief," David said.

Jerry felt it land on his back. He heard David and the others make their way off through the brush. He lay there panting for a moment, then wobbled into a sitting position and pulled a leaf from his mouth. He'd almost died. Could have. Maybe should have. All of a sudden the hero's death had lost its appeal. He picked up and holstered the gun. He staggered in the opposite direction David and his friends had taken. If his life were a movie, it would need a serious rewrite.

Sixteen Candles

by Stephen Leigh

THREE BLOCKS AWAY FROM the Dime Museum, the clock tower of the Church of Christ the Joker tolled midnight.

"Happy birthday to us, happy birthday to us. Happy birthday, dear Oddity, happy birthday to us."

The voice was off-key and cracked. "Look at the present I brought us," it said.

A fencing mask lent a shimmering distance to the heavy .38 cupped in Oddity's hand. Flecks of reflected light from the Jetboy diorama ran along the barrel and glimmered wildly from the mask's steel mesh. The interference shattered the harsh brilliance like a cheap spectroscope into pale, weak colors.

Evan could look at the gun and pretend the weapon was just a fantasy, something seen on television. He could almost imagine someone else was lifting it.

[Sixteen years. Sixteen years of pain in this monstrosity of a body,] Evan said in his interior voice.

[Evan, please don't do this.] Patty's voice. She was Sub-Dominant at the moment, Oddity's eternal pain dampened slightly for her. [I'm asking you to please just let it go. I'll take Oddity for you until John's ready. You can be Passive and rest.]

Evan ignored her. Far below, she could hear John—the third of the trio of personalities who were Oddity. John was Passive at the moment, down in the depths of the strangely-woven mind where Oddity's agony was a faint tidal wash. The passive personality could hear but couldn't intrude. Passive could open the torrent of his thoughts to the others or shield them; the others could listen or not as they wished. The fact that John made no effort to conceal his feelings now spoke more than the thoughts themselves.

[. . . goddamn asshole can't stand the pain like me no courage at all fucking artistic sensibilities Patty may like it but I'm damned tired of the complaining it hurts all of us not just him can't he see the power we wield . . .]

[No, John,] Evan sent down to him. [I don't see power, and I don't care. I want to be alone. Alone. I love you both, but being locked in here—]

Evan stopped. Oddity was sobbing with the emotional under-currents. Evan raised Oddity's left hand. It was mostly John's, though past the lumpy interface the little finger looked to be Patty's and the thumb had Evan's coffee-and-cream coloring. The hand resisted him—Patty, trying to shove him from Dominant and take the body. Evan concentrated his will. The hand came up and slipped back the heavy cowl of Oddity's hood. As Oddity moaned, the fin-gers curled painfully with tendons crossed and overstretched, and lifted off the fencing mask.

The feathery touch of air-conditioning on Oddity's cheeks hurt, like everything else. The chill felt like ice water on a broken tooth. Without the mask, the gun in Oddity's other hand was very present, sinister and compelling all at once. It smelled of oil and cordite and violence.

Three hours past closing, the Jokertown Dime Museum was silent except in Oddity's head, and dark except in front of the Jet-boy diorama, pinned in bright Fresnels with colored gels. Jetboy was caught in midstruggle. Evan had done most of the waxwork sculpture for that exhibit, working in those few hours when he was

Dominant and both hands were mostly his own. Though Patty and John insisted it was all psychological, Evan couldn't work with Patty's hands or John's. They didn't have the touch.

Rare moments, those, when Evan could almost ignore Oddity's slow, continuous transformation as bits and pieces of their three merged bodies came and went, when he could almost believe he was one person again.

[Alone,] Patty echoed sympathetically. [I know, Evan. We'd all like that, but it can't be.]

Evan opened Oddity's mouth. The lips were thin and harsh: John's. Evan placed the barrel of the .38 there and closed John's mouth around it. The burnished metal was a sharp tang against the tongue.

Evan wondered what it would feel like to pull the trigger.

"Oddity—Evan . . ."

The voice was soft and came from behind Oddity. Evan ignored it and struggled to curl Oddity's finger around the forefinger. It wouldn't require but a fraction of Oddity's enhanced strength. Just the smallest tithe of it. Just the tiniest movement and Evan could find oblivion. Solitude.

[Evan, I love you. No matter what, remember that. I love you; John loves you, too.]

"Evan, I think that's my gun you have. I bought it for protection, not this."

[. . . can't even pull the trigger, can't even do the one thing he really wants to do . . .]

Evan gave a heaving inner sob. Oddity's mouth opened. The hand holding the gun dropped to the side of the massive body.

Oddity turned to face Charles Dutton, who stood in the archway of the Jetboy room. Evan knew what the joker was seeing: the melted-wax cheeks, the patchwork, lumpy face that was part Evan, part Patty, part John. The skin would be moving like a veil of cheesecloth laid over a mass of seething maggots. The face would be changing even as he watched, features collapsing and melting back into the pasty sagging flesh. The only unity to it at all would be that each and every one of those mismatched, overlaid parts would be twisted and taut with the torture of the slow, restless transformation.

Dutton didn't even blink. But then Dutton had to face his own living death's-head face in the mirror every single day.

"Dutton," Oddity grated out. Even the voice was harsh and shattered, like some B-movie creature. "It just hurts so much . . ."

Evan could feel moisture on the ruined cheeks. The left hand (Patty's entirely, now), came up and brushed at it.

"I know it does," the owner of the Dime Museum said. "I know and I sympathize. But I don't think you really believe this is the way. May I have my weapon back, please." The cadaverous joker held out his hand.

Oddity looked at the gun once more. Evan hesitated, playing with the control of the shifting, powerful muscles. He could still bring the gun up, place the muzzle against Oddity's horrific, deformed temple, and do it. He could.

Patty tried to force him to give the gun to Dutton. Evan continued to hold it, though it remained at Oddity's side. Dutton shrugged.

"I saw the Atlanta diorama this evening," he said. "It's excellent work, especially what you did with the Hartmann figure. I like the hands even more than the face, the way the fingers grip the podium even though Hartmann's ignoring the carnage behind him. They lend a tension to the entire scene."

The hand that was Patty's twitched involuntarily. An elbow tore from Oddity's chest, ripping muscles and prodding the front of the cloak before subsiding again. "They broke him," Oddity's grating, slow voice declared. "They conspired against him. It wasn't the senator's fault. He wanted to help. He cared, he was just . . . fragile, and they knew it. They did what they had to do to break him."

"Who, Evan?"

"I don't *know!*" Oddity's muscular arm swung wide. Dutton took a half step backward. A blow from that hand could kill. "Barnett, maybe. That Judas Tachyon, certainly. Maybe some conspiracy of the right-wing joker haters. I don't know. But they brought the senator down."

The gun beat against Oddity's thigh again. Dutton watched it. "There's nothing but pain, Dutton," Evan continued. "Every damn joker's life is nothing but unrelieved, bitter blackness. Jokertown bleeds and there's nothing and no one to bind the wounds. I—we—hate it."

"You're one of the few who have done any good, Evan—you and Patty and John."

Oddity gave a short, ironic laugh. "Yeah. We've done a *lot* of good." The weapon's barrel glinted as Oddity started to bring it up again, then let it drop once more.

"Is this what Patty wants, or John?"

Oddity snorted. A glob of mucus spat from one nostril onto its cheek. "John's a martyr. He's almost delighted that Oddity suffers, since it makes us such a fucking noble figure. And Patty"—Oddity's voice softened, and the mouth almost seemed to smile for a moment—"Patty holds on to hope. Maybe Tachyon will find a cure in between his sabotage of the jokers he claims to love. Maybe the virus will go into remission. Maybe there'll be another secondary outbreak like Croyd's to pull us apart again."

Oddity seemed to laugh, but there was no amusement in the sound at all. The gun beat against the heavy cloth of Oddity's thigh.

"It's all bullshit, Dutton. You know what the trouble is? There aren't any happy endings in Jokertown. No happy endings at all."

Oddity shuddered. The huge, misshapen figure brought the cowl up over the face before bending down to retrieve the fencing mask. Oddity placed the mask over its face and stared at the Jetboy diorama.

"It all started here. The hero's supposed to *win*. What a shame. What a horrible, awful shame."

Oddity seemed to notice the gun once more. The hand came up, held the weapon before the fencing mask. "I didn't finish Hartmann's figure," Evan said.

"He can wait. I've been contacted by a source who claims to have Carnifex's actual fighting suit from that night. If I can buy it . . ." Dutton shrugged.

"You're ghoulish, Dutton."

Dutton almost smiled. "So is the public."

"A ghoul *and* a cynic," Oddity said, and its voice was higher and less raspy.

The hand holding the gun trembled, then reversed its grip. "Charles . . ."

Dutton reached with a thin, bony hand and placed the gun in his suit pocket.

"Thanks, Patty," he said. "Where's Evan?"

"Passive," Oddity replied. "We'll keep him down there for a few days if we can. He's tired, Charles, very tired." Shapes humped along Oddity's back and a soft moan came from behind the mask. Then Oddity sighed. "All of us are tired. But thank you for listening and for helping."

"I didn't want to lose my artist."

Oddity gave a dry, rasping chuckle. "I know better. And I think it's time to go. Evan probably won't be back for a while."

Shadows flowed over the black cloak as Oddity turned to leave. "Patty?"

Steel mesh glinted; the head looked back to Dutton but they didn't speak. Oddity lurched heavily away. Dutton watched until she/it/they (Dutton was never sure which pronoun was appropriate) closed the door of the rear entrance. The joker looked back at the Jetboy exhibit, brilliant in the darkness.

"They're right, you know," he told Jetboy. "You were supposed to win and you fucked up."

Dutton turned off the exhibit's lights with a savage swipe of his hand and went back to his office.

He locked the gun in the museum safe.

♣

It was a cool night for May. Oddity's heavy, black ankle-length velvet cloak was comfortable. A cold front had swept the late-spring humidity and smog out to sea. The air was crisp and crystalline. Patty could see the light of the Manhattan towers between the older, lower, and far grubbier buildings of Jokertown.

May 14, 1973, had been a gorgeous night as well, in its own way.

Patty sighed with the orgasm, her eyes closed. "Yes . . ." Evan whispered in her ear, and John laughed in satisfaction, lower down. When the long, shuddering climax had passed, Patty hugged both of them to her.

"God, you two are lovely." Then, giggling, she flung Evan aside and bounded from the bed. Naked, she padded across the room and flung open the doors to the balcony. A breeze lifted her hair, fragrant with a warm, sweet-tasting rain that was scrubbing the city clean. Twenty floors below, New York spread out in noisy brilliance. Patty opened her arms wide and let the night and the elements take her, joyous. Droplets shimmered like crystal in her hair, on her skin.

"Jesus, Patty, anyone could see us . . ." John came up behind her, also naked, hugging her. Evan stroked the two of them in passing and went to the railing. "It's wonderful," he said. "Who cares what they see, John. We're happy."

Evan smiled at them all. They melded into a long triple embrace, kissing and touching as the rain slicked their bodies. When it seemed to be time, they went back inside and made love again. . . .

They'd gone to sleep that night, but they'd never awakened.

Not really. It was Oddity who had opened its eyes on the fifteenth. Oddity, the horror. Oddity, the wild card's mockery of their relationship. Oddity, the torturer.

Gone forever were a social worker named Patty, a rising black artist named Evan, and an angry young lawyer named John. Like a thousand jokers before them, they disappeared into the warrens of Jokertown.

Oddity looked at the brilliant concrete spires of Manhattan and moaned, as much from the memory as the physical pain.

[At least in Jokertown it's harder to feel sorry for yourself, when every day we see the other horrors, the ones who are helpless. Oddity's body has strength to match that of the aces.] John.

[Bullshit, it's all bullshit rationalization. . . .] Evan screamed back, down below. [It hurts, it hurts. . . .]

[Rest,] Patty told Evan. [Rest for a few days while you can. We'll be needing you to take over again soon enough.]

John scoffed. [I'm not rationalizing. It's the truth—in Jokertown Oddity can do some good.] John especially seemed to enjoy the role of vigilante. Oddity: protector of jokers, the strong right arm of Hartmann.

Hartmann's defeat still hurt. John especially throbbed with bitterness. But John was strong; Evan wasn't. Patty sent her thoughts down to him.

[I understand, Evan. John does, too, when he takes the time to think about it. We understand. We do. We love you, Evan.]

[Thank you, I love you, too, Patty. . . .] Evan could have said it only to Patty, but he left himself open to both of them, deliberately.

John was surly; Patty knew he'd noted Evan's intentional snub. [He has a hell of a way of showing his affection, doesn't he?]

[John, please . . . Evan needs the rest more than us. Have some compassion.]

[Compassion, hell. He almost killed us. I'm not ready to die, Patty. I don't give a shit how much it hurts.]

[Evan doesn't really want to die either, or he would have gone ahead. I couldn't have stopped him, John. This was a gesture, a plea. He wants to be free of it. Sixteen years is a long time to be in a room you can't leave. I can't blame him for feeling that way.]

[He's come to hate me, Patty.]

[No.] But that was all she said. John scoffed at her.

"Y'know, if you ignore the fact that there's three of us, we're almost staid," John said one night as they lay on the couch, sipping at glasses of cabernet. "We don't swing, we don't sleep with other people. Within the triangle, we're as monogamous and conservative as some married couple in Podunk, Iowa."

"You complaining, John?" Patty teased him, running a finger along his upper thigh and watching what that did to his face. "You getting tired of us?"

John groaned, and they all three laughed. "No," he said. "I don't think that's ever going to happen."

[Okay, maybe "hate" is a little strong,] John said. [But he doesn't love me or like me anymore. Not for a long time. Do you, Evan?]

[Damn egoist, no, I want out, I just want to be alone. . . .] Then, the barest echo: [John I'm sorry I'm sorry. . . .]

[This might have happened anyway,] Patty said to both of them. [Even without Oddity. Those were different times. Different moralities than now.]

[Sure. But there's no divorce from Oddity, is there?]

[Which is all the more reason we all need empathy and understanding—all of us.]

[You always were the goddamn saint, Patty.]

[Fuck you, John.]

[I wish I could, Patty. God, I wish I could.]

♠

Jokertown had always been a night town.

A little past midnight, the main Jokertown streets were still busy. Darkness hid or amplified deformities as needed. Night was the best mask of all.

Not many nats traveled to J-town in the last several months. Tourism was something done in daytime, if at all. The streets had become too unfashionably dangerous.

At night, Jokertown was left alone like a bad dream.

Still, the locals were out and Oddity decided to keep to the plentiful back alleys. John might find some small enjoyment in being public, in the respect and sometimes outright adulation of the jokers, but Patty didn't. Patty could forgive John's egotism—it was little enough balm for the pain—but she didn't need it or want it herself, especially not tonight.

They were a few blocks from the ruins of the Crystal Palace, in the back alley where Gimli's inexplicably empty skin had been found. The Oddity stared at the stained concrete where Tom Miller's body had lain: another death, another nameless violence. Patty was certain Gimli had been assassinated by a rogue ace, Evan thought that maybe Gimli had been an early victim of the Croyd outbreak, John (always the skeptic) thought maybe Hartmann had arranged it. [And good riddance, too,] John added in counterpoint to Patty's thought.

The Oddity shuffled on, limping because one leg seemed to be mostly Patty's and was attached at a decided angle to the hip. Moving it hurt like hell. The Oddity moaned and moved on.

"Shit, man. She's just a toy. Ain't worth wasting time on taking."

"Yeah, but that cunt'd be nice and tight, wouldn't it?"

Voices stopped suddenly as the Oddity turned a corner into

another alley. There were three of them, all male, none of them looking more than sixteen or seventeen and dressed in grimy leathers. One was prepubescent and childlike; another had a blotchy face peppered with angry blackhead acne. But it was the kid in the middle that made Oddity hesitate for a moment. He was tall and fair-skinned. Under the torn leathers and dirty Levi's he had a fighter's body, lean and hard-muscled. The youth was handsome in a feral way, with intense light eyes half-hidden behind straggling blond bangs. He was almost pretty, until they noticed the bloodshot eyes and the fidgety restlessness. The kid was pumped up, high and dangerous.

The joker Oddity knew as Barbie was sobbing on the ground between the three—a perfectly formed woman with adult features but barely two feet tall. Her face was caught in a perpetual smile. She saw Oddity; her mouth grinned incongruously, but the blue china eyes were pleading.

A quick anger raged through John; Patty could feel its red heat. "Hey!" Oddity shouted, their huge fists knotting. "Leave her the hell alone!"

"Shit," Pimpleface said. "You gonna let a fucking joker talk to us like that, David? Maybe it'd be fun, too. Big enough, ain't it? Maybe it's strong, too."

The leader—David—regarded the Oddity, hands on hips. Patty felt John trying to take control. [Just charge the bastards. Beat the kid's head in before he decides to move.]

Patty didn't need much encouragement. Oddity moved, roaring and lumbering toward the trio like a banshee. The gang suddenly flashed steel. Seeing the knives, Oddity screamed and tore a No PARKING sign from the asphalt. They swung the pole like a flail, it made a deep rumble as it whipped through the air.

There was nothing subtle about their attack. The massive body plowed into the gang like a careening truck. The sign caught Pimpleface and slammed him back against a wall; whipping it around again, they held the other two back. "Get out of here! Now!" Oddity barked at Barbie. The doll-like joker struggled to her feet. She ran, taking staggering, tiny baby steps.

Oddity spun to find David, figuring that if they took out the leader, the others would crumple. They launched themselves at the leering kid.

They were far too late. David's body slumped as if struck. Blackhead caught him before he fell.

[Patty . . . ?]

At the same moment John and Evan felt Patty's presence ripped away from the Oddity. In place of her was someone cool, sinister, and smug: David. For just a second he was Dominant, crowing his triumph inwardly.

Then the pain hit him.

Oddity screamed, loud and long and tormented. The sign and the twisted pole dropped from their hands, clanging on the pavement like an alarm.

John and Evan had had sixteen years to learn the neural mazes of Oddity's odd group mind. They knew all too well the searing agony that assaulted this intruder. Their shared response was almost instinctive: John sent his will surging to the high place they thought of as Dominant, pushing aside the screaming, frightened ego of David.

(Hands grasped at Oddity and a blade ripped cloth: Blackhead, attacking again after shaking off the first blow. Intent on the interior struggle, Oddity simply howled and flung the punk aside once more. The voices of reality seemed to be distant. "Goddamn, something's happened, man. David's *screaming*. Shit!" "Fuck, it's gone wrong, it's gone wrong. . . .")

Blackhead grabbed at their sleeve. Oddity roared and whirled; he heard a body fall hard on the concrete. ("The fucker's too strong! Grab David's body. Let's get back to the Rox.")

They knew it was wrong, John and Evan. "Patty!" they cried together, and the fury gave John enough mental strength to snatch the screaming David from control of Oddity's mind.

As John threw the jumper from the mental ramparts, Evan attempted to slide from Passive to Sub-Dominant. That was more difficult. David could feel himself losing control, and as Oddity's pain became more distant, his will began to assert itself once more.

For a moment both Evan's and David's minds were entirely open to each other as they moved, caught somewhere in the limbo between Passive and Sub-Dominant. Evan *knew* David in that instant, and he hated the mind he encountered. He could feel the jumper snatching at his emotions, his thoughts, his memories, and the feeling of violation gave Evan the power to throw David down again.

Evan screamed with David, thrusting himself past until the jumper tumbled down to helpless Passive.

[John?]

[I've got Oddity, Evan. Just keep that bastard down in Passive.]

Oddity looked around. "Shit. *Shit!*"

The kids were gone. They couldn't even hear the sound of their retreating footsteps. The interior battle might have taken minutes—it was impossible to tell.

[Patty?] Evan queried softly, hopefully, into the matrix of Oddity.

There was no answer but soft, mocking laughter from Passive.

Oddity howled in the darkness of the alley.

◆

She didn't hurt. That was the first thing she noticed.

For sixteen years there had been constant pain. For sixteen years there had been tearing agony as ligaments shifted, muscles were stretched to their limit, and bones scraped against each other in the cage of Oddity's flesh.

She didn't hurt.

And she was alone.

There were the six or seven kids—nats, as far as she could tell—in the filthy room with her, but she was *alone* in a single body.

The others were arguing, but she paid little attention to the words.

"Hey, man, what you're describing is the Oddity. So the Oddity took David. He's gone, man."

"You don't mean that, Molly."

"I don't? Well, he sure couldn't control the fucker, could he?"

"If David's gone, everything's up for grabs. And there's gonna be some people who like that idea. You remember that, Molly. In fact, I'll bet *you're* thinking the same, too." There was rough laughter, footsteps, a slamming door.

The voices were outside. There were no voices in Patty's head.

[Evan? John?] No answer—only silence and her own thoughts.

Patty brought her hands up to her face and marveled.

"Shit, she ain't supposed to be able to *do* that." Blackhead stared at her with an expression caught somewhere between fear and hatred on his pimply face. Patty ignored him, concentrating on the hands and wiggling the fingers, turning them around to see the calluses.

These weren't the hands she dimly remembered from the early seventies. But neither were they the patchwork, marbled, knobbed things at the end of Oddity's arms. The fingers were long, with dirt snagged under the chewed nails and callused hard tips on the left hand that told her the jumper played guitar, for Patty had once had similar calluses.

She could smell the body's own rank sweat, and the dirty, knee-torn Levi's were tight at her crotch. She looked down and saw the bulge of a penis. She could *feel* the cock, part of her. She could make it twitch.

She laughed because that startled her, and her voice was deep and very male. "What's the matter, assholes?" she said with a bravado she didn't feel. "Weren't expecting me to wake up?"

She'd heard the news reports. Everything that had happened tonight added up to the same conclusion: The kids were jumpers. The jumpers' victims had all said the same thing: For the duration of the jump, they'd been in a coma. Patty assumed the jumper's companions had guarded the body until the jumper returned and transferred back. Certainly the transfer was a horrible shock to the victim; it was undoubtedly what drove them into unconciousness.

Patty had felt very little of it. Patty was *used* to existing in a strange body; she was familiar with the sensation of her awareness shifting place. She'd recovered quickly and she knew exactly where she was. Even though the journey here had seemed fantasy (was there really a living, gelatinous globe in which they rode?), she knew where they'd taken her.

Ellis Island. The Rox.

The remembrance sobered her quickly. Depending on who you listened to, the Rox was a refuge where jokers helped one another, or it was a gaping sore, a dangerous seeping wound where the worst of those touched by the wild card had gathered.

YOU HAVE TO DIE TO GO TO THE ROX. Patty had seen that spraypainted in garish colors on the walls of J-town. SEND US YOUR HUDDLED MASSES—WE NEED THE FOOD. Slogans of the Rox had appeared by the hundreds in the past few months. From what she'd heard, death was common and varied here. The bodies floated ashore in Jersey or were found out in the bay.

Patty no longer felt pleased. Refuge or hell, the air of the Rox smelled of garbage and shit and corruption.

[My loves . . .] And she was alone. That was worst of all.

The room itself was a hovel, as bad or worse than anything she'd seen in her years with Welfare Services: corrugated aluminum sides that looked like they'd been pieced together from old awnings, a stained concrete floor, the only light a bare bulb hanging from a frayed extension cord. The door was a piece of warped plywood with a rope handle. Patty was sitting in the one piece of furniture in the room: a Laz-E-Boy recliner, the black Naugahyde hopelessly shredded and soiled with nameless stains.

Patty tried standing. Despite the dirt, despite the neglect, despite the halitosis and the crud in the lungs and the leftover crack buzz, this was a gorgeous body: sleek and powerful and lean. Still, it was an effort. Her knees wobbled and she sat again quickly. Patty forced herself to smile, to look as smug and arrogant as this guy had appeared to be.

The punks stood on either side of the exit, scowling. There were three now; the others seemed to have left. She recognized the one who had been with David. Blackhead had a huge welt on his leg and a bloody nose; a remnant of the fight with Oddity. His face and upper arms were scraped raw and the left side of his head was puffy and discolored. Standing next to him was a slight and pretty girl who looked to be at the most thirteen, with breasts just budding under the tank top she wore. The girl stared wide-eyed at Patty. Her face was round, with a fragile attractiveness. Blackhead had his arm around her; his fingers stroked her right nipple. She scowled at him and moved out from under his arm. She continued to gaze strangely at Patty.

The last of the group was a young woman with a scowl on her face, her arms akimbo over a dirty T-shirt. The way Blackhead looked at her, it was obvious he deferred to her.

"Who the fuck *are* you?" she said.

Patty found that she didn't want them to know she was a woman. "Part of Oddity," she said at last. "You can call me . . . Pat." She laughed mockingly again at that, hearing the strain in the sound. [Ah, Evan, too bad it wasn't you who was Dominant. You'd have to put up with being a honky, but at least you'd be the right sex. You'd be out.]

She was almost startled that there was no answer in her head.

[Alone. God, it feels so *strange*.]

"Molly, we gotta tell Bloat," Blackhead said.

"Not yet. Not yet, man. Maybe David'll be back." She didn't look that pleased at the prospect, but she shrugged. "He knows where we went, huh? He'll come here."

Patty stood again, and this time stayed up. Blackhead blinked hard, scowling at Patty with his right hand fisted around a piece of iron pipe. "We shoulda fuckin' tied him up, Mol'. David's gonna be pissed if we have'ta fuck up his body."

"What makes you think David's coming back?" Patty asked. [God, such a rich voice. A politician would die for it. What do you think, John?] Then: [I have to stop this. There's no one there.] "Hey, I have two other friends in Oddity, assholes. Looked to me like *they* were in charge when you punks ran, not David."

It was a bluff. Patty had seen the battle for control raging in Oddity after the jump. There hadn't been *anyone* Dominant; Oddity had simply been flailing wildly, out of control. The kids had grabbed her and run before the fight had been won one way or the other. Patty had no doubt John was strong enough to be Dominant quickly, but poor Evan . . .

She didn't know what might have happened. If David *had* won, then Oddity could be in J-town at the moment, doing things she'd rather not think about.

[There's nothing you can do about it. Just stay alive. Try to get out of here.]

"He'll be back, and you're stayin' till he does," Blackhead said nervously, licking his lips and looking at Molly for confirmation. The girl beside him was still staring, silent. "You don't know David. He gets what he wants. He's strong. He's got ways. And you— you're in the Rox. You're meat."

"David doesn't know what he hit in Oddity," Patty bluffed. "He may never get out. I rather *like* this body."

Blackhead glanced at Molly. The other girl stared.

"What?" Patty asked. "What's the problem?"

Molly just shrugged, but Blackhead snorted. "He's never been away for more'n a few hours. No one's sure what happens when you stay in someone else's body too long."

"Maybe Bloat'd know," Blackhead said.

Molly scoffed. "And why the hell would you think that? You think Bloat jumps?"

"He reads minds, don't he?"

Molly just scowled harder. "This ain't got nothin' to do with Bloat."

"Everything in the Rox has to do with Bloat," Blackhead insisted. The kid sniffed and wiped his arm across the back of his nose. Snot mixed with the blood on his cheek.

Molly sighed. "All right. Maybe we should let Bloat know what's going on. Hell, he probably knows already. Can you handle this?"

Blackhead scowled. "Shit," he said. "Sure. Me'n Kelly'll stay here and take care a'things."

Kelly's intense gaze had never left Patty. Her eyes were somewhere between blue and gray, and very open.

"You see how she's watching you?" she whispered teasingly to Evan, giggling with the wine. John's fund-raising party for Gregg Hartmann's first senatorial campaign was a noisy swirl around them. "The willowy one with too much makeup, over in the corner by your sculpture. She hasn't taken her eyes off you since she came in."

"Jesus, Patty, you have a filthy mind. That's the Salchows' daughter. She's still in high school. I sold her father two paintings last month."

"I was her age once, too. That's a teenage crush if I ever saw one. I've been there, too. The hormones just run away with your mind. How about it, Evan? She's young, rich, probably willing if a bit inexperienced. White and curious about how it'd be with a big black stud like you."

"Patty—"

Patty laughed and kissed Evan. The girl's face had gone almost angry as she turned away. . . .

Patty gave Runt a half smile. The girl seemed startled; then slowly, behind Blackhead, she smiled back, almost shyly.

[Have to get out of here. Have to find John and Evan.]

Patty knew in that moment how to escape. She hated herself for the knowledge, but she knew.

♥

[You want out I know you do I can feel it and I can do it for you I have the key but it has to be *soon* I can take you to the Rox but *SOON.* . . .]

They were standing in front of the Dime Museum. A poster was stapled inside a case next to the door, a garish drawing of the Syrian exhibit. A waxen Senator Hartmann was gesturing for the others to retreat, his jacket bloody from the gunshot wound. Guards with Uzis gazed at the dais where the Kahina slit the throat of her brother the Nur al-Allah. Braun glowed in a golden spotlight; Carnifex gleamed in his white fighting suit; Tachyon clutched his head and crumpled on the ground.

John wasn't sure how they'd ended up there. For most of the last hour, they'd reeled through the streets of J-town blindly, trying to find the punks and slowly realizing that the quest was useless.

Their fists clenched and unclenched—the right hand Evan's and the left John's. There wasn't much of Patty surfaced in Oddity at all. It seemed that her body had become sluggish since the loss of her presence.

[We've got to go get her, John. David says they'd've taken her to the Rox. He says we have to find Patty quickly. He's afraid. I can feel it. He's scared of what might happen if he's out of his own body for too long. Patty might be trapped.]

[I don't hear him, Evan. We smashed him down to Passive. Stuck him in the basement and locked the door. *We* can't hear the fucker at all.]

[Don't tell him Evan I can get you out I can give you the release you want just help me out of here *quick* I know you I know
you. . . .]

David broadcast the plea desperately, constantly.

Evan knew the truth. John was tiring already; Evan knew that
his own will could not hold David down alone if John fell from
Dominant. The jumper knew that, too. Since then, Evan had heard
David's voice. Constantly.

At Sub-Dominant, Oddity's eternal purgatory sluiced over
Evan's soul, and he could hear the words promising a salvation.

[You want out I know you. . . .] Yes, David knew Evan's weak-
nesses. He knew too well how Evan kept listening and wondering.

A violent shudder racked their body; they could see the right
arm shorten and change color as they watched. The torment was
worse than either John or Evan remembered, as if they had also
taken Patty's share of the agony. The fingers curled with pain, the
nails digging into the palm. When the fists opened again, the hand
was a piebald mixture of John and Evan.

[How long can you stay Dominant?] Evan gasped with the
transformation. [John, the only thing that's kept any of us sane
was being able to go down to Passive and rest. Even Sub-Dominant
hurts too much. John . . . please . . .]

[I'll jump someone else someone you'll loathe someone neither
you or John can stomach at all and you'll be left in the body with
them without Patty without any chance of *ever* getting out at all
unless you help me NOW. . . .]

[Patty's in the Rox,] Evan said. [In the *Rox*. My God—]

[We haven't any plan. We don't know what we're running into
or how to handle it once we do find her.]

[Let's just get there. Now, John. Before it's too late.]

Oddity moaned. The pain redoubled as the body shifted again.
Oddity screamed this time, grasping the fire hydrant in front of
the museum and wrenching upward as if they could drive away

the torture with violence. The top of the hydrant gave way under their assault with a metallic shriek. Water cannoned in a gushing, two-story-high fountain, soaking their black cloak and turning the gutters into dark, trash-filled rapids. Water cascaded over the front of the Dime Museum.

Underneath, David laughed and whispered to Evan.

[When we get there I can do it I can give you the body you want whatever you want just help me. . . .]

♣

"What's it feel like to be a man?"

"Huh?"

Patty kissed Evan and pulled him deeper into her with her hands, wrapping her legs around his back. Next to them, John snored, asleep.

"You know," she insisted, giggling. "To penetrate instead of being penetrated. To feel a woman's heat around your cock. To ejaculate. To have one short blinding spasm instead of a long extended one."

"Is that what you're thinking about?" Evan pretended to be offended and Patty slapped his buttocks, rolling him over until she straddled him. She traced the tight black curls of hair on his dark chest. "So you want to be a man, eh, virile and masterful."

"To surrender my brain to a penis," she retorted. "C'mon, Evan, haven't you ever wondered what it feels like to be a woman?" Evan tried to shrug and she shook her head at him. "Come on now. Admit it."

"Okay," he said. "Maybe a little. But there's no way to ever know, is there?"

But there was, now.

Moving an arm was ecstasy. Feeling the stubble on her cheek was glory. The touch of jeans along her legs was a caress. The tepid beer that Blackhead gave her was a gastronomical delight. Despite all her worries about John and Evan, despite her fear of the Rox, Patty couldn't help but marvel at the wonder of being in this body.

She'd forgotten how *good* it was. It didn't matter that she was male or that she very likely had a crack addiction or worse—she was *free*, able to walk alone and talk alone and not feel anyone else inside her.

[This body's wanted for questioning in New York, and that may not be the worst of it. What if he's got AIDS, what if the wild card has done other hidden things to him or if he's syphilitic or has cancer? What *about* sex? What if after a few experiments you find that you're still attracted only to males? What about John and Evan, trapped in Oddity with that punk?]

But the objections didn't totally convince. She was *here*, in David's teenage body, and Patty had to admit that she enjoyed the sensation. She drank again, savoring the coolness, the odor of the hops, the yeasty taste.

Kelly watched her, always, while Blackhead worried near the door.

"Why do you keep staring?" Patty asked, and the rich, deep voice was a joy.

Blackhead answered for her. "Kelly? She's new. She's got the hots for David but he ain't laid her. She'd love to go down on him, to have him spread her legs—"

Kelly whirled around, stabbing a forefinger at Blackhead. "You shut up, hear? You're just mad 'cause I won't do you."

Blackhead laughed. "Shit," he told Kelly. "That's crap. You'd sure lay down and spread 'em with a smile to get initiated. You ain't really part of us until you can jump, and you can't jump until you get laid by Prime, and *that* might not be for a while, since he don't get out here that often. So don't give me that shy virgin shit. Maybe it don't have to be Prime, Kelly. And you're wasting your time waiting for David. He can fuck anyone he wants. He don't need *you*. I'd do just fine."

"I want more than a pencil," Kelly spat. She huddled on the floor near Patty, arms around knees while Blackhead chortled near the entrance to the ramshackle room. "Son of a bitch," she muttered. Her face was flushed from anger and embarrassment.

"I was her age once . . . . I've been there, too."

"I'm sorry," Patty said softly to Kelly, and meant it. The girl thanked Patty with her eyes, and Patty had to smile again. But Blackhead's words had caused other reactions, too. *"What's it feel like to be a man?"* she'd asked Evan long ago. Now she knew part of it. There was a heat, and her jeans were suddenly tighter in the crotch. "You're very pretty," she said softly so that only Kelly could hear. Though the words sounded strange and awkward, Kelly gave a half smile at them.

Patty hated the rest of what she was going to do. "Kelly, I can give you David, if that's what you want." She whispered it so that Blackhead couldn't hear the words.

"You ain't David," she answered, but without anger.

"No," Patty admitted. "But maybe when David comes back, his body will remember . . . ."

"You were ugly. I saw the Oddity once in Jokertown. No one would go to bed with you the way you were."

"You're a gorgeous woman, Patricia," John said. It was the anniversary of the first time they'd made love as a trio. Their "birthday," they'd jokingly called it. Evan had made a cake. John decorated the apartment with balloons and crepe paper. They'd stuck a silly hat on her head and a champagne glass in her hand when she walked in. "A wonderful person. I can't imagine loving anyone else, and I know Evan feels the same way. We're both very lucky."

Patty nodded, feeling the tears in her eyes and fighting them back. She could feel Kelly's gaze on her.

"No," Patty said. "Not for a long time. A long time."

Kelly's hand reached out and touched Patty/David's. There was a softness in her gaze, a sympathy that made Patty like Kelly despite the hard exterior she tried to maintain. She smiled at Patty and Patty smiled back, feeling the strangeness of David's face.

"Okay," Kelly whispered. "Maybe . . ."

Kelly rose to her feet and went over to the makeshift door of the hut. She spoke to Blackhead in an intense whisper. "I ain't leavin'," Blackhead said loudly.

"Where the hell is he gonna go? This is the *Rox*, asshole. You can stay outside if you want."

"Maybe I'll stay and watch, huh?"

"You can diddle yourself outside." Kelly shoved Blackhead, opening the door.

Blackhead snorted. He gestured with the pipe toward Patty. "I'll be right there. You stick your head out and I'll take it off." He looked from Patty to Kelly, laughed again, and left.

Kelly didn't look at her for a long time. She stayed by the piece of plywood that was the door, facing away. Then she seemed to sigh.

It was Patty who came to her, by the door. She opened her arms and hugged Kelly. It felt strange to be so much taller. Patty was very aware of Kelly, of the breasts pressing against David's chest, of the smell of her hair, of the way her hips pressed against her body. Kelly's hands came around Patty's head and brought it down to her.

They kissed, softly and tentatively, then Kelly's mouth opened. [Very strange . . .] Patty felt her [his] body responding. She leaned into Kelly, pulling her tight. Close. She could feel the unbidden erection aching to be loosed.

[Ah, Evan, so very, very strange . . .]

"So urgent," she breathed. "Impatient."

"What?" Kelly asked.

"Nothing." She hugged Runt again.

There was an insistence to her arousal that differed from anything she'd known before. Maybe it was the years since she'd experienced desire, maybe she'd just forgotten, but this seemed more volatile and dangerous. It wasn't Kelly—Patty had never been par-ticularly sexually attracted to women despite some minor experi-mentation. Patty shuddered as she ended the embrace, as she raised her head from Kelly's lips and held the girl at arm's length. She slipped the shirt over Kelly's head, unbuckled the jeans. Kelly *was* attractive, Patty thought clinically. Very pretty in a young way. Patty stroked her tentatively, then with more passion, her hands going from Kelly's breasts to the fleece between her legs as Kelly closed her eyes.

They sank together to the floor. Kelly's legs wrapped around Patty, her hands sought to unzip her jeans and pull out that odd hardness throbbing there.

Holding back was far, far more difficult than Patty had imagined it would be. Runt's lips and hand were insistent; she seemed to feel the heat coming from both of them. Patty *wanted* to do this, wanted to plunge her erection into Kelly's moist heat. . . .

"I'm sorry," she whispered. Rising up, Patty drove David's fist in a vicious cut across her chin. There was a lot of wiry strength in her new body. Her fist snapped against Kelly's jaw.

Kelly grunted; her eyes closed as blood drooled over cut lips. Her legs and arms went limp around Patty.

Patty got to her feet. She called to Blackhead, outside the door. "Hey, man! How about joining us?"

The door opened; Blackhead stuck his head in and saw Kelly's naked body spread-eagled on the floor. He gaped.

Patty hit the kid in the back of the head with doubled, fisted hands. Blackhead staggered and doubled over, and Patty brought her knee up into his face. She heard the nose break.

As Blackhead fell, Patty pulled on the rope handle and flung open the door.

Patty darted through the opening and into the darkness of the Rox.

♠

Ellis Island was a quarter mile from the shipyards of the Jersey shore and a little over a mile from Battery Park at the southern tip of Manhattan Island.

But you couldn't get to Ellis from either of those places. Certainly some could (and had) *tried*, but they were invariably curious nats, and nats who went to the Rox were treated rudely, violently, and sometimes fatally. The authorities had passed control of Ellis like a legal hot potato from the National Park Service, to the New Jersey authorities, to the New York City police, who had given up any pretext of actual control of the island months ago. Still, patrol boats vigilantly intercepted anyone trying to swim or boat to the Rox. The authorities might not be able to shut down the Rox itself, but they could and would control traffic to and from the island.

Those who went to the Rox knew that to get there safely you had to see Charon, and Charon could only be found on the East River, where the edge of Jokertown touched water.

Oddity could hear the waves slapping the pilings under the rotting wharf. They'd placed a kerosene lantern at the end of the dock—it hissed at their feet, the mesh filament gleaming erratically in the breeze off the river.

Inside, David yammered at Evan, shielding his mindvoice from John.

[Any fuckin' body you want man any fuckin' one just point at it and it's yours free at last just help me when we get to the Rox fast fast *fast*. . . .]

[I don't see anything,] John's usually powerful Dominant voice was weak, but it still drowned out the jumper's constant wheedling. [Maybe Dutton was wrong, Evan.]

[No not wrong Charon will come take us to the Rox that's where they'd've taken her. . . .] David whispered it to Evan alone.

[Charon will be here,] Evan told John. [Be patient.] Even as he said it, he knew how impossible it was. One way or another, this had to be resolved soon. Being Dominant was exhausting and John had only gone down to Passive the day before. It had been hard enough for Evan to move to Sub-Dominant with no rest. John wouldn't be able to hold on much longer. When that time came, Evan would have to take Dominant; if he couldn't or wouldn't hold it, David would. If that happened, they'd lost everything.

John knew it, too. His anger lashed at Evan.

[How can we be patient? God knows what's happened to Patty. If they've hurt her, I swear I'll kill every last one of them.]

[They haven't hurt her, John. She's in David's body—they'll be careful with it.] Then: [John, what if she wants to STAY?]

John wouldn't even consider that. Evan could hear mental doors slamming. [No. Patty wouldn't want that.]

A boot scraped wood, a breath hushed in darkness.

Oddity turned sharply, their heavy cloak swirling. Four youths came from behind a stack of crates. Jumpers. One, with a shock of orange-red hair, held an aluminum baseball bat. Another swung a chain softly at his side. The other two had knives—switchblades. "What the hell do you want?" Oddity growled.

"David?" Chains asked.

Oddity gave a laugh that was mostly grunt. "Dave's not here," the harsh voice said. The bitter laugh sounded again. "So fuck off before you get hurt."

Chains looked at Red, who shrugged. "David's been in there three, four hours," Chains said.

"Hell, that's a long time, ain't it?" Red grinned. He was missing teeth. "Almost as bad as jumping a bar of soap, huh?" He laughed.

Down in Passive, David struggled. [I wonder if Molly sent them or if they came on their own she might like me gone forever I'll fucking kill her if she did. . . .]

"Hey, man, can David hear me?" Red asked Oddity. He slapped the end of the bat against his open palm.

"Why?"

"'Cause I thought I should tell him a few things. Things he'd like to know."

"So talk."

Red grinned. "Tell David there ain't no reason to go to the Rox, man. We're gonna take care of his body." The words sent a shock through Oddity, stunning them all. For a moment they felt nothing. "Now we came to take care of the rest, huh? Just to make sure."

With that, Red took a leaping step forward, swinging the bat like an outfielder swinging for the fences.

He hit the Oddity square in the side of the head.

Oddity staggered and nearly fell. The pain was a burning lance. Oddity screamed, their throat tearing with the sound. John's control tottered, but neither Evan nor David could take advantage. Then John's fury took hold fully. As Red brought the bat back for the next blow and the other three closed in, Oddity forced himself up. A hand caught the bat as it began the downswing; a savage, powerful twist wrenched it from Red's hands—Red's wrist snapped and the kid howled.

Oddity swung now, the bat making an audible and sinister *whuff* through air. Only the fact that Red had crumpled to the ground saved the kid. Chains whipped his steel links in a dangerous arc; Oddity caught them and pulled, catapulting Chains into the pile of crates. The jumper didn't move again.

The remaining two had already fled. Red, cradling his hand to his waist, was limping after them. Oddity screamed again and flung the bat after Red. It clattered into darkness.

[They've killed her! They've killed Patty!] John shouted inside, raving.

[No!] Evan shouted back. [No! I don't believe that. It had to be a bluff, a deception. John, please!]

A soft splash cut off any further discussion. A glowing apparition came up from the filthy water around the dock, garlanded with a bald tire, two green Hefty bags, and a used Pamper. Except for the garbage snagged around the body, it was almost pretty. The thing was a gelatinous hollow sphere eight feet in diameter, nearly transparent except for translucent bands of muscle. Ribbons of light rippled along jellyfish flesh, sparking soft green, yellow, and blue. Near the top of it were two very human eyes and a mouth. It bobbed in the slight swell.

Charon.

"Fee?" it croaked.

[Evan?] John's rage had not abated. It had merely gone cold and dangerous.

[Must find out . . .] David seemed stunned, bewildered. Frightened.

[All right, John,] Evan told him. [We won't know anything unless we go.]

Oddity picked up two shopping bags next to the lantern. Approaching Charon, they showed the joker that they were full of groceries and canned goods. "Fine," Charon said. "Put them inside."

Oddity shoved the bags into the slimy flesh between the muscle. The flesh was cold and wet; it yielded under their pressure, stretching until suddenly the skin parted and they could place the bags on the gellid "floor" of Charon. Underneath the flattened bottom of the joker, they could see hundreds of wriggling cilia.

"You want to go to the Rox? You're *certain?*" Charon asked.

"Yes."

"Then get in." Charon paused. It snorted air from a blowhole atop the sphere and it bobbed lower in the water. "You've got David with you."

"How did you know that?" Oddity grunted.

"I can feel the child's black, wretched soul. Get in."

Charon would say nothing else.

Oddity stepped forward, pushing their way into Charon's body and hating the feel of the clinging, damp flesh. They sat down inside the joker as it began to sink into the waters of the East River. On the muddy, garbage-strewn bottom, in the dim light of the creature, they could see the cilia stirring dark clouds as Charon began the long crawl.

Hidden and silent, they moved south and west into the bay toward Ellis Island and the Rox.

◆

Movement was exhilaration. The running . . . Ah, the running . . .

The wind, the pounding in the lungs and chest, the racing heartbeat—the joy was almost enough to make her forget a groggy Blackhead shouting alarm behind her and to erase the sight of the hovels of the Rox.

Almost.

In the days before Oddity, Patty had devoured Victorian novels with their London slums, the poor waifs, and the quirky, grimy sense of realism. The Rox had the same Dickensian sense of gloom, the same *chiaroscuro* shades, but here the reality was harsher-edged. Makeshift dwellings clung like fungus to and between the decaying buildings of Ellis Island; the lanes between them were muddy, rutted, and filthy under Patty's feet.

Dickens in hell.

In the early morning the lanes were mostly empty. The few inhabitants she glimpsed told her that the Rox was Jokertown distilled, Jokertown boiled down to the raw, bitter dregs. The jokers Patty saw here were the most deformed, the ones just hanging on the edge of what might be called human.

"Where you gonna go, Pat? There ain't no place to hide." Blackhead and Kelly shouted behind her, their voices echoing between the shacks. They hadn't stayed down very long at all. [*Your own fault. They're just kids; you didn't want to hurt them too badly. . . .*] Patty could hear the jumpers' pursuit. She turned left blindly, seeing the lights of Manhattan and the gleam of water through two drunken-angled buildings. A few lights were coming on around Patty as Blackhead and Kelly continued to fling taunts and warnings at her.

Turning the corner, she blundered into someone whose skin felt like soaked velvet. She caught a glimpse of yellow, faceted eyes. "Sorry," she said, and thrust herself away, her hands dripping with whatever oozed from that skin. Two heads leaned curiously from a nearby window, joined at the throat into one bull neck. Something without legs slithered across the lane in front of her, leaving behind a scent of lavender that suddenly turned sour and bitter. A voice roared from the darkness between two buildings, but the words were incomprehensible, hopelessly slurred.

A hand caught at her from behind and Patty screamed. The arm to which the hand was attached stretched like taffy, the hand— clawed like a dog's, but undeniably human—still clutching her biceps. The arm stretched taut and as thin as a pencil, turning her; then the hand let go and she spun and almost fell from the shock of release.

Patty didn't look back to see what or who had tried to stop her. She kept running.

She'd been to Ellis, years ago. She remembered a U-shaped, tiny island, with docks along the central waterway. The administration building dominated one side of the island; the buildings used for holding detained aliens filled the other. Patty could see the administration building on the far side. She could smell the bay. David's body was beginning to pant from the exertion now, but she seemed to have outdistanced the others.

She broke into the open, looking for a rowboat, a dinghy, anything. If she had to, she'd try swimming—she could swim, and this body was stronger than her own had been. Manhattan and New Jersey loomed achingly close.

"Bloat says to ask what good it will do you to be captured by the police patrols, Patty."

Patty stopped. A figure had stepped out between her and the bay. She squinted at it. It looked like a walking, man-sized roach. There were two others with him; jokers, armed with what looked like a shotgun and a small-caliber hunting rifle. The roach-man held up a cheap plastic walkie-talkie. "Bloat sent me to get you."

From the shadows of the buildings, Blackhead and Kelly came panting out. "Hey—" Blackhead shouted. Patty started to run. There was room. Maybe the insectlike joker would be unable to move quickly. Maybe the jokers with the guns might miss. Maybe she could dive into the water and be gone.

Maybe.

The roach's radio crackled. "Bloat says that the water's still very cold this time of year. You'll cramp up and drown before you get halfway there. He says he has a solution for you."

Blackhead and Kelly were very close. She had to move now.

"Bloat doesn't hurt jokers, Patty. He says to remember that you asked Evan not to waste *his* life." The roach's voice was almost a sigh, laced with a strange sadness.

The words were a slash, a mortal wound. Patty's intake of breath was half sob at the memory. And then it was too late. Blackhead grabbed her arm roughly; Kelly, dressed only in her jeans, blocked Patty's path, her eyes accusing, hurt, and cold.

"This is a jumper problem, Kafka," Blackhead said gruffly to the roach-man. The two jokers with Kafka stepped forward threateningly, but Kafka waved them back.

"Not anymore," Kafka answered, softly and almost shyly. "Bloat's seeing her. You want to continue to live on the Rox? Then think about what you want to do here. You're renters; you're here only because you pay Bloat for the privilege."

"We don't take orders from Bloat," the jumper blustered.

Kafka just waited. Blackhead's hand dropped to his side.

What looked like a smile went across the inhuman face under the carapace. "Good. We really don't need this unpleasantness. Please . . . follow me," Kafka said. The joker guards took up escort positions around Patty and the others. Kafka nodded. Scuttling ahead of them with a rustling sound, he led them to the administration building.

And Bloat.

THE ROX CAN'T SINK; BLOAT FLOATS.

THE GREAT WALL OF BLOAT.

Patty'd seen *those* graffiti, too.

Patty's first thought was that Bloat resembled nothing more than a mountain of filthy, uncooked bread dough into which some irreverent child had stuck toothpicks. Bloat *filled* the vast foyer of the administration building. Jury-rigged steel supports jutted through the sagging floor alongside him; concrete pipes stabbed into that monstrous pile of flesh like gigantic IVs. The size of him was almost too much to comprehend; his shapeless flanks receded into darkness and back corridors. His head was a wart nearly lost on the massive body. The shoulder and arms were almost vestigial, stick thin and too short, overwhelmed in the rolling hills of flesh. Bloat could not move, could not *be* moved.

And the stench. It was as if Patty had fallen headfirst into a midden. She gagged.

Bloat's eyes were black and amused.

"A mountain of uncooked dough . . ." he said. His voice was a thin, prepubescent squeak and the words tumbled out in a rush. His statement startled her. "I suppose that's kinder than most, Patty. But then you always considered yourself an understanding woman."

"You mean this one's a fuckin' *cunt*?" Blackhead guffawed behind her. "Hey, Kelly, you almost lost your cherry to a chick."

Kafka motioned. One of the joker guards hit Blackhead swiftly and casually in the stomach with the butt of his shotgun. Blackhead groaned and threw up noisily on the tile floor.

"You should be quiet when the Governor's talking," Kafka said gently.

Blackhead spat. "Hey, fuck you, Roach."

Kafka looked at Bloat, who gestured. The guard hit Blackhead again. The youth went to his knees in the puddle of his vomit.

Bloat watched the violence greedily. His ludicrously small hands clenched and twitched and he smiled.

"Yes, I *know* he's just a child, but he's a vicious, dangerous one," Bloat said, and Patty's intake of breath was audible, for Bloat had once again spoken her thoughts. "For that matter, he's not much younger than me."

Bloat didn't stop talking, didn't stop to take a breath. His monologue rolled on like a freight train without brakes. "There are those who need reminding who controls things here. The Rox is still too anarchic. There's too little direction, too little *real* leadership. We have potential here, nearly unlimited potential and real power. David's group is just one example, even if they're wild and untamed. Still, I've been here less than a year."

The lecture spewed nonstop in Bloat's high voice. He spoke quickly, loudly, giving Patty almost no chance to interrupt the torrent of words.

"What—"

"Do I want from you?" Bloat interrupted, finishing the thought for her. "That's very simple. Oddity. I want the Oddity."

"I don't know where Oddity is."

Bloat's eyes closed. "I do. They're very close. They're coming here now." The eyes opened again and he smiled at Patty. "Such a childish image that puts in your head," he said, the words rushing past pasty lips. "The Noble Rescue. The Happy Ending. But you haven't thought past that, have you? You haven't thought about what happens then. I have. A strength like the Oddity's could be useful. Not essential, mind you, but I could utilize it. The Oddity has been a friend to Jokertown for years. I appreciate that; it makes us siblings."

"I doubt it."

He nodded, more to her thoughts than her words. "In the Rox, jokers try to help jokers. We do what's best for those the wild card has nearly destroyed."

"No matter who it hurts."

Bloat grimaced. "If nats or aces get hurt, I don't care. Fuck them. If that's what it takes, I'll even encourage it. *I* have my own dreams, dreams of the Rox expanding. We've only this little island, twenty-seven lousy acres built on abandoned ship ballast that's filling up quickly. There's a bigger island I'd like to claim."

Bloat took a breath, and Patty plunged into the brief space. "New York? That's impossible."

"Not impossible. Not at all. And spilling nat blood now will save a lot of joker blood later."

Patty saw the attendants listening attentively. Alongside her, Kafka was rapt.

Bloat continued. "The reprisals will be brutal, in any case. I have my dream every night, Patty. The dream tells me that the nats are destined to taste the fruits of their own hatred and bigotry. To fulfill that dream, I need more than the jokers and ragtag gangs. We already have a few renegade aces and jokers with useful powers in residence. We can use more. You have some sympathy with our cause, even if you don't agree with my tactics."

He wouldn't let her speak. The diatribe poured out from him, gasping. "Oh, yes, Patty, I hear your thoughts. 'The Oddity is different.' You're essentially lawful—you helped Hartmann, after all. You think that no one would want to endure the pain of being the Oddity."

Bloat grinned humorlessly. "They don't have to. David, the one whose body you're holding at the moment, our David and his jumpers can transfer people in and out, can't he?"

"Then why haven't *you* done it? Why haven't you left *that*." Patty gestured at the helpless, endless bulk behind him.

The head, so tiny against the body, wrinkled in a grimace. He didn't have to speak for Patty to know that he'd tried it, that it hadn't been successful. Bloat's face suffused with remembered anger. When he spoke, his voice was sharp-edged. "I already know that one new person can be in Oddity and the body still functions. Perhaps *two* can be gone, or even all three. Perhaps not. Perhaps at least one of the original components must always be in Oddity's mind. I don't know. But I *will* find out. I'll find out in any way I have to."

[John, Evan, what do I do now?] The silence inside her head was mocking and Patty felt frightened and very alone. The isolation hurt more than anything she remembered from Oddity.

Bloat had paused. In the silence, a soft and prolonged squilching sound reverberated across the lobby, like someone rolling across a half-filled water bed. Gelid, dark masses erupted from pores all along Bloat's body, which rippled around the large pipes impaling him. The black goo rolled, thickened, and then dropped from the slope of Bloat's flanks, leaving behind umber smears. The clumps piled around Bloat, and Patty saw that the tiles around the huge joker were hopelessly stained.

The horrid stench hit her a second later: the odor of concentrated raw sewage. Patty nearly gagged; around her, Kafka and the others struggled to remain stoic. Joker attendants wearing masks came from an alcove and scurried about removing the filth, shoveling it up and placing it in carts. Others toweled Bloat's side.

"They call it bloatblack," he told Patty, answering the question in her mind. "A body this large requires a corresponding amount of intake. The wild card has made it easier—I can digest anything organic. Anything at all. Kafka has made it simple; these pipes connect directly to the Rox's sewer system. But every body, no matter how efficient, has to excrete waste material."

Patty could not keep her thoughts hidden.

"You're disgusted," he said in his choirboy's tenor. "Don't be. It's what the wild card gave me. Is it my fault that this body needs so much, that I must take in everyone else's shit and spew it out again?" The voice had gone strident. He looked at Patty. "Yes, I'm trapped, trapped the way you were trapped in the Oddity. And I don't need your fucking sympathy, you hear! I'll stuff it back down your fucking throat!"

Patty choked and forced the bile back down. She lifted her chin defiantly to the joker. "We won't run Oddity for you. Not me, not John or Evan. Not for what you want it for."

"We'll see, won't we? Maybe we don't need any of you. Serve, or be served," Bloat commented, and suddenly giggled.

"I won't do it," Patty said flatly. "None of us would."

Again Bloat's lids flickered down over the satin pupils. "*David's* the key, not you. He's only interested in his own ego, but I can convince him. From what I sense of John, he might enjoy life on top for once and kicking some nat ass. Evan . . . Well, maybe your friends *will* be interested. After all, David and his people supply rapture."

"I don't know . . . ."

"Show her," Bloat said, gesturing to one of the joker guards. He came forward; on the doglike face, Patty could see that the lips, gums, and nostrils were stained blue. The joker took out a small penknife. He snapped open the blade and Patty took an involuntary step backward. The joker ignored her, however. Holding out his left arm, he plunged the blade into his forearm to the hilt and as quickly wrenched it out again. Blood pulsed sluggishly from the deep wound.

The joker grinned. He leaned his head back and laughed.

Patty gasped.

"Rapture makes *everything* feel good," Bloat was saying as she stared at the joker. "You could cut your own hand off and it would feel like the most wonderful orgasm. Every sensation is transmuted into bliss, at least for a while. With long-term use, unfortunately, it finally dulls the senses completely, until it is hard to feel anything at all, but that's hardly a problem for a joker, is it? Imagine Oddity's pain transformed into a nearly sexual pleasure, and then slowly, slowly, deadened so you can't feel it at all. Would that be something you might like, or if not you, John or Evan?"

Bloat laughed and smiled grimly at the expression on Patty's face. "Yes, you're thinking it, too. Evan wants out, and I can offer him freedom one way or the other. Are you so sure now, Patty? No, I thought not."

[Evan . . .]

"You're terrified, aren't you, Patty? You hate the separation from your lovers. You listen and there's no one there. But you enjoy being alone, don't you? You wonder if you could stand being in Oddity once again. You wonder if you shouldn't do all you can to stay in David's body. Well, I tell you, you can't. I need David. But I'm not evil, Patty. I don't intend you harm at all. In fact, I've a gift for you. Kafka?"

Kafka nodded. Rustling, he scurried into an adjoining room and came back pushing a wheelchair. Seated in the chair was a teenager, dark-haired and rather pretty. Her eyes were open, but when Patty looked at her, it was like looking into the face of a dead girl. There was nothing behind her eyes, nothing at all. The body breathed, but whoever had once inhabited that shell was gone. Blackhead sniffed behind Patty; Runt gave a cry of recognition.

"I've been saving this," Bloat said. "The girl jumped a polar bear, which turned out to be an animated bar of soap. Unfortunate. But it has left us with an empty body."

Patty glanced at the body, at Bloat. She tried again to blank her thoughts, to make her mind as empty as the girl in front of her so Bloat couldn't steal her thoughts, but Bloat chuckled. [Evan, John . . . I'm sorry, but . . .]

"It is tempting, isn't it? Our jumpers could do it for you. Presto! There you are, a woman again. By yourself. And young, too. You wouldn't be so old."

"I'm not old. I'm only forty."

Bloat chuckled. "So easily offended. Think about it, Patty. We can do it right now. I help you; you help me. Think about it."

♥

Outside the milky, translucent body of Charon, the green depths of the bay were revealed. [John, those are bones out there! Dead people . . .] Down below, David only laughed. John didn't answer.

Oddity moaned. John had paid scant attention to Charon or the ride to Ellis, too intent on the interior struggle and the pain.

Evan could feel John tiring rapidly. Nothing of Oddity seemed to be Patty anymore. Her body was submerged and what remained seemed to hurt them more than ever before, as if they were both taking on the portion of the suffering that once was allotted to her. The boundaries between Dominant, Sub-Dominant, and Passive were growing weak and tenuous. Worse, like some residue of the transfer process, parts of David's memory were drifting loose.

[The killing was a kick better than crack man all the nats running and screaming through Times Square. . . .]

[Evan, this is what he'd do to us. We can't let him take Oddity.]

Evan wasn't listening to John but to David. [I can let you out Evan let you out and and free of Oddity I can do it. . . .]

[What's he saying to you, Evan? He's trying to block me, but the shields are falling apart, too. I can almost hear him.]

Mockingly, more of David's reverie intruded. [With the priest

I took the gun he had in his desk and made one of the nuns get down on her knees and suck his cock until he shot his holy wad in her mouth then I made the other one take the barrel in her mouth like it was a dick "make it come, too" I said and when it did it blew the whole fucking back of her head away and then I jumped when the cops broke the door down. . . .]

[Just more of the same garbage. John, you have to listen to me. What if Patty doesn't *want* to come back in? What then, John? We can't keep David down forever. When he's Dominant, he'll make us do something, something awful, and then he'll jump. He'll jump and leave us with someone else, someone who'll hate Oddity, someone we don't know or love or even like.]

With the thought, their attention was brought back to the outside world. Charon was moving through the sunken grave-yard. Many of the bodies still had ribbons of clothing, shreds of flesh. Fish swarmed around the cages of ribs, nibbling and biting; eels swarmed in eye sockets and wriggled from open jaws like obscene tongues.

And something, som*eone* was pushing at them, pressing Odd-ity's back against the cold, clammy wall of Charon's interior, the flesh beginning to stretch around their back as Charon continued its slow passage. An invisible hand was thrusting at their chest, refusing to let them go any farther even though Charon plodded on. Oddity struggled weakly, but it would not let them loose. [Bloat's Wall Bloat's Wall . . .] David yammered from Passive. [It's you Evan, it's you.]

With the physical pressure, Evan could also feel a mental las-situde. He no longer *wanted* to go to the Rox. This quest was use-less. Even if Patty were alive, it was futile. They could do no good there. John tried to force Oddity through the unseen barrier as they felt the cold waters through Charon's back, but Evan only watched from Sub-Dominant.

"Stop!" Oddity's broken voice shouted. Charon paid no attention.

[Dammit, Evan. Help me!] Charon's flesh was beginning to thin dangerously. The skeletons outside grinned mindlessly at them, waiting.

[This might be better, John. It would be over. Finished.]

[No no *no* please Evan I'll get you out I will. . . .]

[You still want us dead. That's it, isn't it, Evan? That's what you're really saying.] Oddity struggled, took a step forward, but that barely made a difference. The back of their cloak was chill and damp. Charon's flesh bulged dangerously around them.

[You're just barely holding us together, John. I can't keep David back when you fall. He's strong and this time he'll be expecting the pain. He'll know that when it's too much for him, he can just jump.]

[If we're on the Rox, he'll jump back to his own body, Evan. Which puts Patty back with us.]

[I'll have Oddity initiated make you all jumpers so you can get out. . . .]

[Is that fair, John? Are you so possessive of her that you'd punish her like that when she's free? What's better—to let this bastard loose again or to make the sacrifice? We can keep Patty free and take the SOB out with us. What's better, John?]

[I'm Dominant] And with that there was a flailing resurgence of will. Oddity managed two lurching steps back toward the center of Charon. The chill receded. [I'll stay Dominant until we find Patty.]

[And what then, John? What then? It's been *sixteen years*, John. Long enough.]

[John I'll help you too just don't let him kill us. . . .]

David's panic loosed adrenaline. Oddity screamed as John forced them forward once more, trying to keep pace with Charon's slow movement. Fish swirled away from their grisly feast, disturbed by the movement inside Charon's body.

Suddenly they were through. Oddity stumbled and fell as the resistance vanished. Outside, the skeletons were behind them; ahead there were weedy mud flats and the beginnings of a rise. Charon moved between piles of discarded ship ballast as Oddity's lungs heaved and the agony of change lanced through them all. David tried to rise from Passive once more; John only barely managed to keep him down.

He said nothing to Evan. Evan said nothing to him.

Charon hissed. Bubbles rose around them and the body began to rise alongside a rust-stained concrete pier. John forced Oddity to its feet and pushed his way through the body angrily, hating the feel of the wet, cold flesh. There were corroded steel rungs set in the concrete seawall. Oddity swung out of Charon and climbed to the top.

They were waiting for him, a ring of jokers armed with a ragged assortment of weapons.

Oddity howled in frustration.

♣

"What an interesting mind," Bloat commented, but his tiny face was pained and drawn. "The pain makes it unpleasant even for me. Still, the complexity of a shared consciousness is fascinating."

"Where's Patty?" Oddity grated out. Their voice was barely more than a whisper. Most of John's concentration was utilized in staying Dominant against David's mental pushing. They looked from the guards—standing well back from Oddity—to Bloat, gauging distances as the cloak humped and folded over their madly changing body. Bloat chuckled.

"Oh, by the time you got halfway to me, they'd have shot you dead, but then you've already figured that out, haven't you, John? It *is* John, isn't it?" Bloat shook his head. "You should lay down the burden for now, John. It's David I want to speak with."

"No!" Oddity tried to shout; it came out more grunt. "Not until we see Patty."

"I don't think that's a good idea."

[It's a stalemate, John. You see?]

[You give up too easily.] John's ego weakened with each moment, his hold on Dominant crumbling. Desperation colored his thoughts. Oddity gave a tremulous sigh.

Underneath both of them but rising, rising, David whispered only to Evan. [Look at all the bodies here you can have any one of them no need to play goddamn hero just let me past let me take Oddity and I'll set you free I promise don't let us die. . . .]

"We'll see her," Oddity said, "or we'll see how close we get to you. You kill us or you die. It really doesn't matter. One way we get what I want, the other way what Evan wants. *Either* way, you lose."

Bloat sighed. "Such a waste." He sighed, then gestured with one tiny hand. "I didn't care to show my hole card so quickly, but I suppose it can't be helped. Bring her in," he said, then nodded to Oddity. "You need to understand the situation. Can David hear me?"

The fencing mask nodded under the hood.

"Good. It's important he does. David, even if you can, don't jump back yet. Ah, here she is. . . ."

Somehow, thinking of Patty alone in one body had given them a vision of her as she once had been: dark brown hair swirling around her shoulders and wearing the denim skirt she liked so well with a blouse of unbleached cotton. But the person who stepped from the side doorway was in soiled Levi's and a leather jacket. The body was distinctly male, a youthful, handsome face topped with blond and unruly hair.

"John? Evan?" he [she?] said, and the voice was deep. "I love you both. I miss you."

♠

Patty said the words, and felt the truth of them with the tears they set off in her eyes. Behind her, rubber wheels squeaked against tile. She glanced back at the joker pushing the wheelchair with a young jumper's body. The bait. The temptation.

[Yours. It can be yours.] The knowledge tore at her, and she looked back at Oddity, remembering the pain and the hurt and the feeling of being imprisoned.

"Patty?" Bloat said, and her gaze went grudgingly to the joker. "I need to know. Now. Will you cooperate with me? Do it for yourself. Do it for all jokers. Do it for the rapture. Help me."

Patty looked again at the young woman, at the empty, wonderful body. She also saw Oddity watching and she knew that John and Evan could guess her thoughts as well. Faintly, she saw the fencing mask that was Oddity's face nod, as if in forgiveness. [Go on,] she could almost hear John and Evan saying. [We understand.]

Patty reached out and stroked the girl's face with a yearning wistfulness. The skin felt soft and smooth. She knew she would remember that softness forever.

She turned, trying to remember it all. Trying to pack into these few seconds all the sensations of being alone, of being one.

She shook her head.

"No," she told Bloat, not caring that David's body was weeping openly now. "I hate Oddity, but I love Evan and John. You only want Oddity as a weapon, and I won't be a part of that. I'd rather be with my lovers again, as we were."

♦

"I'd rather be with my lovers again, as we were."

Patty's words startled all of them. Evan could feel the surprise loosen what little hold he had.

Oddity screamed.

All at once, everything inside the Oddity had become fluid. The mind barriers crumpled and went to dust.

[John?]

[I've lost Oddity, Evan. You have to—]

The person in David's body was running to them, and his [her?] arms were around them, hugging them and not caring that the body was changing underneath the embrace. Oddity stood there, the arms half up as if unsure whether or not to return the embrace. . . .

[Evan, hold David back. . . .]

[I'm trying, John.]

For a moment, Evan was in control of Oddity as Patty [David?] stared up into the bowl of the fencing mask. "My God, Patty . . ." he moaned. "We love you so much. . . ."

"Evan? It's so lonely out here. I miss you, Evan, John. Please . . . I want back in." She was crying, clutching tighter to Oddity as the powerful, piebald arms went around her at last.

"But you're free," Oddity said, and the voice was slurred, confused. "I don't understand—"

[Hold him, Evan, hold him. . . .]

[Now, Evan. Let me have Oddity,] David insisted.

David's will shoved at Evan's weak resistance. Laughing, David shoved past Evan and into the Dominant position. Immediately the Oddity groaned as the full impact of the pain hammered at the youth. Yet this time, prepared for the torture, David clung to Dominant.

Evan did nothing. Nothing.

He let David have Oddity without a struggle.

[You promised me,] he said to David. [Remember what you promised me.]

[Goddamn son of a bitch, Evan . . .]

"Fucking Christ, Bloat, this *hurts!*"

"David!" Bloat sounded pleased. "Good. Now that you control Oddity, I can say more." He looked down at Patty, who struggled in Oddity's grasp. "I'd continue to hold on to your body. I'd hate to see Patty damage it, which is what she's considering at the moment."

Patty cursed, glaring at Bloat.

Oddity's grip on Patty tightened. "Say it quick, Bloat. I know it ain't your style, but I ain't staying here long."

Bloat smiled. "In a nutshell, then. It's time for us to organize. It's time for the jumpers to help the Rox."

Oddity chuckled, then groaned as another shift in the mutable body racked them. "That's what you were telling Patty. So what? You upping the rent?"

Bloat shrugged, the tiny shoulders lifting helplessly in the immense body. "I imagine there are any number of jokers who would like to be aces, especially here in the Rox. A few judicious triple jumps . . . Imagine what a dozen or so jokers-turned-aces might be able to accomplish."

"Especially with Bloat telling us what to do."

"Especially." Bloat smiled.

[Evan, you can't allow this. . . .]

Evan ignored John's pleading. [David, you promised me. Right?]

[Hey, man. I keep promises. Don't worry.]

[Then go ahead and jump. I'll take Dominant.]

Patty struggled in their arms, biting and clawing uselessly against Oddity's compelling strength. "We'll talk, Bloat," Oddity said. "Maybe you're right. Maybe it's time to organize a little. But in a second, when I'm back in my own skin."

"What about Oddity?" Kafka interjected, looking worried.

"I agree with my counselor, David," Bloat said. "I thought

Patty would help us control it. Perhaps Oddity's simply too dangerous."

[Evan?]

[Just give me a body, David. Like you promised.]

"It'll be cool," David told them. "Don't worry about Oddity."

Inside Oddity, there was a moment of chilling vacancy [. . . Evan! . . .] and then Patty was back, stunned and falling almost immediately to Passive as John made a last desperate attempt to take Dominant.

Evan shoved him back contemptuously. David's eyes had closed. Now they opened again and looked up at Oddity and the hidden face behind the mesh. "Hey, man. You can let me go now."

[John? Patty? I love you both. I'm sorry.]

[Evan—]

[We understand we do . . . .]

Oddity's hands came up. One was Patty's now, one John's. In a swift movement they grasped either side of David's head.

With all of Oddity's power they twisted savagely.

The *snap* of the neck breaking was very loud.

Oddity let the body crumple to the floor. They spread their hands wide, closing their eyes for the last time and waiting for Bloat to give the order, waiting for the bullets to shred their shared body.

[Good-bye Patty, John. I do love you.]

It never happened.

Bloat was staring at David's body. Kafka watched Bloat. The joker guards' weapons were pointing at them, ready.

Bloat only gave a brief sigh.

"David was my key. He was willing to listen to me, to share in my dream. If you were Golden Boy or Peregrine or just another ace, I wouldn't hesitate," he told them, still looking at David's body. "But not the Oddity. Not people who know the pain of being a joker."

The tiny head on the mounded body closed its eyes. The body rippled and more bloatblack oozed from the body. The smell of corruption was strong in the room.

"Get out," Bloat told them savagely. "Get out before I change my mind."

♥

Dutton finally opened the back fire door and stood blinking into the Jokertown dawn. The noseless, living skull face yawned. He tugged the cord of his silk bathrobe tightly around his waist.

"Oddity." He sounded relieved. "I was worried. I'd called some people I knew—"

"We came to work."

"Evan?" Dutton glanced at the hands—for the most part, they were chocolate brown and long-fingered. Dutton stepped away from the door and let the cloaked figure enter, then shut and locked the door behind them. The museum seemed gloomy after the sunshine. "It's six in the morning. What happened? Where's Patty?"

"Here. Passive for the moment. John's with us, too. It's over, Charles. We—I—was wrong. We wanted to tell you."

"Wrong?"

"About endings. Maybe things *do* occasionally work out. The leader of the jumper gang's dead, Charles."

Behind the mask, Oddity laughed, full and loud. The gaiety sounded very strange to Dutton. "It doesn't solve everything," Oddity continued. "Probably not much at all. But it's one little change for the good. A few less atrocities the nats will be able to blame on us, one less excuse they can use to oppress people affected by the wild card."

"And you? What about Oddity?"

"It still hurts. But one of us got out, at least for a bit. We can think of that and hope that maybe—someday—the rest will change."

Oddity sighed.

Under the heavy cloak, shapes came and went.

"You got any cake, Charles?" they said. "It's our birthday."

My Name Is Nobody

by Walton Simons

JERRY WALKED UP THE stone steps into the Church of St. Ig-
natius Loyola. He hadn't been inside a church in over thirty years.
His parents had exposed him to their religious preference, which
was Episcopalian, but had let him stop going after he continually
went to sleep during the service. David had been Catholic, though.
At least the building had a late-Renaissance look that was less for-
bidding than the usual Gothic stuff.

Jerry slipped in and sat behind Kenneth and Beth. They wouldn't
recognize him, though. He was wearing an old look, with sagging
flesh, bad posture, and gray hair. Jerry hoped he could pick up a
comment from Beth saying she missed him, but they sat silently
through David's eulogy. Jerry wanted to stand up and tell everyone that the man they were mourning was a bad one by anyone's
standards, let alone a devout Catholic's. That David was behind
the "jumper" crimes and deserved exactly what he got. Jerry wanted
to, but he didn't. First off, if there was a God, he/she/it would not
be impressed. Second, he didn't have any proof. That chapped him
plenty. All those months of detective work and he had nothing to
show for it. Nobody except Tachyon would ever know he'd found
David out, and Tachyon was all for secrecy.

Jerry glanced across the aisle at St. John Latham. The attorney put his hand to his mouth and coughed. There was strain in his neck and his face was pale. He was breathing in an even, but forced manner. Latham shook his head, then reached in his coat pocket and dabbed at his eyes. Jerry wanted to bend over the pew and get Kenneth and Beth to look Latham's way. They wouldn't believe the tears any more than Jerry did. St. John was the original iceman.

Latham stood, left his pew, and headed for the back of the church. Beth and Kenneth were still focused on the minister. Jerry hobbled after Latham down the church's central aisle. He had to move slowly to stay in character and Latham was nowhere to be seen when he entered the foyer.

A young kid stood at the door to the men's room. He was wearing a new black suit and had obvious blackheads all over his face. Jerry headed for the men's room, wheezing.

"Sorry, old man," the kid said as Jerry approached the door. "It's *occupé* right now."

"My medication," Jerry said, beginning to shake. "I'll die."

The kid made an unhappy face. "Oh, all right. But don't be long."

Jerry heard a man sobbing in one of the stalls as he stepped in. He didn't have to see the face to know who it was. Latham was blubbering like he'd lost his own son. Jerry began running water to wash his hands. The crying tapered off. After a few moments the person inside blew his nose. Jerry turned off the water and reached for a towel. Latham stepped out of the stall.

"He was a fine boy," Jerry said.

"Yes, very fine indeed." Latham turned on the faucet and splashed water on his face. His eyes were completely bloodshot. He left before Jerry could say anything else. Jerry stepped outside in time to see him leaving with the kid.

Something was definitely up.

♣

Jerry savored his last bite of Imperial Duck, chewing it slowly. He'd had to let his belt out a notch already, and it was getting tight again.

"God, that's good," Jerry said.

Kenneth nodded. "Oh, yeah. I'm glad you didn't back out at the last minute."

"It's not you I'm mad at." Jerry took a sip of his hot tea and reached for his fortune cookie.

"Do you enjoy being mad at her?" Kenneth asked, his voice flat and nonjudgmental.

"I don't know. I just feel like she came down unnecessarily hard on me. I don't need that right now." Jerry cracked open his cookie and pulled out the fortune. He paused a moment to read it.

"What does it say?"

"'You will overcome many hardships,'" Jerry said. "I don't think I like that. It means I'll have to deal with them."

"On the plus side, maybe it means you and Beth will get things sorted out. That would certainly go a long way toward making me happy." Kenneth read his fortune and wrinkled his brow.

"How about yours?" Jerry asked. "'Babes in abundance will beat a path to your door'?"

"'A good man has few enemies; a ruthless man has none.'"

Jerry made a face. "Fortunes for the eighties. Get yours and take out anyone who gets in your way. That's real encouraging."

Kenneth paid the bill and the brothers walked out into the crowded streets of Chinatown. The spring air had a freshness that even the smell of garbage couldn't cling to.

"Let's walk awhile," Kenneth said, heading toward Canal.

"Okay by me." Jerry patted his stomach. "I need a little exercise or I'll lose my schoolboy figure."

"Beth told me she called you last week. She said you hemmed and hawed, but promised you'd call her back soon." Kenneth turned and looked at Jerry. "Are you?"

"Yes, she called. And yes, I'm going to call her back when I feel damn good and ready." Jerry knew it was shitty to put her off, but felt like letting her twist in the wind for a while. He really wanted his pound of flesh. "I don't want to talk about this anymore. How about those Knicks, eh?"

"Whatever you say. Just don't lie to her, she hates that." Kenneth looked at his watch. "Maybe we have time to pick up some canoles."

"Time is something I got plenty—" Jerry heard gunfire from inside one of the buildings and flinched. Kenneth pulled him to the pavement as three kids in ski masks and blue satin jackets charged out of an antique shop. All three had guns drawn. They stopped in front of Jerry and Kenneth. Jerry saw two cold brown eyes meet his. The kid's gun swiveled over and past him. Another kid said something in Chinese. The group sprinted off down the street and ducked into an alley. Jerry recognized the bird on the back of their jackets.

"Egrets," he said. Jerry stood, then helped Kenneth to his feet. Someone wailed inside the antique shop.

"What did you say?" Kenneth looked at him hard.

"Immaculate Egrets. They're a street gang. I saw a TV special on them." Jerry smiled. "Nothing like a little mayhem to get your blood going. Should we call the police, or something?"

"I'm sure they've already been contacted. I don't recall any TV special on that particular gang." Kenneth started walking Jerry down the street. "Look, I've heard rumors that you've been doing some detective work. Certain individuals take that sort of thing very personally. So if it's true, I'd advise you to stop it. Now."

Jerry couldn't imagine how Kenneth had found out. Beth wouldn't talk, even though she was mad at him. Maybe someone had tipped him about Jerry having hired Ackroyd at one point. But he'd been checking out David, and David was gone. Jerry decided to do a little fishing. "Who's Kien?"

Kenneth blanched. "So. It is true. You don't want to know, Jerry. Latham is much more dangerous than you can imagine. He's been losing his grip lately, so stay out of his way." Kenneth glanced at his watch again. "I need to get home."

"Latham's got something on you, doesn't he?" Jerry couldn't imagine his brother this scared for any other reason.

"Let's just say the situation is balanced, but very precariously." Kenneth grabbed Jerry by the elbow. "Don't upset the balance. You could get us all killed."

A police car squealed around the corner and bounced down the street, its siren and rotating reds going. "You head on home, Kenneth. Don't worry about me. I'm going to stick around and tell the cops what I saw here." Jerry would also memorize the cops' faces and badge numbers. That could come in handy later, too.

Kenneth gave Jerry a look of troubled resignation. "Watch out for yourself. If you get into trouble with this, I might not be able to get you out. I'd try, of course."

"I know. Tell Beth I really will call her sometime." Jerry waved his brother off. "And don't worry about me. There's more here than meets the eye."

Kenneth gave a weak waist-high wave and turned away. It began to rain softly. Jerry walked down toward the police car. If Latham was putting the squeeze on his family, Jerry was going to dig something up and squeeze back, hard. Thunder rumbled across the sky in the distance.

♠

Jerry sat in the lobby, paging through the sports section of the *Times*. He'd changed his eyes and hair to brown and darkened his skin. His bone structure was thicker. The Knicks were definitely going to make the playoffs. As long as they didn't wash out in the first round, especially to Boston, he could live with whatever happened.

He hadn't turned up thing one on Latham. St. John didn't even have a police record, so he was obviously as sharp as Kenneth said. Might as well shadow him and see if he could come up with something. Anything Jerry could uncover he'd turn over to Kenneth. That way, if Latham decided to up the stakes, Kenneth could match him.

The elevator pinged softly. Latham stepped out of the car, alone. Jerry carefully folded up his paper, stood, and followed him into the street.

It was warm and breezy outside. The sky over Manhattan was clear. The sidewalks, unfortunately, were not. Latham was walking fast and Jerry had to push and shove to keep him in sight. Latham crossed the street at the corner, trotting out onto the asphalt just as the sign across the street started blinking DON'T WALK. Jerry knifed through the crowd, but before he could get across, the traffic surged in front of him.

Jerry stood at the corner, bouncing up and down on his toes. Latham got into a black Cadillac parked in a tow-away zone. There were two young boys in the front seat, and a girl in the back with Latham. The girl had spiky black hair and looked vaguely familiar, but at this distance most people did. She put her arms around his neck and kissed him. They were still kissing when the light changed and the Caddy whipped out into the street. It was gone before Jerry could get a license-plate number.

He changed back in the first-floor men's room. Nobody noticed that the person who went in didn't look at all like the person who came out. Nobody ever noticed. That was one good thing about present-day New York. He checked himself in the mirror on the way out. "Just call me Mr. Nobody," he said. The name felt more appropriate than he wanted it to.

◆

Tachyon was giving Blaise a lecture of some sort. The boy looked like a pit bull who'd just taken a beating from his master, mad and ready to get even.

"Not now, Jeremiah," Tachyon said. "Family discussion."

Blaise gave Jerry a contemptuous look. "Yeah, you don't belong here."

Tachyon reached over with his good hand and grabbed Blaise by the chin. "That will be quite enough. Apologize to Mr. Strauss."

Blaise set his jaw and stared at his grandfather in hateful silence.

"I'll see you some other time," Jerry said, backing out.

Tachyon turned Blaise loose and shook his head apologetically. "Soon, I hope. You've just caught me at a bad time."

Jube the Walrus was standing by the curb when Jerry stepped outside the clinic. His Hawaiian print shirt was a recognizable beacon against the gray of Jokertown.

"Did you hear the one about the guy who played center on the joker basketball team?" the Walrus asked.

"Nope," Jerry said.

"He was a seven-footer, but only five feet tall." Jube smiled around his tusks. "Want a *Cry?*"

Jerry had started to shake his head when he saw the DOUBLE JUMPER INCIDENT headline. He'd been so involved with snooping on Latham that he hadn't paid attention to what was going on in the world. "Sure." He dug out his wallet and handed Jube a twenty. "Don't bother with the change. What do you know about these jumpers?"

Jube shrugged. "Nothing that isn't in the paper. There hadn't been an incident in a while, I thought maybe we were through with those kids."

"Me, too," Jerry said.

"Sure you don't want your change?" The Walrus hadn't tucked the bill away yet.

"Nah. Just let me know if you hear anything else. I know where to find you." Jerry raised his arm as a cab rounded the corner.

"Will do. Did you hear the one about the joker cabdriver?"

"No." Jerry had a feeling he was going to.

♠ ♥ ♦ ♣

The Devil's Triangle

by Melinda M. Snodgrass

HER FINGERS TWINED, WARM and a little dry, through his. Each undulating rise and fall of the horse pulled them apart. Skin sliding on skin. Then the midpoint when for an instant they were side by side, poised in the moment with no retreat.

Tachyon half opened his eyes and watched the colored lights of the carousel whirl past. The music was a little sharp, a little tinny, but it was a waltz.

And in his dreams they were dancing.

He cautiously turned his head, and with that unspoken communication that had arced between them from the moment of their first meeting, she, too, was turning her head. The fine bones of her face were etched in the lights of a Coney Island ride, the eye patch a dark scar on that beautiful face. A deformity, yes, but an honorable one. A wound won in battle. Even on Takis one might be tempted to keep the scars, not replace the missing eye.

The music was slowing, the horses' eager spring dying to an awkward sad sigh as the ride came to an end. Without thinking, Tach patted the arching neck of his steed. His artificial hand struck the wood of the carousel horse, producing an ugly hollow tone.

The violence of his reaction was wearily familiar. Stomach closing into a tight ball, jamming itself against the back of the spine, nausea like a physical pain. Cody's hands cupped his face, but there was no gentleness in the touch.

"Cut it out. You lost a hand. He could have gutted you. I lost an eye. The bullet could have blown my damn head off. If you're smart, you're grateful to just fucking be *alive*."

"I'm sorry, I'm not normally a whiner."

"Yes, you are." She smiled to take away the sting. "You're always agonizing about what can't be fixed. The past is dead, and the future ain't here yet. The best we can do is live for the moment, Tachyon."

They started walking down the midway. The air was redolent with the smell of stale grease, corn dogs, cotton candy. Overhead the sky was a diffuse milky white as the high clouds reflected back the lights of New York. Barkers squalled from their cheap and gaudy arcades.

"See Tiny Tina, the world's smallest horse."

"Three balls for a dollar. Knock over the milk bottles, and a prize is yours."

Screams from the more garishly neon-decorated rides ripped the night air. The Parachute Jump blossomed like an exotic lily against the night sky. Tiny figures plummeted toward the ground only to be caught by the billowing of a parachute. There was something almost grotesquely maternal about the gigantic ride dropping its little chutes like seedlings around its looming bulk.

Tachyon tore his gaze away from the Jump and asked, "Where did they say they were going?"

"The Zipper," Cody said.

"Dreadful."

"They're boys."

The couple stopped at the entrance to the ride. Rock music assaulted the ears, the bass line vibrating in the ground itself. The little cars were opening, spilling their stumbling, tottering passengers like peas from a pod. Blaise had his arm around Chris. The human boy was staggering, but Blaise, his hair almost scarlet under the lights, was fully in control. There was a wild light in his dark eyes, and his teeth gleamed.

"What did you think?" asked Blaise.

"Damn . . . that was awesome," replied Chris.

Tachyon and Cody exchanged glances at the way the child had awkwardly prefaced the sentence with the cuss word.

Boys into men, thought Tachyon. So difficult a transition.

"Chris is what? Thirteen?" he asked.

"Yes," said Cody.

"At thirteen I was just emerging from the women's quarters."

"That's lousy planning. Just when a boy wants to be around girls, you separate them." She studied her adolescent son now exchanging playful blows with Blaise. "On second thought, considering the raging hormones at that age, maybe it's a good thing—before any ad hoc biology lessons can begin."

"We have toys for that."

"What!"

He caught her thought of outrageous sexual implements. "Not those kind of toys, living toys."

"I think that's worse."

She walked away to join her son, and Tachyon chewed on his lower lip. She was a strong woman with strong attitudes. Had his flippant remark offended her? Made her think that he regarded her as a toy? He hurried after the threesome wondering how to make amends. ·

The boys were walking across each other's lines, each trying to draw Cody's attention. Blaise danced out in front of her, walking backward with easy hip-swinging grace, somehow avoiding the oncoming crowds.

Maybe he has more telepathy than I think, Tachyon mused as he studied that lean figure. At fourteen Blaise was already three inches taller than his grandsire, and already showed signs of developing

a linebacker's shoulders, and the whip-lean hip of the true athlete.

*And you're having a hell of a time taking him during your karate
workouts*, a disquieting voice reminded him.

Tachyon shook off the worry. Blaise had been much better since
Cody had entered their lives. Putting aside that it was a celibate
relationship, it had all the qualities of a marriage. Cody alternately
scolded and mothered Blaise, and he loved it. Her interest in the
boy had soothed his mercurial disposition. In fact, it had been
months since Tach had felt actively afraid of his grandchild.

"Cody," Blaise was saying. "Would you like me to win you a
stuffed toy? I can do it." He jerked his head toward the shooting
gallery.

Tachyon stepped up to join them. Cocked a grin up at Cody.
"Perhaps you better rely upon me. I've been at this a little longer
than he has."

Blaise frowned, and Tach felt a flare of embarrassment. Prancing and snorting in front of his fourteen-year-old grandson. Who
was in competition with whom?

The woman sniffed. "Thanks boys, but I'll win one for myself."
She allowed her fingers to ruffle lightly across the curls on the top
of his head. Tach felt as if his lungs had been replaced with stones.
It was tough to draw a breath.

"A contest," said Blaise, his eyes bright.

The three males followed Cody to the gallery and laid down
their money. She was already testing the weight of the weapon. Tach
hefted the rifle. It was awkward left-handed. Despite his thrice-
weekly sessions at the range he still had much to relearn.

The operator fired up his machine, and a line of rampant bears
trundled across the back wall. Blaise and Chris blazed away. Blaise
was better than the human boy, but neither of them succeeded in
scoring the requisite number to continue. Blaise threw down the
rifle and backed off, muttering petulantly in French.

Tachyon and Cody stepped up to the counter. Began firing. The operator stared openmouthed at their competence. Charging bears fell supine onto all fours and were swept away. The numbers mounted. Chris's cheeks were red with excitement. He hung close to his mother's left side. Blaise's glance was smoldering fire between Tachyon's shoulder blades.

Tachyon had missed two shots. Cody only one. One more and he was out. He sighted, drew in a breath, held it, squeezed the trigger. The bear remained smugly, stubbornly upright. It seemed to be sneering as it rounded the corner. Tachyon laid down the rifle. Cody kept shooting. It took five more minutes before she had finally missed three shots.

The man pulled down an enormous white tiger and handed it with a bow to Cody. Tach as a consolation prize got Roger Rabbit.

The man and woman, with their children in tow, headed back into the shifting color of the midway.

"Aren't you ashamed of yourself?" Tachyon scolded as they waited for Blaise and Chris to buy cotton candy.

"For what?"

"Demolishing my fragile Takisian ego."

"Takisian, my aunt Betsy. *Male* ego." She gave him an ironic glance out of her one eye. "Going to win a prize for the little lady," she mocked.

"Be kind, I am a one-handed shootist."

"And I'm a one-eyed shootist. So much for excuses."

But Tachyon had lost his taste for the banter. He was reliving a nightmare. *Blood and bone fragments fountaining into the air. Agony, agony, agony!*

Her cheek was warm against his. Her arm a welcome support.

"What is it? What's wrong?"

"Memory," he forced out. "We remember more clearly than you humans. It's our curse." He drew his thumb across his forehead. It came away wet. "Oh Ideal, I am sorry, it is passing now."

Her hand slid down and gathered his prosthetic hand into hers. "You remember the pain . . . ?" Her voice trailed away in a question.

"As if it were yesterday."

"Oh, God, I'm sorry."

Her lips were against his cheek. Whispering the words. The warm breath puffed against his chilled skin, and suddenly Tachyon realized he was in the circle of her arms. Since that day at the clinic they had never done more than touch hands. Now her arms were around him again. Their thighs were lightly touching, and he had a full erection.

Simultaneously they began muttering apologies and inanities and backed away from each other. Cody hurriedly swept up the boys. Tachyon went in search of a men's room.

"Meet you at the car," he called to them as he fled in search of cold water to splash on his face and a long pee to relieve the pressure—sort of.

♥

Roger Rabbit sprawled on the sofa in the office. The tensor lamp threw an almost painful yellow light across the welter of papers on the desk. The rest of the room was in shadow. Tachyon rubbed gritty eyes, picked up his fountain pen, and laboriously scrawled his signature across the bottom of a grant request. His prosthetic right hand was serving as a paperweight at the top of the page.

Most of the grants had dried up after the bloody events at the Democratic National Convention last July. This grant was for fifteen thousand dollars from the greater New York Franco-American society. Fifteen thousand dollars would keep the Blythe van Renssaeler Memorial Clinic open and operating for about two hours and twenty-seven minutes, but all the little thousands added up to joker lives saved.

Tachyon heard the distinctive quick tap of her heels in the hall outside his office. The door opened, and Cody was there, backlit by the fluorescent bulbs in the hall.

"What in hell are you doing here? It's two A.M."

"And why are you here, Madam Surgeon?"

"I had patients to check on."

"As do I."

"Those"—she waved a hand toward the paperwork—"are not worth killing yourself over." She crossed to the desk. "People we either cure or bury. These"—she swept up a handful of paper from the desk, crumpled them and dropped them into the trash can—"we handle in a different way."

"Cody, behave yourself." Tachyon dug out the abused paperwork.

She cocked a hip up onto the desk. Tachyon's mouth went dry. At the amusement park she had been wearing blue jeans: now, unaccountably, she had changed into a skirt. Her pose left a lot of thigh visible. Tachyon was noticing.

She noticed him noticing and smiled. With the eye patch and the scar it gave her a dangerous predatory look. But sexy: God, she was sexy.

"You had one hell of an erection at the carnival," she said conversationally. "Made me realize just where I stood with you."

After swallowing his stomach, Tach forced his voice into the same matter-of-fact tone she had used. "Cody, we have been working together for almost a year. Frankly I'm surprised at my forbearance, and I can hardly be blamed for my body's betrayal."

"I'm a professional. Soldier, doctor, your chief of surgery."

"And a woman," he reminded softly.

"And you want me."

"I would be a liar if I denied it." He picked up his hand and fitted it onto the stump of his right arm. "Could you ever want me?"

"I don't know. I'm nervous about getting too close to you."

"Why?"

"You've had too many women. I don't want to be just another notch on your gun."

"You make me sound very spoiled . . . heedless."

"You are. In some ways you're a real user."

"As long as we're being this honest—you should know that I have been incredibly forbearing and patient with you. I have been willing to wait—"

She slid off the desk. "Yeah, but I'm worth it," she interrupted.

"God damn it, woman. I want you!"

"Tough. Until you lose the revolving door, I'm not interested. If I walk through your bedroom door, I better be the only one."

"What are you asking for?"

"Commitment. It's an important word to me. I'm the most loyal friend you'll ever have, Tachyon. But if you betray me I'll kill you. Are you still certain you want me walking through that bedroom door?"

"I don't know. You frighten me . . . a little."

"Good. The game's not big enough if it doesn't scare you."

She suddenly leaned in and kissed him quick and hard on the lips.

"What was that for?" Tachyon asked.

"For being man enough to admit that we women really are the more dangerous sex."

He combed back his hair. "You have me totally confused."

"Good."

The door closed softly behind her.

♣

Tiny, gaudily dressed figures whirled past in a kaleidoscope of colors. The rifle butt was slick against his cheek. *Her* eyes warm on the back of his neck. He squeezed convulsively and bullets sprayed like light rays from the barrel of the gun. Tiny Tachyons shattered and died.

The man was handing down a *gigantic* toy. He turned to face her. Her expression of pride and love warmed him. Her hand reached out, and stroked down his cheek, unzipped his pants, pulled out his penis. Her lips were hot on the head of his cock. His heart squeezed into a tight painful ball.

Sperm jetted hot and sticky across his belly. Blaise sat up in bed, breath coming in hoarse gasps.

Cody, Cody, Cody.

♠

Cody was just leaving as Blaise and Chris arrived at the apartment. She kissed Chris on the cheek, lifted Blaise's Dodgers cap, and ruffled his hair. Fire shot through him, and he stared at her with hot, suggestive eyes. Blaise noticed with satisfaction that she turned away quickly to gather up her purse and briefcase.

"Okay, outlaws, I'm off to the hospital. There's a chocolate cake on the counter *and* Coke in the fridge, so no excuses for not studying. The sugar rush ought to be enough to propel you into next week."

"Okay, Mom," said Chris

"Blaise, are you all right?" Cody asked, a hand on the doorknob. "You keep staring at me like a boy with acute constipation."

Blood flamed in his cheeks, and Blaise's fantasies deflated like his suddenly flaccid penis. "I'm fine," he muttered.

The door closed behind her, but the scent of her perfume still lingered in his hair.

Chris was already in the kitchen hacking off two enormous slabs of chocolate cake.

"Algebra," he said as Blaise walked in. "Do you understand it? And *why* do we have to understand it?"

"You might not have to, but I do. It's the first step to calculus and trig, and you have to have all three for astrogation. I've got a spaceship that's going to be mine someday. I have to know how to navigate her."

"That is so neat," Chris mumbled around a gigantic mouthful. "A spaceship, *and* a granddad who's an alien."

"It's not so great."

Chris gaped at him. "You gotta be kidding. What could be better?"

"The life I had before." Blaise carefully cut away the icing, and mashed it with his fork. "No school, no homework, no *clean up your room*. My father did that. Uncle Claude said I was too important to be irritated by the mundane."

"You've got a father?" asked Chris in honest amazement.

"Yes, of course."

"So . . . where is he?"

"In a French prison."

"How come?"

"He's a terrorist. Tachyon put him there."

"That's good."

"Why?" asked Blaise.

"Because . . . well . . . because—"

"Chris, it's *fun* to be a terrorist."

"Yeah?"

"You're always on the run. Always changing houses. Passwords, meeting arms dealers at night on the river. Always a step ahead of the stupid flics. You're always walking a step to the left of ordinary people. They have to work or go to school. We watched the artists in Montmartre, ate pastries in cafés on the Left Bank. We walked through the museums and he told me all about the painters, our history. '*Vive la France*,' he would say, and then he would laugh and hug me."

"Who?"

"Uncle Claude."

"And was he a terrorist, too?"

"Yes."

"What happened to him? Is he in prison like your dad?"

Very levelly Blaise replied, "No, he's dead." Blaise mashed cake, and watched icing erupt through the tines of the fork. "I think my grandfather killed him."

"Blaise!" Chris's eyes were wide, and he had chocolate icing around his mouth. It made him look absurdly young, and really stupid.

"Your mother really likes me," Blaise said, changing the subject abruptly. He was tired of the past. Thinking about it made him sad. Made him mad.

"Huh?"

The younger boy's incomprehension infuriated Blaise. Gripping Chris by the hair, he yanked back the human boy's head.

"She wants me! She's in love with me!"

"You're crazy!" yelled Chris. "You're just a kid. Like me. You're like my brother, except I don't *want* you for a brother when you act crazy."

"We'll never be brothers." Blaise's tone was quiet, dangerously rational. "For us to be brothers . . . that would imply that Cody and my grandfather—"

"It could happen."

Blaise was on Chris again, his long, slim hands closing around the boy's throat, but he exerted no pressure. "No," he said softly. "That is *not* going to happen."

He released Chris, and walked out of the apartment.

♦

"Tachyon, we've got to talk."

The alien looked up from the microscope. Blinked to clear the moisture from his eyes brought about by too-close concentration. The woman's agitation beat at him despite her level tone and calm expression.

"Cody."

He held out his artificial hand. She laid her hand on his forearm where the prosthesis met flesh.

"What happened to Chris?" Tachyon said.

"Damn." She bit her lip. "Why has this happened?"

Humbly he said, "I do not mean to read your thoughts. They are just there for me."

"I'm my own woman, Tachyon," she warned.

"I know." He cocked an ankle onto his knee. "Now, tell me what happened."

"I'm concerned about my son, but the reason for my concern is Blaise."

Tachyon knew his expression had grown wary. He fiddled with the focusing mechanism on the microscope.

You may hide it from yourself, but the world sees, mocked a little voice.

The Takisian steeled himself.

Cody continued. "Blaise scared Chris half to death last night."

"Did he mind-control him?"

"No, but he wrapped his hands around my kid's throat. He made some crazy remarks about me." Cody made a weary gesture. "Now it sounds so stupid, but I saw the fear in Chris's eyes."

"Blaise is . . . erratic at times. In the months since you've been here I've seen an improvement in him. You've been the mother he never had, and he wants to please you. There is less anger in him—"

"It's not the anger that worries me. There's a coldness in Blaise that's almost inhuman."

"He is inhuman. He's a quarter Takisian."

"That's bullshit, and you know it. Genetically humans and

Takisians are identical. Maybe you were our ancient astronauts—I don't know, and none of this is relevant. The point is that—"

She broke off abruptly.

"Say it, Cody."

"Tach, he needs help."

"I can help him."

"No. You're the problem."

He rose and walked away from the truth of that statement.

Spinning back to face her, he said, "You have to understand. What he's been through. The horrors he has seen and endured." Tach was nervously washing his hands. He noticed and forced himself to stop.

"His childhood was spent in the hands of a violent revolutionary cell in Paris. Then last year he became a host for a hideous creature. While in its thrall, he experienced his first sexual encounter. He mind-controlled a joker and forced the wretch to *literally* tear himself to pieces."

Her hands closed about his, and he looked up into that single fierce dark eye.

"Tachyon, I'm willing to be understanding. This is all very sad, but it doesn't alter the relevant, dangerous fact. Blaise is a sociopath, maybe even psychotic. People are going to continue to get hurt."

"I am willing to take that risk."

"Fine! But you don't have the right to place others at risk."

"What can I do! With his mind powers do you really think he's going to submit to analysis?"

A new, worrisome thought intruded. He watched it etch itself momentarily on her face. Concern rose in the back of his throat, snatching the breath from his lungs, and Tachyon realized it was *her* emotions he was feeling. She was afraid for him.

"Tachyon, *you* can control him, can't you?"

"For now."

"What does that mean, for now?"

"As he matures, he gains power. I've taken to maintaining shields against him constantly."

"How hard are these shields to . . . ?"

"To break?"

"Yes."

"Exceedingly," he soothed.

"I'm afraid."

"Don't be. I will protect you." Her hair was soft against his fingertips as he brushed it back from her forehead.

Sharply. "I don't need your protection!"

Startled, he pulled back. "I meant no offense. I assumed you would be a shield to my back as well," he stuttered, backpedaling frantically. The militant light died from her eye.

"Damn it!"

"What?"

"It's so damn hard to hold my own against you."

"Why must you?"

"Because you're too fucking seductive. Too glib. Too polished. Too attentive. I *won't—*"

She whirled and was out of the lab as if every ancestor ghost in her pedigree was on her heels.

♥

The bright June sunlight spilled into the gloomy interior of the Jokertown Dime Museum and set dust motes to spinning. Blaise liked that. Had they been there all along, he wondered, just waiting in the darkness for his coming? Or had his arrival created them?

Do other people think those kinds of thoughts? Blaise mused as he sauntered past the "Hideous Joker Baby" display and the Jetboy diorama. Cody was standing in front of the waxwork figure of his grandfather. Blaise felt a flare of irritation.

The woman thoughtfully stirred her cup of Italian lemon ice and took a bite.

"How young he looks," Blaise heard her say.

"No different than now," said Dutton, owner of the Dime Museum.

The joker was standing behind her, hands hidden in the folds of his cloak. The hood was back, revealing the death's-head. Blaise wondered if the man was trying to shock Cody, or if this was a measure of how well accepted she had become?

Cody was speaking again. "No, that's an illusion. When I look at him, I see every one of those forty-three years etched in his face."

"You care for him," suggested Dutton.

"I'm fascinated by him," Cody corrected, then added: "It's the face of a dissipated saint."

"I'll leave you to a contemplation of a face for which you care . . . er . . . with which you are fascinated."

"What lovely grammar you have," said Cody dryly as Dutton retreated back into his office.

The stones were a sharp, hard pressure against his thigh. Blaise cupped his hand protectively about the bulge and moved swiftly to intercept Cody as she moved to survey the Syria diorama.

"Hi, Cody."

"Oh, God, Blaise, you startled me."

She had pressed her hand against her throat. He could see where her tan ended and the milk white of her breast began. He noticed she was wearing a thin gold chain. He liked the way it echoed the gold of her skin. Maybe colored stones didn't suit her? Maybe she didn't like them? *Oh, God, I love you so much!*

But what he said, in a voice jumping with nervousness was, "I got something for you."

He dug into his pocket, the supple leather of the pouch was soft against his hand. The knobby bundle pulled free and Blaise tugged open the drawstrings. With a sound like hail on glass the gemstones spilled across the surface of the diorama console. Emeralds formed a drift about the button controlling Sayyid. A diamond skittered hysterically toward the edge of the console, and Cody automatically caught it. Her fingers closed tight about the jewel. Slowly she raised her hand to eye level and cautiously unfolded her fingers, as if fearful of what her hand contained.

Blaise frowned down at the rainbow spill and worried his lower lip between his teeth. The sapphires looked almost fake—too blue. The rubies weren't bad, but the topaz was best. The boy swept up a golden topaz the size of a small robin's egg and held it against the hollow in Cody's throat. A nervous pulse was hammering there. Blaise liked that.

"Here, this suits you best. I know it's only semiprecious—"

"*Where* did you get these?"

Her voice was rough, commanding, not the breathless excited coo he had expected. Blaise flinched, felt stomach acid starting to churn.

"You don't *ask* about a gift, you just accept it."

The jewels rattled as Cody began sweeping them into a pile. She twitched the leather pouch from his hand and began shoveling in the gems. "Blaise, you're in *big* trouble. Tell me where you got these. Maybe we can work out something without your grandfather having to find out. You are a minor—"

"*Cody!* They're for *you!*"

"I don't want them. I don't want stolen gifts."

"I just wanted to make you happy," said Blaise.

"Well, you've managed to achieve just the reverse."

"Cody." His voice was a plaintive whine. "I love you."

Her hand was soft on his head, the fingers stroking through the rough short ends of his brush cut. "Every kid feels that way. I fell madly in love with my high-school history teacher. It's something we do when we start to notice there's a difference between boys and girls. When you're a teenager, everything seems so insecure.

If we can fall in love with an older person, it helps give a sense of order to a very uncertain world."

"Don't talk down to me!"

"I'm not. I'm trying to show you that I do care. I do understand, but understanding is not permission."

His power was beating against the confines of his skull. His entire body was one great pressure-filled ache. He wanted to explode, to lash out.

"I *love* you." The words had to squeeze past clenched teeth.

"I don't love you."

"I can make you!"

For the first time he saw a reaction. A flicker of alarm in that single dark eye. But her voice was cold and dead level as she said, "That's not love, Blaise, that's rape."

His arm executed a wide, uncontrolled arc. "It's him! It's *him*, isn't it?"

"What are you talking about?"

"I'm better than he is. Younger, stronger. I can give you *every-thing*. Anything you want I can give you. I can take you anywhere."

He began to pace, long agitated strides that carried him across the narrow confines of the aisle and back again. Cody was so still it was frightening.

"Anywhere in the world," he continued. "Off the world. And Chris is okay, he can come, too. You don't want *him* pawing at you. You don't want the stump rubbing your boob, or feeling you up—"

The blow was so unexpected that it stopped the words in his throat and rocked him back on his heels. Cody slowly lowered her hand. Blaise could feel the stinging imprint of her palm on his face. A pressure was building in his chest as if all the unspoken endearments, curses for Tachyon, descriptions of prowess were piling up like cars on a gridlocked beltway.

"Now, you listen, and you listen good! I have allowed you to ramble on in this very silly and very immature fashion out of concern and love for your grandfather, and out of consideration for your youth and folly."

Each word struck like a lash, and Blaise writhed under the withering scorn in the deep, husky voice. His love was curdling until it lay like an oily foul-tasting slick on the back of his tongue.

Cody continued. "But I'm out of time, and I'm out of patience. Somewhere out there"—her arm swung in a wide arc encompassing the city—"there's a lovely young girl who's learning to prove geometry theorems, or cut out a dress pattern, or play tennis, and someday the two of you are going to meet and be very happy together. But that girl isn't me."

She hefted the pouch of jewels and stared sternly down at him.

"Now, tell me where you got these, and I'll see if I can keep you out of reform school. And you keep your mouth shut to your grandfather. I won't tell him what a fool you've been if you'll work with me and we get these jewels back to their owner."

"I *hate* you!"

A mocking little half smile curved her lips. "I thought you loved me."

He backed away, held out a shaking hand. "I . . . will . . . show . . . you."

The Tachyon waxwork was directly opposite him. Blaise coiled and lashed out with a spinning back kick. The head flew off the wax figure, and it toppled to the floor. Then quickly and methodically he kicked it to pieces.

Dutton ran out of the office.

"Hey!"

His voice trailed away as he looked from Blaise to Cody, who was standing as still as one of the waxwork figures surrounding her.

"I'll . . . show . . . you," Blaise said again, and strode out of the museum.

♣

"It should have sounded silly and melodramatic. Hell, it did sound silly and melodramatic, but frankly it scared the pee out of me."

Tachyon pressed a glass into her hands. Folded her chilled fingers about it.

"And when he kicked that waxwork to pieces . . ." Cody took a long swallow of the brandy.

Tachyon returned to the bar and poured himself a drink.

"Are you sure you are not overreacting?" he asked.

"No!"

He held up a placating hand. "All right."

Cody tugged a pouch from her purse and flung it down on the coffee table. It landed with a sharp crack. "And I know for damn sure this isn't an overreaction."

Tach shook out the contents and stared in amazement at the multicolored gems that glittered against the crimson of his glove. His eyebrows flew up inquiringly.

"I called the police and pretended to be a journalist," Cody said. "Nobody has reported a jewel theft."

"I will handle him," said Tachyon. "You need be afraid no longer."

Cody joined him on the sofa. "Tachyon, you moron. I'm not worried about me. I'm worried about you. What I saw in Blaise's face was—"

She broke off and bit down on her lower lip. Tachyon tried to reschool his features. He sensed that he looked like a stricken deer.

"He hates you."

There it was—bald, ugly, stark, the truth. He had been hiding from it for over a year.

Her shoulder was close. He laid his head against it. Cody's arm went around his shoulder.

"What am I going to do?"

"I don't know."

♠

Like a shadow's vomit. Children in the darkness. Following. Watching. Blaise whirled, lips drawn back in a snarl. They retreated. For an instant he considered reaching out with his power. Coercing one of them. Shredding his mind. Finding the answer. *Who are you? What do you want?* But one thing life with Tachyon had taught him—caution. There were too many of them. He might hold eight or even ten, but their sheer numbers would beat him down.

Blaise ducked into a Horn and Hardart. Bought a sandwich and coffee. Cody had kept his jewels, God damn her. But maybe that wasn't so bad. He had taken them for her. Let her keep them and consider what she had rejected. She'd pay soon enough.

And money was better than jewels anyway. He had mind-controlled a limousine driver and the elegantly attired passenger. That had netted him almost a thousand bucks. He could go a long time on a thousand bucks. But the jewels would have been better.

The turkey sandwich was dry, the bread forming a soggy expanding mass on the back of his tongue. Blaise choked it down and wondered again where the fat old joker news vendor had come by a fortune in precious gems. Maybe he should go back to Jube's apartment and make him tell?

A slim form slid onto the stool next to him. Blaise tensed. Studied her out of the corner of his eye. He didn't bother to slide a hand down to the .38 tucked into the waistband of his pants. His mind powers could subdue her faster than a gun could fire.

The girl was young. Fifteen, sixteen with spiky multicolored hair, deliberately tattered blue jeans, unlaced high-top sneakers.

"We've been watchin' you."

"Yeah, I know. Any particular reason why?"

"You look like you need a place to go."

"I've got plenty of places to go," said Blaise.

The girl popped gum. "What are you gonna do when you get there?"

"Take care of myself."

"Think you can?"

"Know I can." And there was something in his face that made the girl edge as far away as the stool would allow.

"I'm not sayin' you can't," she said. She thrust out a hand. Blaise noticed she had bitten the cuticles into the quick. "Molly Bolt."

Blaise ignored the outthrust hand. "What do you want?"

She pulled back her hand, thumb rubbing lightly across the tips of her other fingers as if she were startled to find the hand at the end of her arm.

"Just this. You need a place to go. You ever need a team . . . people to handle something . . . come to pier eleven on the East River. We'll find ya."

The cold coffee had a slick oily taste. "I'll keep it in mind."

"Fine."

She was gone as quickly as she had appeared. Suddenly the well-dressed businessman seated a table away stood up, unzipped, pulled out his cock, and pissed down his own leg.

Blaise left. The food wasn't very good. And he'd lost his appetite with the realization of just who or rather *what* he had been dealing with.

Jumpers.

Jumpers were after him.

◆

"Would you stop worrying? Go already. Go to Washington, and bring back that grant. Mama needs a new laser surgery center."

The connection on the car phone was terrible. Cody sounded like she was calling from the center of an electrical storm. Tachyon pictured her: hair brushed back, one hand thrust into the pocket of her lab coat, knee jiggling as she longed to get back to her patients. For an instant his concern and fear for Blaise receded. He laughed.

"What are you chortling about?" Cody's voice was sharp with suspicion.

"You. How many times per second is your foot tapping?"

"You *are* interrupting me."

"Take the time. I'm worth it."

A slight choke of laughter as he threw her words back at her.

"Prove it to me," Cody said. "Get down to Washington, and lobby like hell." She added, "It really is a shame about Senator Hartmann. He might have been a loon, but at least he was our loon."

The missing hand flared in agony as Tachyon remembered the bite of the assassin's buzz-saw hand. An assassin sent by Senator Gregg Hartmann, Democratic presidential candidate. Or at least the candidate for a day until Tachyon had destroyed forever Hartmann's political ambitions. But Cody did not know—could never know—any of this.

"Tach, are you still there?"

"Yes, yes, sorry. Take care of yourself. I'll see you Monday." He started to hang up, then hurriedly added, "Please, please, be cautious. Be careful."

A disconnected buzz was all he got back. Had she heard? Did she understand? Tachyon stared out the windows of the gray limousine at the city like a jeweled ship sailing away from him in the darkness. Blaise was out there somewhere.

The thought chilled him.

♥

Troll was propping his nine-foot length against the front reception desk, chatting up the Chickenfoot Lady when Blaise entered. The joker straightened abruptly, his face twisting into an expression of surprise and concern. It looked like tectonic plates in motion.

"Blaise, your granddaddy's been worried sick. Where the hell have you been? I ought to whip your ass."

Troll suddenly turned, lowered his head, and ran full tilt at the far wall. He struck with a sound like a cannonball crashing into a fortress battlement and went down in a heap. Chickenfoot let out a hysterical cackle and ran through the big double doors leading to the emergency room.

Blaise walked on, brows knitted in a frown of concentration, hands thrust deep into his pockets.

Cody wasn't in her office.

She wasn't in surgery. Finn was, and he shouted from behind his mask about the sterile integrity of the room and advanced on dancing pony feet on Blaise. Blaise didn't fuck with Finn's head. He kind of liked the pony-sized centaur.

Cody was in the morgue. What appeared to be an enormous wasp was on the table. Blaise watched as she carefully cut open the joker's chest cavity and surveyed the lungs. Cody then leaned over a small tape recorder. Her voice was so low he couldn't distinguish the words, just the soft, husky timbre like a chuckling brook. The sound made him shiver, but whether with anger or desire he couldn't say.

Suddenly Cody looked up and stared directly at him through the tiny window in the morgue door. Blaise jumped, hating that she had thrown him off balance. He stiff-armed the heavy door, and it flew open. She didn't retreat before his furious entrance. And that, too, made him angry.

"Hello, Blaise. Had a good time for the past week?"

"I've come for two things. My stones and you."

Her smile was crooked and a little hateful. "Your problem, my son, is that you've always thought your stones were bigger than they are."

"I can *make* you love me!" Blaise cried.

"No, you can make me hate you. Love you have to earn."

Cody was standing stock-still. A pillar of ice and darkness. Blaise ran his eyes down that slim tall form. Noted her hand tucked into the fold of her lab coat. The glint of the scalpel between her fingers. He smiled.

"Cody, you're so stupid," Blaise crooned.

The scalpel fell from nerveless fingers.

"I don't give a fuck how you *feel*."

The coat fell with a sigh to the linoleum floor.

"Because I can . . ."

The blouse joined the coat on the floor.

". . . *make* you . . ."

She stepped out of her skirt.

". . . love me."

♣

Had it connected, the blow would have ruptured a kidney.

But Blaise's karate training gave him a split-second warning. The young man spun away from Tachyon's thrust kick and caught his grandfather by the ankle. Floor met chin with head-ringing force, and Tachyon tasted blood as his teeth snapped shut on his tongue. He rolled to the side. Blinked in consternation as the heel of Blaise's boot slammed into the floor where his head had rested only a second before. Tachyon got his legs beneath him and bounded to his feet. Blaise charged, and the older man fended him off with the artificial hand. The digits couldn't be bent to form a proper spear hand, but the hard plastic fingers still managed to sink a satisfying distance into the teenager's solar plexus.

Blaise let out a sound like a dying air brake, and Cody lunged for her surgical gear as Blaise's mind control broke.

"Would you fuck this macho bullshit!" she screamed. "And just mind-control him!"

For an instant Tachyon was distracted by the sight of the completely naked Cody snatching up and wielding a chest separator like a modern-day Hippolyte.

First rule of combat—never, never, never get distracted.

Blaise landed a palm strike to the face. With a dreadful mushy sound the cartilage in Tach's nose let go, and blood fountained over his chest, forming a red bib on the elaborate peach-colored coat.

Belatedly the Takisian brought up his hands in defense. He and Blaise circled each other warily.

Feint, feint. Tachyon lashed out with his mentat's power and struck the glass-smooth surface of Blaise's shields. Struck again and a tiny cobweb of cracks appeared in the structure. At this rate it was going to take until next Tuesday to breach the boy's shields. And Tach didn't have that long.

Too much booze and not enough exercise was taking its toll. He was panting like a ruptured hog. Blaise landed a body blow that resurrected memories of broken ribs from the year before.

Suddenly Cody was there. With a deft twirl of the chest separator she landed a walloping blow to the back of Blaise's head. He staggered, but then Cody froze and began advancing stiff-legged on Tachyon.

"You see, Granpere." Blaise's smile was feral. "I can control her *and* fend you off. Mentally and physically. All at the same time."

Blaise's coercive ability was the most powerful Tach had ever confronted, but it was brute force. The subtleties of high-level mentatics were beyond him. Contemptuously Tachyon batted aside Blaise's grip on Cody. Interposed himself between the teenager and the woman. His mental shields enfolded her close as an embrace.

Cody was raging. Her thoughts ripped off her like sparks off a shorting fuse.

Damndamndamn. Stags. Runtingbedamnedstags. Me a damn shuttlecock. Notatoy! Release/makefree!

Cannot. Dare not. Tachyon sent to her. *Help me*, he begged.

Tachyon licked blood from his upper lip and endured three punishing body blows as he closed with Blaise. Clawlike, the artificial hand closed about Blaise's arm just above the elbow. It could exert enough pressure to crush a metal cup. Its effect on human tissue was also quite satisfying. Blaise screamed, and Tachyon's nostrils flared with wild, joyous pleasure as he slammed his left hand over and over again into Blaise's face.

Touch her, will you? No! None but me! She is mine! Mine! MINE!

Blaise tried a ball shot, but Tach was too quick for him. The blow landed on his thigh. The older man responded with a hammer blow to the boy's nuts. A scream ripped through the morgue.

Tachyon could feel Blaise's mind control scrabbling at his shields, but the teenager was in too much pain, too disoriented by hate and interrupted lust to muster any effective challenge to Tach's power.

Suddenly there were hands tearing at his shoulders.

"Stop it! *Stop it!* You're going to *kill* him."

Tach snarled, ignored her, continued the pleasurable business of reducing his enemy to a bloody pulp. The hands were gone. Tach heard the slap of Cody's bare feet on the tile as she ran.

Agony! The formaldehyde burned like acid in the cuts on his face, his eyes. Tach and Blaise both fell back. And at last it penetrated. Blood lust, the killing. He had been on the verge of *murdering* his own grandchild. Horrified, Tachyon stumbled back, lost his footing in the slick blood, and went windmilling to the floor.

Blaise, his face a mask of blood, cradling his mangled arm, snarled down at Tachyon. "You're *dead!*"

Crablike, Blaise scuttled for the door. Flung it open and bolted from the morgue. Tachyon shook off the fear that held him and struggled to his feet.

"Where are you going?" cried Cody.

"Must . . . catch him. Apologize. Help him."

"It's too late for that!"

Tach tottered for the door, but the pain from his broken nose made him dizzy. Tach sent out a telepathic bellow for Troll and was amazed when the nine-foot-tall joker appeared a second later.

"Doc, are you okay?" the security guard asked.

"Of course he's not okay," snapped Cody.

Troll opened and closed his mouth several times as he contemplated the stark-naked chief of surgery.

"Blaise," Tach mumbled around a split and rapidly swelling lip.

"He lit out of here like a scalded cat," said Troll, then added ruefully. "Sorry I'm so late getting here, but I knocked *myself* clean out."

"Help me get Dr. Tachyon to emergency," Cody ordered. "We've got to fix that nose."

"Put on some clothes," ordered Tachyon.

"What's the matter? You've never seen a naked woman before?"

"I do not wish the entire world to see my woman."

"*Your* woman? *Your woman?*"

Tach retreated from her acid laced thoughts. "Slip of the tongue," the Takisian muttered weakly.

♠

"Owwwww! What are you using?" Tachyon complained nasally. Cotton wadding and splints clogged his nose, and his throat was becoming sore as he struggled to breathe through his mouth. "An entrenching tool?"

"Don't be such a baby." The probe hit the steel tray with a metallic clatter. "You're going to need a new nose. Any preference?"

"How about just like the one I had."

"Don't waste a golden opportunity."

"Why should I change it?" It annoyed him that she didn't like his nose.

"It was a trifle on the long side," Cody said coolly.

"It was patrician and aristocratic."

"It was a honker."

Tach absorbed this. Reluctantly admitted, "My great-great-great-great-great-great-great-grandmother always hated my nose."

"Then allow me to be creative."

"All right."

Cody worked in silence for several minutes, then a little gruffly she asked, "How did you know?"

"We were halfway to Tomlin International when I realized I had forgotten a grant application."

"The one from HEW?" she interrupted.

"Yes."

"I've got it. I inadvertently picked it up when I was in your office this afternoon. I'm sorry."

"Sorry? You should thank whatever ancestors guard your back. So fortuitous a gift should not be demeaned. Anyway, Riggs started back, and at about Fifth Avenue I heard you screaming your head off. Riggs spared no effort, and as a result we had a police escort all the way to the clinic."

"Well . . . thanks." She made a minute adjustment, and Tach sucked in a pained breath. "I seem to be making a habit of having you rescue me."

"It is my pleasure."

"Well, it's no pleasure for me. I'm accustomed to taking care of myself."

"You would do the same for me," said Tach gently.

Cody prefaced her words with a long sigh as if she regretted the emotion that drove the response. "I suppose I would."

◆

That girl was back. Lips skinned away from his teeth as Blaise whirled on her.

"Why the fuck are you following me?"

"You look like you need that place to go." The angle of her cigarette as it hung limply from her lips seemed to mock him.

"I don't need dick from you."

"I can show you something you'll like," Molly Bolt said.

Blaise smiled. "You're a really skinny, ugly little runt. I doubt your pussy's going to be much nicer."

The girl's face closed down like a series of slamming doors. "You're so fucking stupid. Okay, fine, we'll show you."

He felt the pressure of a mind. Then a second, a third, more and more joined in a desperate attempt to do *something* to him. Molly's tough-girl act was starting to fray at the edges. Blaise grinned at her. Reached out and closed his power about the watchers in the shadows. Last of all he took Bolt. It felt sweet to save her until last. Blaise commanded, and eight kids walked out of the shadows of the alley. Stood shoulder to rigid shoulder with their leader. Molly's eyes raged at him.

"What are you?" whispered a girl whose white-blond hair formed a shimmering nimbus about her little face.

Blaise considered the question for a long time. It deserved a lot of consideration. Finally he said, "Inhuman."

Blaise patted down Molly Bolt and pulled out a package of cigarettes. Lit one. Took a long drag. "Now, what was it you wanted to show me?"

"Read my mind," spat Molly.

It angered Blaise that he couldn't. Tachyon would have been able to. That cranked the anger a little higher.

"What are you going to do with us?" Molly asked.

"Sell you as lawn jockeys." The laugh emerged as a tight little whinny.

"Let us go . . . please," cried the blond girl.

"You won't fuck with me?"

"I swear it," said Molly, pleading a little now. "We need you. Now I know why."

"What were you going to show me?"

"Let us go."

Blaise released them. Truth was, his overstretched mental powers were starting to quiver like a too tightly wound guitar string. But his little humans never suspected.

Molly ran a hand across the spikes of her multicolored hair. Sauntered to the mouth of the alley. The sidewalks were filled with rush-hour humanity. The sun sank like a bloated red sack into an ocean of brown-green smog. In the canyons between the buildings night had already fallen.

"So, pick one," said Molly.

"One what?" asked Blaise.

"Person," said a skinny kid whose face seemed to be one angry blackhead.

"For what?" Blaise asked. He hated to ask. It made him look stupid.

"To humiliate," said the blond teen in her soft little-girl voice.

"Or kill," offered another of the gang.

Blaise scanned the crowds. Listened to the blare of car horns. The thrum and rumble of hundreds of tires racing across the uneven asphalt of Broadway.

"Hurry," prodded Molly Bolt.

Blaise ignored her. Eventually he spotted what he was looking for. A carefully combed head of carrot-red hair, a business suit on the inexpensive side of nice. Not too tall. A little too slim.

An incline of the head. "Him."

"And do what?" asked Molly.

"Kill him."

♥

"I am fine. It is just a broken nose. I do not need to be in bed."

Cody ignored him. Folded back the comforter.

"I must reach Washington."

She stripped him out of the blood-covered coat.

"I must locate Blaise."

She unbuttoned his shirt.

"Make up your mind," Cody said. "Blaise or Washington."

Tach considered. "Washington."

"Fine. You'll fly tonight. Dita's already rescheduled your tickets."

"Damn it," he raged. "Don't manage my life."

She pushed his shirt off his shoulders. "Somebody has to." She pointed at his pants. "Finish. I'll get you some water so you can wash down these pain pills."

It's useless arguing with a shut door. Meekly Tach stripped off his pants and shorts and crawled beneath the sheets.

Cody returned with the glass and an ice pack. Tach obediently swallowed the pills.

"I'm sorry," he said quietly.

"Now what are you apologizing for?"

"Mind-controlling you. I know how fiercely independent you are, but I could not effectively protect—"

"I know why you did it. Let's just drop it, okay?"

"Nonetheless, your reaction shamed me. Cody, please understand and do not reject me. My defense of you is not meant to demean you."

"I know."

"Perhaps it manifests as somewhat proprietary, but that is because I am still hoping—"

"Tachyon, would you just shut the fuck up."

"But I do not want you angry—"

"You know what your problem is? You talk too goddamn much!"

♣

Black, oily. The water looked really disgusting. And the smell . . .

Blaise swallowed hard. Wished his elbow didn't hurt so bad. Out in the bay a police patrol boat droned past, spotlights sweeping across the choppy waters.

Blackhead—Blaise had discovered his name was Kent—set down the bags of groceries on the end of the pier. Molly knelt and lit a kerosene lantern.

"One if by land?" asked Blaise sarcastically.

Molly didn't reply, for there was rippling in the dark water and a *thing* rose up from the water.

"Shit!"

"No, Charon."

Kent thrust the bags of groceries through the semitransparent body wall. Blaise's initial disgust was passing. It was just another version of *Baby*, Tachyon's living spaceship. Blaise took a step toward Charon. Molly held him off with a hand to the chest.

"How bad do you want it?" asked Molly sternly.

Blaise remembered. *Shrill screams. The wailing of sirens forming a frantic counterpoint. The small redheaded man pinned against the wall of the cleaners. Vomiting his blood across the hood of the big Caddy.*

"Enough to do anything to get it."

"Then ya gotta trust us. You gotta be one with us."

"And if I don't?"

"You can't make us give you the power," the blond girl said. "You can only scare us so much."

Blaise slid his eyes toward her. "And do I scare you?"

"Yes."

Startling in its simplicity and honesty. Blaise took another look at her. Fine-boned. A few pimples on her chin, but otherwise unflawed. Fawn's eyes, but smoky gray with a dark circle surrounding the iris. The pale hair hung below her hips; it stirred softly in the breeze off the river.

"What do I have to do?" Blaise asked, turning back to Molly.

"Die."

"Huh?"

"Symbolically speaking," Kent explained.

"This is bullshit."

"No," said Molly. "This is real." She lifted a long chain with shackles attached to the end. "You walk behind Charon. We've got the end of this." She shook the chain. "Eventually we pull you in."

"Eventually." Blaise turned the word over and over in his mouth.

"You have to trust us to pull you in before it's too late," said the blonde.

"What's your name?" Blaise asked abruptly.

She was surprised and replied without thinking. "Kelly."

"Stop farting around," interrupted Molly. "Have you got the guts for it or are you a jerk off and a coward?"

"Try saying something like that after all this bullshit is over," warned Blaise. "And just what *is* the point of this bullshit?"

"You have to die to live with us," a boy called out.

"Great," muttered Blaise. "This is so stupid."

"In or out, Blaisy Daisy," crooned Molly.

Tachyon vomiting blood. Cody, eyes wide with terror and desire. Her body fiery hot beneath his. Bloody froth on her lips as his fingers sank deep into her neck.

Blaise thrust out his hands. The shackles closed around his wrists. Blaise eyed Charon. The two small eyes regarded his thoughtfully, closed in a slow blink. Blaise laughed as a white-hot surge of lust and anticipation shot through him.

This was going to be fun.

♠

They had clipped a heavy diver's belt about his waist, replaced his tennis shoes with lead-soled boots. Charon had slid beneath the water, Blaise plummeting like a stone behind him.

Blaise concentrated on the thousands of wriggling cilia that propelled Charon across the muddy bottom. How long could he last? How long until the last stale bits of air exploded from his aching lungs and the filthy waters of the river rushed in?

Charon's body cast a greenish glow into the dark waters. Occasionally a fish brushed against Blaise's body, fluttered hysterically away. His feet tangled, and Blaise fell to his knees. Almost . . . *almost* he gasped. His foot had caught in the rotting rib cage of a body. There was a jerk of the chain, the shackles biting into his wrists. Awkwardly Blaise staggered to his feet. Hurried to catch up with Charon.

There was a roaring in his ears, and his lungs were laced with fire. His eyes focused desperately on the chain. Noted how the vaguely defined bands of muscle in Charon's body closed lovingly about the metal links. Blaise fought the urge to reach out and seize control of Molly.

No! He'd fucking *die* before he'd break.

And that was beginning to seem very likely. Blaise lifted his hands and pressed them against his nose and mouth. Suddenly the slack was taken up on the chain, and he was being reeled toward

Charon's glistening body. He struck and began flailing desperately at the rubbery wall. It stretched reluctantly open. Water and Blaise poured into the slimy interior.

Kelly was yanking him up out of the water, which washed sluggishly across the floor of the joker's body. *Air.* Gulp it down, taste it, revel in the cool rush that filled his starved and aching lungs. Molly unlocked the shackles. They were cheering, laughing, suddenly he was captured in their embrace. A ten-headed animal with twenty arms holding and caressing him. Blaise realized he was crying and he couldn't figure out why. But it must have been okay because several other jumpers were crying, too.

Blaise became aware of a mental barrier. It whispered of terror, death, loss, loneliness. He blocked it. The jumpers were shifting nervously. Molly soothed them with a constant soft murmur.

"Just a little more. Almost there."

"What the fuck is that?" asked Blaise.

"Bloat," came the terse reply.

Kent suddenly jumped to his feet. He was whispering as he shuffled toward one moist gelatinous wall. Blaise grabbed his wrist, forced him down next to him.

"Sit down! You can take it. It's just a stupid mind power. And a pretty wimpy one at that."

The jumpers were regarding him with awe. All except Molly. She looked pissed.

"No wonder the Prime wanted you," breathed Kelly.

"Who's the Prime?"

Bolt tersely replied, "You'll find out. Someday. Maybe."

Charon gave a little lurch as if all the thousands of cilia had pushed against the muddy bed of the river. They were rising. Water cascaded off Charon's back. They had arrived.

Once on shore, Blaise folded his arms across his chest and gazed across Ellis Island. The trees covered it like spikes on a dinosaur's back, and above the shadowy foliage loomed massive buildings topped with turrets and fanciful cupolas. It reminded Blaise of the Takisian fairy tales Tachyon used to tell. Lost kingdoms that existed only in the clouds and mist. Elaborate palaces that lured a man to explore their treasuries and ballrooms only to fall to his death with the sunrise.

◆

But it wasn't a palace. It wasn't even livable. At least Blaise didn't think so. They had led him through the darkness to the main immigration center, and now they stood in one of the side rooms. There were a couple of cots, and twenty or thirty sleeping bags. Some were rolled like somnolent caterpillars against the walls, others were spread out on the stained and buckled tile floor. Candy wrappers, crumpled snack-chip sacks, empty Vienna sausage cans littered the room and formed junk drifts in the corners.

Gray-green paint peeled like a bad sunburn from the wooden walls. High overhead, filthy windows barely indicated the presence of a waxing moon. Some were broken, the shattered glass like jagged fangs embedded in petrified jaws.

"Pick a place," said Molly with a broad, gracious sweep of the arm.

"Do I get a sleeping bag?" asked Blaise.

"You can share mine," offered Kelly as she sidled up next to him. "Until we can get one for you," she hastened to add, wilting a bit under his cold stare.

"Better rest, Blaisy Daisy," said Molly. "You're gonna need it."

Blaise pivoted slowly to face her. "Don't . . . ever . . . call me that . . . again."

Arms militantly akimbo, Molly sneered in a singsong tone, "Or what?"

"I'll kill you."

The matter-of-fact tone left the girl gaping. She suddenly

recalled herself. The watching jumpers, eyes bright like a hunting rat pack, eagerly waiting for the fight. Molly tossed her head and laughed.

"You can try, Blai—" The word cut off and she whirled and exited.

"She's a quick learner. I like that in a slit."

The boys laughed. The girls shifted uncomfortably and exchanged glances.

Yes, Blaise decided. *This was fun.*

♥

The lights made interesting effects on her face. At times it seemed as still as a white marble effigy. At others it was soft and vulnerable.

Tach hugged his briefcase to his chest. Winced as a bus released its air brakes with a sound like a dying pig.

"This was not necessary. Riggs could have driven me."

"I wanted to," said Cody.

She drove as smoothly as she did everything else. No wasted movement, hands lightly gripping the wheel, the tiniest wrist movements as she wove through the beltway traffic.

"I wanted to make sure you got on that plane," she continued, and Tach forced himself back from a rapt contemplation of her hands.

"I'm not going to collapse from a broken nose."

"It's not your health that concerns me."

"Thank you." A little ironic and she caught it. She cocked her head to get a better look at him out of her one eye. "Should you be driving?" Tachyon suddenly asked.

"Little late to worry now. And as for the plane. I was afraid you'd take it into your head to go looking for Blaise, and frankly, funding the clinic is a hell of a lot more important."

"You can be very cold."

"No, I just know when to cut my losses."

The cars up ahead suddenly braked and the red flare of their taillights punctuated and underscored Tach's sharp reply. "I don't think he's a loss!"

"Then you're a delusional fool."

Tachyon dropped his head briefly into his hand. "All right, I don't *want* to think that."

Cody spun the wheel and they shot up the ramp and under a sign marked DEPARTING PASSENGERS.

"Better. God damn it, Tachyon, in maybe twenty or thirty years I'll have you past the guilt, out of the wallow of self-pity, and you'll have figured out when to shut up."

"Thank heaven I'm a big enough man to listen to this catalog of my flaws."

Cody's eye raked his diminutive form. "Well, your *ego* is big enough to handle it."

"I'm also highly encouraged."

"By what?"

"That you are willing to devote your life to the reclamation of my mind, body, and spirit."

The seat belt nearly cut Tach in half as Cody slammed on the brakes in front of the terminal.

"I don't think my original statement went quite that far."

"It was implicit."

Tach closed the prosthetic hand around the handle and pushed open the door. Cody moved to the trunk and pulled out his two big suitcases.

"How long are you going to be gone?" she asked.

"Three days."

"You've got enough here for a round-the-world cruise."

"But, my dear, one must dress."

He was smiling bravely up at her, but inside he suddenly felt like he was filled with broken glass. Tears sprang to his eyes, and he muttered a curse.

Cody laid her hands on his shoulders. "What is it? You look stricken."

"I don't know. Nothing." Tach shook his head. "I am suddenly just so very, very unhappy."

For a long moment she looked at him, then bending down, she placed a soft feather-light kiss at the corner of his mouth. Tachyon stared at her in amazement.

"Smile for me, kid," she said, a crooked smile curving her own lips.

Tachyon burst out, "Cody, come with me to Washington."

"What? You're crazy. I've got no ticket, I don't have any luggage, what about my kid—" She paused for breath. "And who's going to run the clinic?"

People were shouldering past them as the couple blocked the automatic doors into the terminal.

"Please, I am frightened for you."

"I'll holler if I need you."

"It will be too far to come."

"You're hysterical. It's the pain pills talking."

"Cody, he means to harm us."

"Do you or don't you want me to call the police and have them search for Blaise?"

"No." Tach stared seriously up at her. "For if he's found, I shall surely have to kill him."

♣

When you're stark naked and dressed only in a scarlet robe that had obviously been ripped off from some local Episcopalian church choir, you can feel like a real dork.

Add to that the fact that nerves were giving Blaise the most amazing hard-on it had ever been his pleasure to experience. Or maybe he just got off on big black candles and a droning tape of Tibetan monastery chants, he thought ironically as Molly led him into the dark, echoing room.

Molly glanced down at his penis thrusting aggressively from between the folds of his gown, and grinned. "You're gonna do just fine," she muttered as if to herself, but intending for Blaise to hear.

He didn't respond. This and anything that followed could be endured. The ultimate prize was too great to blow it with a fit of temper now.

Jumpers lined the walls. Blaise did a quick head count. Forty-two. But many of those weren't jumpers. You couldn't jump until you'd been initiated. Most, like Kelly, were still waiting. Blaise noted that two-thirds were boys. Why? Did it—whatever it was—affect males more strongly than females? How did one make a jumper?

A lurid green pentagram had been painted on the stained tile floor. On the walls were painted other occult symbols. The swastika, a leering goat's head, 666. The enormous room was lit by a score of black candles, but they did little more than chase the shadows into the corners of the roof where they hung like brooding bats.

In the center of the pentagram was a low table. It was an odd height if it was meant to serve as an altar. And the three red satin pillows tossed on its polished black surface really ruined any hope of suggesting blood sacrifices.

Molly closed her fingers around Blaise's left wrist and led him three times around the pentagram. At the eastern point they stepped into the figure, and the jumpers let out a weird, undulating cry. Blaise had to bite back a laugh.

Then from the darkness a man's voice asked, "Who comes to be made?"

"Only one, Prime," called Molly.

"Is he worthy?"

"He is brave. He is trustful."

"Will he serve?"

Molly nudged Blaise.

"I'll serve," the boy replied. Apparently it was the right answer.

Molly signaled and Kent hurried forward to pull off the choir robe. They were all staring at him. Kelly especially. Blaise ran a hand across his chest. Noticed that he was starting to grow hair. He had become a man. He could pinpoint the moment. He had gone into that morgue a child. Emerged a man.

"Lie down on the table," whispered Molly. "With your stomach on the pillows."

For a moment he bridled at the undignified position—his bare ass thrust aggressively skyward.

Patience. Patience.

Tachyon vomiting his life out across the hood of his limo. No, even better across Cody's lap.

Paper-dry hands cupped his rump, and Blaise almost lost it.

Didn't take a genius to figure out what was coming.

Parted his buttocks.

Oh, I'm gonna get you for this, Grandpa!

Tearing pain as the man thrust deep within him.

A lifetime later and it was over. Blaise rose stiffly from the table. There was blood on his ass and legs.

The man gestured a broad sweeping motion that set the hanging sleeve of his gown to swaying. "Reach out. Seize one of them. Trade with them. For you it should be child's play."

Yeah, snarled Blaise internally, and he reached out for the man.

Nothing happened. Behind the mask the man's eyes glittered. The mouth twisted stiffly into a smile.

"You beautiful bastard," the Prime said. "You *would* try to fuck with me. Forget it, I can't be jumped."

"Can you be killed?" Blaise asked sweetly. From behind him he heard Molly gasp.

"Oh, yes, but without me there are no more jumpers. Don't shoot yourself in the foot, Blaise, in a fit of pique."

The hem of the gown whispered about his feet as the Prime turned and slunk back into the shadows.

Blaise turned back to his peers. They peered back at him like bright cardinals in their scarlet robes.

"Come on, let's play," said Molly.

And Blaise reached out. Seemed to bounce out of his skin. Shoot like liquid fire. He came to rest in Kent's body. He looked out at the world from new eyes. Glancing down, he studied the overly long thumbnail on the right hand, the callused finger pads. Would the body remember how to play guitar? Blaise wondered. Then he was on to other sensations. Like the fact that Kent *smelled* funny. Blaise looked across to his body. Molly and Kelly were easing it to the floor. It . . . he . . . Kent—damn!—seemed to be conscious, but frozen in some kind of fugue state.

Blaise made the jump back. Shook off Kelly's patting hands. Climbed to his feet. Raucous laughter rang through the rafters, skittered among the shadows. The jumpers stood in shocked silence.

Blaise threw back his head and screamed like a banshee.

"Oh, Tachyon! You're going to *wish* I had only killed you!"

♠ ♥ ♦ ♣

Nobody's Home

by Walton Simons

KENNETH WAS LATE. CENTRAL Park baked in the August heat. Most of the animals in the zoo were napping. Jerry sat in front of the seventy-five-foot-tall cage that had been his home back when he was a giant ape. A lone pigeon walked up to him, head bobbing. Jerry shooed it away.

He felt a strong hand on his shoulder.

"It's just me," Kenneth said, sitting down beside him. "Sorry I'm late."

"What's up? You sounded pretty mysterious on the phone."

Kenneth nodded. "It's Latham. He's going around the bend, I think. He's involved in more than you can imagine. For years he's been a major figure in the Shadow Fist Society. Which includes everyone from punks like the Immaculate Egrets and Werewolves up to very respectable businessmen. And Latham's in it up to his neck."

"But he's got something on you, too. Right?" Jerry leaned forward. He'd been trying to come up with material on Latham for months, and hadn't turned up anything other than a few interesting reports from his time in Vietnam.

Kenneth looked away. "There are some things I'd rather Beth didn't know about. Other women. We've made such progress since almost getting divorced. I don't want to jeopardize my marriage. Latham has some pretty graphic evidence. One of the women I saw was working for him." He turned back to Jerry. "This isn't to be repeated, you understand."

"Only under torture," Jerry said. "Who's Kien?"

"You're better off not finding out, but it may come to that soon."

"What do you mean?" Jerry wiped his sweaty forehead.

"Latham knows I have information on him. He wants to trade it for what he has on me." Kenneth shook his head. "But I've known St. John a long time. He'll hold back something to keep me in line."

"So what are you going to do?"

"Give you my file on Latham, if you'll have it. He's made some threats lately. I wouldn't put it past him to break into the house trying to get them. Beth might get hurt. This way I can let it drop that the papers are no longer in my home. He'll suspect you might have them, of course."

Jerry shrugged. "The day a native New Yorker is scared of some high-class thug from Beantown will never come." Jerry paused. "Well, maybe he does make me a little nervous."

"Good, because he's a very dangerous man." Kenneth looked straight at Jerry. "You're sure you don't mind?"

"Nope. Look over there." Jerry pointed at the chimp cage. One of the apes was high in a tree, throwing its shit at another on the ground. "That's what we'll be doing to Latham soon."

"I'll settle for a return to the established balance of fear," Kenneth said.

"We'll manage," Jerry said, putting his hand on his brother's shoulder.

"Thanks." Kenneth opened his briefcase. "Now, let's discuss what you're going to do about your appointment with the city officials next week."

"Right." Jerry sighed and stared back at the chimp cage. Sometimes the shit got thrown at you, as well.

♠

Jerry sat on the worn, orange couch, shifting his weight. It was hot outside and his sweaty legs stuck to the cushion through his pants. The waiting room was quiet, except for the male secretary's fingers on the keyboard, muffled voices from inside the offices, and the breathing of the joker woman sharing the couch with Jerry.

Kenneth had shown him what to sign and told him what to say. He'd even offered to come along as legal representation. Jerry said no. It was time he started taking care of a few things on his own. Still, the back of his throat was dry. Several trips to the water cooler hadn't helped. City officials could do that to you. Especially in New York.

He turned to the joker, who was normal except for her grotesquely overmuscled jaws and mouth. "Did you sign them?" he asked.

She shrugged. "Do I have a choice?" Her voice was soft. Talking seemed awkward for her.

"Always." He straightened his shoulders. "I'm not going to."

The joker nodded, but didn't seem impressed. "You an ace?"

"I was once, but not anymore." The lie needed all the practice Jerry could give it. "You remember the big ape in Central Park?"

"Yeah. They took it away to make a movie or something. Right?"

"Right. That was me." Jerry felt a chill crawl halfway up his spine. "Dr. Tachyon cured me, but my power doesn't work anymore."

"Too bad," she said.

"Not really," Jerry said. "It'll keep the government goons off my back. Why are they interested in you?"

The woman smiled, revealing two rows of large teeth like polished marble. "I'm what's classified as a type-two joker."

"What's that?"

"Any joker who's something other than just ugly, I guess. My teeth and jaws are pretty strong. I can bite through almost anything." The joker looked around, presumably for something to demonstrate on.

"That's okay, I believe you." Jerry unstuck his legs from the couch. "What do they call you?"

"Susan," she said. "How about you?"

"A long time ago I used to be called the Projectionist," Jerry said. She looked at him with polite blankness. "That was before your time, I'd imagine. Now I'm nobody. People just call me Jerry."

"Regular names are best, anyway," Susan said.

The office door opened across the room. A man in a suit showed a visibly shaken six-legged joker out. "Mr. Strauss?"

Jerry nodded and stood.

The man let him go inside first. He was middle-aged and slightly overweight. His hair was thin and gray. His eyes brown. He took Jerry's hand. Jerry shook it and squeezed hard. The man squeezed even harder.

"Sit down, Mr. Strauss. I'm William Karnes."

Jerry sat. Karnes eased into his chair behind the well-ordered desk. He put a finger to his mouth and opened a file. "I see you failed to sign forms fifteen and seventeen-a. Why is that Mr. Strauss?"

"Well, I'm no longer an active wild card," Jerry said, "so I don't see why I should be subject to conscription in the event of a national emergency. And I believe the other one said I was to notify your office if I were to take any kind of extended vacation. It just seems unnecessary."

Karnes rubbed the end of his bulbous nose. "The government has its reasons, Mr. Strauss. Failure to cooperate now may mean some very serious inconveniences for you later on. You're aware of the rumblings in Congress about reinstating some of the old Exotic Powers laws."

Jerry took a deep breath. He didn't want to let Karnes get under his skin. That had been Kenneth's advice. "Yes. I do keep up with current events. But, as I say, I'm no longer a wild card, except in the most technical sense. I believe you have a medical report from my physician to that effect."

Karnes stared at Jerry. "From Dr. Tachyon. We can hardly give that much credence. If you want to undergo testing by some of our staff, I might agree to that. But we don't pay much attention to alien quacks."

Jerry could feel the blood hammering inside him. "I don't think I have anything else to say to you, Mr. Karnes." He stood.

"Sit down, sir." Karnes pointed to the chair. "I can make more trouble for you than you can imagine. I have a job to do, and none of your kind is going to stop me."

Jerry felt something go hard inside him. "Really? Well, let me clarify something for you, Mr. Karnes. You're a low-level bu-reaucrat with a stick up his ass. I'm a multimillionaire with lots of very powerful friends. If I were you, I'd be extremely careful who I threatened. If you're lucky, I'll only come after you with lawyers. Do you feel lucky, punk?" Jerry quoted a cop movie he'd just seen.

Karnes opened his mouth. Shut it.

"Stay out of my hair, then." Jerry left the office, shutting the door loudly. He walked over to Susan, who was still sitting miser-ably on the couch. "He's an asshole. Don't trust him."

"I don't trust any nats," Susan said. "Not anymore. It's just that I can't find a way around them."

Jerry patted her on the hand. "Right. Well, good luck, then."

Susan smiled. It wasn't pretty. Maybe she'd bite a hole in Karnes's desk. Probably not, though. That kind of thing only happened in the movies.

◆

Jerry sat on the bed, oiling the pistol. He'd bought and read a couple of books on gun care. If he was going to have a weapon, he was going to take care of it. He'd been target shooting for a few weeks and the pistol no longer felt awkward in his hand.

There was a sharp knock at his apartment door. Jerry put the automatic in his dresser drawer under some T-shirts and crossed the room. He peered through the peephole and saw a middle-aged man in maintenance clothes. He opened the door.

"I'm here to get you plastered," the man said, smiling.

"Right. Just follow me." Jerry closed the door and led the man to where his wall safe had been installed. All it needed was plaster, paint, and something to put in front of it.

The man walked to the wall and looked it over. "Nice safe," he said. "This whole building could burn down and anything inside would be fine. Yes, sir. I kind of hate to be working on the anniversary of the King's death, though. I'll drink a few beers for him later on. Are you a fan?"

"I'm not sure I know what you mean?" Jerry said.

"Elvis. The King. He died twelve years ago today. I remember that summer. We had the second big blackout. You remember that?"

"No. I was around for the first one, though." Actually, Jerry had caused it, but didn't feel like telling this guy the story. "I liked Elvis when I was younger."

"Can't stop liking the King just because you get older. That's no kind of fan to be. I listen to Elvis every night before I go to bed with the wife. Makes it just that much more exciting."

"You mind if I watch TV while you work?" Jerry asked.

The man shrugged. "Don't see why not. You're the one spending a fortune to live here." He spread out a piece of canvas on the carpet in front of the wall and sorted through his spatulas.

Jerry picked up the remote control and punched up the local news.

". . . another apparent jumper crime. A mime says someone else entered his body while he was performing in Central Park, removed his clothing, and inserted a chrysanthemum in his anus. The jumper then paraded the mime around the park and made obscene gestures at passersby."

"Jeez," the maintenance man said. "That's three in the last two weeks. When are the cops going to do something about those jumper assholes?"

"Maybe they're scared," Jerry said.

"I can understand that. It's a sorry day when New York's finest can't handle a few snot-nosed kids, though. Even if they are aces."

"You like aces?" Jerry turned away from the TV and looked over at the man.

"Hell, no. Can't stand them. Put them all in prison." He pointed a spatula full of plaster at Jerry. "That's what they should have done to the fat guy, even if it was just a joker he killed."

"There's two sides to everything," Jerry said.

"Yep, and the lines are getting drawn. If you're for aces and jokers, you're looking for trouble. And a young man like you doesn't need any trouble."

Jerry considered telling the man that they were probably the same age, but that would just make him curious. He turned off the TV and picked up his *Cosmopolitan*. He was trying harder to understand women, but just couldn't seem to turn the corner. Maybe Irma Kurtz could enlighten him.

♥

Kenneth was expecting him for lunch, but this time it was Jerry who was late. Traffic was at a standstill on Third Avenue. He'd paid off his cabbie and started walking uptown. Within two blocks his shirt was soaked in sweat. He'd started out walking fast, but had gotten stitches in his sides and was just keeping pace with the tide of bodies on the sidewalk.

Kenneth hadn't actually said so, but Jerry figured his brother was going to turn over the material on Latham. He'd mentioned several times that Jerry shouldn't cancel out. That had to mean something. Kenneth didn't waste words.

He was in the same block as the restaurant when his right leg cramped up. Jerry leaned against a wall and rubbed the back of his calf. The searing pain began to go away after a minute or two. Every other person that walked by looked at him and shook their head. He reached down and pulled the toe of his shoe toward him, stretching out the muscle. The pain lessened. He started limping toward the restaurant. Ahead, he saw three people go in. They were young and well dressed, but their clothes seemed wrong on them. They looked like kids playing dress-up. Jerry only saw them for a moment, but they seemed familiar. One of the girls was wearing a wig. Jerry had a few of his own and could spot one a mile away. He tried his bad leg and it quickly cramped up on him again. He started hopping slowly down the sidewalk. He started walking again when he stepped inside the restaurant. His leg was sore as hell, but there was nothing he could do about it. The cool air inside chilled his sweaty back. He smelled sauerkraut and schnitzel.

They were sitting in a booth. The girl in the wig and the boy held on to the other girl. She looked passed out. A body brushed past him. Jerry saw his brother leave the restaurant.

"Kenneth?"

There was no answer. Jerry hobbled out after him. He grabbed Kenneth as they neared the sidewalk and tried to turn him around. Without looking, Kenneth threw an elbow that caught Jerry in the chest and knocked him backward. Jerry fell onto the sidewalk, skinning his hands. Kenneth stepped out into the traffic.

"No," Jerry screamed, and struggled to his feet.

Kenneth turned, looking disoriented, just like the girl inside had. He snapped his head around at the sound of squealing brakes. The car turned sideways. Its right fender slammed into Kenneth, knocking his body up and back. Kenneth screamed. Jerry heard the crunch of glass. Kenneth bounced off a parked car and slid down into the street.

Jerry ran over, the pain in his leg forgotten. Blood was coming from Kenneth's nose and mouth. His body was twisted in a way that meant a broken back. Jerry knelt down next to him. "Kenneth, it's me. Don't try to move." He turned to the gathering crowd. "Somebody call an ambulance, now."

"Jerry." Kenneth's voice was garbled by the blood in his throat. "They did it to me. Switched bodies. So . . . weird." He closed his eyes, reopened them. "Hurts so much. Had to be . . . Latham behind it. Tell Beth . . ." His body shuddered and then was still.

"No," Jerry said quietly. He held his brother's hand for a moment, then let it go and stood. He looked up and saw the trio of kids disappear around the corner. The boy was carrying a large folding envelope. Jerry ran a couple of painful steps, then stopped. "No."

Someone took Jerry by the shoulders and guided him back into the restaurant. He could tell they were saying something consoling, but he couldn't pick out the words. They sat him down. A waiter put a glass of water and a shot of whiskey in front of him. "You wait here until the police arrive, sir. If there's anything you need, just ask."

Jerry downed the whiskey without feeling it and clenched his hands into fists. Underneath the disbelief and the pain, there was something cold growing inside him. Something that would have to be taken care of sooner or later.

Jerry thought about Beth and slumped in his chair. She wasn't up to this, couldn't be. He'd been a shit to her for so long, it wasn't likely he could be much of a comfort now. But he was damn sure going to try.

Jerry heard sirens approaching. He raised his hand for another drink, then reconsidered and waved the waiter away. This wasn't the time.

♣

They were alone on the couch. After the funeral Jerry had hustled the friends and relatives out of the house as soon as courtesy would allow. Beth had held up well, but he could tell she needed another big cry soon.

"I know we haven't had time to talk about it, but I want to apologize for the way I've acted the past few months. I know I hurt your feelings, and you didn't deserve that." Jerry sniffed. Beth wasn't the only one with a cry coming on. "I'm really sorry, and if you'll give me another chance, I'll never let you down again." He touched her tentatively on the shoulder.

Beth put her hand on his and looked over at him. "Oh, Jerry, that doesn't matter. I know you're not really hateful. Sometimes these things just happen. What's important is that you're here for me now." She scooted across the couch and put her head in the hollow of his neck. "I need people around me who I can trust, who I can be myself with."

Jerry put his arms around her. He couldn't tell if he started crying first or if she did. They held on to each other, hard. After they were both done, he went and grabbed a box of Kleenex. They blew their noses together and Beth managed a smile.

"I really do love you, sis," he said. "Sometimes I just don't show it very well. It's one of the things I'm working on. I'm trying not to drink so much anymore, either."

She nodded, then dabbed at her eyes. "I'm proud of you for that."

"Are you going to stay here?" Jerry was afraid to hear the answer.

"My brother said he'd be glad to put me up for a while. I haven't been back to Chicago for years. I'm probably due for a visit."

Jerry nodded. He looked at her, but it felt like she was already gone. "That might be best for you."

She took his hand. "It'll only be for a while. I'll be back."

"I'll be waiting," he said.

♠

Tomlin was packed wall to wall with bodies. It was still summer-vacation time for a lot of people and everyone seemed to be trying to get into or out of New York on the same day. He and Beth sat next to each other in plastic row chairs. She hugged her gray carry-on valise and stared out the window at the taxiing airliners. She was quiet. He couldn't imagine how she felt. As terrible as his pain and loss were, hers was worse.

"Eastern flight 178 now boarding for Chicago, with connections to St. Louis and Atlanta," came a soft voice over the public address.

Beth stood and fished her boarding pass out of her purse. She set down her valise and hugged Jerry tight. He knew he was going to cry again, but figured that if he started now, Beth would, too. She didn't need to be a wreck getting onto the plane.

"Good-bye, bro. I'll be back soon, I think. I just have to get out of here for a while. I'll keep in touch."

Jerry picked up her bag, put his arm around her, and steered her toward the boarding entrance. "God, I'm going to miss you. You're all I've got left."

"That's not true, or I wouldn't leave you." Beth kissed him on the cheek.

Jerry handed her the valise. "Call me when you get in."

"Absolutely. Good-bye." Beth turned and handed the man her boarding pass. He took it and smiled at her. Then she was gone.

Jerry sat back down and stared out the window at the plane. He rubbed his eyes and tried to think of his favorite song. Nothing came to mind. He watched until her plane taxied out of sight.

♠ ♥ ♦ ♣

Dead Heart Beating

by John Jos. Miller

"IT'SSS THE GENERAL'SSSS ORDER, Fadeout," Wyrm hissed, his foot-long tongue lolling out disgustingly over his chin, his eyes as expressionless as a pair of cuff links stuck through the sleeves of a frayed, cheap shirt.

"Since when have I had to be frisked before seeing the old man?" Philip Cunningham asked Kien's loyal watch joker.

"Sssince the General ordered it." Wyrm's stare was unrelenting.

Cunningham gave his best put-upon sigh. "All right," he said, good-naturedly raising his hands over his head as Wyrm patted him down.

But the easy smile and air of practiced indifference hid the sudden unease running through Cunningham's mind. He knows, Cunningham thought. Somehow the old bastard found out about New Day. That's why he called me in to see him.

Wyrm grunted, stood back. "Okay," he said almost grudgingly. "You can go in."

Cunningham hesitated. He was sure that an angry Kien was waiting for him beyond the closed door to his private office, an angry, vengeful Kien, ready to confront Cunningham with his knowledge of the scheme that would have put Cunningham in his place as head of the Shadow Fists. Cunningham wondered briefly who had betrayed him to Kien, but decided to worry about that later. Now he had something more basic on his mind. Survival.

He could try to make a break for it, or he could bull his way through by putting the blame for New Day on someone else. Loophole, maybe. Or Warlock. That might be his best bet.

He squared his shoulders and opened the door to Kien's inner office. Inside, it was quiet and dimly lit. The only illumination came from the shaded lamp on the edge of Kien's desk. The room's atmosphere was dark and sepulchral, with the glass cases housing the fabulously expensive Asian antiques scattered around the room playing the part of the grave offerings.

"You wanted to see me?" Cunningham asked as he entered the room. He stopped, frowning. "Kien?"

The shadowy figure sitting behind the huge teakwood desk was only dimly lit by the small lamp. Cunningham stepped forward cautiously, then suddenly realized that the Shadow Fists would have a new master much earlier than even he'd anticipated.

Kien was dead.

If that indeed was Kien seated behind the desk. Cunningham approached slowly, disbelievingly, wondering if his boss was playing some kind of macabre gag. But it wasn't anywhere near April 1 and Kien wasn't the type to pull practical jokes. The body slumped behind the desk was headless, but Cunningham could tell it was Kien from the half hand flopped carelessly in the fine blue powder scattered on the desk surface. And Kien wasn't the only deader in the room. The watchdog joker that Kien normally kept in a jar on his desk was pinned to the desktop with Kien's platinum letter opener, horribly marring the wood's glossy finish.

Cunningham gingerly leaned over the desk, first shifting the lampshade to throw a little more light on the body. Carefully keeping clear of the blue powder sprinkled on the desktop that had mixed with a massive quantity of congealing blood, he reached out cautiously and laid two fingers on the back of Kien's whole hand.

The flesh was still warm and pliable. Kien's fingertips were stained blue, and more of the powder clung to the front of his blood-soaked shirt.

"Rapture," Cunningham said to himself, stepping back from the desk. The blue powder was manufactured in Kien's own Shadow Fist labs. It enhanced the pleasure of anything, turning food into ambrosia, a simple touch into an orgasm. It also had some unfortunate side effects. In a way, Cunningham thought, it was ironic justice rarely seen out of bad television shows that Kien had been using his own wares.

Cunningham didn't think of himself as a stuffed shirt, but he was old-fashioned in his choice of recreational vehicles. He stayed away from the pernicious new stuff, with the often correct notion that he wasn't going to fool around with any kind of chemical until it was proven relatively safe by countless others. He was too bright to be anyone's human guinea pig.

The thing of it was, though, Cunningham could have sworn that Kien had a more conservative attitude toward drugs. When Kien played Kubla Khan In His Pleasure Dome, he would occasionally indulge in a pipe of opium, which had a long history of acceptance in Chinese culture. But that was it. He used no other drugs and was only a light drinker. It was a surprise to discover that Kien was a rap head.

Or was he?

Cunningham carefully considered the death scene. Why would Kien kill his own watchdog joker? And if Kien hadn't killed the sorry little bastard, who had?

The person who had taken Kien's head as a souvenir.

But why steal the head of a dead man?

To keep the memories locked in Kien's dead brain away from Deadhead.

Perhaps. If that were the case, then this was an inside job.

Knowledge of Deadhead's unique ability to access the memories of dead brains wasn't exactly widespread outside the Shadow Fists.

Cunningham tugged the letter opener from the batrachian joker's chest, then set it aside. A small box stuffed with elegant wrapping paper sat on the edge of Kien's desk. The box was stamped with the name "Lin's Curio Emporium," an expensive antique store that was part of Kien's far-flung commercial empire. Besides importing costly Asian antiquities, Lin's was also a high-class drugstore where well-heeled clientele could pick up anything from marijuana to heroin. To rapture.

Cunningham put the joker's body in the box. The joker might be dead, but that didn't mean he couldn't be questioned. Not as long as Deadhead was available.

Cunningham took a long, careful look around the room. There were no windows and the room's only door led to the antechamber guarded by Wyrm. He sighed. It looked like a classic locked-room mystery. Too bad he never read Agatha Christie.

Only the door to the office wasn't locked. It suddenly opened and Wyrm stuck his head in, saying, "Excussss—" and stopped before he got the first word out.

Leslie Christian stood behind Wyrm. Cunningham didn't like the weathered-looking British ace who'd appeared from nowhere the previous year and had somehow stepped right into the Shadow Fist Society as Kien's personal confidant. He was a smug, supercilious bastard who stank of unsavory secrets.

The two in the doorway stared at the scene inside Kien's office, then Christian said laconically, "So, finally made your move, old boy?"

There was a moment of shocked silence, then Wyrm howled in anger as Christian's words finally penetrated his stunned brain. The joker rushed into the room, his foot-long tongue whipping back and forth, his fangs bared and dripping poison.

Wyrm wasn't very bright, and he was intensely loyal to his master. When he got an idea through his skull, it tended to stay there. And now he had the notion, neatly planted by Christian, that Cunningham had killed Kien. Cunningham knew he wouldn't have the opportunity to talk things over with the insanely jealous joker.

He faded. Fading made Cunningham as blind as he was invisible, but his other senses had been sharply honed by continual practice. He called a picture of Kien's office onto the video screen of his mind, and moved around a freestanding glass case that contained a selection of delicately inlaid and enameled snuff bottles. He headed out of Wyrm's path and to the office door.

But Wyrm's angry screams got closer. Rapidly.

Cunningham ducked and there was a loud crash as Wyrm hurled himself forward, barely missed, and smashed through the front of the display case. The angry joker floundered through shards of shattered glass and broken bits of priceless antiquities, hot on Cunningham's trail despite his total invisibility.

What the hell was going on? Cunningham thought, then felt on his face the wet caress of Wyrm's ultrasensitive tongue. The bastard can smell me, Cunningham realized. Then Wyrm was on him.

He twisted away as the joker grabbed at him and one of his flailing hands caught in Cunningham's shirt. Wyrm pulled him close. Cunningham could picture the wide gaping mouth, sharp fangs running with saliva like the drool of a mad dog.

He was no match, Cunningham knew, for Wyrm's wild-card-enhanced strength.

He faded in his eyes to see Wyrm ferociously biting empty air and brought his right knee up hard between Wyrm's legs.

Wyrm screamed and Cunningham pulled away, glancing quickly around the room. That bastard Christian had disappeared, pulling the office door shut behind him. Crossed on the wall near the door were a pair of antique ceremonial daggers, their hilts encrusted with pearls, rubies, and emeralds. Cunningham sprinted across the room, cursing Wyrm under his breath as the joker hobbled after him. He ripped the daggers from their wall mounts. Wyrm's hot breath was on the back of his neck as he faded again, taking the daggers with him to invisibility.

Wyrm slammed into him, smashing him hard into the wall. The breath exploded from Cunningham's lungs as he turned and slashed with both daggers. But the weapons, centuries-old antiques, were no longer useful for anything but show. One glanced harmlessly off Wyrm's forearm, the other snapped on his rib cage.

Cunningham wanted to swear, but he couldn't catch his breath. Wyrm caught his face with one of his inhumanly strong hands, his clawed fingers raking furrows on Cunningham's cheeks. One of the joker's fingers found its way into Cunningham's mouth, and the ace bit down hard.

He tasted blood in his mouth as Wyrm screamed and instinctively pulled away. His lungs laboring for air, Cunningham staggered back across the room to where he remembered seeing a viable weapon: the letter opener he'd put down next to the lamp on Kien's desk. He faded in his eyes just as he ran into the desk. Pain flashed through his knees as he bashed them against the edge of the desk, then he skidded across the stinking, sticky mixture of congealed blood and blue powder. He slid over and off the polished surface and landed on the desk chair and Kien's cooling corpse. Somehow he managed to grab the letter opener as he went sailing by.

Wyrm followed him, leaping over the desk with outstretched talons and dripping fangs. Cunningham thrust out his right hand, holding the letter opener, as Wyrm slammed into him, flipping the chair, Cunningham, and Kien's corpse all to the floor.

Cunningham was stunned by the double impact of colliding with Wyrm and smashing into the floor. It took him a moment to realize that he was still holding the letter opener and that something wet and sticky was running down his hand. The letter opener, he finally realized, had penetrated Wyrm's throat, angled upward through the joker's mouth and into his brain. The joker's blood was pulsing thick and warm on his hand.

Cunningham lay there for a moment breathing in the cloud of swirling blue powder.

It tasted so good to be alive.

◆

Kien's chair felt comfortable against Cunningham's body. It was soft and plush and swiveled silently on well-oiled casters. Cunningham spun around in it idly, knowing that he should get going, that Christian could return at any moment with a goon squad, but somehow he just couldn't help savoring the feeling of complete triumph over his onetime boss. He stopped twirling around in the chair and rested one foot on Kien's headless corpse, another on Wyrm's rapidly cooling body.

So this is what it felt like to be head of the Shadow Fists. It was a heady mixture of power and mastery flavored with the anticipation of sweet riches to come. Of course, Cunningham realized, some of this flight of fancy had been caused by the rapture he'd breathed. He had to get it in gear. He couldn't afford to get caught napping now.

He reached out gingerly, careful not to disturb any more of the fine blue powder that had settled back down upon the desktop, and picked up the telephone hanging precariously on the desk's edge. He dialed.

"Fadeout," he said into the phone. "Put me through to Warlock."

He hummed as he waited for his co-conspirator, the head of the Werewolf street gang, to get on the line. Warlock was tall and strongly built; no one, not even Cunningham, knew what form his jokerhood took. He always wore a mask. The Werewolf custom of wearing a common mask originated with him, as his followers aped whatever celebrity mask he wore for however long he chose to wear it.

"This is Warlock." The head Werewolf's voice was deep and emotionless, though there was something of cold, dispassionate danger in it. The Werewolves were, in Cunningham's opinion, mainly just a bunch of jokers with delusions of toughness. Warlock, though, was authentically dangerous. Even his ace power, which Warlock called his death wish, was eerily perilous.

Warlock would simply wish a target dead, and within twenty-four hours he'd get his wish. Sometimes the victim's heart would give out, or a blood vessel would burst in his brain. Sometimes they'd be in the wrong place at the wrong time and a runaway taxi would do the job. Once one of Warlock's victims had had the cosmically bad luck to be drilled between the eyes by a micrometeorite. No one knew how he did it, but Warlock's death wish never failed.

He was a man to be cautious around.

"New Day is on," Cunningham told him with rapture-induced exuberance in his voice. "Now."

"Already?" Warlock asked thoughtfully. "It wasn't scheduled until next week. No one's in place—"

"We have to move now," Cunningham interrupted, and told Warlock about Kien's death. "I don't know who did it or why, but Christian's got to be involved somehow," he finished. "He showed up here too damn conveniently, and left after siccing Wyrm on me."

"What's his motive for wanting Kien dead?" Warlock asked.

"I don't know," Cunningham admitted. "But we'll find out when we get ahold of him. Right now we've got to move. Fast. He's already tried to pin the killing on me once. I figure he might bring Sui Ma in next."

Warlock made a sound deep in his throat and Cunningham knew that he'd pushed the right button. Even though both gangs belonged to the Shadow Fist Society, there was no love lost between the Werewolves and the Immaculate Egrets. The Wolves were jokers. They had the smell of the street on them. The Egrets were nats, for the most part smug, snotty nats. Though they worked the streets like the Werewolves, somehow they thought themselves superior to their brothers in the Fists, an attitude actively encouraged by their leader Sui Ma, Kien's sister.

"Put the Wolves on alert," Cunningham said. "Find Chickenhawk. Contact the Whisperer. I have a feeling we may need him before this shakes out."

"Lazy Dragon?" Warlock asked.

"Still missing," Cunningham said. "Last time I checked his place his sister was living there, and she hadn't heard from him in months. I'm afraid that Christian—or whoever's behind Kien's killing—might have already taken him out."

"What about Loophole?"

Cunningham made a dismissive gesture. "Leave him for now. He probably knows where a lot of the bodies are buried, so he may be useful later. But I can't see how he can hurt us now. He's just a lawyer."

"All right," Warlock said. "You want me to send a few of the brothers along to keep an eye on you?"

"That's a good idea," Cunningham said. He looked at the box with the tiny joker body in it. "I'm going to head for the Lair, but first I have to find Deadhead. I've got a little something for him here."

Fortunately Cunningham knew just where to look.

♥

Cunningham knew the rapture was still playing tricks with him when he had to fight down the urge to buy half a dozen sandwiches at the Horn and Hardart at Third Avenue and Forty-second Street.

He walked firmly through the food line, reminding himself that he was there looking for someone and not to stuff himself with mystery-meat sandwiches.

Although the eatery was crowded, Cunningham spotted Deadhead sitting by himself in an otherwise deserted corner. It was as if the automat's patrons—not usually considered a finicky crowd—were instinctively avoiding the half-mad ace. Cunningham couldn't blame them. At the best of times Deadhead was a repellent figure. His clothing was one step up from a bum's, his hair hadn't been washed since the Reagan presidency, and his corpse-white face was continually dancing with nervous twitches and tics that made him look like he was suffering through electroshock therapy.

"Hello, Glen," Cunningham said carefully as he approached Deadhead's table. He looked at the empty plate before Deadhead and sighed. The deranged ace was often difficult to handle after a meal. "What'd you have to eat, Glen?"

"Not much," Deadhead said defensively. He refused to look Cunningham in the eye. "I can feel the sun and see the rolling plains. The grass tastes good."

"Christ," Cunningham muttered. "You didn't have a hamburger, did you?"

"Mooo," Deadhead said, loud enough to make people stare.

Cunningham pasted a smile on his face and put a hand on Deadhead's arm, lifting him from his seat. "We have to go now," he said. "I have something for you to do," he added quietly.

Deadhead nodded and got down on all fours.

"Up we go," Cunningham said in a voice that tried to be casual. "Time to go home."

"Mooo," Deadhead replied.

Cunningham kept a smile on his face, but leaned down and whispered fiercely, "Get ahold of yourself. I'm not going to drag you to the damn car."

Deadhead nodded and stood, straightening his clothes as best he could. His eyes darted around the automat. "I'm fine. Really. Just wait a moment."

He went to the cash register and bought a pack of gum. He unwrapped all the sticks with shaking hands and popped them into his mouth one by one. He let out an ecstatic sigh and chewed contentedly. Cunningham flashed a knowing smile at the cashier and led him out of the automat.

"Come on," he said, pulling him down the street to the parking garage where he'd left his Maserati.

Deadhead followed him meekly, his eyes fastened on the faraway scenes playing in his brain as he relived the life of the cow who'd been part of his lunch. At least, Cunningham told himself, counting his blessings, Deadhead hadn't collapsed into an insensate stupor like he often did after ingesting meat.

He deposited Deadhead in the passenger's side of his Maserati, locked the door, and stood. A man was standing in front of his car. He hadn't been there a moment ago. He was Asian and wore mirror shades that gave his youthful face a blank, hard-edged look. His hands were in the pockets of his satin jacket that Cunningham just knew had a large white bird embroidered on the back. He could afford to act casual. The two similarly attired thugs standing behind him were carrying Uzis.

It took Cunningham a moment to put a name to the face: Jack Chang, a lieutenant in the Immaculate Egrets. He smiled at Cunningham. "Sui Ma," he said, "wants to see you. It's about her brother's missing head."

♣

"Careful," Cunningham said as Chang parked the Maserati by carelessly wedging it between a pair of overflowing garbage cans in a narrow Chinatown alley. "You'll ruin the paint job."

The Egret grinned. "What's the matter? Don't you have insurance?"

Cunningham didn't like Chang's attitude, but he kept quiet about it as they got out of the car and waited for the other Egrets to show. Macho posturing was a waste of breath. He preferred to remember insults, mark them down, and act on them later under the proper circumstances. And Chang had just made his list.

The Egrets following in the van screeched to a halt right behind Cunningham's Maserati. The driver laughed as he tapped Cunningham's car with the van's bumper, pushing it forward gently against the brick wall in front of it. Cunningham kept his expression impassive, but added another to his list as the Egrets piled out of the van, laughing. Two dragged a stupefied Deadhead by his arms. His payback list, Cunningham thought, was going to be very long before this day ended.

"Let's go," Chang said. "Little Mother is waiting."

Like her late brother, Sui Ma was something of a sinophile. In her case, she made the Egrets who guarded her headquarters wear costumes out of what looked to Cunningham like the road show of *Anna and the King of Siam*. Though, Cunningham noted, discreetly holstered opposite the guards' stubby-bladed Chinese swords were very modern-looking machine pistols.

Sui Ma's headquarters always made Cunningham feel uncomfortable, and it was not just because of the feeling that he was entering the den of the Dragon Lady. Behind the staid brick facade that was the outer wall was a fantasy land of silken tapestries and screens, electric torches glittering in wall sconces, and the heavy scent of incense billowing on the air.

Sui Ma herself was waiting for them in her reception room, sitting on her intricately carved wooden throne that was decorated with hundreds of peacock feathers. She wore robes of dark blue silk embroidered with the dazzlingly white birds that were the sigil of the Egrets. She was a short woman, rather plain and chubby, just coming into middle age. But her mild appearance masked a powerful mind as ruthless as her brother's. And right now she didn't look exactly pleased to see Cunningham.

"Your ambition," she said coldly to Cunningham, "has finally driven you too far. Not only have you slain my brother and his faithful bodyguard, but you then mutilated my brother's corpse. You'll pay for both acts."

Cunningham couldn't tell if she sincerely believed that he had killed Kien or if she was just using the circumstances as a convenient excuse for taking him out. He shook his head. "I'll take the blame for Wyrm, but it was self-defense. Christian sicced him on me. I'll give you even money that he was the one who told you that I'd killed Kien."

An expression flitted across Sui Ma's face that told Cunningham he'd given her something to think about. He spoke rapidly to press his advantage. "If I killed the General, what did I do with his head?"

She smiled. "You took it to feed to that disgusting creature of yours to learn all the secrets of the Shadow Fist Society."

"That's a fine theory," Cunningham admitted, "if I had the head in my possession. I don't."

"Then why," Sui Ma asked triumphantly, "did you go immediately from my brother's murder to pick up Deadhead at the automat?"

"Because I had something else for him," Cunningham explained. "The body of the watchdog joker that Kien had kept in a jar on his desk. The murderer killed the joker to keep it from blabbing about Kien's death. Someone seems to be running around behind the scenes trying to pin the blame on me."

"Christian," Sui Ma said thoughtfully. She gazed off into the distance for a long moment as Cunningham felt something like hope sweep over him for the first time since he'd been brought into her presence. "Where's the body of this joker?" she asked him.

"In a box in the glove compartment of my car," Cunningham said. Sui Ma glanced at Chang and nodded. He gestured at one of his goons, who immediately left to fetch it.

"And Deadhead?" Sui Ma asked.

"We have him in the antechamber," Chang said.

"Bring him."

Chang nodded and also left, leaving Cunningham alone with Sui Ma and the half-dozen impassive guards who stood behind and around her peacock throne. She continued to stare silently at him, as if weighing the value of his life. He decided that now wasn't the time to annoy her with idle chitchat.

The goon returned with the joker in the box. He presented it to Sui Ma. She looked in the box, nodded, and gave it back to the Egret who placed it at her feet on the upper tier of the throne's dais. A moment later there was another short, respectful knock on the door, and Chang led in two Egrets dragging Deadhead between them.

The disheveled ace stared around the room with his dark, confused eyes, mumbling something to himself that no one else could understand. He looked at Cunningham, nervously licking his lips. "You have a job for me?" he finally asked.

Sui Ma nodded and pointed at the box. "In there."

Deadhead stepped forward and removed the box's lid with shaking hands. "It's so little," he said.

Cunningham nodded. "Consider it an appetizer."

Deadhead's smile turned broad and fixed. A line of spittle ran down his chin as he reached into his pocket and took out a small leather case. Inside were a number of small, shiny, sharp implements. He chose one and began to saw, humming to himself. Cunningham looked away as Deadhead cut through the tiny skull. Sui Ma watched fixedly.

It took Deadhead only a few moments to cut away the top of the joker's skull. He glanced furtively at Cunningham and Sui Ma as he finished, then hunkered over the body. Half hiding his actions, he scooped out the joker's brain and popped it in his mouth. He chewed hastily, noisily, then swallowed. He knelt on the middle step of the dais before Sui Ma with a dreamy smile on his face, the tics and spasms that usually contorted his features subsiding into satiated serenity. His eyes closed.

"How long will this take?" Sui Ma asked with more than detached interest.

"It depends," Cunningham said. "The corpse was rather . . . fresh . . . so that should cut down on the time it takes him to assimilate the memories."

It took a few moments, but then Deadhead finally began to groan and squirm. "Noooo!" he cried, twisting as if to avoid a fatal blow.

Cunningham leaned forward eagerly.

"Who killed you?" he asked.

"Red hair," Deadhead panted in his trance. "Smiling face. The boy likes it, he does." He squirmed again and let out a long, keening cry.

"Is he alone? Is there another in the room?"

Deadhead whipped his head back and forth. "Another. Too far back. Blurry. Can't see who—"

Cunningham cursed to himself. The joker who'd guarded Kien's desk had been terribly myopic. "What about Kien? Is he in the room?"

"At his desk."

"What's he doing?"

"He is afraid. He opens the box, though he doesn't want to. He is saying, 'Why are you doing this to me? I don't want to. Don't make me do this.' He puts his face down in the box—"

Cunningham and Sui Ma looked at each other. "Mind control," Cunningham said, and Sui Ma nodded. "Someone—the redhead—made him inhale enough rapture to kill a whole platoon of r-heads."

"Redhead," Sui Ma said. "Mind control."

"Dr. Tachyon," they said together.

Sui Ma frowned, shaking her head. "I don't get it," she said. She looked critically at Deadhead, who was panting like a dog and tossing and jerking spasmodically on the floor, caught up in the after-effects of brain-eating. "Why would Tachyon make Kien kill himself?"

"Maybe it wasn't him. Maybe it was some other redheaded mind-control artist." Cunningham shrugged. "Deadhead can draw a picture of our man when he comes out of it." He looked at Sui Ma. "You can see, anyway, that I was telling the truth. I didn't have anything to do with your brother's death."

Sui Ma again looked into the distance. "That may be true," she admitted, "but since when did truth have anything to do with deciding upon the proper course of action?" She looked at Cunningham. "My brother is dead and I shall be the new supreme power in the Shadow Fist Society. I do not think that you'd care to work for me, Fadeout, and frankly I don't think that I would trust you."

"So I'm still dead," he said with as much flippancy as he could muster.

"Let us say that the firm is eliminating your position," Sui Ma said with a smile.

"Okay," he said. "In that case, fuck it."

He faded to total invisibility. He didn't know the layout of Sui Ma's room as well as he did Kien's, but he'd done his best to memorize it in the last few minutes. He hit the ground, rolled, and came up dodging as he heard Sui Ma shout and her guards blunder around the room. There was a short burst of gunfire, an anguished scream, and then Sui Ma shouted, "Use your swords, idiots, and guard the door!"

He moved toward the sound of her voice, and stumbled over what sounded like a moaning Deadhead. He landed silently, rolled, stood, and bumped into someone else. His hand slashed out and sunk into firm, muscular flesh, and he felt sudden, searing pain as a sharp blade chopped down into his upper thigh. He stifled a scream, and struck up at where he judged the sword wielder's wrist would be.

He struck flesh again, and pulled away. The blade came with him, still lodged in his thigh. He set his teeth together and yanked the sword from his leg, fading it out. Clasping both hands around the hilt, he swung in a great figure eight, feeling it slice through meat like a hot knife through butter.

Sui Ma shouted again at her guards, and that was a mistake because now he knew where she was. He started to circle toward her, holding the invisible sword out before him like a blind man might hold out his cane, and to the confusion and panic running through the room something new was suddenly added.

There were deep, hoarse shouts in new voices, and the sound of gunfire blasted deafeningly through the chamber. Cunningham risked fading in his eyes for a moment and had to stifle a cry of relief as he saw that the cavalry had arrived in the form of a Werewolf squadron led by Warlock himself.

There were more than a dozen Wolves wearing leathers and delicately featured Michael Jackson masks, and armed to the teeth with automatic weapons and combat shotguns. One of them had a portable boom box, and the song "I'm Bad" was blasting through the chamber louder than the reports of their weapons.

Sui Ma was standing before her throne, more anger than fear on her face, braced by two of her guards, who were dropping their swords and fumbling for the guns holstered at their sides. Cunningham gauged the distance between them and slipped back into total invisibility. He lunged forward silently, swinging his razor-sharp blade.

He felt something warm and sticky splatter on his face and faded in his eyes, knowing that the mask of blood he was now carrying would give him away anyway.

One of the guards was down, but the other was turning toward him, gun up and ready. Cunningham tensed to dodge, but before the Asian could fire, a shotgun blast from the hands of a Werewolf cut him down. He fell forward, thudding down the steps of the dais, and Sui Ma was standing unprotected and alone before her throne.

She looked at Cunningham. "You seem to have won for now," she said, almost graciously.

He nodded. "You were right," he said. "I could never work for you. And I don't think that you could ever work for me."

He thrust the blade up and into her stomach, and she gasped, collapsing backward onto her chair. She looked at him for what seemed a long time before her eyes glazed over. Cunningham sighed and turned away. He'd killed before, but it made him feel funny to kill a woman like that. He couldn't totally console himself with the thought that she'd been prepared to do the same for him.

In the rest of the chamber the Werewolves were wrapping up the last few of their surprised, outnumbered foes. Warlock stepped over Deadhead, cowering on the floor, and came up to join Cunningham at the top of the dais.

"Got here as soon as we could," he said, "after one of the brothers spotted you being hustled out of that laundromat. Finally figured, what the hell, bust in and—"

He stopped and stared at Cunningham. Cunningham supposed that he was quite a sight. His leg was throbbing like hell. The sword cut he'd taken on the thigh was bleeding like a goddamn river, and the blood of the guard he'd killed was splattered all over his face. Warlock was staring at his face. From the look in his eyes, peering through his Michael Jackson mask, he looked like he'd seen a ghost. The blood, Cunningham realized, must make him look like he'd taken a bad head wound.

"Don't worry"—he laughed—"I'm all right. This isn't mine." He wiped at the blood, smearing it but managing to remove some of it from his features.

Warlock seemed to catch himself. "Right," he said. "Glad you're okay. But we'd better move it before more of these damned gooks show up." He gestured at Sui Ma's corpse. "They're not going to like that."

"Okay," Cunningham said. He looked away from the corpse-littered room. Most of the bodies were Egrets, but a few Werewolves had gone down at the hands of Sui Ma's men. "It's back to the Lair. We've got to figure out where that damned head is."

But despite the death surrounding him, despite the pain he himself felt, Cunningham couldn't keep back a wide smile. It was over. The New Day had come. He was the new head of the Shadow Fists.

♠

In the far-gone days when the Bowery had been noted for its fashionable nightspots, the decrepit building now known as the Werewolves' Lair had been a famous luxury hotel. When things started going bad for the neighborhood, the hotel had been turned into apartments. When the neighborhood really hit the skids, it had degenerated into a flophouse, then been abandoned for well over a decade, sinking even further into pathetic decrepitude before the Werewolves took it over as their headquarters.

They'd made some effort to clean it up, though Werewolf sanitary standards were not exactly those of the Ritz. It was a smelly warren of dirty little rooms, the heart of which was Warlock's Sanctorum. This was a large chamber behind double wooden doors that had a crude pentacle surrounded by the legend 666: LAIR OF THE BEAST sloppily lettered on them in drippy red paint. It was dimly lit and cluttered with books overflowing their shelves and piled against the walls and sitting on the dusty furniture where they competed for space with occult gimcracks ranging from real human skulls to bundles of dyed chicken feathers that looked like they'd come from Auntie Leveaux's Hoodoo and Love Potion Shoppe.

Cunningham had co-opted Warlock's normal seat behind a desk piled high with more occult stuff, under a rather badly executed portrait of a bald and jowly Aleister Crowley, Warlock's patron saint. Warlock sat in a chair across the desk that was usually reserved for visitors. He was watching Cunningham closely. The ace sat with his bandaged leg held stiffly in front of him, his voice low and thoughtful as he mused on the day's wild events.

"It's Christian," he muttered, "it's got to be Christian. But how did that limey bastard think he was going to get away with taking over? He's too much of an outsider in the Shadow Fists to have a real power base."

"Unless he was conspiring with Sui Ma," Warlock suggested.

Cunningham shook his head. "She seemed genuinely surprised that her brother was dead. I think she really thought that I did it."

"There's Loophole," Warlock said. "He might figure in somewhere."

"He might," Cunningham agreed. "That's why I sent a few of the brothers to his office to pick him up. Maybe he can clear up some of the mystery." He fingered a sheet of paper lying on the desk in front of him. "Like who the hell this is."

It was a sketch done in colored pencil of the red-haired mind-control artist who'd killed Kien's watchdog. Deadhead was really a talented artist, and he'd caught an expression of cruel delight in the kid's smile that was doubly horrific on such a young, otherwise sweet face.

There was a respectful knock on the Sanctorum's double doors, and Cunningham looked up from the sketch to see two Werewolves come in with Edward St. John Latham between them.

Latham was a lean, handsome man in a dark gray Brooks Brother suit with a light, almost imperceptible purple pinstripe. His face had no expression at all as he entered the room and nodded at Cunningham. He ignored Warlock as he sat down in the chair next to him, crossing his leg casually, ankle over knee. "I suppose congratulations of a sort are in order," he said.

"Thanks, Sinjin." Cunningham knew that Latham disliked being called Sinjin as much as he could be said to dislike anything. He was an emotionless, supposedly utterly loyal bastard. It was hard to see where he'd fit into a conspiracy against Kien. "But there's still some things I'd like to clear up."

"Such as?"

"Such as are you with me and Warlock, or the General and his sister?"

Latham smiled without humor. "I've already heard about the late General and his late sister. There's not much of a decision to make, is there?"

"I'm glad to see that you're being sensible. Tell me. What do you know about Leslie Christian?"

"Christian?" Loophole frowned. "Why?"

"He's the missing ace from the deck. I've got the Werewolves scouring the city for him, but he seems to have disappeared. Not, however, before trying to pin Kien's murder on me."

Loophole looked faintly surprised. "Then you didn't kill Kien?"

Cunningham shook his head. "No. Would I do a thing like that? I figure Christian had to have been involved in the killing somehow. He showed up right after I'd found the body and tried to frame me, then he disappeared."

"Why would Christian kill Kien?" Latham asked.

"I don't know. But what do we really know about him?" Cunningham asked, ticking the points off one by one on his fingers. "He's an ace of some kind. He's foreign. He drinks. Somehow he wormed his way into Kien's confidence. He could have half a million reasons for wanting Kien dead, but we don't know enough about him to guess what they might be."

"Whereas," Latham said dryly, "you just had one reason for wanting the General dead."

"Okay," Cunningham conceded. "We're being honest with each other. I admit it. I wanted to be head of the Shadow Fists. I had . . . plans. But I didn't kill Kien." He reached across the desk and handed Latham the drawing of the youthful mind-control artist that had skewered Kien's batrachian watchdog. "He did."

Latham took it, glanced at it. Something flickered across his face, and for a moment Cunningham could swear that the usually unflappable lawyer was unsure of himself.

"The joker saw this kid mind-control Kien and make him shove his face into a bag of rapture. Then the kid killed the joker."

"Interesting," Latham murmured.

"You have any idea who this could be?"

Latham looked at him a long while, then said, "Perhaps."

"Do you want to let me in on it?"

Latham considered it for another long moment, then nodded. "In the interest of truth," he said without a trace of irony in his voice, "and justice."

Cunningham suppressed a smile, but Warlock let out an audible snort.

"He runs with a street gang that's done some work for the Shadow Fists," Latham said. "His name is Blaise. He is Dr. Tachyon's grandson."

◆

A half-dozen derelict jokers were sitting around the entrance to the boarded-up old movie theater in the heart of the Bowery, sharing a bottle wrapped in a brown paper bag and soaking up the last rays of the autumnal sun like a clutch of bloated lizards.

"How's it going, fellows?" Cunningham asked the bums. A few

looked up as he spoke. "Maybe you guys could help me. I'm look-ing for someone. This kid." He waved Deadhead's drawing. "I heard he hangs out here with a gang." He pulled a roll of bills from his pocket and peeled off a twenty. That elicited a little more interest.

One of the joker's eyes rotated forward like a chameleon's and focused on Cunningham. "You a cop or something?"

"That's right," Cunningham told him.

"You look like a cop. Kind of clean-cut, anyway. A cop on tele-vision. That right, boys?" There was general murmured assent, and Cunningham decided that he'd better bring the conversation back on track.

"What about the kid?"

"That bratty asshole. Him and his gang of assholes. The theater used to be ours before they moved in. Now it's loud music every time of the day and night and you really gotta be careful. They know when the welfare money comes in and they'll take it right from you."

"Is he inside now?"

"Yeah," the joker said. "Him and his expensive clothes. You can tell he's rich. He don't need to hang out here. He should give it back to us and go home to Manhattan. Him and all those brats."

Cunningham smiled, and dropped the twenty-dollar bill. It flut-tered onto the bum's lap and he grabbed at it as the other derelicts surged to their feet. Cunningham watched them scramble for the loot, and then weave and stagger to the liquor store across the street in the wake of the lucky stiff who'd grabbed it.

He crossed the street himself and looked into the window of the car idling at the curb. Warlock was driving. Deadhead was in the seat next to him, looking jittery and unsure as always. Latham was in the backseat, flanked by a pair of fierce-looking Werewolves. There were three cars parked at discreet distances behind this one. All were loaded with heavily armed Werewolves.

"Okay," Cunningham said. He took a deep breath. "This looks

like a job for Fadeout." He smiled. "I'm going to try the back door. I want you guys to wait here for now."

Warlock nodded. "Be careful," he said.

"I will. Trust me on that." He nodded to the Werewolf and re-crossed the street.

The theater's back door was locked, but the lock was old and cheap and yielded easily to Cunningham's probe. The door opened into musty darkness, a dank, garbage-choked passageway that apparently led behind the movie screen, then forked into the auditorium. Cunningham froze in his tracks as the sound of gunfire suddenly blasted through the theater. He crouched in the darkness, listening. The sound had an unreal quality to it. The voice shouting over it was familiar and almost inhumanly loud. There was a thundering crash, the sound of roaring engines, and the plaintive cry, "I can't die. I haven't seen *The Al Jolson Story* yet!" and Cunningham suddenly realized what was happening.

Someone was screening a movie, apparently the hideous remake of Howard Hawkes's classic *Thirty Minutes Over Broadway*. Cunningham waited in the darkness as the sound of a plane going down filled the theater. There was a loud explosion as it crashed on the Manhattan shoreline, then cheers and whistles from the audience. There were apparently few Jetboy fans in attendance.

Cunningham went on down the passageway. He brushed past a thick, dusty cloth hanging and found himself in the auditorium. It wasn't crowded. There were twenty, maybe twenty-five kids sitting close to the screen in the center section. Few seemed very interested in the images flickering before them. Some were gorging themselves on candy and ice cream, others were making out—though making out was a rather tame term for some of the acts Cunningham witnessed in the light reflected from the huge white screen.

One boy, though, was riveted to the action on the screen, despite the underaged siren rubbing up against him like an affection-starved cat. Even in the darkness, Cunningham could make out his gorgeous red hair and delicately handsome features. It had to be Blaise, the kid Latham had identified as Tachyon's grand-brat.

His eyes were glued to the screen, where people were now turning into rubber and plastic monsters courtesy of cheap special effects as the wild-card virus rained down from the sky. There was a scene cut, and Dudley Moore was suddenly strutting across the stage in a grotesque parody of Tachyon, wearing a ghastly red wig and an outfit that would have done justice to a drag queen.

Moore clutched at his hair as if he were searching for cooties. "Burning sky!" he swore. "I warned them! I warned them all!" Then he broke into an hysterical fit of weeping.

Blaise stood, throwing aside the girl who had been squirming against him and licking his ear, and drew a handgun he'd had holstered at his side. Cunningham shrank back against the wall as Blaise squeezed off a round. The report was startlingly loud within the confines of the auditorium, making the soundtrack explosions sound like harmless popguns in comparison.

But Blaise wasn't shooting at Cunningham. He hadn't even seen him. He'd put a bullet through the screen right between Dudley Moore's eyes. The ragtag audience of juvenile delinquents cheered, and Blaise sat down, a malevolent smile on his lips. In that moment Blaise looked as hardened and evil as the most twisted characters Cunningham ever had to deal with in the Fists. It was frightening to see such an expression on such a young face.

Cunningham shuddered, and moved on.

The lobby was dirty, dark, and deserted. The afternoon's last light filtered in through the cracks between the plywood boards haphazardly placed over the theater's glass doors. The concession stand was empty and dusty, though fresh popcorn was in the popper and cardboard boxes half-full of candy treats were stacked atop the counter. The confections all looked recent, probably brought in by the gang to devour while watching the main feature.

They had, Cunningham remembered, also been eating ice-cream bars.

He went to the portable ice-cream cart parked next to the candy counter and opened the door in the top. He looked in it for a long moment. There, nestled among a couple dozen ice-cream sandwiches, was Kien's head, raggedly cut off at the neck.

Cunningham found himself oddly reluctant to touch the cold, dead flesh. He wasn't squeamish, and he'd had no great love for Kien when the General had been alive, but there was something ghastly about his manner of death that disturbed him. He looked down at the glassily staring eyes and sighed.

There was no way he was going to get any answers unless he got the head to Deadhead. He picked it up. It was cold as a block of ice. Somehow he felt better after he'd dumped a box of candy bars behind the counter, put the head in the box, and faded it all to invisibility.

He peeked into the auditorium. The movie had progressed through the scene where Tachyon had saved Blythe van Rennsaeler from a gang of crazed joker looters—to accompanying hisses and boos from the watching gang.

They were just raggedy-ass kids. Sure, some were armed and Tachyon's grand-brat was a mind-control artist, but Cunningham had a couple of carloads of Werewolves outside waiting for his call. He crept back into the lobby and set the box with Kien's head in it on the candy counter. He went up to the lobby doors. They were pulled shut with a chain looped around their bars with an open padlock dangling from the chain. He creaked the doors open cautiously and peered out the front of the theater.

The bums were back, but they were too engrossed in squabbling over the newly purchased bottle of booze to even notice Cunningham. He gestured at the cars parked at the curb across the street, waving vigorously, and doors opened and Werewolves got out. They crossed the street. The derelicts noticed them and realized at last that something was about to happen. They moved off silently down the street, clutching their paper-bag-wrapped bottles as if afraid the Werewolves were going to try to take them away.

"What is it?" Warlock asked as they approached.

"It's Blaise and his fellow delinquents, all right. Round 'em up, but don't start anything rough. Watch out for Blaise. He's got a gun and some kind of mind-control powers, but he should be smart enough not to start anything when he sees there's a bunch of us. And Deadhead." The insane ace looked almost guiltily at Cunningham. "I've got something for you."

"The head?" Warlock and Latham asked at the same time.

Cunningham nodded.

The Werewolves filed silently through the lobby. There were a dozen of them, big, tough mothers dressed in leather and armed to the teeth with automatic weapons and shotguns. Cunningham was at their head, after showing a happily drooling Deadhead the cardboard box on the candy counter and leaving him to it.

"Remember," he warned the Werewolves, "keep it quiet, but if that Blaise brat tries to start anything, blow him loose." He turned to the Werewolf leader. "Warlock, stick close to Latham. Make sure he behaves."

"You heard him," Warlock said. "Let's do it."

Inside the auditorium the movie had progressed to the famous scene between Dudley Moore as Tachyon and Pia Zadora as Blythe van Rennsaeler, with Moore, rose in mouth, playing an elephantine melody on the piano while Zadora sang of "alien love" and the audience roared with laughter.

Time to end this, right now, Cunningham thought. He stepped into the auditorium, drew his pistol, and fired off a round into the ceiling.

That got everyone's attention. Candy and popcorn went flying as the teenage delinquents leaped to their feet and made abortive attempts to flee.

"Hold it, everyone!" Cunningham shouted in his best authoritative voice. Either his tone of command worked or the sight of a dozen heavily armed Werewolves did. Everyone froze. Everyone but Blaise.

He stood slowly, and faced Cunningham from across the auditorium. "What do you want?" he shouted over Zadora's sudden squeals of ecstasy as Dudley Moore had his way with her on the piano bench.

"Just to talk," Cunningham said. "There's nothing to fear."

"Sure," Blaise said. He sauntered up slowly to the head of the auditorium, fully aware that everyone's eyes were on him and playing his role as gang chieftain to the hilt. "What do you want to talk about?" he asked Cunningham casually.

Cunningham jerked his head back to the lobby. "In there." He looked at the Werewolves. "You five keep an eye on the kids. The rest of you come with us."

The Werewolves followed Cunningham, Blaise, Warlock, and Latham back into the lobby. Deadhead looked around guiltily. "Chinese food," he said through a full mouth, and turned back to his task.

Blaise frowned. "Oh," he said. "I see you found it. Too bad. He said I could have it."

"He?" Cunningham asked, leaning forward eagerly in anticipation.

"Me," a new voice drawled.

Everyone turned to look at the stairs leading up to the projection booth to see a middle-aged, blond, weather-beaten man standing there, smiling. Something in his smile made Cunningham feel cold.

"Christian," he said, swiveling his gun toward the British ace. "I knew it! Why did you do it? Why did you kill Kien?"

Christian's sardonic smile widened as he ambled casually down the remaining stairs and joined the others on the floor of the lobby. "But I didn't," he protested.

"You can't deny that you were this brat's accomplice."

"I'm not denying that at all," Christian said blandly. "I'm simply denying that we killed Kien."

"What?" Cunningham asked.

As if on cue, Deadhead suddenly moaned and turned and faced them. "Why are you doing this to me?" he whined. "Why are you stealing my body? Why, Kien?"

A cold wind blew through Cunningham. "Kien?" he repeated softly.

Christian leaned against the candy counter. "Of course," he said with a sardonic smile on his tanned features. "You've been plotting and planning to take my place for a long time. I got sick of it. I decided to flush all the conspirators into the open, using," and he nodded at Blaise, "my jumper friend here to provide me with a perfect cover."

"No," Deadhead whined. "Please, no. I've been loyal. . . ."

"Jumpers?" Cunningham said. The realization that Blaise and the others were jumpers made him turn cold. "You changed bodies with Christian and faked your own murder?"

"Exactly. Latham had brought the jumpers into our sphere of influence some time ago. I decided, however, to bypass him this time and approach Blaise directly. I used him to switch bodies. Since then I've been using Christian's astral projection to keep track of you and the others."

That explained a lot, Cunningham thought, grateful that he was surrounded by a band of friendly Werewolves. "Too bad, in the end, you miscalculated." He turned to Warlock. "Waste him," he said.

Warlock's face was unreadable behind the Michael Jackson mask. He lifted his pump shotgun, then turned and placed its barrels directly under Cunningham's chin. "Sorry," he said.

Christian—Kien—laughed. "Splendid!"

"What are you doing?" Cunningham demanded. "Kill him! Kill him and it's all over."

"It is over," Warlock said gently. "You see, my power allows me to see death on people's faces. I saw it this morning on yours at Sui Ma's. I knew then that you would die before the day ended."

Cunningham felt sudden sweat spring up on his forehead. "But kill him! All you have to do is kill him!"

Warlock shook his head and Kien laughed and laughed.

Cunningham turned to face him. "You were dead. I thought you were dead—" he started, but Kien held up his hand, stopping him.

"No excuses. No lies. I have flushed out a traitor, but find myself trapped in an old, badly abused body. I think," he said, looking hard at Cunningham, "that I would like to trade it in on a younger model."

"No!" Cunningham screamed. He tried to fade and run, but he heard high, tittering laughter from Blaise and a hand of cold metal clamped down on his naked brain. The room spun and he was somewhere else. His legs were young and strong, but everything was whirling about, making him dizzy and nauseated, and he couldn't get them to work. His perspective shifted again almost immediately and he fell against the candy counter. He bounced, hit the floor, and started to crawl away, but his body was old and tired and his head was swimming and confused.

He heard faraway laughter, and an eager young voice said, "Let me!"

Someone turned him over and he saw blazing red hair and a young, horrible grin, but most of all he saw a huge gun barrel pointing right at his face.

He closed his eyes and tried to speak, but no words would come. He may have heard the horribly loud, terribly frightening explosion.

But that was all.

♠   ♥   ♦   ♣

Nobody Gets Out Alive

by Walton Simons

JERRY STOOD ACROSS THE street from Latham's apartment building. A cool wind stirred up the dry leaves around his feet. The late-September heat had given way, at least temporarily, to the first cold snap of the season. He was dressed in a maintenance man's outfit. The steel blue .38 was tucked away in his work box, along with a few other things. He was as ready as he was going to get. He waited for the light to turn and walked across the street.

He showed the doorman a fake work order he'd manufactured. The doorman was more bored than suspicious and let him in. Jerry walked quickly to the far elevator and put an OUT OF ORDER sign over the button, then pushed the button and stepped into the waiting car. Latham, naturally enough, had the penthouse apartment. Of the two cars, this was one that went all the way to the top. One of the things Jerry had learned about in the last month was how elevators worked. He opened the control panel and set the car to go all the way up. His knees almost gave way as the elevator started. Jerry made his features and skin tone Asian. He pulled his change of clothes from his work box. It was mostly leather. The finishing touch was a fake Immaculate Egrets jacket. He'd had it made from the videotape he'd gotten from Ichiko. Once fully dressed, he tucked the gun into his jacket. The car stopped. Jerry clipped one of the wires. For now, the elevator was going nowhere. He could rig a bypass in a hurry if it came to that.

Jerry stepped out and walked to Latham's door. He fingered the lock and let himself in, closing the door softly behind him. The penthouse was quiet. Except for a light in what appeared to be the bedroom, it was dark as well. Jerry took a deep breath, padded across the carpeted floor to the lighted doorway, and stepped in.

Latham was lying naked on the bed. His body was covered with sweat and his hair was a tousled mess. The sheets were knotted on the floor with a red robe. Latham looked lost in a moment of private satisfaction. He glanced up and saw Jerry-the-Egret. His narrow smile slipped.

"Who sent you? How the hell did you get in?" Latham's voice lacked the assurance Jerry was used to hearing.

Jerry pulled the .38, but didn't point it. "I'll ask the questions. Tell me about the jumpers." He had to have the truth before he could shoot Latham. He wouldn't be able to deal with killing him otherwise.

A young naked woman stepped out of the bathroom. It was the bald-headed girl. She had powerful, well-defined muscles, almost to the point of being unattractive, and bikini-waxed blond pubic hair. Jerry leveled the gun at her chest. He'd been watching for two hours and hadn't seen her go in. He didn't know if he could kill a girl. Even if she did have a part in Kenneth's death.

"He made us," she said. "All of us. With that." She sat on the bed, bent over, and kissed Latham's flaccid penis. It twitched under her tongue.

"Not just yet, Zelda. Business first." Latham put his hand under Zelda's chin and pointed her face at Jerry.

Jerry felt something that might have been pain if it had lasted more than a few seconds. His vision blurred for an instant. When it cleared, he was looking down at Latham's penis. There was a pleasant warmth between his legs, like nothing he'd ever felt before. He tried to sit up, but his body felt heavy and clumsy. A hand grabbed him and pulled his head back.

There was an Egret in the doorway pointing a gun at him. Jerry felt his hands being twisted behind his back. Cold metal surrounded his wrists, and he heard twin clicks. He opened his mouth to speak, but it was his Egret body that screamed.

The Asian face began to melt and flow. The Egret tore at the satin jacket and shirt, exposing his chest. Breasts began to form there. Jerry's pirated body closed its eyes and screamed again. He felt another moment of vertigo and found himself staring at Latham and a handcuffed Zelda. She was still screaming. The lawyer pushed her off the bed. Jerry brought his body under control and squeezed his trigger finger, but Zelda had dropped the gun. He ran.

He dove into the elevator and pulled a bypass from his work box. It slipped from his sweaty fingers. He picked it up and clipped it into place, then punched the ground floor. He looked up. Latham had the gun pointed at him. Jerry dove to one side and heard the shot at the same time. The bullet tore into the car wall behind him. The doors closed and it started down.

Jerry changed his clothes and appearance back to the maintenance worker. His insides tingled and his skin was cold. He straightened himself and took several deep breaths. It didn't help. He was still shaking when the elevator doors opened on the ground floor. He walked in measured steps across the lobby and out into the cool New York night.

He stopped at a bar near his apartment and ordered a double. He figured he needed it. Jerry knew he'd been lucky. He hadn't counted on Zelda being there. But she hadn't counted on not being able to control his shape-changing ability. Jerry was so used to it himself that he didn't have to think about it anymore. Without that, he'd have wound up like Kenneth and the rest. Latham probably wouldn't figure out exactly what happened, but he'd damn sure be paranoid from now on. That would make him even harder to get to.

"Have another?" The bartender looked down at Jerry's empty glass.

"Why not?" Jerry slammed the whiskey down before the glass could make a ring on the polished wood bar.

♥

He sat down next to the grave and tossed pebbles into the newly cut grass. He didn't look at Kenneth's headstone. It made talking to his dead brother seem more stupid than it already was.

"Sorry, I screwed up again," Jerry said quietly. "I don't know what to do now. Got any ideas?"

The wind gusted in the treetops, tearing loose leaves with a whistling clatter. He heard a car pull up down the hill. A car door shut. He turned. Beth was walking slowly up the hill. She waved from below the shoulder. It looked like it took all her strength. Jerry stood and started down to meet her. When he reached her, they hugged silently.

"You didn't answer at home or at the apartment, so I figured you might be here." The wind whipped her hair into her face; she pushed it back and held it.

"I wish I'd known you were coming. I'd have done something special," Jerry said.

"I'm not up to anything special right now." She shivered. "I'm not up to staying at the house yet, either. Can we go to your apartment?"

Jerry blinked and opened his mouth, but said nothing.

"It's not that," Beth said. "I just want to be with somebody who cares about me. I just want to be held."

Jerry nodded, both disappointed and relieved. She'd given him a big compliment if he was willing to see it that way. "Let's go," he said.

♣

Jerry did his best to clean up the apartment while Beth unpacked her luggage. He tossed all the dirty clothes in the hamper and stacked his film magazines and books at right angles. Beth opened a drawer and giggled, then held up a pair of crotchless, tiger-print panties. "What's this?"

Jerry covered his mouth for a moment, then recovered. "Relics of a bygone age." He sighed, remembering. "Veronica."

Beth set them back into the drawer. "Did you really love her?"

"I thought I did. I obsessed about her. I wanted to make her happy. I damn sure wanted to fuck her." He shrugged. "I've learned just enough about love to be very confused about it. Maybe I've got ape residue in that part of me, or something."

Beth smiled. "I think that part of you is fine. You just don't know what to do with it."

"Neither does anybody else, apparently. I haven't had a date in months." Jerry sat down on the couch. He and Veronica had used it often. He tried not to think about that.

"Give it time." Beth sat down on the edge of the bed and shook her head. "Way to go, Beth. Say one thing and do another."

"What are you talking about?"

"Well, when I was in Chicago, I spent some time with an old boyfriend and we wound up in bed together. I think he was just trying to make me feel better." She bit on an already ragged fingernail. "I knew it wouldn't help, but I guess I had to prove it to myself anyway. The sex was nice, but it really didn't matter. When it was over, Kenneth was still gone. And I'll never get him back."

Jerry got up quickly and walked over to her, but she was already crying. He didn't want to start himself. He wanted to be strong for her. "I wish . . ." There was nothing he could say that would comfort her, and he knew it.

Beth leaned into him and held on tight. He could feel the warmth of her tears through his shirt. "There are some things you can't really share, and I have to sweat out the worst of this on my own. But, Jesus, I'm glad you're here."

Jerry held her for a few minutes, stroking her hair, not saying anything. She stopped crying and looked up at him with puffy eyes.

"You want a Coke, or something?" He needed something himself, but wasn't going to drink in front of her.

"No." Beth pulled away from him, picked up her overnight bag, and headed into the bathroom. "I just need to go to bed. It's been a long day."

"It's been a long year," he said. "And I could use some sleep, too."

♠

Jerry told her his entire supply of stupid jokes before they got into bed. He was tense and wanted to defuse the situation if he could. It had been months, since Fantasy, since he'd actually been in bed with a woman.

Beth turned out the lights and curled up facing away from him. She pulled his arm around her and kissed him lightly on the back of the hand.

"I love you a lot, Jerry."

"I love you, too, sis." She'd never felt more like family to him than now.

Beth slipped into sleep quickly. Jerry had tried for hours, but just couldn't manage to relax. His penis had gotten hard a couple of times, but he clamped down on it with his legs until it calmed back down.

Finally, he went to the bathroom for a couple of sleeping pills. He washed them down with a drink of water and looked at himself in the mirror. His face was the same. It hadn't shown a day of age since Tachyon saved him from apehood. He felt changed, though. Felt like he finally had something to offer people, like his affection and caring made a difference to them. Maybe this was what growing up was.

He resisted the temptation to change his face to Bogart's and said, "Here's looking at you, kid." He flipped off the light and went back to bed.

He settled carefully in between the sheets. Beth moaned and jerked her free arm. Jerry took her gently by the wrist and pulled it down to her side, then kissed her on the back of the neck. She quieted and her breathing became even again. He looked outside. The sky was turning dull red behind the curtains. He hadn't realized it was that late. Jerry pressed his body close to Beth, closed his eyes, and gave sleep another try.

♠ ♥ ♦ ♣

About the Editor

GEORGE R. R. MARTIN is the author of the international bestselling A Song of Ice and Fire series, which is the basis for the award-winning HBO series *Game of Thrones*. Martin has won the Hugo, Nebula, Bram Stoker, and World Fantasy Awards for his numerous novels and short stories.

www.georgerrmartin.com
Twitter: @ GRRMspeaking